HAL ARNOLD

We Who Pave the Milky Way

To everyone paving their way through life.

Preface

We Who Pave the Milky Way is the culmination of the emotions of ten years of my life. Every time I was angry, sad, or happy, I put my pen to the paper and wrote the stories of Jacob, Samuel, Saul, Emmanuel, Jana, Derrick, Wei, and many more. Writing this book was the most terrifying and thrilling experience of my existence. Through each character, I created people who I loved and respected. My foggy, dissociated feelings, my anxiety and my anger at the disappointments of a life in which I didn't feel like I had any control, became the beginning emotions for my characters and the unfortunate people of Yalk.

At first, the people of my novel were just ways to express feelings I felt unsafe to communicate to the others around me in any other way. Where Jacob was representative of my anger, anxiety, and willpower Emmanuel was representative of my conflicted, ever-changing self, and Ana was a desire to want back the childish and the impossible. The longer I wrote, the more my characters developed and became more than singular emotions and needs. In many ways, I think this is representative of my own mental and emotional growth occurring over the ten-year writing span of my novel.

Some parts of the novel happened as accidents. For a long time, I had no intention of writing the novel I have, let alone the trilogy quickly following. *We Who Pave the Milky Way* started out as a desire to write a short story in which the unwatched children of a society unknowingly exterminate their own kind. This idea became the base for Jana's part of the memory stream, and shortly after, the idea of an unnamed character and a "Historian" followed.

Equally, there was no deep intention put behind the naming of "Jacob" who was originally given his name as a placeholder so I could continue writing. The name was chosen originally as a joke because I believed it to be the most cliché name for a male main character. This joke of mine became the bane of my existence as I could no longer call him anything else.

The rest of the story, however, was not strewn together with so little attention. The crafting of the characters and their twists and turns was done lovingly and painfully as I pulled them in different directions toward the inevitable conclusion of the novel and the trilogy. I made every sentence with a desire to seem authentic in terms of the reactions of the characters and the descriptions of the events in a high science-fiction scenario. In many scenes, I have cried for the pain of the characters or become angry with their actions. There were scenes that left me empty for days, namely the final scene with Candace and Derrick. Which was written originally to communicate my own experiences of abandonment. I was critical of Candace, who could not love her broken spouse unconditionally enough and didn't notice when her own husband had disappeared. I was also critical of Derrick for not having the strength to take on the responsibility of her love but instead chose to be self-destructive and ruin both of their possible happiness.

There was also a lot of joy in writing this story. Many names of beloved friends were mixed into the names of planets, people, and cities. These special people were those who I admired and many were those who first encouraged me to push through my publishing anxieties. I hope, too, that anyone reading this will have such an inspirational group of people to feed you when you're in a creative frenzy and don't remember, get you out of your room when you haven't seen daylight in over a week, and will talk to you long into the night.

I wrote this book first in the hope that people who are feeling oppression from any place will see there is a point to fighting back, whether that's because you're suffering from mental illness, abuse, lack of acceptance, ableism, or racism. I wrote it secondly hoping people will realize advocating change is better than doing nothing even if your work is fruitless. We can't pretend things are good enough "as is" when so many people are still being lost to these important issues. To the former people, I hope you, too, can fight off your "Lovindians" as I continue to fight off mine.

I

No Need for a Grave

"Free people know the boundaries of their freedom."
~My mother

1

Chapter 1

We used to be something quite different. That much we know. Our bones pop and crack in protest of their sedentary life. When I look down at my fruitless hands and think about who I've left behind, I can't believe this is all there's ever been. That's why people stand up on crates and cry their grievances. That's not me, though. I don't want to disappear.

The wind whistles over the top of the dome. It always does. I used to think one day I would be able to ignore it, but that day isn't today. A voice chants over the wind, but I don't look up. If you look at them, they'll be encouraged to try harder.

"Don't you want more?" the voice cries. "Don't you want to create? Don't you want a life of your own? What about your children? The Lovindians keep us under their thumb! They tore us away from our homeland and from our pride! Shouldn't our children have more?"

I'm never going to have children.

A guard watches the man closely but from a distance. The guards are all of a species called Gromptu. The Gromptu are molting right now. Their oily, gray skin is covered in sparse patches of downy feathers. They are an ugly race with huge eyes and short, furry, funnel-shaped ears. Their strange, broad, board-like arms end in three awkwardly long fingers, and their feet end in talons. At some point in their evolutionary history, it was likely their arms had been wings instead.

I don't have to look at the Talker to know that the Gromptu towers over him, even standing on his crate. It's not their size that's so intimidating, though; it's their eyes. Their eyes are emotionless, white, round orbs that seem to watch you no matter where you stand.

Whenever I feel a Gromptu watching me, I try to imagine myself drifting above the planet in my transporter craft. I try to imagine how small the three ovular, gray domes that mark Yalk's surface look from space. We belong to the middle building, Unit B. The rest of mankind dwells in units A and C. I feel the white eyes on me now and picture how the volatile atmosphere pushes constant waves of dust over the domes. I picture how it all fades away with just a little space— how the planet becomes just a round dot in the dark.

I turn the next corner of tall, gray, block apartment buildings. The place is a jumbled maze, but we have enough time on our hands to learn to navigate it well. The maze continues not just on the ground but also in the air. From where I am, I cannot see the top of the dome. A tangled web of clotheslines hangs a wide range of different thin, beige cloths from window to window, lacing Unit B together. Even if I could see the top of the dome, all I would see is a screen of artificial light created to simulate daytime. It only feels like real sunlight if I stare at it too long and let it hurt my eyes.

I turn twice more and reach the court where we play. The court is really an alleyway where two apartments face each

4

other at just the right distance. Each apartment has one large circle drawn at the second floor. These circles are the goals, called the "Scrab's eye." "Scrab" is a Yalkian insult describing a person who is like the filth that gathers in long undisturbed places. Looking up at the two enormous circles on the walls, I shudder. It's not hard to imagine which scrab the eyes belong to.

"Jacob! You're already here!"

Samuel tosses me the bugger, a hardened bread roll, and I catch it against my chest.

"Been waiting forever!" I lie.

Samuel takes me seriously and mumbles words of apology. He uses one of his awkwardly long limbs to scratch the back of his head with his hand.

"He's messing with you, genius." Emmanuel pushes past him, holding out his swatter for me to pass the bugger to him.

I tap the bugger up with my swatter, a kitchen spatula, and he bounces it up and down. The two of them are brothers. Samuel is the elder brother but he's far more good-natured and gullible. He's too good for us, in all honesty. Samuel smiles in relief, never even considering being irritated at my lie. Too good.

We don't have enough players to play the game properly, so we naturally fall into a triangle, bouncing the bugger off of our swatters while we talk. There are very rarely enough players to play the game, so we are pretty good at passing it to one another. We don't even have to look at the ball directly; hitting it has become second nature.

"Where's Saul?" I ask.

"I guess he couldn't come today," Samuel replies with a lopsided frown.

5

A deep red shines through Emmanuel's copper skin.

"You're full of scat, Samuel! You know why he didn't come. He knows Maan doesn't want us around him."

Samuel freezes and the bugger rolls to my feet. I bend and pick it up. The bread is really hard. They must have hidden it from their mother for a long time. They might be able to hide bread from her, but no one can hide Unit B's gossip from their Maan. The rumors about Saul's father have been circulating for days.

"I don't think that he'd actually avoid us..." Samuel frowns.

I bounce the bugger off the end of my swatter. They aren't paying attention anymore and we've only just started. This is why we need Saul here. He always knows what to say to shut them up.

"He would too! He'd never want to cause us any trouble!"

Emmanuel flips his swatter at me, indicating for me to pass, and I pass it a little too low. He pops the bugger up just before it reaches the ground.

"Maybe we should go talk to him then. We can tell him we don't care what Maan says," Samuel says hopefully.

The roll falls back down to Emmanuel's swatter and he hits it at me a little too hard. I step back and manage to catch it right before I'm hit.

"Won't work, Sam," Emmanuel sighs bitterly. "You know once he's decided something, not even a pregnant Rodavian can change his mind, and you know their reputation for a bad temper."

Emmanuel knows Saul best, so he's probably right. There's not much to be done about it. I don't have any parents to tell me to stay away from the son of a Talker sympathizer. I transferred from Unit C, where my family lives, to Unit B

6

when the com-panel said I'd become the legal age to transfer. I was fourteen years old in Lovindian time. I haven't visited my family since. We might as well be a planet away because none of them can fly a transporter craft, and I'm not going to visit them. I didn't even tell them I was going. That was six years ago now.

Saul knows family is important to these two, though. They aren't like me. When Saul found out their Maan didn't like the rumors about his father, he backed away. He probably thinks he's being some kind of hero by isolating himself. Saul's dramatic like that.

"Will you talk to him, Jacob?" Samuel asks.

I pass him the bugger before answering.

"I don't think it will help." I echo what Emmanuel said. "He won't change his mind if he thinks he's protecting the two of you."

Samuel grimaces. I know that's not what he wants to hear. He holds the bugger in his hand and frowns. My stomach clenches guiltily. I could have said I would at least try. I open my mouth to change my answer, but Emmanuel shakes his head at me. I close my mouth. Samuel passes back the bugger, addressing me again.

"What do you think of the Talkers?"

Why does he always want my opinion? I hate it when he looks at me like that. I used to have someone else who looked at me like that, and what did I do? I left her behind. I was the only person she could depend on and I left her. His open trust always makes me uncomfortable. Not everyone is trustworthy.

I shrug, not looking at him. "I don't get their purpose."

"Whaddya mean, scat-brain? All they do is shout their

7

purpose at anyone who walks by. They think the Lovindians are parasitic creeps that enslaved us all and we deserve better." Emmanuel scoffs at me and smacks the bugger hard. He grumbles when his lanky brother manages to reach it before it hits the ground.

"I mean that I don't know what they hope to get out of it," I say laughingly. "We all know what's going on. What's the point of spreading awareness? Just adds to the depressing vibe in this dump."

"You're right about that, redling." Emmanuel smiles halfheartedly.

I self-consciously bring a hand to my reddish-brown hair. Red hair is traditionally a trait from Unit C, just as black hair and darker complexions are traits of Unit B. Even in Unit C, the trait is rare now, and if it's matched with green eyes, it's said to make for a lucky soul. In Unit C, there is even a Redling Festival. It's rumored that the heartbeat of a redling extends down to their strands of red hair. I certainly can't feel a heartbeat in my hair, but maybe it's muffled because it's reddish-brown and not a true red. My hair is too muddy for me to be a true redling, and my brown eyes seem far from lucky. Emmanuel and Saul just like to tease me.

The artificial lights dim a little, and they both glance up uneasily. It's getting late, and they don't want to be in the corridors when the lights become too low. Even the Talkers know to go inside then. Emmanuel talks a tough game, so it's sometimes hard to tell that he's still young. Add this to the fact that he's stocky, broad-shouldered, and his closest friend is Saul, and it becomes easy to forget. When the lights dim, however, the fact that he's the youngest out of all of us starts to show. He runs a hand through his wavy, black hair.

Samuel looks at me a little anxiously as if asking permission for us to start back towards their home. I nod to him. Emmanuel doesn't notice.

"Let's head back, guys; I'm starting to feel a little tired." I lie. Samuel smiles gratefully and I attempt to smile back. His gratitude continues to unsettle me. I walk them back to their apartment, but I won't go in. I can hear their mother fussing their siblings into bed, and I have no doubt that she's preparing to go out into the corridors like the others. In the same corridors that Emmanuel and Samuel are so quick to exit, adults everywhere in Unit B are preparing to enter.

They both pause before the door. I feel a wave of awkwardness, but I'm not sure of the source. I catch Emmanuel shooting a side-glance in my direction. Do they want me to do something? Is this about Saul? I don't know what to say about that!

"Don't worry about Saul," I say to them, trying to make my voice sound like that of an older brother.

"Pshh— not doing that." Emmanuel runs a hand through his hair and disappears quickly inside.

"Thanks. It'll be okay," Samuel says searchingly.

Is he trying to console himself?

"Yeah, it'll be okay," I repeat.

He follows his brother, his shoulders a little more relaxed. My jaw tenses. I start to walk toward my own apartment. I feel the pull that the darkening lights create but I'm not interested in walking tonight. I don't want to be with the others. I open the door of my apartment and the light turns on. I slide the door closed and the light turns off. The only things we need the doors closed for are sleeping and couple's activities. Neither of these things requires light.

I don't have to see my room to feel my way to my cot and lay down. People were already starting to gather in the halls as I was coming home. I've been with them before. We don't really know why we do it. Maybe it's just because we can't get all of our energy out in the day. For whatever reason, though, Yalk becomes alive at night with humans marching the corridors. My mind automatically thinks of the crowds passing through each other again and again. My legs stir restlessly. I turn toward the wall, away from the door.

I dream of Keren.

I see her— so small. She holds an infant— so, so small. Her gold eyes blaze through her waves of messy, red hair.

"Jacob, you left me to do it all alone. I don't have any big brothers to help me." It's not a whine. She's too tough for that.

Old tear stains line her face, but she's not crying now. A little hand tugs at her tan skirts. She puts a hand on the child's head. She was willing to bear the burden of her younger siblings. I want to reach out and touch her. I want to tell her I'll come home soon, but I'm not moving and no words are coming out.

"You can't lie to me." She smiles sadly.

I try again to reach her, but no matter how big the steps I take are, I never get close enough. Moving is awkward. I'm weighed down.

"You can't lie to me because I'm too much like you."

The distance between us grows. I'm leaving her at the same speed I left her in my transporter craft all that time ago.

2

Chapter 2

I sit outside my apartment, back against the wall, with a bowl of reheated, black, mashed legumes in my lap. I don't taste any flavor as it goes into my mouth, but I'm hungry, so it keeps going in. No one is in the corridors yet. They all spent restless nights and will sleep in as late as their bodies allow them. I've grown accustomed to the permanent, black rings around my eyes. I have the same dream every night, which means every night I don't get much sleep. I stopped trying to get adequate sleep shortly after I moved to Unit B.

The air on Yalk is heavy with the heat of over fifty thousand warm bodies that are the inhabitants of Unit B. There is no breeze that lifts the stench of sweat as the vents near the top of the dome barely push out air. The only sense of cool comes from leaning up against the thick, block walls of the apartments, which are made of some type of natural material likely mined from the planet. It's not rare to see groups of people pressed with their backs against the walls for relief.

Maybe today I'll take a trip to Yahbi. The others think I'm weird for having my transporter craft license. It was a little more popular to get a license in Unit C, where I grew up, but here in Unit B, I'm an outlier. Even when I asked Saul if he wanted to join me on a trip to Yahbi, he just mumbled something about flight sickness and turned bright red.

To get a transporter craft license, you have to take all the assigned lessons on the computer panel, which is assigned to your apartment. After I completed the lessons, a command key to control the transporter craft's basic functions was delivered to my apartment. Getting the home's com-panel away from my mother and siblings was hard, so I frequently woke up early and took it away before they were awake. I used to sit in the transporter craft that I wished to pilot and listen to the computer panel tell me what to do. I felt productive back then. I had a dream, but I never thought I'd do it. I never thought I'd actually leave. It was just a fantasy. When I left, it was almost as big of a surprise to me as it was to my family. After I left, I was too much of a coward to go back. It didn't matter how much I regretted it.

I pull out my fennele from my pocket. The instrument was made so that you could carry it at all times. You expand it by pulling out the metallic neck and spreading out the sides like a fan. I pluck a string, and it has a light, twinkling sound to it. I've set down my bowl for now, and I pick playfully at the strings, not trying to make a song.

Unit B wasn't the dream that I'd hoped it to be. I thought that I would escape the weight of my childhood by leaving Unit C, but I still have yet to feel the freedom I expected. It was nice to finally have my own space, my own choices, but then the boredom came. At that point, I could have returned home, but I didn't.

It wasn't long after moving into my apartment in Unit B

that I started taking trips to Yahbi, the only other planet that humans can travel to. There are plenty of species on the planet Yahbi, but it is rare to see a human. Yahbi is what might be referred to as a "recreational planet." I stab my spoon at the mush in my bowl. They have *real* food on Yahbi; not like the Yalkian stuff ordered from com-panels with the Lovindian allowance of Baunti. Yahbiin merchants line the streets with the smell of meat cooking in hot pots and on stickers.

I leave my bowl on the ground and stand up. The corridors are still quiet. I want to run off on my transporter craft and get a meal improvement, but my feet take me in a different direction. I sigh but don't stop walking toward Saul's apartment. Talking to him isn't going to do any good, but I'm going to lose my mind if I have to watch Samuel and Emmanuel sulk around until he comes back.

Saul's apartment isn't far from mine, which is another reason why I feel like I can't just go off to Yahbi without trying to talk to him. If I talk to him before the other two wake up, they won't even have to know I tried. As long as Samuel doesn't know, he can't look at me like I'm something special.

I turn the corner, but the door to Saul's apartment is already sliding open. Did he have a similar idea? Was he coming to talk to me? The person who emerges is too tall to be Saul. Saul only lives with one other person. Saul's father slinks out of the apartment. He looks over both of his shoulders uneasily and turns the corner.

I'm stunned. I remember the rumors that were sprouting about him. When I had heard about him being a sympathizer of the Talker's Movement, I hadn't thought about what that might entail. To some degree, I hadn't even believed it at all. Does Saul know? Talking to Saul is going to have to wait.

Breathe. I can't jump to conclusions. His suspicious behavior doesn't look promising for his reputation.

I start after him. His loose-fitted wrap-shirt billows out behind him, and I catch sight of it just as he disappears again. I leap after him. The wind will cover the sound of my footsteps, so as long as I stay far enough away, he probably won't notice me. I am so caught up with my chase that I almost make the mistake of stumbling into him. I hunker back into the alleyway just as he looks over his shoulder. I realize that I have never actually seen Saul's father before. He looks like an older version of Saul. He has reddish blonde hair, pale blue eyes, and a bulking figure. At the moment, though, the comparison stops there. His eyes are frantic and his cheeks are sunken. He coughs in an attempt to catch his breath. Like most people on Yalk, he's out of shape. He stumbles forward, but I hesitate.

The only thing in this direction is the landing bay, but what could he have to do there? To my knowledge, there's nobody in Unit B who is qualified to fly a transporter craft besides myself. At least, I've never seen anyone else using a transporter craft. I rub my eyes to make sure I'm seeing correctly. He's just standing there in front of the landing bay doors. The Gromptu chirp a bit in their Lovindian tongue. I wonder if they are as confused as I am, but it's impossible to tell. The massive doors lift with a groan that could have been heard all over Unit B if the wind were not so loud. I must have been wrong. Someone else on Yalk must be able to pilot a transporter craft, or why else would he be here?

Saul's father disappears through the doors. The alarm indicating that the doors are about to close starts to blare. If I go now, I'm taking the chance he might see me, but if I

14

wait, I'll lose sight of him. I rush the space between myself and the doors. The Gromptu at the door ruffle their feathers, but they are used to seeing me, so they don't try to stop me.

To my relief, Saul's father isn't entering the craft that I flew from Unit C to Unit B. At least he hasn't been taking mysterious trips in my craft. It would have been embarrassing if I hadn't noticed that before. Technically, none of the crafts are mine. They're all the Lovindians' and can be used by any certified humans. Any command key would work for any craft, but I have a personal attachment to the craft I voyaged here on.

I notice that the craft door lowers without him using a command key. So someone else is inside. I can barely fight my curiosity. The door to Saul's father's craft lifts and seals behind him. I push back my thin, beige sleeve and look at the command key wrapped around my wrist. I press my thumb to it and whisper, "Open craft door."

The hatch lowers and I slip inside. What's the plan? I look around the small interior of my blocky-looking craft. There's a massive bench in the middle of the craft which looks at the display screen. There isn't any actual windscreen on the craft; it just shows me a projection of the outside. I slide into the bench, which was obviously constructed for a much larger species. I imagine that these crafts were probably owned by a conquered race and sent to us because they are clumsy and poorly made.

If I move too quickly, the viewer screen of Saul's father's craft will pick me up in space. I can afford to wait. It's not like I don't know where the craft is going. There is only one place they can go, and I know exactly how much time it will take them to get there.

The landing bay doors open, and I watch the other transporter spit itself clunkily into space. Whoever is piloting the other craft clearly hasn't put the love and maintenance into their craft that I have. The Gromptu could technically do the work for me, but I enjoy having something to do, and they've never stopped me from doing it. I set my transporter craft to launch just as the other craft should reach Yahbi's surface. Now I wait.

The engine stirs in anticipation. I lay back on the bench to think. Saul's father looks like more than just a Talker sympathizer to me. I haven't seen him jabbering like a twit on a crate before, so how is he connected to them? I bite my knuckle thoughtfully. The guys' Maan might be right. Anything connected with the Talkers is probably dangerous. I start to doubt myself. I followed Saul's father out of curiosity, but this might be linking me to something more treacherous. They always say "curiosity killed the cat." I don't know what a cat is, but maybe that's the point. Maybe they all got killed by curiosity. I sit up to stop the engines of my craft from engaging.

"I don't think I should do this," I say out loud to myself. I scratch the back of my hand anxiously.

Samuel's worried face pops into my mind. *It'll be alright,* I had promised. It's too late. The preset timer goes off, and the craft automatically launches itself past the landing bay doors. I could turn the ship around, but it's already set to autopilot. I could take it off autopilot, but I'm already on my way. The yellow planet glows on the viewer screen. I lay back down on the bench again.

If Yalk is dust, Yahbi is sand. The Yahbiins tell me that there are places on Yahbi which aren't all sand, but there's no landing pad for my craft there. Yahbiins have offered before to take me to the brighter sides of Yahbi on sand pedalers, commercial vehicles that roll over the dunes, but I imagine they'd be more likely to rob me and leave me for dead in the middle of the dunes. That's the one common theme about Yahbiins, they're greedy little merchants that would sell their soul if it meant they could make some baunti. I assume that selling their souls has something to do with the reason they're able to autonomously sell in the marketplace. Maybe I'm underestimating them, though. Maybe they managed to swindle even the Lovindians.

Like all of the planets in the galaxy, Yahbi is owned by the Lovindians, but it is special because, for the most part, it isn't run by the Lovindians. It is run, instead, by what is called the "Second Generation" of Lovindians. The Second Gens aren't necessarily like them. However, it isn't all that unheard of for a Second Gen to take on the horrific habits of their forefathers. To my knowledge, the Second Gens give a good deal of leeway to the crafty little Yahbiin natives.

It's impossible, of course, to tell a Second Gen from a Yahbiin native. That's how the Lovindians work. It is impossible to tell a Lovindian from anyone else because "Lovindian" isn't a single species. The best that is understood is that the conquering race has some ability to take over the bodies of those they conquer. They live forever at the expense of their conquered people. No one knows what the original Lovindian species looks like, and many believe that the original Lovindian species completely died out centuries ago because of their preference for other species. I've always thought that, if that were true, it would be incredibly ironic.

Second Gens are any of the following generations born to the original Lovindian souls. Seconds are the lucky children.

Lovindians inhabit whatever bodies they want to, which has consequences if they want to reproduce. Any child born to them while they're in another body has the instincts, mentality, and mental capacity only of that species. If the species is similar to that of the original Lovindian race, then they are raised as Lovindians, given Second Gen authority, and are allowed the privilege of using conquered bodies.

Third Gens, or Thirds, are the unlucky ones. If the species their child is born into isn't compatible with their own, the child is abandoned or shunned by the Lovindian society. They, however, are lucky in the fact that they aren't going to be used for their bodies, and they can hold positions for the Lovindians. Thirds don't last long. They're not embraced by their own species or the Lovindians. Suicide frequently occurs across all species of Thirds.

This is all common knowledge, but for me, it's impossible to tell if anyone is any type of Lovindian unless they come out and admit it, which of course, they never do. Emmanuel is quick to call the Gromptu "turds," but there's no way of telling if they are second or third generation.

Sand quickly finds its way into the folds of my fabric-wrapped feet. I learned not to take the fabric off my feet on my first trip to Yahbi. That just encourages Yahbi's smaller, insectoid inhabitants to come looking for a nibble. It took almost three days before I could walk without hobbling.

The booths in the marketplace can be as small as a single table or as large as a tent canopy. I step off the landing pad and jog toward one of the booths. A native Yahbiin with naturally purple-tinted skin and orange-brown hair looks up at me. He grins his orange teeth.

"Human being!" he says with outstretched arms.

"Hey, Sabo. You been watching the landing pads?"

"As always, as always." He grins wider, seeing a financial opportunity.

I flip a piece of baunti from my pocket and set the value on the coin to "15." The green coin sits on the counter of his booth, glinting in the sun. A triangle touchpad in the center indicates its worth.

"Human being! You always understand me so well! How can I assist you with my vast wealth of information?"

"There was a Yalkian transporter craft that landed here just before me. I'm sure that wasn't beneath your notice." Flattering Sabo is always a good strategy.

"Of course! I thought it was you, but it was two different human beings. That one human being has been bringing people here for days. They think we don't notice that they haven't been leaving, but we do. We keep track of everything. Everything is business and everything is our business."

I have to force myself not to roll my eyes at the Yahbiin mantra. I press the baunti coin on the table but don't take my thumb off of it.

"Where are they camping out, Sabo?"

"It would be immoral to reveal where a secret meeting would be carrying out and when it would be happening." He pouts comically and glances down at the coin under my thumb.

I double tap it and the number goes up to "25." Sabo smiles toothily.

"But it would be terribly immoral to not help an old friend reach his human being friends! Your friends are camping in a green, canopy-style tent in the southwestern market. You'll know it when you see it. The canopy is too dark for Yahbiin colors. For a secret meeting, they sure did choose a suspicious tent!"

It is bad that even Sabo, whose booth is in the southern market, knows that the Talkers are trying to have a "secret" meeting. Saul's father and his friends are being more than a little sloppy. My blood rushes. If Sabo knows, everyone on Yahbi knows. The Yahbiins might not care about what they are doing, but there are sure to be Thirds and Second Gens hovering on the planet. If it is profitable for the Yahbiins to tell the Thirds and Second Gens where the Talkers are, they will tell the Lovindians before the baunti hits the table. I double-tap the coin again to encourage our future business and leave it on the table.

"Human being! Wait!" he calls after me.

I stop. He plays with the coin nervously in his hands.

"Human being, if these friends of yours are not close friends... I would not go to the green tent this evening."

For a moment, I don't move, but then I smile and nod. I watch him dematerialize my coin into his computer panel. I wonder if he told me this information because he felt some kind of actual kinship to me or if he just wanted to make sure I was alive to secure future business. Either way, the information he just gave me says a lot. It means that the Lovindians are more than aware of what is happening this evening, and that doesn't bode well.

I knew that figuring out where Saul's father was going was the easy part. The hard part is navigating through Yahbi's crowds. For a lot of conquered species, Yahbi is the only marketplace available for them. The recreational planet lures all kinds of creatures whose species I don't know the name of, and I have no plans of asking them. The best knowledge to have on Yahbi is which species to stay clear of, and I'm happy to know just that alone.

"Command key, show southwest."

The command key projects an arrow just above my wrist. I follow the crowd flow. Even aggressive species follow the crowd flow. If you don't, navigating Yahbi is impossible. The downside of this is that sometimes to go southwest you have to go another direction. There are no straight lines to go anywhere on Yahbi.

There's nothing that can describe the noise on Yahbi. Arriving on Yahbi for the first time, you quickly learn that there are species capable of making sounds that you never could have imagined existed. On Yalk, everything is so quiet that the windy atmosphere outside drowns out the sound. On Yahbi, there is a cacophony of trills, honks, growls, hisses, chirps, and clicks. Once, I was next to a creature that made a noise so shrill that I was nearly deaf for several hours.

One Yahbiin moon sets and two more rise from the north. It's growing dark when I see the top of the dark-green tent canopy. Sabo was right; it stands out terribly. The tent they've chosen is meant for the winter climate. I can tell because there are two layers of tenting.

I'm sure the Talkers chose it for privacy, but there's no reason for privacy on Yahbi. Yahbiins want to gain prospective buyer's attention, so if they have a booth with any type of covering at this time of year, it is going to be a bright-colored, net curtain that allows merchandise to be visible. The winter tent in front of me is meant to block out wind and sand, so the outside is solid and thick. There is a second inner layer called a thermal screen which locks in heat. Normally, the winter tents are painted with images and descriptions of the merchandise inside. The bare, closed-off, tent walls look horribly suspicious. A knot forms in my stomach.

I walk around the back of the tent and lift a stake from the ground. I slip between the two layers to listen to the inside. It's hot. The space I find myself in is only as wide as my forearm. I'm not as thin and lanky as Samuel, and for the first time, I can see the advantage of being built that way. At least I'm not stocky like Emmanuel. Beads of sweat form on my forehead and drip down my cheeks. Sweat leaks into my eyes and it stings. I don't dare wipe it away because the movement could make the thermal screen ripple.

I put my ear close to the thermal screen and try to block out the sounds of the Yahbiin marketplace. Nothing. At least the sun is setting. If it were much brighter out, I would start baking in here. Sweat runs down my leg and it itches. I want to reach down and scratch, but I'm not about to be found snooping around. Instead, I focus on the ray of light shining through the curtain. It's already beginning to sink down. Sunset on Yahbi happens fast.

Sabo said the meeting is this evening. Maybe they found out the Lovindians suspected them and decided not to come. That would be good. Sweat tickles my ear, and I toss my head uselessly. What am I doing here anyway? This is stupid. What do I have to gain from knowing what they're doing here?

What about Saul?

I shake the thought from my head. Risking my safety for someone else is stupid. I'm just here because I'm curious. I don't do anything for anyone else's sake. I proved that when I went to Unit B. I can't talk to a Talker without the risk of being seen as a sympathizer, but hiding here between the tent and the thermal screen, I can listen. This is an opportunity—that's all.

The ray of light reaches my feet. I wiggle my toes at it. Now my sweat is cool. The tent in front of me tremors. For a second, I almost think that I imagined it, but raspy breaths come from inside the tent. My heart flips. I don't know whether to be excited or worried. Since they've decided to come, they must not know that everyone on Yahbi knows what they're doing. I clench my damp hands into fists.

"It looks as though Abraham has not arrived." The voice is soft and young.

"No scat."

The second voice has to be Saul's father. I've heard that gruff bark yelling after Saul before. Maybe I should tell them now. I can sneak into the inner tent, warn them, and then slip out the back before being noticed. The tent rustles again, and I freeze instinctively.

"Rachel," the young man whispers, "thank goodness they didn't get you!"

"No," comes the soft and tired voice of the new arrival. "They didn't, but that was too close. I can't keep scrambling the travel logs; they're eventually going to look into those couple seconds of signal distortion. The Gromptu may look slow, but they are Lovindians just the same. All Lovindians are clever bastards no matter what ranking they are or what form they take."

"Rachel is right," says a deeper voice, who must have entered with Rachel. I recognize his voice. He's one of the Talkers who goes on the crates. I think his name is Benjamin, but I can't be sure. "We can't keep coming to Yahbi to meet like this. It's safer than Yalk, but this place is still crawling with Second Gens. That's not even including the Second Gens who aren't openly Second Gen or any Lovindians which might

23

be lurking here, completely unidentifiable."

If only he knew how right he is. I try once again to stir up the courage to go into the tent, but I'm frozen solid. If I go in, I've helped them. The Lovindians are terrifying creatures. No one has ever seen their true form because they take on the bodies of their conquered people. A Lovindian could appear as anything, or anyone, at any time. One of these people inside the tent could already be... I bite my tongue at my cowardice.

"There's no point in being careful. We're only delaying the inevitable," Saul's father growls. "You're all fools if you think we'll be around for much longer. The Lovindians likely already know what we're doing. For all the hell we know, we're already infiltrated, and one of us isn't even one of us anymore. Oh, and Isaiah, don't start with the whole code system again." I assume that Isaiah must be the younger man. "Rachel is fantastic at running codes to us, but if one of us were found out and taken in, we all know the Lovindians could get the codes or any other information that they wanted out of us."

"If you believe we're going to get caught, then why are you here?" Isaiah shoots back.

"Isaiah," Rachel says softly.

"I'm here, nit-prick, because Abraham told me to be here. If I'm already done, then I might as well keep a promise to my oldest friend."

The whole tent shakes and I almost fall into the room. I steady myself the best I can, hoping that they're all too distracted to notice my mistake.

"Abraham!" Rachel gasps.

Abraham's voice is warm and deep. "They have us. You all have to go. We have the coordinates of the red planet. Each of you, take a slip now with the coordinates on it. We will each go to our assigned safe house, but I think it's unlikely that the Lovindians aren't already there."

"What's the point of a safe house if it isn't safe?" No one answers Benjamin.

I hear paper rustling. The red planet? The coordinates? It's time for me to leave. If I don't get out of here, I'm going to be trapped with them. What if they associate me with them just because I'm on Yahbi? Cold sweat starts to pour down my back.

"But Abraham, this is madness!" It's Isaiah's voice.

Abraham ignores him as well. "Go now. If you are trapped, try to pass the coordinates on to someone; it doesn't matter to whom it's passed. We have to believe that if the information is available, the right hands will find it. Don't let this die here. We worked too long to find the coordinates. The Historians are within our reach! They're our last chance to hear the story. This is the only direction we can hope to press forward. This might be humanity's last chance. Go! Go now!"

The tent rustles as someone tries to flee. I'm shaking. There's a sudden cry of surprise, and then silence.

"They're already here!" Rachel breathes in.

"I'm sorry," Abraham whispers. I think I hear tears in his voice.

"Don't sweat it, Abe; we had a good run."

No. No, no, no. I want to scream, I want to run, but nothing happens. It's just like the dream where I reach out to Keren but can never touch her. There's no sound as it enters the tent, but I see its glowing eyes through the thermal layer. All of my blood drains to my feet and makes them heavy. A light flashes and the inner tent is suddenly illuminated, revealing the solemn, black outline of a single Gromptu. The mysterious white light flashes again, and I'm blinded. I shouldn't move, but I can't help but touch my eyes. I can't get the image out of my mind. It's burnt on the back of my eyelids. I see the dark lumps lying on the ground motionlessly.

There's no way to run now. The brightness starts to fade from my eyes, and everything seems darker than before in the aftermath of the blazing light. Still, there's a soft glow coming from inside the tent. I squint to see better. My breath catches in my lungs. A pair of white eyes floats inside the tent.

It sees me.

I swallow hard. I'm trapped! My heart thunders in my chest so loud that it can probably hear it too. I breathe in and shut my eyes. It was fast. Whatever it did to them was fast. *I'm sorry, Keren.*

Minutes pass. I open my eyes. The Gromptu is gone. Had it not seen me after all? No, I know for certain that it had. I hadn't imagined that. My knees collapse. I fall into the room and vomit violently.

My stomach emptied, I blink my eyes to adjust to the darkness. There's a stillness to the room that's unlike any other I've ever felt before. I crawl towards Saul's father, who lays face-first on the floor. His pale blue eyes are the same shade as Saul's. My chest tightens. I put my hand on his back, but I fail to feel the rise of air going through his lungs. The life is gone from him, but I can't see any wound to patch up. It's like the white light just swallowed the life from his body.

She is the most shocking. The young woman, who must have been Rachel, has warm, olive skin and red lips. Like Saul's father, there's no mark on her to explain how she was killed. Her black ringlets of hair spill out across the ground. Underneath her hair, I can see the slip of paper they had exchanged caught between two of her slender fingers. I stumble toward her, and my nausea returns.

I brush away the web of hair covering the paper. Her fingertips are still warm as I take the coordinates from her. I wonder if she was from a different unit—maybe Unit A. I would have remembered seeing someone as shockingly beautiful as she is. My stomach turns. Whatever passionate life she had lived is gone. If I had known I would see this, would I still have followed them to Yahbi? My head spins.

I stagger up to my feet and back out of the tent. It's dark. None of it feels like it's real. Business changes on Yahbi in the night. The streets aren't crowded. The curtains on the tents all come down, and the customers are either nocturnal or customers who would have reasons for not wanting to be seen in the daylight. In the night, there are people on Yahbi like the Talkers, people that are involved in race wars unapproved by the Lovindian government, and privateers. Privateers are Second or Third Gens, who operate almost completely free of Lovindian control. They steal from Lovindian allies, which are unknown to me, under the guise of being terrorists.

I wonder how many of the shrouded figures are Lovindians or war criminals and shiver. I'm made aware of how inappropriate it is for me to be here. It will be a long walk to the transporter craft. I numbly trudge back in the direction of the craft. The shock that stagnates my mind somehow still allows my feet to keep going.

3

Chapter 3

I wake to the beeping of the transporter craft's system panel. "ENTERING ATMOSPHERE" flashes across the screen. I arrived back to the craft in the early hours of Yahbi's dawn and attempted to catch a few moments of rest during the trip back to Yalk. I can see Yalk clearly on the viewer screen. My thoughts feel as thick as Yalkian mash. I struggle to sort through them.

What does this mean? In some ways, it doesn't mean anything at all. People disappear. It happens. We all know that it happens. But I saw it. Now I know what it means to "disappear." I see the bodies lying there in the sand all over again. If I had any food left in my stomach, I would feel sick again. Saul's father is just gone. A sharp pain digs into my chest.

When Saul was a child, his mother died during the wheeze. The wheeze was an outbreak that had been eradicated by the time I had arrived at Unit B. We had outbreaks in Unit C, but not like the wheeze. A third of Unit B's population died. It was one of the reasons why it was so easy for me to transfer—there were plenty of open living spaces. Saul had lost his mother, and his father never found another pairing. His father became a quiet recluse, keeping to himself. Many said that he blamed the Gromptu for bringing the infection to the planet. With humanity's limited contact with the rest of the galaxy, it was easy to believe that the Gromptu were the easiest way that a disease could enter the unit. Just bringing in any outside germ could cause an outbreak. After the wheeze, the transporter crafts were redesigned to spray decontaminant when their doors opened. That didn't save Saul's mother, though, and now Saul is about to learn he's all alone.

The landing bay doors open and the craft lands using autopilot. I feel the safety of the too-large seat of my transporter craft. What will happen when I exit? The Gromptu on Yahbi may have already reported back to his friends on Yalk. I was spared before, but maybe it just needed time to decide what to do with me.

My hands tremble as I reach into the folds of my shirt for the slip of paper. They called them coordinates, but they don't look like any coordinates I've ever seen before. It's just three words. I pinch them hard between my finger and my thumb, and my hand steadies a little.

This is what they died for. This is what I might die for, and I don't even understand what it means. They said that it leads to a red planet, but I don't know how to use them, what the red planet signifies, or if my craft could even get me there. The limits on my fuel tank could make it impossible for me to even reach the planet they were talking about.

I raise the command key on my wrist to my lips. If I lower the door to my craft, there's a good chance I'm going to be greeted by a white light. I breathe in, thinking of Keren. What does she think of her older brother? Will she ever learn of my disappearance? I shiver. Maybe she thinks I've disappeared already. I never even bothered to explain why I left. My stomach swims. By now, I probably have siblings that I have never even gotten the chance to meet—I may never get the chance to meet.

A million times over I have regretted the decision to leave Unit C, but now I regret it more than ever. I felt so suffocated there. I'm fraught with images of my mother staring blankly at the walls as Keren learned to crawl. The obligations, the responsibilities, the repetition ate me up. The contentment others had with pretending to be content—it disgusted me. I judged them for trying to find ways to survive their lives. Now I wish that I hadn't been such a selfish child.

I stand up with a sinking feeling. The craft is small. A few steps won't delay my impending death for long.

"Open hatch door."

Nothing happens. I peek out and spot a Gromptu across the landing bay preening a feather on its shoulder. Something about it must not have been to its liking because it plucks it coldly. I guess that whatever they plan to do with me, they don't plan to do it now. I pass through the doors into the core of Unit B and sigh a deep breath of relief.

I need to tell Saul. I need to tell the others what I witnessed, while I still have the chance. Just because I'm not dead now doesn't mean that they will allow me to see what I've seen. The buildings are a blur. Heads turn as I pass and children point. I'm causing a scene. I pass a crate, but there's no one standing on it.

"Jacob?" He grabs my sleeve. "Hey! What are you doing running like that? Have you cracked?"

"Let me go, Emmanuel! I'm not cracked! I have to talk to Saul!" I yell, snatching away my arm.

Emmanuel curses at me.

"Why do you need to talk to me so badly?"

The voice stops me. Saul. Samuel is standing with him too. They are holding their swatters as if they've just come back from a game of Scrab's Eye Ball.

"Saul? I thought you weren't going to be around us anymore," I pant.

He turns red until I can't see the freckles on his face. "Didn't realize I was so unwelcome."

"That's not what I mean!" I roll my eyes.

Samuel steps in. "We made our Maan apologize for what she said. It was just gossip anyways, right Saul?"

I look at Saul to search his reaction, but he just nods, appeased by Samuel's peacemaking. The red drains a little from his face. Saul looks like the complete opposite of Samuel. Saul is pale and freckled with reddish-blonde hair. He is closer to my age but not as tall as Samuel and his stomach is much rounder.

My heart still thunders in my chest. Saul, although looking at me strangely, appears to be completely unaware of what's happened.

"That's good." I force a smile.

It's impossible to tell if Saul even knows the validity of his father's ties with the Talkers. My words catch in my mouth. How could I even begin? I can't tell him in front of the others. They've only just gotten permission to see him again. I stare at him dumbly.

"Saul, what's that Gromptu doing outside your apartment?" Emmanuel points.

31

The hairs lift on my arms. Saul's eyebrows knit together in confusion.

"I don't know," he says, wiping the hair from his forehead.

I turn to follow their gaze. The Gromptu places something on the door and moves away.

"What did it put on your door?" Emmanuel whispers.

Samuel is very pale, but Saul shrugs.

"It didn't put anything on anyone else's door," he mumbles.

I'm dumbstruck as they start walking curiously toward his apartment. My determination to tell Saul what happened on Yahbi extinguishes. I don't want him to read what's on the door. There's security in ignorance. I don't want to watch, but I'm drawn in as if I'm watching a video.

He pulls the slip from the door. He stiffens. The slip falls and swings down to the ground.

"What? What is it?" Emmanuel lays a hand on his shoulder.

Emmanuel never studied the Lovi-dex and he can't read it. Samuel walks forward and picks it up off the ground. He mouths the words to himself, and his eyes go wide. He looks to me. I don't have to read it to know what it says, but Samuel extends it to me, and I take it from him obediently.

Hereof Kish is no longer a citizen.

"Samuel! Jacob! What does it say?" Emmanuel shouts.

Samuel's eyes don't leave me. He shakes his head. Without another option, Emmanuel looks to me. I open my mouth, not knowing what I will say. Saul beats me to it first, and though I didn't know what to say, I wouldn't have said this.

"It says my father's dead."

I can hear the anger burning in his voice. We all watch him now. He wipes away tears from the corners of his eyes, and I don't know if they're from grief or fury.

"It doesn't say he's dead," Samuel breaks in quietly.

Guilt washes over me. Why can't I just tell him the truth? Why can't I tell him what I saw? I should have said it as soon as I found them. I shouldn't have hesitated.

"He's dead!" Saul snaps back, turning on us, but not looking at anyone in particular.

"Saul—" Emmanuel starts. His voice is filled with worry.

"It's probably best that you stay away from me from now on. You know why they killed him." He shakes.

"Saul, we would never—" Emmanuel tries again.

"I said stay away!" He slides open the door to his apartment and slams it behind him.

Emmanuel stalks away, and I know he's trying to hide tears that he's too proud for. I wish that Samuel would follow him, but I know that he won't. My heart clenches.

"Do you think Saul's right?" he whispers. "Did they kill him? Did they do it because he was a Talker?"

I grit my teeth. If I tell him what I know, it changes everything. He will have to live with the burden of knowing that we are just as easily extinguishable as bugs. Over the time that I've been in Unit B, these three have unknowingly become like brothers to me. I want to protect Samuel. If I can protect any of them, let it at least be Samuel with his good heart.

"I think you should follow Emmanuel home," I say. "It's going to take some convincing to make him believe that Saul didn't mean what he just said."

Samuel nods understandingly, and I'm relieved that he doesn't pressure me for an answer.

"Are you going to try to talk to Saul?" he asks instead.

"Yeah," I surprise myself by replying.

"Alright, good luck." Samuel smiles sadly at me, and then

jogs after his brother.

I give a big sigh and knock on the door.

"I said swat off, the whole lot of you!" Saul hollers back.

"It's just me," I say, not knowing why I think it will make a difference.

To my astonishment, the door opens just a crack. The doors don't actually lock, so technically, I could have come in either way, but I prefer to have his permission. I'm hit with a wave of stale air as I enter. It's obvious that Saul's door stays shut for the majority of the time. I respect Saul's wish to sit in the privacy of the dark and shut the door behind me. The lights turn off. At first I can't see anything at all, and then my eyes adjust to the dark. Light from the hallway seeps in through the cracks of the door and shoots a ray of light across his face.

"You wanted to tell me something before," he says quietly.

I'm surprised to find that he's not crying. His hands are folded behind his head as he lies on his cot staring at the ceiling. I don't know what he's thinking. This is somehow much worse than finding him in shambles.

"It was nothing," I lie.

He nods, willing to accept my lie. For a moment, he's quiet and I don't know if he intends for me to leave or not.

"They murdered him," he hisses, barely audibly.

I sigh, relieved that he was the one to break the topic. I take a seat on the ground beside his cot, taking care not to sit on his father's empty one. I realize now, in the dark, just how tired I am. Only hours ago I was wandering through the dark on Yahbi. My arms fall limply. Nothing feels real. It's like I'm watching everything happen just outside of my body.

"You don't deny it like Samuel did," Saul whispers.

Does he think I know more than I'm saying? My heart

quickens. I wish that I could see his face better, but my eyes haven't entirely adjusted yet.

"It's because you're older than they are," he says.

I jump on the excuse. "Yeah, I am."

"I wonder if it was true then. I wonder if he was a Talker sympathizer. I never even thought about it before. I never paid attention to what he did. He was so bitter after Mum died, I didn't ever want to be around him. We never even talked about it."

I nod, not knowing exactly how to respond. I can't shake the feeling that he should be talking to Emmanuel. He's his closest friend. I'm just a guy they asked to play Scrab's Ball one day.

"Saul, there's something—" I try to say it, but his expression makes me hesitate. His jaw is clenched tightly in anger. It's not so much that he's grieving but that he's furious.

"They have to pay." He pounds his fist against the wall.

"What do you mean?" I ask tentatively. My heart patters.

"You know what they are, Jacob! They are monsters! They take our bodies so they can live forever! They're secretive, horrid, nasty parasites!" This speech sounds hauntingly familiar. "They took him from me! What threat was he? Even if he did sympathize with people who yell in the corridors, what did it matter? What could they even do? We don't have any power!"

I can feel the piece of paper with the coordinates in the folds of my shirt. I suspect that the Talkers did a little more than yell in the corridors. They must have gotten a little too close to the truth, and it all had to do with that red planet they were talking about.

"I'll tell them all. I'll tell all of Yalk what they did."

Panic arises within me. I think of the white light which almost reached my hiding place between the tent layers. I'm suddenly very thankful that I didn't tell him what I saw. The more that he knows, the more he's likely to make himself a target.

"Saul," I caution, "you know what they did. You know what they're capable of."

He jumps up to a sitting position and swings his legs around to face me.

"That's exactly why I have to tell everyone!"

"Saul, it won't make a difference," I say evenly. "People on Yalk won't listen, and what do you possibly want them to do about it?"

"I'll make them listen!" His eyes blaze. He ignores the second half of my question.

"Whatever you're thinking, Saul, don't do it."

"I thought of all people, Jacob, you would get it. Out of all of us, you've been the most restless." I hadn't thought it was that obvious. I can't meet his gaze. "You think we don't get you? You think we don't notice the way you sulk, all hung up on some guilt you won't tell us about? You think we don't know the reason you slink off to your transporter ship is that you can't stand to let yourself relax? That we don't know you hate yourself infinitely?"

I'm shocked. I don't know what to say. My face burns. He's only saying it because he's hurting, but he's telling the truth. The truth is that I've always held myself away from them. I hate myself more for his words. I want to respond to his accusations, but I don't know how. I deserve it—I deserve this for not returning to Unit C.

"You don't even like us! You think we're beneath you!" he

36

barks.

"That's not true!" I defend myself finally, jumping to my feet.

"Then why can't you even look Samuel in the eye!"

My chest hurts. What did I do wrong? How did I somehow make him angry at me? It was a bad decision to come here.

"Samuel knows you don't like him, and he's still your creeping little shadow!"

"That's not why! I do like Samuel!" I fight back.

"Then why do you treat him like that?" he challenges me.

"I—" I can't get the words out. I can't tell him the truth. I can't tell him that I'm unreliable and undeserving. I can't tell him that I only hurt people like Samuel. I can't tell him any of this.

"You shut us out like it's nothing!" he hollers.

"Like you just did to Emmanuel?" My anger boil up from inside. It pours over the top and I'm seething. I came here to console him, but now he's picking me apart. He doesn't know anything about me! He doesn't know how I feel!

"That was different." He says this, but his face reveals more pain than he's letting on.

"It wasn't," I state.

"Get out of my apartment."

I don't bother to argue with him. My head is burning. I try to clear my head, but all I see is Samuel's dejected face and Rachel's limp figure. The white light flashes through my head repeatedly as the images pass through. It's too much to process.

When I sleep, I dream of Keren.

4

Chapter 4

My mother used to tell me, "Free people know the boundaries of their freedom." It's expected that a good citizen not only knows what is considered incorrect behavior but can also anticipate what might be incorrect behavior before making a mistake. The Lovindians are good at drawing lines, and it's our responsibility to see where they are without having to be told. By now, we don't have to touch the burners to know which ones are hot. The Talkers told us that freedom shouldn't have boundaries, and now they're gone. I guess they should have known their boundaries.

I feel the teachings of the mother I left behind itching under my skin. Goosebumps form on my arms. Samuel looks at me with big, pleading eyes, but I can't force myself to look at him. Saul's words echo in my head, and I wonder if deep down Samuel really does believe I don't like him.

It has been many days since my fight with Saul. When he told us what he was planning to do, Emmanuel had been behind him all the way. Emmanuel managed to convince Saul that there was no way he was going to keep his distance, mostly by just following him silently wherever he went until he accepted it. Samuel and I tried to talk him out of it, but he wouldn't even look at us. We were on his side, or we were against him. Word had gotten around that all the Talkers on Yalk had vanished. No one had been watching to see it happen, but everyone knew it had.

Saul knows what he is doing is wrong. Every human in Unit B knows. That's why we are squirming just to look at him. He stands up on his crate chanting like a member of the Talkers' Movement. My stomach clenches.

"Listen! Listen to me! You and I were once kings and queens! We were gods over our lives—gods over a planet of our own! They stole this from us! They stole our heritage, our history, and our homeland, yet you stand around, living off the tit of the conquerors, satisfied and growing fat!"

"Give it a rest, kid, geez! You're one to be talking about growing fat," growls an onlooker.

Saul's chubby, freckle-pricked face turns a deep shade of red. For a second, just as he's thrown off his speech, he looks like the Saul I used to know, used to be close to. His head shakes in anger and disbelief, and reddish-blonde hair falls into his pale blue eyes. He shuffles his feet awkwardly back and forth on the crate. Samuel tugs at my sleeve. What does he want me to do? He should know by now I can't get him down from there. Saul sucks in a deep breath and blusters back at the man.

"Do you want to just forget what the Lovindians stole from us? Do you want to forget what was taken from our ancestors?" he says accusingly.

"Kid," the man shakes the can in his fat fist, "can't I have my morning drink in peace for one damned day?"

"Peace? What can we know of peace? The Lovindians, those parasitic beasts, have taken away our peace of mind."

"Ah, can it, kid!"

The can goes up too quickly. I don't notice it until it hits Saul square in his nose. The brown liquid soaks instantly through his beige-colored clothes and drips from the tips of his blonde hair. Trails of brown stain his cheeks, but he bears the humiliation.

"Didn't you learn from your father?" the man shouts over his shoulder as he walks away.

"Scat off!" Emmanuel goes to rush after the man, but Saul stops him.

I grimace. Even if Saul has chosen this path of his own accord, it's still painful to see. I finally take a glance at Samuel and see a matching frown on his dark-complexioned face. Even he can see that Saul's continuous preaching is going to mean trouble. I had heard stories that Saul was becoming more emboldened lately, to the point of directly insulting the Lovindian guards, but I had tried to ignore the whispers.

The man who'd thrown the can is right, as much as none of us would ever want to admit. Saul needs to learn from his father's mistakes and keep quiet. If people were scared of the Talkers before, they are even more scared now after they disappeared. It's not like the Talkers Movement were the first group of Yalkians to speak out against the Lovindian regime, but they were the most memorable in recent history. I once heard of a group of men and women who protested for medicine outside the doors to the shuttle bay during the last Wheeze. I can't help but wonder if Saul's father was protesting while Saul's mother was sick. I feel the hair rise higher on my arms.

Every day I wake up surprised that a flash of white light hasn't taken me during the night, but here Saul is, knowing the consequences and speaking out. Saul is a reckless idiot, but I'm a weak coward. This is the first time I've seen him do this, though. Samuel practically dragged me. I didn't tell him about our fight, but since Saul and I fought, he's been tense when bringing up his name. Samuel is a lot more perceptive than I was giving him credit for. He clearly knows something has happened between us.

Emmanuel has found a rag to give to Saul and he passes it to him to let him wipe the drink off of his face. Saul dries his face with a few unheard curses. He pulls the rag away from his eyes and notices us for the first time. His eyes bulge with rage and embarrassment.

"Wonderful! Glad the two of you could catch the show!"

Samuel starts talking before I can stop him.

"No, we didn't enjoy that. I mean, we didn't think it was funny or anything." He stumbles over his words and finishes lamely, "That guy was awful."

I cringe for him. Things have changed. Samuel can't be the peacemaker for us anymore.

"Why don't you and Jacob go find a nice, quiet place together, and leave me the hell alone? Maybe Jacob can play you the fennele."

His jab about my little, metal, stringed instrument sends a wave of nostalgia running through me. Saul always teased me about my playing, but at the end of the day, they'd always want to listen. There aren't many musicians in Unit B. His comment, although trying to be snide, only serves to remind me that he was and is my friend.

I want to say something, but Saul is already jumping off his crate. He hefts the box onto one shoulder and marches away, probably to yell his cause at citizens across the Unit Building. Emmanuel glances between us and Saul but, with a strained look, walks guiltily toward us.

"Hey, Sam. Hey, Jacob," he says tiredly.

Samuel nods at his brother, but his eyes follow Saul. He's still hurt by his rebuff.

"How are you doing, Emmanuel?" I ask to fill the awkward silence.

Looking for this invitation to vent, Emmanuel jumps right into what he wants to say.

"Tired. I've tried to get him to stop. I don't know why he won't give it a rest. He doesn't even know that his dad was really one of them."

I don't comment on this. In the passing days, I've decided that I can't tell any of them what I saw on Yahbi. As volatile as Saul is, I don't know what he would do with the information I have. Plus, he already knows the truth—he just doesn't have the details. If I told Samuel, he'd be traumatized, and if I told Emmanuel, he'd probably become as fanatical as Saul. The only thing keeping them all safe is the fact that they don't have the same knowledge as I do.

"You don't think anybody would take Saul seriously do you?" Emmanuel whispers.

I know he means the Lovindians when he says "anybody," and the truth is that I have no idea what the Lovindians think of Saul's antics or what they might do about them. As ridiculous as Saul looks up there and as little attention is paid to him, he is bound to pique the Lovindian's interest eventually. The Gromptu are always watching. It's impossible to pretend like this is going on beneath their notice.

"I don't know," I say pathetically. "I hope not," I add on.

Emmanuel nods with a lopsided frown, "Me too."

He straightens himself up and smiles weakly. I try to smile back some reassurance, but I don't feel it.

"See ya tonight," he tells Samuel and runs off in the direction that Saul went.

"Maan's worried sick about him." Samuel sighs.

For the millionth time in the last several days, I don't have anything to say back. I'm worried too, but I'm trying not to show it for Samuel's sake. We tried to convince Emmanuel to at least stay away from Saul while he's talking. "Someone has to look out for him," was all he said back.

Saul doesn't know about the white light. There's no fighting it. It doesn't matter how loud Saul hollers, there's nothing that he will be able to do to save Emmanuel, let alone himself, if the Gromptu are ordered to make them disappear.

"You haven't gone anywhere in your transporter craft since what happened," Samuel observes. Saul was right about one thing; Samuel really does pay a lot of attention to me.

I'm uneasy at the mentioning of Yahbi. I'm not ready to think about the place again, but at the same time, waiting for a Gromptu to kill me in my sleep has made me more restless than I ever was before. I scratch the top of my hand, and I'm surprised to see that it's been rubbed raw. "You only just noticed?" Samuel says concernedly. "You've been scratching like a lunatic lately."

I pocket my hand, feeling my fennele in there with it. I know that the slip of paper I had gotten from Rachel is in the pocket deeper still. Those two objects alone are a lot of baggage to be carrying. Without going to Yahbi, the feeling that I'm trapped here has increased tenfold. The acute attention that

43

my brain likes to pay to the restless, dead nature of Yalk is exhausting. At least on Yahbi everyone has some sort of goal to fulfill. Their goals are usually self-serving or illegal, but they're goals nonetheless. I don't know how much longer I can resist returning, even with the memory of my last trip.

Samuel is waiting for me to say something, and I smile at him apologetically. It's the first time in a long time that I've really looked at him. Samuel is much better looking than me and kinder too. Someday, once he gets interested, he's going to be popular. He's grown a lot lately. He's even beginning to fill out a little so that his long limbs look less awkward.

I rarely understand what people are thinking or what they want. Keren used to say that I was so in my head that I was incapable of understanding anyone else's. For once, though, I can tell what my friend is thinking. He wants me to tell him what I think about Saul. He wants my opinion on what will happen to his brother. He wants to know why I'm itching my hand to pieces. I grin tightly and scratch my neck with the hand I'm not hiding in my pocket.

Samuel smiles back, but I can see his disappointment. He doesn't ask me anything.

5

Chapter 5

Two months pass. I return to Yahbi. My hand has started to bleed from all of the scratching. If I spend any more time simmering in my guilt on Yalk, I am going to have only bones for a left hand.

On this side of the planet, Yahbi's surface is covered in sand dunes. The outer perimeter of the market, called the landing zone, is littered with ships of various classes. It's common to see many transporter class ships like my own, but there are also cruiser class and an occasional fighter class. Cruiser class ships are used by Lovindians as luxury vehicles and have a wide range of quality depending on the prominence of their owners. Most of the fighter class ships are ones that have been repurposed to serve as cruiser ships— or to serve the appearance of having been repurposed.

When I land, groups of young Yahbiin scavengers take advantage of the sand swirling in the air to decide whether there are any parts of value worth snatching from my craft. Parts stolen from inside the landing zone are frequently the beginning treasures of a Yahbiin booth. For young Yahbiins building a hoard of objects that they can sell is a rite of passage. My boxy craft fails to capture their interest, partially due to the black Lovindian craft logo on the side and partially due to its lack of worth. Private crafts from Thirds and Seconds of lesser importance are easy targets but a military owned craft isn't worth the risk.

I dive into the crowd as a Rodavian strides by with trailing pods. I pull my left leg up to avoid touching the soft, fleshy skin of one of the pods. Rodavians are monstrous, nine-foot-tall, insectoid creatures with massive pincers and dreadful personalities. The Rodavians carry their unborn young in fetal-fluid-filled pods outside their bodies, which are attached to the creature in a way not unlike the human umbilical cord. If I had touched even just one...

"Hey! Kid, get outta the way!"

I jump. In my haste to get away from the Rodavian, I had nearly run into one of the Yahbiin's carts. The Yahbiin inhabitants can be just as violent as a Rodavian over their merchandise.

"Oh, I'm sorry; I was just—"

"You were just leaving! Go on, shoo!" the thing says with orange, bared teeth.

I listen to him and attempt to slip into one of the crowd currents. I always make sure to spend my allowance in the market square of Yahbi and not by submitting a list of needed goods to the officials on Yalk through a com-panel. I like the noise of it all. There's something about the activity which causes my mind to focus. On Yalk, my mind feels so muddled, and my spirits sink with the monotony. Yahbi, in comparison, is full of colors and light. There is a real sky above me and there is real ground below my feet. Yahbiin traders include a multitude of species, and the planet attracts multitudes more.

A wall of people stops the crowd current in front of me, and I'm forced to join a group of consumers hovering over a booth.

"Shoes here! Shoes with real soles!"

People fork over baunti with their usual mob-like mentality. I roll my eyes, but the sheer beige cloth wrapped many times around my feet looks pretty worn. I wiggle my toes and see my big toe nearly pop through the front. Despite wanting to be above the mob, I start to reach for my baunti.

"Wait, wait, kid, you don't want to spend your baunti on that!"

I ignore the speaker at first, but a meaty hand grabs my wrist.

"Hey, let me go!" I shout.

The Yahbiin is strong. I feel ridiculous as I'm hauled away from my new shoes. I can't even dampen my pride enough to call for help. I will only add to the stereotype that humans are weak if I do. The little monster only comes up to about my hip. It takes too much effort trying not to run into someone that I can't attempt to fight back.

We arrive at a booth surrounded by a sheer purple curtain. I wave the curtain away with my one arm, spluttering curses, and look around at the dust-covered tables circling the inside. "Dingy" doesn't even begin to cover it. The Yahbiin drags a wooden crate from under one of the tables. The crate is nearly taller than he is, and he huffs as he pushes it to the center of the floor. He gives a toothy grin and breathes heavily through his teeth. I think I'm supposed to be impressed.

Then he launches himself at the box. Is this some kind of embarrassing attempt at entertainment? The man misses, but admirably, and humiliatingly, tries again to heave himself on top again.

"Do you need help?" I ask, trying not to watch.

The Yahbiin shakes me away with a hand. With a groan, he summons all of his upper body strength and successfully topples onto the box. Brushing himself off, he gives me a grin of confidence, which is so sleazy looking that I shudder. Even standing where he is now, he's shorter than me. His skin is a dark purplish color and his nose is fat and squat on an already fat and squat face.

"Good sir, you do not want to waste baunti on trivial things! You want the big things!" So he's just going to pretend that didn't just happen. I roll my eyes. "Oh yes, the big things! You see, for the last year and a half, I have been trading around the galaxy with the permission of the wonderful Lovindians."

Is this a scripted speech? More importantly, the last bit he said in a way that suggests he doesn't think the Lovindians are so wonderful. I'm instantly suspicious. What is he playing at, saying something so bold? Who paid him to say this?

"You don't like Lovindians?" I dig.

"Ah, no, who does? Never will get used to that nasty habit they have of taking bodies. It's one thing to conquer people, but that's taking it to another level. Still, they gave me a chance to make some money, so they can't be all bad. Plus, the Second Generation isn't too bad. I mean, they're raised in Lovindian schools, so who knows when they might pick up that nasty aforementioned habit, eh? Nah, guess you can't really trust them either." He chuckles.

"I guess that's true. It's a little scary to think they might want your body to be their next one." I shrug to the Yahbiin.

It's easiest to play the game this way. He doesn't act like a Lovindian, but I've never known one personally, so maybe

48

they are ridiculous and inclined to theatrics.

"Er, yeah." The short man looks down at his feet, and I think I see him shiver.

The shiver is too instinctive; he can't be a Lovindian. I don't relax, though. He still could have been paid to do this. It could still be a trap.

"Why don't you look around? Yes, look around! I'm sure you'll find something that will pique your interest!"

He recovers quickly, but he hops off of his box and sidles away from me. I've made him nervous. Good. Now we're on even ground. Most of what I see sprawled out across the tablecloths is covered in a layer of filth. What I can make out beneath the grime are strange trinkets and possible parts to machines that I can't even pretend to guess at. Hanging from the top of the tent are more gadgets that I can't recognize. A Yahbiin should know better than to think that a human could be interested in anything like this. Of course, there's not a ton of humans visiting Yahbi. So maybe he genuinely doesn't know.

"Oh, of course, you're a little overwhelmed with the diversity of it all. I feel like you're a good kid, a smart kid. You probably want to know about the good stuff."

If there is anything that could be said about the Yahbiin people, it is that they sure are good at swindling. This one was willing to drag me from the street just to get a sale. From inside his raggedy jacket vest, the Yahbiin retrieves a round, flat disc, which is about the size of his grubby palm.

"I'm sure that you've never seen this before," he boasts happily.

"No," I return irritably.

Other races love to pick at humanity's ignorance. Humanity

is one of the least privileged species out of the ones that the Lovindians have collected. The species that are removed from their home planets and unitized always are. It's not surprising. At least species that get to stay on their planet know the societies around them. Humanity was completely uprooted, and who knows where they were developmentally. We might never have even achieved space travel.

I could have gotten a new pair of shoes; they are probably all gone by now.

"No, of course you haven't!" the Yahbiin restates. I roll my eyes. This is dramatic even for a Yahbiin. The man looks around through the sheer curtain and lowers his voice. "Would you like to know how I knew that?"

"Because I'm human," I grunt.

The Yahbiin is taken aback. "Because you're hum—no, boy! Species has nothing to do with it! I bet not a creature on Yahbi 'sides me knows what this is."

"Oh, yeah? Why's that?" I try to make myself sound sarcastic, but I'm actually surprised.

"Well, sir, this little gem was smuggled into the galaxy. It was made by a Lovindian competitor."

I squint to see it better, and the Yahbiin uses the power of his wooden crate to hold the object above my head. It doesn't look like anything particularly special. My cheeks burn. For the millionth time, I feel my ignorance of the world. This man could be showing me a compressor to a Quadrinian Herbal Mixer for all I know.

"What does it do?" I ask.

"What? This little do-dad? Well, I'll tell ya." He looks around suspiciously and leans in to whisper. His hot breath comes over my ear. "It blocks the sensors of Lovindians ships."

"Sure it does," I say sarcastically. That settles it. I'm going back to see if any shoes are left.

"Stop! Wait! If I could prove it to you, would you be interested?"

He grabs my sleeve just before I reach the purple curtain. I look down at him, doing my best to show him my complete disinterest. The creature's already bulbous eyes bulge a little more around its squat nose. He places the device against my chest, and I shirk away from it, but not before it falls into my hands. Holding it doesn't change anything. My skin crawls just looking at it.

"You're a human, right?" The Yahbiin guides me back to the center of the room, and to my embarrassment, rolls back on top of the crate.

"I've already pointed that out," I snap.

"We don't see many of you around here. That's why I knew you had to be special. That you might be... in need of such a thing."

"What are you insinuating?"

"Well, most humans are pretty grass-fed now, if you catch my drift." He winks. "Oh, no offense, of course," he adds as my eyes narrow. "You, though, I had you pegged as an anti-Lovindian type of guy. Who were those humans that used to cause trouble? The yappers? I don't know. You remind me of one of those types. They were originally why I went to great lengths to get this thing. They were going to pay me massively."

The Talkers. Why had they wanted this thing? It hits me. The red planet. Using a sensor blocker would be the only way to travel to the red planet. My stomach drops. I flip the device over in my hands. It's circular and fits perfectly in my palm. It radiates a cool feeling.

What if this is a test? The Lovindians don't know why I was in the tent, but seeing my reaction to the device is a good way of judging my intentions. All the Yahbiin has to do is report back if I've bought it.

"How does it work?" I ask impulsively. Stupid.

"Ha!" the Yahbiin barks. "You've got gall, kid; that's for sure! What kind of project could you possibly have in mind?"

"Forget it." I turn to leave. "I don't have a purpose for that."

"Wah—wait, wait!" The Yahbiin tumbles off of the crate, landing on his stomach. "Oof!"

I stop only because I'm startled.

"Do you need help?" I say, half-exasperated.

The Yahbiin is so overcome with a sudden kind of hysteria that he doesn't answer my question. Instead, the creature licks his lips with a yellowish tongue, and spits out, "Nine baunti!"

I pause. It is insanely underpriced. I couldn't have even bought the shoes for nine baunti. If this Yahbiin isn't a Lovindian spy, then he is definitely trying to sell me a useless part to some obscure object.

"Look, you just click this third button, and BAM, it's taken care of." The creature exaggerates the motions with his stubby arms. I notice the Yahbiin is sweating, and it has a distinctly different smell than human sweat.

"Why?" I ask.

"I don't think I understand you, my good human." He grins in a way that he is incorrectly assuming looks like innocence.

"Why are you selling it so cheap?" I demand.

The Yahbiin sighs in what appears to be a mix of frustration and relief. "It's a death sentence! You said it yourself; I could be their next—you know! If I got caught with this contraband! Ha! I'd be done! I'm not fighting for some cause. I don't wanna die for this thing. I just wanted to make a little baunti."

"Ah," and for the first time, I start to believe the slimy, little man. I don't know if this is because I want to believe him, or if it's because I actually think he's telling the truth. I see myself counting out the nine baunti in my hand. The Yahbiin snatches the coins away and simultaneously puts the device into my palm. It happens so fast.

"You won't regret it!" The Yahbiin flashes me a wretched smile and shoves me from the tent as quickly as he pulled me in. "Have a great day!"

If I'm not executed by white light in the middle of the night, and I get the chance to return to Yahbi, I have a feeling that I won't be welcomed back again inside that tent. Good riddance.

6

Chapter 6

The shuttle bay door closes as quickly as it opened. The air outside on Yalk isn't dangerous in small doses, but extended exposure can become toxic. The Gromptu barely stir as I land beside the five matching transporter crafts. Their lack of reaction after what I've just done both relaxes me and gives me anxiety at the same time. I scratch the top of my bandaged hand. The wind whistles over the dome.

Yalk is a desolate planet on the surface. Humans have been freely allowed to settle on the planet in the unit buildings, and the Lovindians lost nothing because there is absolutely nothing of value on Yalk. The planet has been mined, farmed, and even logged until not even grass can grow. Of course, with no plant-life, there is no oxygen. The lack of oxygen makes it necessary for the Lovindians to construct oxygenated unit buildings for us to live in.

The wind on the planet constantly shifts the dirt and whips it up against the unit buildings that we call home. The unit buildings are ovular shaped because it makes them less likely to be blown away in a tornado of wind and dust. The thrum of the dirt outside is barely separable from the sound of acid-based rain that, in some seasons, comes down in heavy sheets, turning Yalk to a planet of mud. The rainy season makes a formidable obstacle for the small transporter crafts, and I hesitate on days when the rain roars.

The com-panels say that humans were transported from a planet called "Earth" many generations ago. We are labeled "war refugees." I get the feeling that "prisoners of war" is probably a better term. Our transporter crafts only just span the distance of the furthest permitted planet, Nivri, and back before running out of fuel. Nivri is a gas giant. It's pretty to look at, but unless you want to watch mineral miners circle the planet for a few moments before your low fuel warning goes off, there's no point in going.

We don't have any information about Earth in the com-panels. We don't know why we were removed from Earth, and I'm sure that no species ever knows why they're removed. Our planet, our oxygen, our crafts—all given to us. The planet Yalk hums of human life, but it's not progressive life. There is a sense of being a pet—living a purposeless and well-fed existence.

Then there is this other feeling. It's the feeling that rises up in the shiftless compound just as the lights start to dim. I can see it in an occasional cringe or shadowed face. This feeling resides in a suggestion buried in the back of every human's mind. The suggestion that we aren't pets but cattle.

"Humans are pretty grass-fed now."

I think of what the Yahbiin said and cringe. I'm hit with a wave of this intoxicating feeling as I exit the craft and step into the landing bay.

"Jacob!"

A Lovindian guard lifts an eye as Samuel waves wildly from across the shuttle bay. The attention of that staring, white globe makes my hand drift automatically to my pocket where the sensor blocker is hidden. Looking past Samuel at the Lovindian guard, I start to understand the fear that wracked the Yahbiin when he sold the device to me.

"Hey! I'm right here, you heap of Larvak dung!" Samuel says waving a hand in front of my face. I snort. He doesn't even know what a Larvak looks like. I laughingly push away his hand, and the dark feeling starts to lift.

"How was Yahbi?"

"It was—" I can feel the device against my thigh.

"Geez! You trying to kill me with suspense or something?"

"Oh, sorry. It was—weird," I finish awkwardly.

"What do you mean weird?" He scrunches up his face.

"I almost got in a fistfight with a Rodavian," I offer. At least it's true.

"Those are the giant insectoid ones, right?"

"Yeah, the ones with the big, nasty claws!"

I mimic the claws and Samuel laughs, but then he scratches his head nervously.

"What is it?" I ask.

"Nothing, I'm just relieved that it was just the Rodavian, I guess. You know, after everything that's been going on…"

"Hey, a Rodavian is nothing to shrug at!" I say as an attempt to joke off the deeper conversation.

"Yeah, but I might rather face a Rodavian than do this stunt that Saul is about to pull," he mumbles.

"You haven't seen a Rodavian, though! W-wait. What?" I stumble, realizing what he said. "What stunt is Saul about to pull?"

Samuel shrugs. "I don't know exactly."

Samuel's eyes drift off to somewhere darker, and they land on the guard who is busy preparing to open the door so we can enter the housing area. The Gromptu shuffles, stops, and preens through a whitish-gray feather. Its cold, white eyes pause on us for a moment, and then it continues on with its duties.

"What do you know?" I whisper.

"Just that he's planning something to catch attention," he whispers back.

That's not good. I liked it better when he was getting brew cans thrown at him. The doors wail loudly as they close behind us. It's a safety precaution for wandering children. The inside of each Unit Building is lined with rows of apartment buildings stacked high with tiny, little rooms. The apartment buildings climb up so far that the highest ones aren't far from the top of the dome. People at the top frequently complain that it's hotter nearer to the artificial lighting.

A room in the apartment buildings is only about five hundred square feet. They're fine for one or two people, but they're misery for three or more. It is fairly common for a family to outgrow their apartment, but there are only so many rooms per apartment building, and it can split families. In lucky cases, families are able to obtain two apartments side-by-side, or at least nearby one another. However, it isn't unheard of for a family to be split into completely different units.

I turn to look at Samuel. He looks uncharacteristically grim. I can't help but think he might know a little more than he's letting on. How badly would it hurt him if the Gromptu made me disappear? I shouldn't have followed Saul's father to that tent. Samuel finally breaks the silence.

"My parents wanted me to come right back from the port; they want me to rearrange some furniture."

"That's too bad."

Samuel gives a passive shrug. With a smile and a wave, he turns the corner toward housing block nine, where he lives. The unit was originally sectored off into blocks to lock down outbreaks of the wheeze. Now we just use the blocks as a way of directions.

It is weird to me that families are always doing silly, tedious tasks, like rearranging furniture. Sometimes Samuel's family rearranges the furniture three times in one day. It's like they think that if they arrange their table and five beds enough times, they can finally find a layout that will give them enough space for their family of seven.

I remember what Samuel said about Saul. I wonder if his decision to do something bold had anything to do with us watching him get hit with the can. For a while, I had hoped that his anger would subside with time as he failed to get people's attention. "I'll make them pay," he had said behind the closed doors of his apartment. I sigh, feeling heavy.

The loud thrumming of the wind outside of the unit seems to emphasize the stillness of the air inside. I note that the lights are already starting to dim. People stir in the occasional doorway, and once in a while, a child's laugh, if nearby, breaks the unbearable quiet. I've often thought that if the wind would stop, if only for a second, the quiet rolling of human tongues might make Unit B a little restful. Instead, our words are swallowed up in the weather's moans and whistles. I decide that I'm not going home quite yet.

"Ah, the Wind Wraith is angry today..." A woman says across

one of the apartment windows as she and her neighbor hang up the wash on the lines.

There's a legend of a young warrior who used to live on Yalk before the Lovindians invaded. He wasn't a particularly strong man, and he didn't even like to argue, but he was enlisted in the military just the same. When the Lovindians attacked his village, he was at the very back of the battalion. The further he marched, the more the people in front of him started to thin. The warrior stood alone in a land of bodies.

The warrior died like all of the rest, but when his spirit should have soared to the heavens, it sank into the ground. He felt the blood of his people soak in the soil and the fires butchering the treetops. The young warrior, who never wanted to fight, wailed a war cry like none other has cried. Until this day, he forces the wind to bash against the sides of the units, wanting to get revenge for his people. They call him the Wind Wraith.

A woman walks briskly past me. There's no way that she has anywhere important to go, but I've noticed that many people here seem to walk with importance. Her thin, wide-legged pants pull back around the fronts of her knees with the swiftness of her pace. Most people on Yalk wear wrap shirts and these loose-fitted pants. My mother once had a dress and it wasn't beige. My grandmother had found dyes and painted it for her tying day with my father. My father always talked about how remarkable it was before he left our family for a younger woman. I remember that when my sister was born, she cried for days after she realized the dress would no longer fit her rounding figure. It was probably for the best; the thin fabric was fraying apart, and I'm not sure it was ever meant to take the dye.

I turn so that I can watch the woman go. Maybe she walks with importance because the most important thing she has to do is to walk. I grimace at the thought, and a man who is watching mistakes it for a grin.

"Quite a pretty thing, huh?"

I cringe, shaking my head. I don't know how this sludge can even see past her blatant unhappiness. It's hard to feel attraction when seeing a person's smile is so rare. Some might be thinner, some might be taller, but Yalk is just different shapes of the same exhausted people. None of us know why we walk. There are two types: those who shuffle aimlessly, caught up in their lack of direction and those who plow through their lack of direction, never accepting that they have no idea where they're going.

The halls have darkened considerably more. It's a good thing that Samuel went home. It's going to start soon. Water drips down from above and lands on my forehead. I look up to see freshly cleaned linens, poorly wrung, hanging on the line. The damp, stifling smell of laundry is constant company in the hallways. I shuffle, looking up once in a while to see if I want to turn this corner or the next. There's no sound in my steps. If I could hear my footsteps, maybe I could go home and rest. The wind wails, and I give a tired sigh.

I'm drifting, wandering around corners, apartments. People are joining me now. A set of Gromptu stand apprehensively at the end of the corridor I'm walking. A couple of men stagger out of their rooms, looking exhausted. I breathe in. The walking is starting. It's been a long time since I've walked, but it happens naturally.

In the day the Talkers had spit rebellious anecdotes, but even they gave up to the walkers of the night. The walkers are those who are old enough to shudder when they think about their existence. They're men and women who know why their cousin didn't come home. It may look like a protest but it's not.

No, this is something else—a mindless exertion of energies that could be focused on something productive. It isn't a protest because there's no direction. There's pain, frustration, animosity, and a numb hatred—too far repressed to be acted upon usefully. Walkers walk at night because they're not strong enough to walk in the day. That takes a different kind of energy—a different mindset.

A woman slams into my shoulder as she marches to nowhere, and it almost knocks me off my balance. I notice that the nearest Gromptu flinches with me as if it felt the blow as well. One of them gurgles something in Lovindian, and it's lost just like any other words. I turn the corner and another Gromptu is trying to herd a couple of people so that they won't injure themselves by walking into one another. He will have to stop trying soon. It isn't worth it.

People have filled the walkway, but I just sigh. I feel heavy. The children who linger outside their apartment a little longer are ushered inside and sent to bed. Parents emerge separately to walk about in the darkening dome. I wonder if they would walk if they could hear their footsteps. I wonder if they wouldn't just tuck their children in at night and sleep in peace.

I recall what Saul had said on the crate that one day.

"Peace? What can we know of peace? The Lovindians, those parasitic beasts, have taken away our peace of mind."

Maybe if someone would stomp or march, but I don't, and no one else does. Our steps are swallowed up—swallowed up in the hissing, thrashing wind. If we could just hear them, then we could find peace. If we could just hear them, then we would know that we are still walking—still walking for a reason. I bump into the person beside me. A Gromptu slides past my vision. Do they know why we walk? Do they mock, or do they pity? Who would know with those massive, inexpressive eyes?

The crowd whirs with intensity. I struggle just to put one foot in front of the next. Then—what? I think I hear something. We all pause together to register the sound. Then, I find myself retreating back to block seven. My heart is thundering in my chest, but I can't do anything more than walk stiffly in the direction of home. I know all over the compound parents are returning home, and they will say nothing to their wide-eyed children who had listened to the haunting sound as they pretended to be asleep. Now the parents will go to bed themselves, the beating of their hooves still echoing in their ears.

7

Chapter 7

"Jacob! Jacob, wake up if you're in there!"

I groggily wipe the sleep from my eyes. There's a loud series of rapid knocks at the door.

"Jacob! Come on! You have to be in there! Wake up, you lazy Scrab!"

Scrab? I laugh. That's a word that usually only comes out of Emmanuel's mouth. When did Samuel pick it up? I don't even bother to straighten my hair as I totter over to the sliding door. My muscles are sore. I notice that there's a purplish bruise on my arm from being shoved by someone last night.

I hit the panel by the wall and the door rushes open with a "ffssshh." Samuel is still holding his fist up to knock, and he shuffles awkwardly away as he lowers his arm back down to his side.

"Who are you calling a Scrab?" I say playfully.

Pink rises into Samuel's cheeks, and he embarrassedly tries to laugh it off.

"I just thought it might get you out here faster. I don't even know what it means, to be honest," he admits sheepishly.

I chuckle but am interrupted by a big yawn.

"What on Yalk is so important that you had to bang on my door and call me names?"

He instantly becomes more serious. Dark circles lurk under his eyes. He looks like he's stayed up all night. He didn't join in the walking, did he? No—he couldn't have. He's still too young, too innocent, but deep down, I know that's not true. I was younger than Samuel when I first walked. I gesture weakly for him to come inside.

He takes a seat on a stool, the only other piece of furniture I have besides my cot. Samuel sits hunched uncomfortably and I see again just how tired he is. It takes a while before he gains enough momentum to speak.

"Saul has a terrible idea. They're going to take him. He's going to disappear too, just like his dad."

I'm flooded with relief. It's just Saul. Samuel still hasn't been tainted with the misery of Yalk. His pleading gaze brings me back to the current moment, and what he's said starts to process. He wants me to do something about it, but he doesn't know that I've already tried. Saul already made it pretty clear that he didn't care about my opinion. On the other hand, though, if Samuel is worried about what Saul is doing, then it has to be something pretty reckless.

"What's he doing?" I say with a full sigh.

Samuel looks up with encouragement that he shouldn't feel. "He's going to try to do his talking while the people walk tonight."

Stupid. Insane. Scat. If Saul tries to do that, he could incite the rage of the mob upon himself. I rub the purple bruise on my arm. The outrage of the walkers is blind. It's not a fury that's capable of being directed. Saul has to know this. He also has to know that by risking something like this, he is bound to attract the attention of the Gromptu.

Samuel is right. It's a terrible idea. Still, I can't help but feel a burn of inspiration in my chest. I imagine it would be therapeutic to scream at those mindless idiots. He can't get them to stick around long enough to listen to him, so he's going to try to get them interested while they're all out in the walkways. It is impossible not to respect his dangerous, horrible idea. He's wrong, though. There's no reaching them like that. I know what it feels like—you can't listen to anyone when you're walking.

I become aware that Samuel is watching me intently. I want to tell him that I can save our friend from harm and that everything is going to be okay. I want to, but how can I? Saul won't listen to me, and it's not like I don't understand why he's doing this. Everything we do is useless. Everything we do is just leading toward death. If that's true, then why not let Saul do this useless thing if he knows the consequences and gets a few moments of freedom by doing it? Isn't that what we all want? At least he would be fulfilling some sort of obligation he feels that he has to his fellow man. The fire, the life that was in the Talkers when they died in that room—I understand it. It's the death that I can't understand. It's Rachel's pale, cold face that I can't understand. Saul is my friend.

"What do you want me to do, Sam?" I finally answer.

His shoulders slump further, "I don't know. I just can't stop thinking..." He trails off.

I grit my teeth and answer truthfully. "There's not going to be any dissuading him. Hopefully, he'll just end up getting scared before he goes too far."

I feel like a coward by saying it. I have coordinates from

65

the Talkers, I have a possible sensor blocker, and I can fly a transporter craft. Still, I don't have any plans to do anything with the information. I know the coordinates by heart, but what will I do with them? Saul is walking in the dark more confidently than I am walking with so many tools.

He's walking toward death, I remind myself.

A quiet sniffling wakes me from my thoughts. Samuel. Too tired to fight his tears, he watches them fall onto the edge of his stool. I grimace. Of course, Samuel can't understand this at all. He doesn't understand the anger that Saul and I feel. All he understands is that Saul is in danger.

"It's not just Saul... Emmanuel—" He coughs and can't get the words out.

Of course. The image of his foul-mouthed, swaggering little brother tailing loyally at Saul's heels pops into my head. He must be how Samuel learned about Saul's plans in the first place.

"You're worried he's going to join Saul tonight," I say.

He nods. "I can't reason with him. I tried all last night."

I can't help but feel shocked.

"So he's set on joining Saul?"

He nods again.

This is bad. It would be bad enough if Saul planned to walk, but Emmanuel—Emmanuel is barely old enough to be considered a man. Saul can do what he wants, but getting Emmanuel involved in his fight is out of the question.

"Where are they now?" I ask.

Samuel jumps off his stool, looking like a transformed man. "Thank you! I knew you'd help me! He will listen to you! Saul still sees me as just a kid, but he'll listen to you. He respects you."

I wince. *No, Sam, you respect me.* I expect that Saul has a lot of feelings toward me right now, but I doubt greatly that any of them is respect. I'll be lucky if he doesn't hit me, let alone allows me to talk to him about Emmanuel.

Samuel is chattering away already, leading me toward the back of Unit B. How does he manage to keep that bounce in his step even when his shoulders are slumping from exhaustion? I yawn, feeling tired just by looking at the effort he is making. His eyes are bright and hope-filled when he looks at me, jabbering about how the other day he stole another bread roll from his mother and it is starting to look like a really good bugger.

I never understand how he can put away his worries so quickly. If it is because he wholeheartedly believes I can fix this, then he is going to be in for a disappointment. Whatever image he has built up of me in his head is about to be let down. Maybe it is for the better. He has to learn eventually.

I hear Saul before I can see him.

"We are given allowances of baunti! They feed us, they give us shelter, but in return, they limit where we go and what we can accomplish. We were gods of our own land! We fed ourselves, made shelter for ourselves! Look at us now! What have you done today? Yesterday? The day before that? How many of you have even experienced sunlight? How many of you have never even taken a transporter craft to leave this planet? I bet most of you have only seen the artificial light! What is day and night to you anyways? It's not a force of nature, not the turning of the planet, it's the light controls set by the gods of this world! Our all holy Lovindian overlords!"

I never could understand how the Talkers could rant so passionately when they were shouting at air. No one is walking in the walkways anywhere near Saul. It's like he has a massive invisible wall surrounding him. They're probably scared into their homes by all of his yelling. Saul stands proudly nonetheless. Maybe the yelling in itself is therapeutic.

Emmanuel lies up against the side of Saul's crate. His feet are unwrapped, and he entertains himself by carefully picking the grit from between his toes. I grimace as he examines a piece between his finger and his thumb. Samuel has gone stiff beside me, clenching his fists at the sight of his brother's carefree attitude.

"When Maan finds out about this, he's going to be dead," he whispers.

"At least we won't have to worry about him disappearing if she kills him."

Neither of us laughs at my joke. Saul draws a breath in between sentences, and I take the opportunity to step in front of his crate. He breathes out through his nose, looking at me narrowly.

"What do you want?" he growls.

"Don't get stage fright now that you actually have an audience," I say evenly.

Air hisses through his clenched teeth.

"Just want to talk, Saul," I say quietly so that the others can't hear.

Saul laughs unnaturally, giving a wicked grin. "Well that's what I'm up here to do, right pal?" He gestures at the empty hallway.

"Sounds like a bit of a one-sided conversation from where I'm standing, but I'm not here to discuss the neighborhood's noise complaints. Although, the community has been begging me to shut you up for a while now."

Saul steps off the crate. He's bigger than me on or off of the crate. He raises his lip into a snarl. Damn it, why did I have to go and pick at him? I need to have an actual conversation, and here I am walking halfway across the Unit just to insult him.

"Don't you have something better to do, Jacob? Shouldn't you be running away on your transporter ship to hide from the realities of this scat planet?" Saul sneers.

I bite my tongue. I can feel Samuel watching me. The truth in Saul's comment makes my face burn.

"I need to talk to you. Privately," I say tiredly.

"I'm on the clock right now, Jacob. I can't just take a break whenever you want to speak love words to me," he says with an infuriating smile. Emmanuel chuckles, and I shoot him a glare he pretends not to see.

"Saul, if we were ever friends..." I hate the begging in my voice.

"Apparently, we were not," Saul hisses. The hairs go up on my arms, and I'm using all the restraint I have to keep myself from punching him.

"Fine. If you give me this, I'll owe you."

His lips widen into a nasty grin, and he reminds me of a Yahbiin trader right before they rob you blind. I ignore the feeling and gesture for him to follow me out of earshot from the other two. Saul nods in agreement, and I'm surprised by his willingness.

"What do you want?" Some of the fire in his voice has died now that he doesn't have to impress the others.

"It's about tonight," I start.

Saul rolls his eyes. "Emmanuel's got a big mouth."

"I'm not going to try to talk you out of it," I say.

"I should hope not. That would be a waste of both of our

time." He shoots a glare over my shoulder, and I follow his gaze. A boy, who was trying to sneak out of his home without being caught by Saul's rantings, stops dead in his tracks. His eyes are on Saul. Slowly, he shuts the door, deciding it is better to stay locked up than risk a confrontation with Saul.

"You're a real terror, Saul." I chide him.

"Huh?" He is still distracted with the boy he is keeping prisoner.

"I'm here to talk about Emmanuel." I try to get him back on topic.

"What about him?" He is genuinely surprised.

"He shouldn't go with you tonight, Saul. The walkers are dangerous, and you have to know your crusade is going to end badly. Don't bring him down with you tonight. The Talker movement is your fight—not his."

Saul's eyes narrow, full of fire. "It is his fight; it is your fight; it is all of our fights. If I believed this wasn't all of our fights to fight, then I wouldn't even try to stand on the box in a river of mindless lunatics." So he does know how insane what he's doing is.

"Saul—" I try, but Saul holds up a hand and continues.

"Nevertheless, I told him not to come with me. I tried explaining it to him, but he's a stubborn brute. He says that I'm not going to my death on my own. I would spare him if I could, but the truth is that he's already in the middle of this either way. If he dies out there with me, it's at least a nobler death than the one he would be granted further down the line. Maybe he'd live a longer life not coming with me, but I don't think he'd live a more purposeful one, and I can't change his mind anyway.

"He's a rough kid, but he has a lot of spirit in him. If he could get older and think for himself, I think he could do better at this than I am. He's smart, but he's lazy and would rather someone else think for him. Maybe that's why when he does make a decision on his own I can't change his mind even if I threatened to burn down Unit B."

The sadness in his voice means he is telling the truth. He really had tried to convince Emmanuel to stay home. I look away. I see my friend and it hurts.

"Don't do it then, Saul. Please."

Saul laughs. The passion that was in his eyes when he talked about Emmanuel is gone. It reminds me that we aren't friends after all.

"If I don't do it, then no one will."

"And what's wrong with that! What's wrong with not throwing your life away?"

"We're all throwing our lives away! Even my idiot father! He didn't do scat!"

"Then why—?"

"Have you not noticed we are at the ripe age to disappear? Don't blame me for wanting to do something before I vanish and my friends forcibly try to forget me. I talked to you, Jacob. That's all I agreed to." His voice is cold.

He looks to where Emmanuel and Samuel are waiting for us. Emmanuel sits on top of Saul's crate, arms crossed and his bare feet swaying. Emmanuel is laughing at something that was probably crude by Samuel's reaction. Both of them look up at once, and their resemblance is uncanny. I make a motion at Samuel to tell him it's time to go. He trots toward me, and I wince. If I were the one standing on the crate, would Samuel follow me just like Emmanuel follows Saul?

"What did he say?" he asks hopefully.

"He said he'll try," I lie.

"That's great!"

"I don't know that he'll listen," I warn, feeling like scat.

"Do you think I could keep him in the house?"

I smile, raising an eyebrow. The idea of Samuel being able to keep wild, headstrong Emmanuel from doing anything is amusing.

"Yeah, you're right." Samuel's shoulders sag.

"They'll be alright." I reach up to tussle his wavy, black hair.

He gives a small, thankful smile. My stomach turns, but I do my best to smile back. If Emmanuel won't stay in, then I will be forced to go out. Maybe I can keep Samuel's faith in me for just a little longer.

8

Chapter 8

The wind blows stronger than usual. The people of Yalk would say that the Wind Wraith must be angry. I close my eyes, and I can almost feel the wind rolling over the top of the dome. Thick, gray dust pours unendingly over and around the ovular-shaped compound. Many times I have watched the dust swirl around the planet from the viewing screen of my transporter craft.

I open my eyes. The lights are starting to dim. I am very familiar with the long hour that starts with the dimming of the lights. The restless energy of Unit B's inhabitants will reach a point of being tangible. The worse the wind, the more violent the walkers are. Saul has picked a bad night to stir up trouble.

No sound of Saul yet. I don't dare hope he's changed his mind. He's probably preparing himself to go out even as I sit here waiting. Emmanuel wasn't home when I walked Samuel to his door. I didn't tell Sam what I was planning. It would only make him worry more. I have never told Samuel that I have walked before. It's something you don't have to tell someone. They can sense it about you.

A woman strides by. A child is ushered inside. I stretch my legs and yawn widely. I have to get up. Men and women are bustling through the walkways already. People stream into the walkway to join the swarm, but it's not possible to trace where they come from. They just appear. The crowd grows and grows, moving as one bumbling mass through the corridors. Somehow they all find their place in the chaos and follow their made-up lines in the mixing currents.

Where is Saul? I start to pick my own lines in the crowd. It's easy enough. One foot in front of the other. Instinctual. The wind howls outside of the dome. I can't hear my footsteps. No noise. Nothing but the wind.

Where is Saul?

Turn left, turn right, a man wanders in front of me, but I don't turn to avoid him. We brush sleeves but don't hit.

Where is—?

The wind lets out a long whistle and it spurs the crowd to move at a greater intensity. Faster. Faster. Turn. Turn.

Where?

I stop. The world is spinning. I fall forward into another person as a woman slams unapologetically into my back. I panic. I'm out of the current and spiraling out of control. I'm forgetting something. Everything is so clouded. An elbow finds my ribs.

"Aghhghh!" I yelp in pain.

I hear my cry above the wind, and it's all terribly clear. I hear something else—all of the feet rampaging at once. It's painfully, overwhelmingly, loud. How have I never noticed this before? The men and women of Yalk surge around me—a mindless mob. They aren't operating within currents! They're a mad stampede of angry, scared, dumb animals. Nausea

74

swims in my stomach.

"SAUL!" I holler. My voice soars over the heads. "Saul! Where are you?"

I listen but don't hear an answer. I have to focus. It was when I started moving by instinct that I lost my mind to the mob. I have to think! AGH! This is insanity! If Saul and Emmanuel try this, they're going to be trampled. I have to get to them before they attempt anything.

I dodge right as a middle-aged man switches paths in front of me suddenly. An older woman almost catches my shoulder, and I dive left to compensate. I have to think about what I'm doing; I can't risk becoming mindless like the mob and forget about Saul and Emmanuel. Another elbow flies toward my head, but I've learned my lesson. I duck just as a voice screams out over the roar. I almost forget to move. I feel my blood drain.

"Look at what you have become! Look at the animals that you are! Hear me! Hear me and be awakened from this spell they have put upon you! We are not the servants of their machinations! They may have bound our forefathers, but they do not have to have you! Don't you want to rest easy in your beds and cradle your children close until they sleep? Instead, your children lie awake in fear of the mindless bodies which go crazed in the night!"

I run the best I can toward the voice, popping my head out above the crowd when possible to look for the speaker. I bob up and down until I see a tuft of reddish-blonde hair. How did he get up on his crate in this madness? Where is Emmanuel?

"Saul!" I cry.

He starts to turn just as a wild arm is flung in my direction. I curse quietly as I'm forced to dive down. I desperately resurface to the top. Scat! I've lost him again! I listen as hard as I can for his voice. Please. Please.

"Grtgah-at gah-gaht grahz." Not Saul.

I feel cold, but hot tears form in my eyes. Somewhere in the crowd, there's a reply to the Gromptu's call. The clicks are accompanied by a series of hoots and chortles. This is wrong. This is very wrong. *Saul, you idiot!* He doesn't have the attention of the people, but he has gotten attention nonetheless. I push forward with a renewed determination.

"What do we have to lose? WE'VE LOST EVERYTHING! WE HAVE NOTHING!"

I see him. He's noticed the Gromptu's calls. He searches the crowd, scanning it anxiously. The hooting grows louder. *Please, Saul. Please get down. Run! Please, run!* He's so close. Not even an apartment-length away, but he hasn't seen me yet.

"Saul! They're coming!"

He still doesn't hear me and opens his mouth to speak again.

"Hear me! Our lives are up to you! The future of our sons and daughters is based on the decisions we make today! Do we choose to roll over and die, or will we become the threat that all of the Lovindians know we can be? Fight for humanity! Fight for your children! Fight for yourselves! It is we who pave the Milky Way!"

I pull all the air into my lungs.

"SAUL!"

He turns—his eyes are lit aflame.

The wind howls and a cold, bottomless hooting rises with it. The box falls.

"SAUL!"

I throw out both of my arms, hitting hard bodies on both

sides. Flesh and bone slam against my body. Fingernails peel through my skin. I plow through. Pain boils deep within my stomach, and I feel like an angry beast awoken from a deep slumber.

"SAUL!"

Their long fingers wrap around his arms. He kicks and screams, but they carry him away almost effortlessly. The Gromptu chirp in their strange Lovindian tongue and ignore my friend completely. A couple of bristled feathers between their shoulder blades is all that his efforts are worth.

"Jacob!" Saul screeches. His voice is high-pitched, young, and filled with terror. His fear-filled eyes lock on to mine. "Go, Jacob! Fight with all you have!"

I claw my way mercilessly toward him. I'm thrashing uselessly against the tide. I take deep, sobbing breaths.

"Stop! Jacob, you have to stop! Not me! You can't save me!"

I don't understand what he means. He's lost his mind completely. Saul lashes out against the guards using his teeth and claws. He looks like a rabid creature, but his eyes are cold and calculating.

"Not me! Fight for them! Save them!" he screeches.

If someone would just look up and see what is happening! The Gromptu could easily be overpowered by the masses, but the humans are oblivious. No, they're apathetic. Their greatest champion is being torn down in front of them. Even as they are towing him away, his words are crying out for their sake. It's hard to see him through all of the tears. I thrash, but I can't get any closer.

"I will! I will save them!"

I lie just like I've lied to Samuel a million times. I lie like I lied when I said I would keep Emmanuel safe. At my words,

77

Saul goes limp. He gives me a toothy grin. His eyes still burn, but he stares into the crowd—past me. Past it all. He's being drug away into the swarm. Every muscle in my body lurches forward to follow him. I burst through the people in front of me just as a flash of red goes through my head. I feel my brain rattle inside my skull. I'm falling. Falling down into the nightmare. Beneath the feet of the people I have promised to save.

9

Chapter 9

Saul? Saul!

"Jacob? Jacob, stop! You need to calm down!"

Samuel pushes me gently back into the cot, and the pain in my sides makes it impossible to resist him. The thin, beige sheets are cool. The light flooding in from the door makes my head swirl.

"You can't thrash like that in your condition! You about gave me a heart attack screaming like that."

I screamed? My arm is heavy as I lift the sheets to peak beneath them. Bandages. A lot of bandages.

"What happened?" My voice sounds hoarse and unfamiliar.

Samuel sighs and gets up to pour a cup of water.

"I was going to ask you that. When I couldn't find you the next morning, I ran around asking anyone I saw if they knew what might have happened to you. Finally, a woman gestured toward apartment three, and I find you lying in the middle of the walkway. Can you imagine what I thought?"

He hands me the cup, and I spot tears in his eyes. I know what he thought. I lift the water to my lips and find myself abruptly at the bottom. It is the best water I have ever tasted.

"I shouldn't have asked you to watch after him! To think that after all that, he just turned up the next morning like nothing was wrong!"

I cough hard in surprise; sharp pains wrack my sides. How many ribs have I broken?

"Emmanuel came home?" I finally spit out.

"Yeah, and he hasn't come out of his room since." Samuel frowns.

Relief floods me until I spill over into tears. I can't control them. They feel hot on my cheeks.

"Does he know?" I ask softly.

"Know what? Jacob, are you okay? You're crying!" Samuel's eyebrows come together in confusion.

Of course. Samuel doesn't know what happened to Saul. I wince at the daggers in my head. My promise to Saul echoes on.

"What can I do? My Maan wrapped you up the best she could, but we didn't know..."

"Your mother did a fine job, Samuel. I'm not in much pain." Samuel doesn't even pretend to believe me.

"What happened six nights ago?" he whispers.

Six nights? I'm surprised, but I shake it off. I can't protect him much longer, but I don't want to tell him now. Samuel lays a hand gently on my shoulder. His eyes are full of concern. He reminds me of Keren. I look away.

"I need to talk to Emmanuel," I say.

"What on Yalk for?" he exclaims.

"It's important."

Samuel frowns. "He won't leave his room."

"Alright." I lean down excruciatingly to set my cup on the

floor.

"What are you doing?" he says anxiously.

I scoot my hips slightly up, using my hands to support me. My abdomen screams as I put pressure on it. All of my life, I have been selfish, I've run away, but now I've made a promise. I think about it and only it. These first steps are going to be painful—literally and metaphorically.

"Whoa, whoa, whoa, where do you think you're going?"

I search my ribs, gritting my teeth together as I feel down them. Maybe two broken and another two badly bruised? It's hard to tell. I studied the basic medical modules on the computer panel, but my education is limited. I attempt a deep breath, and my sides agonizingly protest.

"I owe your brother a visit. He deserves one," I reply through raspy breaths.

"Emmanuel can wait! You need to rest! You're lucky you're alive!"

I see the feet coming down all over again and shudder. Samuel is more right than he knows. I toss back the blanket and slide each leg across the cot. The outlines of purple bruises are just visible through my thin, beige pant legs. As I look down, a piercing pain runs up the back of my head to just behind my right ear. My fingers dig to find the spot, and as they make contact, I almost vomit; the knot there is huge. That's where I must have been hit when I fell and was—trampled. How am I supposed to do anything for these people?

The coordinates! I pat my pant pockets rapidly.

"Are you looking for this?" Samuel asks, extending my fennele.

Momentarily I forget the coordinates. I take the instrument

and extend it carefully. I sigh in relief when I find it intact. I slide it into my pocket.

"Was there anything else?" I ask.

"Just a piece of paper." He pulls the coordinates from his pocket and hands them to me.

I take them a little too quickly. He raises an eyebrow but doesn't say anything. He's clearly exhausted. Circles from lack of sleep are imprinted under his eyes, making his dark face seem darker still. A wave of guilt rumbles through me. I'm not about to make his life any easier.

"I need you to help me get to your house. I need to speak to Emmanuel."

Samuel shakes his head. "I'm not helping you. You need to stay here."

I narrow my eyes and grab the edge of the cot. Samuel has never refused to help me before. This time isn't going to be any different. He's going to help me whether he wants to or not. I'm not going to lie back down.

I force myself to press my feet into the floor and manage to rise to a half bent, standing position. I saw the bruises, but I hadn't felt the pain in my legs until now. I sway but keep myself up. The tops of my feet are bandaged; I hear the sounds of bones popping. Scat. If Samuel doesn't decide to help me, I'm as good as done. I have to pretend that I can make it on my own.

"I'm going with or without you, Sam. I would appreciate it if you would help me with my shirt, though; I'd prefer not to startle your family or the neighborhood more than I have to."

"Stop! Please! Okay, I'll help you! Just stop, you're making me hurt to look at you, and you can't make it there on your own."

I hold in my sigh of relief and take a seat on the cot. Samuel rushes to the closet and pulls out one of my wrap shirts. I do my best to sit straight, but my sides ache with the exertion. Sweat beads on my forehead. Samuel is too busy helping me put my arms through my sleeves to notice. He is very careful in the way he wraps the one long strip of cloth around my back and ties it at the front. I'm thankful that he ties it loosely.

"This is stupid, Jacob. Just stupid," Samuel mutters, but he puts my arm around his shoulders to help me up.

Intense pain runs in waves down my body. My sweating increases. The pain in my legs is almost unbearable. My feet crackle, and I wonder how many little broken bones are beneath the bandages. My knees are fat and swollen. I stagger forward a step and bite the side of my cheek until I taste blood.

"Jacob..." Samuel starts.

"I can do it!" I snap.

I analyze the floor in front of me deeply. Step one, step two, step three. My feet crackle as I walk, and it makes my skin crawl. Four. Five. I manage to make it out of the door. The light in the walkways is intense compared to the darkness of the apartment, and nausea rolls over me. Sharp pains in the back of my head accost me constantly. Samuel's house is two blocks down and three to the right. It's all I can do to stand. Samuel waits patiently. He's no longer arguing with me. I don't know if this is because he's struggling to hold me up, or if it's because he's finally resigned himself to the task at hand.

"Sam," I say as I force a step, "I know this seems insane to you, but if I don't do this right now, I couldn't live with myself."

Samuel grunts in response. I'll have to settle for that for now.

Neither of us is fit for talking. Each step is agonizing. The pain in my legs goes dull from the inflammation, but everywhere else, the pain is sharper with every move. I can feel the tiniest weight put down on my foot and the smallest inhalation of breath into my lungs. I don't know if I'm actually moving on my own or if Samuel is carrying me. I have to try harder.

It's a wretchedly slow trip. My knees don't bend; it is like hobbling on stiff boards. The makeshift bandages are unraveling as I sweat profusely. The pressure the bandages created around my ribs disappears as they loosen, and the pain increases immeasurably. I can't see the ground in front of me. It fades. I'm not sure I'm lifting my legs at all anymore. Am I sending any commands to my body?

"Jacob? Jacob! Samuel! How could you possibly bring him here? What were you thinking?"

The screeching, lecturing voice catches my attention, and I try hard to focus on it.

"I know, Ma, but he was determined to go. He tried to walk out on his own. What did you want me to do?"

"Samuel! The boy couldn't have walked it on his own. Hold him in bed by his shoulders, threaten to strangle him, or hit him in the head with a pan! He couldn't have fought you in that state! Why on Yalk did he want to come here?"

"Maan, I couldn't have done that! He told me he had to see Emmanuel."

"Emmanuel! Emmanuel has locked himself in his room for days!" She dismisses him quickly and continues to lecture. "After—the incident—Jacob should have stayed in bed for weeks!"

The incident. So they do know what happened to me.

"He knows that, Maan. Please let me take him inside."

"Fine! Fine! Hurry up, he's half-dead now! Look, his bandages are all unwrapped!"

My eyes dart around the apartment. I have never been inside it before. The "rooms" are separated by pull-out walls. The open rooms reveal only a simple cot-style bed. Through all of the fuzziness, nostalgia creeps in. My childhood was spent very similarly to this. Samuel's mother pounds on a set of pull-out walls in the corner of the apartment, which have been sealed together.

"Emmanuel! Emmanuel, come out this instant!"

There's no reply.

"Emmanuel, please, it's important!" Samuel tries.

I focus on the floor again and force my feet to support my weight. My knees don't seem to agree with my decision. I pull in a big breath and fall against the door.

"Emmanuel. It's me," I say as strongly as I can manage.

The walls snap apart just enough to admit me. Emmanuel's mother starts to lecture her son, but I seal the walls shut as I step inside.

"You look like garbage."

Emmanuel is shorter than his brother, but he's broad-shouldered and he fills up the room almost wall to wall. He doesn't bother to give me the cot, or even to move over to let me sit. I shake with the effort to keep myself up.

"Emmanuel, I can't stand." I start to sway.

Suddenly realizing the severity of my condition, he moves to let me sit. I close my eyes and breathe. My body screams.

"Did you come all the way here just to die in my bed, because I really think you could have done that somewhere else." I still detect concern beneath his snide comment.

I do my best to gather myself.

85

"Where were you, Emmanuel?"

Emmanuel deflates in front of me. I note that the front of his wrap shirt is soaked. I know why as I watch his cheeks stain darker with little trails of tears. Emmanuel wipes them away immediately into his sleeve. His deeply brown eyes look at me with a fury. It's weird how much his eyes look like Samuel's, but Samuel's eyes have never looked like this before.

"Don't blame me for what happened to you! It's your own damn fault if you went out and got... you know!"

"Trampled," I say flatly. Emmanuel turns away blushing. "But you're right; it wasn't your fault."

"I know that!" he snaps and starts to chew on the nail of his left index finger.

"Where were you that night?" I repeat evenly.

Emmanuel chews harder on the nail, and it snaps audibly. His other hand clenches into a fist.

"He tricked me," he whispers, looking at his bedsheets.

"Who? Samuel?" I vaguely remember Samuel's scheme to keep Emmanuel at home.

"No! Not Samuel! That idiot couldn't trick anyone. Saul! Saul tricked me!" I lean in, trying to understand him as he cries.

"What did he do?" I ask quietly.

"He told me we were in it together! He lied to me!" Emmanuel wrings his hands, tears falling into them. "He grabbed my wrists and tied them together. I fought him so hard, but he was so much bigger. I begged him not to go without me. I begged! Then he tied my ankles."

"It wasn't your fault, Emmanuel; he was trying to keep you safe."

"I let him go!" he moans.

"You didn't let him go. There's no fighting Saul when he's set on something."

"What happened to him? Why hasn't he come to apologize? Why are you here?" The words come to him in between raspy gasps.

I feel hot. My chest tightens until all I can focus on is the hard knot in the middle. The pain in my sides and back increase as I fight back emotions that I'm not yet ready to handle. Emmanuel has lost his best friend. I have to keep it together.

"I'm sorry."

"You're sorry? Where is he?"

My mouth is dry.

"Where is he?" he demands.

Please don't ask me that. I summon all the willpower in my body to look into his desperate eyes. Emmanuel grabs my arm, and I notice blood on his fingers from chewing his nails. I shiver as I look into Emmanuel's dark, wet eyes. I swallow hard. I see Saul smiling madly as he's drug away. Saul wanted this. He chose it.

"I failed you, Emmanuel. I failed Saul, but I'm going to avenge him. I'm going to do what I should have done since the beginning."

"What are you saying?" Terror fills his eyes. "WHERE IS SAUL?"

I grunt as I rise to my feet. It hurts so bad, but I can't feel it. I can't feel anything.

"WHERE IS SAUL?"

Emmanuel reaches out, trying to clutch on to my clothes.

"WHERE IS SAUL?"

I slide open the wall.

"Don't ask me."

It's time to go. I drag myself away and collapse onto Samuel in exhaustion.

II

Pave the Way

"Hear me! Our lives are up to you! The future of our sons and daughters is based on the decisions we make today!" ~ Saul

10

Chapter 10

I'm healing. That's what Samuel keeps saying. Healing is exhausting. I flip over the paper with the coordinates on it again and again. Samuel comes daily to feed me and keep me company. I itch to be back behind the viewer screen of my transporter craft. Fourteen days have passed since I visited Emmanuel.

I stop flipping the paper when I see some older children playing Scrab's Eye Ball between the apartments. They stare for a minute at my bruised and weak body. I'm used to it. They all want to see what happened to me. After a moment, they forget about me and continue to play. I settle on the ground with a groan. I lean up against the apartment wall. A boy with reddish hair glances in my direction and misses his shot, much to the dismay of his teammates. I wonder if his family is originally from Unit C.

When I moved to Unit B, Scrab's Eye Ball was something completely new to me. It was a game that had developed completely on its own in Unit B. It was Saul who had asked me to join in a game when they needed an extra player. For days I had awkwardly found reasons to walk by the courts and take a long look at the players. I had never spent time with anyone besides members of my own family, and I might have never gotten the courage to speak to them if it hadn't been for Saul.

Scrab's Eye Ball is usually played with two teams, three players per team. Each player is equipped with a swatter, which are almost always stolen spatulas from mothers' kitchens. There are only two places in Unit B where Scrab's Eye courts are set up. The courts are both built in the space between two apartment buildings. At the second floor of the two facing apartments are two black circles drawn directly on the sides of the buildings. Rebelliously, Unit B inhabitants call the circles the "Scrab's eyes."

The players, armed with their swatters, have to work together because they each have to hit the bugger once before shooting for the eye. The game is usually played to three points. I'm pretty good at the game because of its unpredictable nature. It doesn't matter how athletic you are or how strong you are or how good you are at calculating trajectories. The bugger is never perfectly round and the swatters are always flimsy. There is almost no way to predict which way the bugger goes when you hit it, and even if you get used to playing with a certain bugger, it eventually breaks, and the next time, the bugger is different. That's what happens when your ball is made of bread.

I'm good at focusing only on the bugger. I can clear my head to focus only on where it's falling at a particular time, and I can get there before it hits the ground. That's really the trick of the whole game. Emmanuel always loses patience and ends up flinging the bugger at full speed away from our swatters. Keeping the bugger in play so you can gradually get it closer to the Scrab's eye over time is your best chance in a game where you can't properly control anything.

Watching the game now, I feel a bitter irony. The teams are so focused on keeping the bugger to themselves and keeping it off the floor that they don't notice how infrequent it is for either team to score any points in the Scrab's eye. It's often people play for hours and never score a point. It's funny how people can be so focused on getting nowhere.

Still, watching the children play does relax me. If I have to sit inside for another second, I'm going to lose my mind. Saul's face haunts me. I hear Emmanuel's voice echo in the back of my head, and I try to shake it free. Just listen to the sound of swatters connecting with the bugger. The children aren't experts at the game, though. The smacks are awkward, fumbling sounds as they barely connect with the bugger.

I sigh. My shoulder aches. I keep my left leg out in front of me. My ankle isn't healing quite right. It pops and snaps when I walk on it, making me grit my teeth. My headache hasn't gone away since I woke up. Everything seems too bright. My head buzzes when I try to think.

Why did Saul think I could do anything for these people? Why does everyone always trust me? Saul and I never got along completely smoothly, not even before his dad's death. I feel guilty as I look down at the coordinates. I hadn't wanted to tell Saul about what happened to his father. I didn't want him to know his dad was gunned down like an animal.

Even more so, I just didn't know how to even start. The Gromptu's merciless, white eyes staring into me through the tent had filled me with horror.

Now, though...

What if I had told him? I didn't always understand Saul.

Maybe he would have understood why the Talking Movement wouldn't work. Maybe he wouldn't have tried the stunt that he did. If I had said just something! Ugh! I grab my head and rub my temples with my thumbs to ease the pain.

Each inhale stings and each exhale feels like my chest is trying to slowly slip out through my feet. I'm exhausted, but my mind is tormented with endless thoughts. The redling boy misses the bugger and falls to the ground. The other children help him up. The corners of my eyes burn.

The children decide to go home. The two black rings are inky and watery as they look over the children. There they were—always watching. They stare back at me, and I feel their challenge. They're bigger than me. They were bigger than me long before I was born, and they will be bigger than me long after I am gone. They challenge me to disagree. My palms sweat and my nails dig in clenched fists.

They just took him away. They just made him disappear, and I'm supposed to forget. I'm supposed to repress it like the people of Unit B repress my trampling. My head pounds. My body seems to radiate heat. They made him disappear, and for what? He posed the same threat as a bugger to a Scrab's eye, but they swatted him away.

I lived by the rules. I did what was expected of me. I let them take Saul's father. My anger burns on.

Why? Just because they could!

I burn and burn.

I have to do something. I have to fix this.

I feel hot.

I stagger toward the eyes, and I can almost imagine them glowing. The children left behind the bugger, and I snatch it from the ground. With all the strength I can muster in my tired body, I launch the bugger into the center of the eye. The bread explodes. I collapse to my knees. I just want to make them hurt. I just want to make them hurt a little bit. Bread isn't going to hurt a Gromptu. What can hurt a Lovindian?

I feel so hot.

I will save them!

Save them? Save who? I can't save anyone. I had just said that in the moment. Saul couldn't have expected me to do anything. I'll look after Samuel and Emmanuel, but I couldn't possibly do anything to save all of them. Not against the white light. Pathetic. I'm pathetic.

"Jacob? Jacob, why on Yalk are you here? Damn it! You really have a death wish!"

I grit my teeth. They just drug him away. Like I wasn't even there.

"Jacob? Scat. You're burning hot! Hey, are you in there?"

Samuel? When did he get here? His brows meet in worry over his dark, concerned eyes. What does he think of me? How much of what happened to Saul does he understand? Does he blame me? I try to stand, and Samuel helps me to my feet.

"I'm sorry," I grunt.

"You should be," Samuel scolds. "You should be in bed."

I shake my head. "I'm sorry for all of it. I'm sorry for what happened. I'm sorry for Emmanuel."

"Emmanuel will be fine. Come on, brother, we have to get you home. You need to let yourself heal and stop making me drag you home. Oh—don't say it! If you say sorry one more time, I'm going to lose it!"

How had he known I was about to apologize again? Samuel rolls his eyes at me.

"Jacob, you can't blame yourself. If anyone is to blame, it's me. I didn't even try to reason with him. I just asked you, and I've known him all my life. It should've been me to try and stop him." Samuel's jaw tenses, and I don't know if it is from anger or from the force he is exerting to help me walk.

I hadn't even thought about how Samuel was feeling about Saul before now. He is closer in age to Saul than Emmanuel is, and they all grew up together. I've been in Unit B for such a short time. It didn't occur to me that Samuel would feel guilty about what had happened. Samuel continues on.

"Emmanuel doesn't blame you either. He just blames himself. I think he feels like he should have tried harder to keep him from Talking." Samuel wipes his black hair out of his eyes and smiles sadly. He tightens his lips into a thin line. He looks uncomfortable with the conversation.

He hasn't said his name once. Maybe it's too hard for him. I hope that he isn't trying to forget him. I have always struggled to figure out what other people are thinking. I never thought that Emmanuel and Samuel might blame themselves for what had happened to Saul. Understanding people was something Keren had always been better at. My head throbs, and this time it feels like it is more than guilt causing the pain. I feel dizzy.

Samuel is right; I need to rest.

11

Chapter 11

I like to sit in the corridors when I eat breakfast. Being in the silence of my apartment for too long makes me anxious. The fever comes and goes in waves, usually after I've tried to get out of bed for any length of time. Samuel's mother came to check on me after I collapsed again and said it was likely caused by me not giving my body adequate rest. So now I'm doing what I'm supposed to be doing—resting. Mostly.

I poke at the mash in my bowl disinterestedly. A warm-colored hand suddenly reaches over my bowl and reveals a bread roll.

"Thanks, Sam." I take it and look up.

Emmanuel looks away awkwardly; his wavy, black hair falls into his face. "Sorry."

I'm too stunned to wonder why he's apologizing. Emmanuel slides down next to me, propping his back against the side of my apartment wall too. I roll the bread around in my hand, not sure if I should eat it now. Guilt wells up in my stomach, turning me off from my meal. It would be rude not to eat it.

"It's from Maan," he says quietly.

My face burns. I dip it in the mash to soften it and take a large bite. Emmanuel sighs, seeming to relax a little. His face looks tired, but there's no trace of the manic person that I had left crying weeks before. I note that the skin around his nails is still bloodied from chewing. He's a pregnancy younger than Samuel, but right now, he looks like the older of the two.

"If you're expecting me to burst into tears, it's not going to happen," he snaps. I look away, embarrassed for staring. "I don't want to talk about Saul either, so don't worry," he adds. There's more silence. I'll wait for him to start again. "I've been studying the Lovi-dex lately," he finally says.

"Why?" I ask. It's not like him to study anything.

"I'm just sick of being so... ignorant. I've been thinking about getting my transporter craft license too."

My twisted fingers go instinctively to the paper with the coordinates in my wrap shirt. Emmanuel raises an eyebrow but doesn't say anything. I wonder if Emmanuel would go to the coordinates if he had the opportunity. I half-expected him to do something crazy like Saul and start Talking, but I guess that's not really him. It's impossible for me to guess what he would do with the coordinates.

"Why a transporter craft license?" I ask.

"Just want to see some things," he replies vaguely. I feel slightly suspicious, but I don't have any right to pry. "What are you going to do, Jacob?"

The sensor blocker is heavy in my pocket. I scoop the last bits of mash onto the roll and stuff it into my mouth. All the saliva in my mouth works hard to make the dry mass into something edible. What am I going to do? Save them. I shake the thought from my head. It's plagued me over and over, especially when my fever escalates. That's not me. I don't want to disappear. Emmanuel breaks my train of thought.

"You know, I never liked the Talkers. I always thought they were a bunch of scat-brained blowhards." His tone carries an unexpected bitterness.

"Yeah," I agree.

"But... sometimes I wonder if they didn't have something right."

"What do you mean?"

"Well, I'm not such an idiot to go yelling my intentions in the street, but if the humans of Yalk were made to really face their situation, I wonder what we could do."

"Nothing," I say confidently.

"Probably." He nods, running a hand through his hair. "I just wonder if there is a way to do it different than the Talkers did."

"Don't wonder about it too hard," I say hypocritically.

Emmanuel laughs as if calling me out. My fingers run over the strip of paper. I really hope that he is just talking. He doesn't need to get involved with anything risky like Saul. But someone does. I shake my head to try to get the invasive thoughts away.

"You look like you're healing up good."

"Thanks. It's mostly thanks to your mother and Samuel."

"They're like having two mothers," he grumbles.

I laugh and my sides pinch sharply. Emmanuel squints his eyes at me, and I think for a moment I detect worry before it disappears. I wonder suddenly if that's why he's actually here. Maybe he is actually worried about me, and he didn't just come to deliver a bread roll. I feel a second rush of embarrassment. I don't like being so pitied, and I'm not used to being so looked after.

"You know, you're not too different than they are some-times." I smile.

"I'm not anything like them at all." The cold honesty in his face is startling. He's not insulted or complimented; he just disregards it completely. Does he wish he were more like them? Do I? Emmanuel chews carelessly at the corner of his finger.

"Emmanuel, if you—had a way of learning something more about the Lovindians, even if it was dangerous, would you do it?" What am I rambling about to him? I shouldn't be asking him this.

He looks at me blankly. "Depends."

"On what?" His vagueness is annoying.

"If it's a calculated risk." He blinks.

Calculated risk? I don't understand him, but at least that much is normal about the situation. I wish for him to continue, but of course, he doesn't. He stands unexpectedly and brushes off the front of his pants.

"But right now—I'd do about anything to keep myself busy. It makes life more bearable." He frowns.

He drags his feet as he heads off in the opposite direction of his home. It's strange seeing him weighed down by something. I feel like I've looked in a window and seen through his carefree exterior. I don't know what he means by "calculated risk." How can I calculate the risk of doing something when I don't know what there is to gain? All the Talkers ever said was that these coordinates lead to a red planet and a story.

I squeeze the paper in my fist. Calculated risk doesn't matter anyway. I made my decision a while ago.

12

Chapter 12

My middle finger is crooked now, and I'm still stiff when I walk. At least Samuel is letting me walk around without nagging me constantly. He would definitely have a few words to say if he knew what I'm about to do. I flip the paper with the coordinates over one last time, pocket them, and head for the door. My feet still aren't right; they're swollen and blue in places. My ribs, though, seem to have found a way to heal. They are still sore, but the pain has eased immensely.

It's time to see if the Yahbiin has sold me a random piece of junk. I've had a lot of time to think about what I'm going to do. I've traced each action over in my mind so many times that walking toward the shuttle bay seems like routine. I type the three words on the paper into the guidance system:

P-A-V-E T-H-E W-A-Y

The words trigger coordinates already in the transporter craft's database. The Talkers were more impressive than I gave them credit for. I click the third button on the sensor blocker. For the first time, I feel an eerie quality to the black on the viewer screen. Space, which has always felt like an endless escape, now feels too open, too vulnerable to eyes which will know that I should not be here.

I check where the craft is taking me. If the red planet is too far for my craft to take me there and back, then I'll have to turn home. It almost certainly has to be further than the craft can go, or else my guidance system would have picked up on it before. Taking this trip just to find out I don't have enough fuel will at least let me rest knowing that I've tried everything in my power to avenge Saul's death.

A blue dot blinks on the guidance screen. My heart drops. The destination marked is so close that I should already be able to see it on the viewer screen. I search wildly across the viewer screen. There's nothing after all.

Scat.

After all of that, the coordinates are just Larvak dung. The Talkers probably bought them off some Yahbiin trader who thought it would be funny to make "human beings" fly to nowhere. I roll my eyes. So much for the truth seekers of the human race—the last of humanity's fighters. It makes sense this way. Humanity can't be a threat no matter how hard they try.

Then why did they kill him?

A little red dot shimmers on the viewer screen.

No way.

It's a dwarf planet. It's barely large enough to be called that. It is likely just a piece of rock that fractured off of a larger planet, but there it is. A red, beating pulse in the silent dark.

A thin layer of artificial atmosphere ripples as my craft approaches. The computer panel shows that the atmosphere is breathable, but just barely. Spending any extensive time here isn't a great idea. The oxygen levels are slightly high and the nitrogen levels are just a little low. As the craft idles into the planet's gravity, I get a good view of the surface. Red. Dry. Flat. A blip on the surface rolls across the screen. It's a rocky-looking outpost that could be the remnants of a past civilization. Is that where I'm supposed to go?

I take over the manual controls to lap the planet again and prepare to land next to the only unnatural feature on the planet's face. The craft slides down unexpectedly smooth. There is no wind to cause turbulence upon landing. Red dust, stirred up by the ship, rises up from the planet's surface and covers the viewing screen completely. I set the craft down.

The ship lurches as it makes contact with the surface. The hatch door lowers, and a flood of red dust instantly coats the inside of the craft.

Scat.

How on Yalk am I supposed to clean that up? The Gromptu won't miss that. Coughing, I stumble out into the dust. As the dust settles, I understand why my little craft caused such a massive cloud. The planet is disgustingly still. Little red dust tornadoes spin around my linen-wrapped feet as I walk. I walk toward the sun, in the direction that I had seen the building on the viewer screen.

The sun is disappearing below the skyline. The planet grows darker with every step. I hadn't seen any life on the planet from above, but I can't help but be fearful of what kind of creatures might come alive in the dark. I quicken my pace. A round hump, unnatural to the red planet's surface, slowly rises from the ground.

The building is much larger than I thought it was. The outside is made from some kind of dark-red clay, obviously taken from the planet. I brush away layers of dust to see that it is intricately engraved underneath it all. Dried vines hang down from the top of the edifice as proof that vegetation had once attempted to take on the inhospitable environment.

One thing is for sure: the massive building emphasizes just how small and barren the planet is. It is dark inside the gaping archway, but I'm used to the dark indoors. I don't see any signs of life within. I try not to feel let down. Maybe this place was the answer long ago, but the Lovindians found it and destroyed what was left. It sure looks like the resources were mined from the planet. Maybe the Talkers were just too late.

The inside is dark and cool. The sound of my cloth-wrapped feet brushing against the cold rock floors echoes hollowly off of the dome ceiling. My eyes slowly adjust to see that although the room is domed at the entryway, further down the ceiling is flat and supported by many rows of pillars. It creates the effect that the building goes on forever. It is beautiful by itself, even without any great secrets.

Whatever I was looking for, this place doesn't have it. I sigh. At least I can stop feeling guilty about not telling Saul about the coordinates. It was just another dead end.

"I wish they would not come."

I jump. The deep, grumbling voice bounces off the pillars, distorting my ability to tell where it is coming from. I scan the room wildly. Finally, I see the owner of the voice—a bulking mass of a creature. Although the speaker arrived suddenly, he makes no effort to conceal himself. His voice intensifies slowly as he speaks, like a boulder rolling down a hill.

"I wish they would not come, but they always come. The freedom-fighters, the past-dwellers, they always come for the truth."

I'm frozen. I try to focus on what the creature is saying, but as he slowly approaches, I'm able to see more of its warped appearance. What is it? The creature speaks in a common Lovindian tongue, making me naturally apprehensive. Thin, crackled lines of age create a marred, rocky texture across its long face. It almost looks as if the creature emerged from the building itself as it so resembles the crumbling stone. Its skin is softer than stone, though—like a human's if it were dried and hardened by infinite years of sun. A train of fur runs up the creature's back and drags behind as if it is just a cloak and not physically connected to his being.

I can't make words, but the being seems to be doing fine on its own. It rambles on in a one-sided conversation.

"People come, see the empty room, and I watch their dreams die in their eyes. They always come, and the damned Lovindians don't even care. No need to block their sensors. The Lovindians never saw the others as a threat. They would let them come in, see the emptiness of what used to be greatness, and then, defeated, they would return to their despondent lives."

"Others?" My voice seems small. How did he know about the sensor blocker?

"Oh, of course! Every conquered, once great, race will eventually breed a hero, but they're never strong enough to learn the knowledge that they seek. No, the Lovindians will always win. Curse them! Why do you think the Lovindians let the rumor of the great Historians persist? So that those still with hope will crawl out of the dark, find their way here, and see that there is no hope after all. It's a pest-killing system. A strong bug finds a food source, but it's poison. He goes back to the hive and tells all the others, killing them too."

I struggle to keep up with all of this new, free-flowing information. So it was a Lovindian scheme after all. It pulled out those who still had rebellious hearts by promising some kind of hidden knowledge. People would put their hopes into this place and find it completely empty. I remember Abraham saying something about finding the Historians. Just another part of the legend, probably.

"Who are the Historians?" I finally manage to ask.

The creature is over top of me instantly. Its boulder-like body moved soundlessly and nimbly. Its massive head looms above me. A hard vice grabs the bottom of my chin, and I cry out instinctively. My heart thunders in my ears. I've done it now. Samuel won't be around to clean me up after this thing is finished with me. Tears from pain leak down my cheeks. It blows hot, earthy breath across my face.

"Not possible," it whispers. I wiggle uselessly in its grasp. "You're human." I stop struggling and look into its solid-gray eyes. I can't read its expressions at all. "Who are you?" Its already stony face somehow becomes more intense.

"Let go of me!" I demand.

To my surprise, my feet hit the floor.

"Who are you?" he rumbles again.

"Why on Yalk do you care about my name?"

"I let go of you," he says with a hint of a threat.

"Scat! It's Jacob! My name is Jacob. Okay?"

"I haven't seen a human in so many lifetimes. I didn't think I'd ever see one again."

Cold rushes over me. I suddenly know what I'm looking at, and I look in horror. It is one of them. It's over. I knew from the beginning that this might happen, but even after looking death in the face so many times, it doesn't come easy to do it again.

"You're a Lovindian." I don't move. If I have to go, then I'm going standing my ground.

"I was," it says almost thoughtfully. He scans me with his cold eyes.

"You were?"

"I can't transfer anymore. I was banished here to slowly die in this body."

Transfer. I hadn't known what they called it before. I feel sick. If the Lovindian is telling the truth, then it would make sense. Here I am showing up with a fresh body to deliver right on the desperate creature's doorstep. It's interested in me because it must like human.

"You say you don't know who the Historians were? Why did you come here if you weren't searching for the Historian's legacy? That's what the heroes always come for."

So there had been some truth to the stories.

"I have a debt to pay. Your friends murdered the real heroes, and I'm the scat that was left to pay the debt," I say coldly.

The creature's eyes widen, and a strange rumbling emits from its open mouth. I shift from foot to foot uneasily as I recognize it to be laughter.

"The Historians were an ancient society of different species whose sole duty was to keep a record of history throughout the universe. This place," he gestures at the room around us, "is called the council building. The Historians would come from all over the galaxy to meet on this neutral ground, where it didn't matter if their peoples were at war. Although they weren't the same species, they all had one important attribute in common: they were memepaths."

"They were what?"

"They were capable of reading memories."

"They could read your mind?" I shiver.

"It was more than that," he rumbles. "The Historians could read memories from something called the memory stream. The memory stream was a collective of every conscious memory. All that was necessary was for you to find the strongest memories of a certain time, and you could watch history unfold before you. This was long and tedious work because, although they might be able to narrow it down to the planet, time, and species, it didn't mean the memories would be clear, perfectly accurate, or important. The memory could be faded, it could be biased to the person you were watching, or the strongest memory of that day could have been someone sitting at home eating Wanango nuts all day."

I'm reeling. The Lovindian gives me the knowledge as freely as a mother gives her daughter the last slurp from her bowl. I don't understand why it is telling me what it is, but I can somehow sense that this is priceless information.

"Jacob," I'm called back, "if someone was going to hurt you, what would they need to do?"

My thoughts turn to Saul. I'm scarred with the image of him going weak after my hopeless promise. Suddenly it's not Saul but Samuel. It's Emmanuel being trampled beneath the people's feet. It's Keren falling limply after a burst of white light. I shudder.

"That! That thing you just thought of! I could see it on your face. I don't know what you've seen, where you've come from, or what is close to you, but there's definitely something out there that could hurt you. If I knew what your story was, I would know what would hurt you the most."

A story—that's what Abraham had said that they were after.

He had said that the coordinates were their last chance to hear the story. If they were after a story—then whose story did they want to hear?

"The Lovindians," I whisper. "The others were looking for the weaknesses of the Lovindians. They wanted the Lovindians' history."

"It's a sad story."

"Could you tell me?" I don't know why I say it. The creature is surely going to kill me. What am I thinking? Do I think the Lovindian is going to wrap me up and tell me stories in the dark?

"I can," it boomed.

This is too easy. What does it want from me?

"Why?"

"It's my duty to him."

"To who?" I ask.

The Lovindian steps back and gestures with an abnormally long, gnarled arm from its head to its bare feet. My mouth goes dry. He is referring to the body's rightful owner. The creature settles down on the floor and is once again limber, showing no age. My eyes dart toward the exit. I can see my transporter craft from here. I wet my lips with my tongue. I could probably make a run for it.

"Who was he?" I ask, hoping he doesn't hear the shake in my voice.

The creature sits with its eyes closed. Its face has become an illusion of rock. His voice is gritty when he answers.

"He was the first and the last Historian."

13

Chapter 13

This creature used to be a Historian of time itself, and now it is just a corpse inhabited by a parasite. It's a tragedy.

"You killed the last Historian; why would you want to honor him?" I accuse him.

"I didn't kill him willingly."

I can't tell if he's telling the truth or not. My knees are shaking uncontrollably under the pressure of his gaze, but I try to stand tall. If he's going to kill me either way, let me at least not die as cowardly as I lived.

"Then you've never willingly killed anyone over hundreds of years?" I challenge him.

"I didn't say that." His voice seems somehow heavier than before. "I only say that I did not willingly kill him."

"Then how am I supposed to trust you?" I grind my teeth.

"What do I have to gain from lying to a human? I can kill you now if you'd prefer."

"I want to know the story." The building echoes back my impulsive request.

"It will take time." The Lovindian's gray eyes are unreadable as he continues. "You will see and feel things that you cannot imagine—things that will damage you."

I don't know what he means. How can I see and feel a story? How could a story damage me?

"I don't understand," I say honestly.

"This body," he lifts his crackled hands, "is still telepathic and memepathic. I can access the memory stream and transmit the memories directly into your mind. I can allow you to live history. You will understand the Lovindians better than any other living creature in the galaxy."

It's like I'm in the Yahbiin's tent all over again. Here I am on the brink of another deal. Another major decision. What would Saul have done? Would he trust one of the killers? A person who openly admitted to murdering an ancient Historian? His kind is why Saul is dead.

"I have to know."

He slowly extends a crumbling hand.

"Take a seat, and when you're ready, take my hand."

I settle down awkwardly across from the Lovindian. I start to scratch at the back of my hand, but the bandages stop me. A strange kind of numbness has taken over my body. My decisions suddenly seem very impulsive. It was impulsive to take the coordinates from Rachel's hand, impulsive to buy the blocker, and it was impulsive when I shouted to Saul that I would solely take on the responsibility of saving all of the people in Unit B. It's easy to walk a path when there are walls on three sides.

I reach out my hand, and the Lovindian takes it. My hand becomes so cold that it burns. I try to pull away, but it is like my hand is wedged between two boulders. Is this part of it? What is happening? Dread fills my stomach. What if this is how Lovindians steal bodies? Am I offering myself freely to the beast? I raise my other hand to knock the creature away, but when I look over, my hand hasn't been raised at all. My arm refuses to obey my mental commands. Move! Pull away! The rest of my body has slipped away as well.

"The connection has been made. Please stop struggling! I don't want to hurt you!"

If he's a liar, he's a good one. My mind starts to give in to disorientation. I can't fight him anymore. My thoughts turn. My own voice pressures me from the inside. I hear me speaking, but I'm not speaking at all. The words are not my own.

"From the articles of The Council:

Year: 2772

Subject: Jana"

"Due to the violent nature of the Lovindian race, it was not surprising that the first toy created on the planet of Lovindo was a gun. The toy was made of a cheap compound similar to plastic and bore a resemblance to the Lovindian UV-D gun. Thus, the toy was given the uncreative but child-friendly name "Lovi-gun." However, the very existence of any toy, of any kind, being manufactured by a people who possessed a planet as crater-ridden as their hearts was peculiar.

"Similar versions of the toy were created on other planets, but there was one significant difference that made the Lovi-gun so popular: it could be used in daylight. Other toy guns would emit a huge flash of laser light to signify a hit and, of course, laser light is impossible for the eyes of most beings to see in daylight. This was a problem for two reasons: The obvious being that children, who were not nocturnal, would have to go to bed at night, and then they wouldn't get the chance to use the guns. The second problem was that on many planets there were very few hours of darkness. (On Zenthro-3 there is almost no 'nighttime' due to its three suns.)

"The Lovi-gun created a short pulse of air, in addition to the regular blast of laser light, that worked with an armband to notify the children when they were 'shot.' Other toy companies had previously considered the idea of air pulse toys but were too afraid to manufacture them. This fear was due mostly to the threat of lawsuits from the parents of kids who had stumbled and injured themselves after being hit with an air blast. Lovindo, however, was unique in the fact that it did not have to worry about these hot-tempered complaints.

"No parent was going to file a lawsuit against the battle-ready inhabitants of Lovindo."

I don't hear my voice any longer, but I'm not returned to the Council Building. The world melts like a thousand brilliant shades of wax. It mixes brown and fades to white.

I emerge from the colors and clutch my arms tightly around my body. Surprisingly, though, I'm not cold. I step and snow crunches beneath my feet. My eyes blur with the quickness of the passing trees, but I'm not running. A fallen tree blocks my path, and my legs course with power as I leap over it. I hear a low grunt as I hit the ground, and it's mine and not mine at the same time. Dizziness overwhelms me, and the world starts to melt away again.

"Stop resisting! Let her tell you the story!"

I put aside all of my suspicions and focus back on the snowy woods.

"Don't fight her! Become her!"

Become her? I don't understand! But wait? For a second, I think I see the snow. Icy air fills my lungs. It's going to be dark soon. I'm in the body of the person and out of the body. Jana, her name is Jana.

The snow made the night seem earlier than it was. Pockets of moonlight emerged through the trees and lit up the white below. Her light step left no footprints since the steady wind was constantly sweeping the top layer of fresh snow away to reveal the unyielding ice beneath.

Jana tossed her sandals away for the weather to hide. Her hand slipped down into the hood of her coat, and she dropped the Lovi-gun inside. With the dexterity that only a youth could have, she flexed her clawed fingers and toes and started the long climb up the Silatine tree beside her. As the girl pulled herself up the tree, the bark peeled away, like sunburnt skin hoping to rid itself of the invader. Jana skillfully evaded the tree's meager attempts to remove her and lifted herself onto the first limb forty-five feet above the ground.

Jana lifted a fan-like ear from her furry face and listened. A blast of icy-cold air swept across the bare skin of her inner ear. Jana flinched but continued to filter the silent planet for life. Long ago, the majority of creatures on Octorn adapted into being born without vocal cords. With a predator as sharp-eared as the Octornians, silence became survival.

Her ears rotated suddenly. Sandals. Four miles off. They would be there soon. A gust of wind tugged loose a few Silatine needles from the tree; they spiraled end-over-end to the ground. She was gambling on the elements being loud enough to disguise the sound of her presence.

Gingerly, Jana reached around the back of her head and lifted the Lovi-gun from her coat. She was ever-conscious of the slightest weight transition. If the branch creaked, she would be discovered. With strong arms, Jana aimed through the foliage around her. The armband on her wrist glowed a soft blue.

Her ears tilted again. Six thundering feet. Gentha's gang, no doubt. Jana smiled. Louder, louder, louder still! Her ears pinned tightly against her head. She breathed out. Click.

A spectacular burst of laser light exploded from the end of her gun, and for a moment, the entire world was white. Then, her little eyes adjusted to see three Octornian children sprawled out on the ice. Even a pulse of air as soft as the air pulse was violent at the high speeds the Octornians could travel. The taller, middle child moaned as her armband made a little chirping sound and turned from light blue to red. The other two groaned with her as their screens did the same.

Jana let out a burst of laughter. Nothing left to fear, she slid gracefully to the ground.

"How fast do you think you guys were going when I hit you with that pulse? Probably would've passed right by me if I hadn't—alerted you to my position."

"Alerted us! You knocked the wind out of our lungs!" Gentha screeched.

Jana laughed. "Shouldn't have made yourselves such easy targets!"

"We could have been hurt! Who knows what a pulse might do to a person moving at that speed!"

Eto and Lantha brushed the snow from their fur. Eto yawned loudly, distracting Gentha momentarily. Lantha didn't pay any attention to the others but started to rub her lower back, which had taken the worst of her fall.

"You hurt Lantha!" Gentha used it as an excuse to throw a clawed hand at Jana.

Jana saw it coming, having grown up with Gentha since she

was very young, and dodged her easily. Eto, Lantha's older brother, caught Gentha's shoulder.

"Come on, Genth, it's not so bad! We got pretty far in the competition!"

Gentha stumbled forward, but her snow sandals stopped her from falling.

"So who's left?" Jana pretended to ignore Gentha entirely.

"Seems like it's just you, Grel, and Netto," Eto responded but started to examine the girls. Lantha seemed to have taken the brunt of the burst and she looked a little green around her eyes. Everyone expected Eto and Gentha to be paired when they came of age. Gentha whimpered a bit, gaining ever more attention from Eto and Lantha both. "I think we should probably return to Delyre tonight since you've finished the game for us," he said to Jana.

Jana was momentarily overwhelmed with the desire to return to town with them. Their useless Lovi-guns laid deactivated on the ground. Lantha gathered their guns and drug her feet behind her older brother as he cared for Gentha. Even as she watched them go, snow started to fall and gather in her fur. She could hear them talking about warm food and beds long after she could no longer see them. It had been a long time since she had gone home.

It was not uncommon for a young Octornian to venture off for up to a month without returning to the comforts of society; however, it had been a little over a month since Jana had gone home. Jana sniffled and started to follow the sound of her companions. They would forgive her, and it was unlikely anyone else from the game would suspect her to go home for the evening.

The sky had melded into a very solidified black, and no

moonlight shined through the thick snow clouds that had formed almost instantaneously. Enough snow was now gathering on the hardened ice that Jana found herself plowing through with her shins. She was traveling much faster than her friends, who had limped away, and she knew that they could not be far. A large gust rocketed through the trees; the branches were bent back, but they didn't snap. They probably would not be able to make it to town and would have to find a tree to wait out the storm. The wind had reached a volume that made it impossible for Jana to listen for her friends, and she knew that there was no way she could navigate any further. Jana reached out to the nearest Silatine tree and scrambled up to see if she could spot them in the snow.

Ahead and to the left of Jana's plowed path was a wider path that was taking the weather a much longer time to fill. She had been right to think that she was close. Jana opened her mouth to call out to the others but was stopped when she noticed that the wider path had branched out a little further up the way. It would have made more sense for the three to take shelter in the same tree rather than face the storm individually. Why, then, had they decided to separate? Had they argued? No, Eto would never abandon Gentha in weather such as this over a quarrel. She continued to uncomprehendingly look at the path that her friends had made and found that her hesitation to call out to them had been wise. Beneath her, a small Octornian drudged through the snow.

Jana's path in the snow was now entirely filled-in, and the new Octornian seemed adamant on following the large path of the others. Jana watched him slink across the ground with the agility of a small animal. The snow he walked on was conveniently packed down by the others' feet, and so he could move fairly quickly. He held his Lovi-gun at his chest and, in doing so, revealed that he was one of the three still left in the game. He must have followed the trail of the others, not knowing that they had already been shot by Jana. Jana was happy to take advantage of his ignorance; smoothly, she lifted her gun to shoot.

Her ears were clamped down hard against her face to block out the torrential sound of the wind, and for a moment, there was silence. Her cold hands fumbled for a second but then steadied as she readied to aim. The planet was dark enough now that the light from the laser gun could be completely admired when it was shot; she grinned, expecting that wonderful satisfaction. Then the light seemed to bounce brilliantly off of everything. Jana jumped back and fought to regain her balance on the branch. Spontaneous blue light sparkled in the back of her eyes even after it had faded. Her surprise was complete; no single Lovi-gun could produce so much a show. Besides, she hadn't even pulled the trigger.

The Octornian stumbled backward at the force of three combined air pulses. Eto stepped to the side of the Octornian and lifted him by an arm so that he could see his face more clearly. Jana leaned in and identified the Octornian as Grel. In the excitement, Jana had lifted her ears a bit so that she could hear Eto pronounce some words that she didn't understand.

"Grz'gtgaht t'ga aht." The wind must have muffled the words.

How had their guns turned back on? She had shot them; she had seen them deactivated. She inched forward a bit further and was repelled back again by a blast of snow. Gentha had come to Eto's side, and they worked together in dragging Grel out of the elements. They disappeared, and Jana leaned back against the tree, brushing off the worst of the ice frozen in her fur. And for a long time, there was nothing to do but hunker down and embrace the misery of the weather.

"Come on back, boy; you've been out for too long."

I blink away the film smear from my eyes. Heat rushes back to my body, and I twitch uncontrollably. The cold is gone; my friends are gone. I jolt into a sitting position and scoot back across the floor.

"Jacob! You're back; it's okay!"

Jacob, Jana, Jana, Jacob, Jana, Jana, Jana, Jacob.

I touch my face and feel unkempt bristles but no fur. Any remainder of the Octornian is gone. One of the cracks deepens in the Lovindian's face, and I foggily connect it to a smile.

"People always act differently when they come out of the memory stream. You seem to be recovering quite well; you've clearly come to terms with your motor skills."

I didn't remember him warning me about not being able to move before we started. What else did the Lovindian conveniently leave out? I'm tired, though. No—I'm exhausted. Every movement feels like it's sucking all of the energy from my body.

"So she was from the past?"

The Lovindian's eyes widen in surprise. I scowl. The bastard didn't expect me to be able to speak either.

"She was. Are you feeling okay? The transaction usually leaves people a little bleary."

My fingers come up to rub my temples. It is a little difficult to recall what I saw in her memories.

"I think I'm fine. Those words, the ones that Eto spoke—they were Lovindian, weren't they?" I ask.

I hadn't even noticed the Lovindian leave in the first place, but now he approaches with a cup of clear liquid. He holds the cup out for me to take, and I wrap my hands around it. It swirls peculiarly.

"It's not water; it helps to clear off the sick feeling. It's called nyauta," the Lovindian explains.

I draw in a long swig of the nyauta, and almost immediately my mind starts to clear. I set the cup down and pull my hands away. I see the pink in my palm and instantly the pain registers. I clutch my hand quickly to me. Along the seam of my hand, the skin had pulled apart in a thick but unbloodied tear, leaving the edges pink and tender. I trace the marred area with a finger, and the hair goes up on my arms.

"It's the cost of knowledge," the Lovindian says. "The telepathic connection requires an entry point."

"An entry point? Is that why your body looks the way it does? Will that happen to me?" My mind is racing.

"Unfortunately, yes," the Lovindian says heavily.

My mouth drops. Why on Yalk had he not mentioned that before? This is insanity!

The Lovindian rumble laughs, and his laughter is so forceful that it stirs the dust around him.

"You're joking," I growl.

"Yes, Jacob. My body is just very old. I have been stranded here for a very long time. It's rude to point it out."

I never expected a Lovindian to criticize my manners. I remember suddenly that the creature had claimed that the Lovindians had banished him to die here.

"Why were you banished?" I ask.

The creature lowers his head. I've hit a nerve. Its rocky face turns so that I cannot see it when he replies.

"I'm a murderer."

I laugh loudly. I know that it's not appropriate, but I start and I can't stop. It's the most ridiculous thing I've ever heard. The creature turns on me, and his gray eyes seem to burn.

"Why do you laugh at me? Explain," he states.

"You're all murderers!" I say in exasperation.

The creature blinks in surprise. My bitter laughter stops and my stomach feels hot. It's not murder when you are killing cattle. It's just nature.

"What was the point of what you showed me today?" I demand.

"The point?"

"Yes. You promised to help me find the weaknesses of the Lovindians, and so far, you've just shown me some furry aliens running around playing games."

"They're one of the first of this galaxy."

"One of the first?"

"To be conquered."

"The guns," I whisper.

"Yes."

The back of my throat fills with bile. I had been Jana. I felt what she felt. My feet find the grainy, barren soil outside. The planet is dead; a perfect place to harbor the past.

14

Chapter 14

The quiet whir of the craft's engine is comforting as I carefully wipe the red dust away from the inside. My thoughts keep drifting back to the story. The Lovindians preyed on the children of the Octornians. It's not that I thought it was beneath them; it's just a reminder of the level of ruthlessness that the overlords are willing to go.

With that in mind, I don't know what to think of the Lovindian on the red planet. If the Talkers had reached him, would they have trusted him? I scrape at the dust in the creases of the control panel. The ends of my fingers start to feel raw. It's so frustrating doing this on my own. I don't have any guidance or experience. I can hardly tell what the people closest to me are thinking, let alone an ancient creature inhabiting the body of another.

The transporter craft eases into orbit above Yalk. I activate the autopilot tour to have more time to clean the innards of the craft. The program exists so that Yalkian children have the opportunity to see their planet from above. I still remember when I first signed up to go on one of the tours. The Gromptu placed us into a group of about seven children. I remember entering the landing bay for the first time and feeling thrilled at the closeness of the outside world—no more peering inside when the doors were opened.

We jumped about excitedly, trying to see the shuttle we were going to board. However, once we boarded the shuttle and zoomed out the bay doors, all of the other children started to scream and cry. In the confines of space, there was no parent to comfort them, but I was used to not having to rely on my parents for this kind of attention.

The world outside the viewer screen spins. My insides whirl, just as they did that day in the craft. The program continues with a series of sharp, jarring motions. The children had cried, begging to be let down, but the Gromptu just stared wordlessly. It was only later, after I learned how to fly, that I realized the cruel purpose of the program. It is so easy to glide the craft seamlessly through space, but that's not what the Gromptu let the children feel. They were supposed to hate the feeling of flying. Space was supposed to be intimidating. There was no adult there to comfort them; just a dark, unspeaking Lovindian.

The surface of Yalk almost always looks the same from above. It's either all dust or all mud. At the moment, it's all dust, just like the first day I entered a transporter craft. I hadn't cried with the other children at first. I looked around, trying to take in everything I could, but then I felt them—the eyes. I glanced around at the others' faces; they were red and tear-stained. That's why the eyes glowered down on me, and me alone. I knew then that I needed to react like the other children. Something told me that it was the only way to react.

The planet is sad and barren. The shuttle shivers from

the wind and dirt whipping up against the exterior as the craft breaks through the atmosphere. A blast of sand shoots through the bay doors, following my craft as I enter. There's a grinding click as the landing gear catches the ground. I breathe out deeply as I hover my hand over the control for the craft door. Someday I'd like to exit my transporter craft without having to fear the white light. The only light this time is fluorescent.

"Jacob!"

Scat. I jump in surprise.

"Jacob, how could you just leave like that? You're barely able to walk around; just look at you!"

Of course, Samuel is waiting for me. I think of Emmanuel calling him like a mother. No, he is worse than a mother. He looks at me strangely.

"Why on Yalk are you red?"

Scat. I forgot about my clothes! I was so busy cleaning the transporter craft that I forgot that I was red too! I try to think of some convincing reason. Anything. Fell in powdered dyes? Spices?

"You know, I don't even want to know! How do you even manage to come back looking *that* terrible?"

I assume that this question is also rhetorical.

"It's not all that bad. Just a little tired is all," I lie.

"You know disappearing like that just isn't fair, Jacob," his voice falls, "not after what happened with him."

Saul.

"You're right. It wasn't fair, but you wouldn't have let me go if I told you I was going. You've been watching after me like a Gromptu lately, Sam, and I had things I needed to do."

"That's why I've been watching you. All you've been doing

lately is simmering about what happened to him."

My face burns. He is refusing to say his name on purpose. I stop walking.

"Say his name."

"Huh? What are you talking about?" Samuel asks, turning red.

"Say his name, Samuel."

"Why are you doing this?" He knows what I'm talking about.

"Just say his name!"

I feel the Gromptu's eyes. Let them stare stupidly with those lens-like eyes. That's all they are, lenses for the real Lovindians.

"Say his name, damn it! Stop hiding from it!" I bellow. He flinches at my words, and I hate myself immediately. I step back, but he's already shaking.

"Saul!" he screams and I step back in shock. "Are you happy? Are you happy now?"

Fire burns in his eyes, and for the first time, I really see the resemblance between him and his younger brother. I look away.

"I'm sorry." He has spent so much time looking after me, and this is how I repay him?

"It's fine," Samuel grumbles, sounding embarrassed. "I do understand, you know. I get what happened. I just—can't quite believe it."

I nod and rub the back of my hand. When I get the courage to peek up at him again, he's deflated. We awkwardly continue our walk back toward our apartments. He avoids eye contact with me.

"How's Emmanuel?" I sigh.

"He leaves his room sometimes now."

He doesn't mention Emmanuel's visit with the bread. His mother must have sent him when Samuel wasn't around.

"I'm going to be taking trips to Yahbi a little more often, Samuel. I just figured I'd tell you so that you don't get nervous when you come over to my apartment and I'm not there."

"Uh-huh, sure." Samuel rolls his eyes but doesn't ask any questions.

"What?"

"Just don't get hurt, Jacob."

We reach my door. He stares at me long and hard, and then turns and runs toward his apartment. Since when does Samuel seem to know so much? The less he knows, the safer he'll be from the Lovindians. He seemed to grow up overnight after what happened to Saul. His happiness will be more secure if he doesn't know what I'm doing. Cattle taste better when they don't know the blade is coming. If we really are just cattle, I want to be the toughest piece of meat the Lovindians ever chew on. That's my choice, though. If Samuel would rather pretend what happened to Saul never happened, that's his choice.

Emmanuel's face comes to mind. The hate and pain that burned in his eyes—that's how I feel. I can't bury that. If I do nothing, I'm going to go insane. What is Emmanuel doing now? Is he just going insane? He said something before about trying to stay busy. I wonder how he's progressing at mastering the Lovi-dex and learning to fly a transporter craft.

The lights are dimming. My muscles are weak with exhaustion. If I'm going to continue the story tomorrow, then I need to rest. As I lay down, my mind drifts through all that I saw. I see the layers and layers of snow, which I have never truly seen before. After seeing it through Jana's eyes, though, it's just as familiar as Yalk's dust or Yahbi's sand. I try to recall how it felt, but it's still not quite my own memory. I can only hear the crunch that it made as my feet broke the top.

The Lovindian said that Octorn was the first planet they invaded in this galaxy. A galaxy is huge—is it possible that the Lovindians have more than one under their control? Fighting the Lovindians might be like fighting space itself. What knowledge could save me from that? I shake the thoughts out of my head. It's not like it matters whether I am saved or not.

15

Chapter 15

Maybe it would have been stealthier to pace out my visits to the red planet. The truth is that I don't know what stealthiness should look like in the face of the Lovindians. The Talkers thought they were being clever, and look where that got them. What I do know is that, like the Talkers, I'm on a time limit.

This time, I wait for the dust to settle completely before opening the door. I hop to the ground too quickly, and a wall of red dust shoots skyward. I cough violently. After a humiliatingly long period of time, I wipe my eyes of tears and filth.

On my first visit, the planet had been nearing the end of its light cycle. This time, it almost seems like a completely different planet. The midday heat is almost unbearable, and after the coughing fit, I'm covered in thick sweat. The perspiration dries on my forehead, making the dirt stick where it is. I already feel like I need to wash. I would wish for wind to relieve the heat if I didn't fear what the planet might become with just a light breeze.

The stillness of the planet is more powerful than the heat.

As I walk, it is like I am stirring the air for the first time in years. The same tiny, red dust tornadoes spin wildly about my feet. I watch them dance ahead of me and dissipate only to kick up new ones to replace the old.

I stop at the massive entrance and peer in. In the daylight, the room is better revealed. I brush away the dirt from the floor with my clothed foot. For just a moment, I see light blue tiles before the dust rolls back over them. Hands that weren't owned by Lovindians laid these tiles. My heart yearns for what this place may have looked like before. I wonder how long ago they stripped the planet.

"Welcome."

I startle and the Lovindian chuckles. The hair prickles on my arms and the back of my neck. It's terrifying how easily this being could kill me.

"Sorry, I was just looking." I don't meet its eyes.

"What did you see?"

"I was wondering what this place looked like before it was strip-mined," I tell him.

The Lovindian nears, and I'm struck again by his massive size. The fur that drapes down his back makes a swishing sound as it drags the ground. There's a strange weight to its presence. If I didn't know that it was a Lovindian, I think that I might be in awe of it instead of fearful. My stomach twists a little. It's revolting to think of a Lovindian stealing the life of this ancient being.

"It was a place of dreams," the Lovindian rumbles.

"Why did they even bother to destroy it? It's so small."

"If you neglect too many of the small things, it will add up with time," he says. "It seems cruel and excessive to strip-mine a dwarf planet, but it wasn't always this small. The mining process took quite a toll on its size."

"Did it have a resource that was highly valued?"

"Not really. The Lovindians don't like to waste time or productivity, but it's part of their protocol to strip-mine the planets when they've been conquered. Time management is something they've had a long time to perfect." He chuckles and I don't. "Bad humor, my apologies."

"Are you telling me that every planet the Lovindians conquer has completely been destroyed?" How many ecosystems have been destroyed because of "protocol?" I shudder. It's more senseless destruction than I can imagine.

"Not all," the Lovindian says.

"How many of them?" My muscles tighten in anticipation of the answer.

"Most." The word is hollow.

I want to feel anger, but all I can feel is emptiness. I can't even begin to fathom the amount of death the Lovindians have caused. I can't comprehend the type of evil that could cause so much pain. It's not just conquering planets. It's mass genocide on all planetary life.

"How can they do something like this?" I swallow hard.

"Jacob; why are you a terrorist?"

"A what?" I stammer out.

"A terrorist." The Lovindian lets out a rumbling laugh. "That's how you'll be charged anyways. Okay, I see you're going to be proud about it; why are you a—Yalkian rebel?"

"I have a debt to pay," I repeat for the second time.

"Right, right, a debt. It's love or hate, boy. I'd be interested to know which is more powerful these days." My face burns. "People only fight back when there is something to be gained or when there is absolutely nothing to lose. When Lovindians off-world a people, they strip the planet because then there's nothing for them to wish for. Why would they rebel to go home when there is no home to go to? All their belongings, all their culture, all their history—their identity—poof!" He makes an explosive motion with his hands.

"If a Lovindian chops off one of your hands, then you thank them for leaving the other. The people might be in outrage over their home planet, but they can't go back to it. If they fight, they might lose their family, and what is left to gain? By destroying the planet, Lovindians squelch out rebellions before they even have a chance to start. That's why they strip every conquered planet. This planet had far too much significance to be allowed to flourish."

I feel hot. The back of my hands itch. I can see what he's saying in my own species. They dedicate all their time to their families and friends. All of Yalk is a tight network of homemakers. Family is Yalk's great treasure. Losing his family was what drove Saul to do what he did in the first place. He fought back only when he had nothing to lose.

"If you're a rebel, it's important to know what you're fighting for. I'd tell you not to fight for hate, but then you might not fight at all. You have to have a big imagination and a lot of wishful thinking if you're fighting for love."

"What about justice?" I ask.

"Justice?" He sighs. "Never heard of it."

I don't argue with him. For a while, the creature stares at what I can only surmise is dust particulate in the air. I know it's time for the story to start, and a hard pit forms in my stomach. The thin, pink scar on my hand burns in memory of the last time. The creature settles on the floor, and I wait for some signal of what to do. I listen to the heavy huffs that come with the creature's breath.

"Please, sit."

I sit.

"Tell me where you last were." His voice is surprisingly soft, like sand running through your fingers.

"I—I don't understand what you're asking."

"In the story." The Lovindian grows increasingly impatient. He twitches slightly, and I wonder if it's causing him discomfort to speak. "Tell me where you last were in the story."

I close my eyes and try to concentrate. I see it almost immediately, and I'm shocked at the clarity before I realize he's already taken my hand. I can almost feel Octorn. I can hear Jana's breath. She's frightened—very frightened, and very cold too. It's the kind of cold that no amount of fur or clothing can block out.

"She's cold."

"Mmm."

"And very frightened."

"I'm going to need a little more than that."

I don't have to think much anymore; I can remember every detail. Her back was firmly pressed up against the tree, digging in uncomfortably. She was too afraid of being noticed to shift her body, as bodies regularly need, and the result was sharp, trembling pains that ran up her legs. The fear was irrational; her friends couldn't see her.

"She wants to go home. Her friend that spoke in the weird language had dragged Grel away with the help of the others. Grel was one of the other two Octornians still in the game. Why did they shoot Grel? How did they shoot Grel? Their Lovi-guns were turned off until the game's completion; I shot them. I know the game isn't over; Eto told me that Netto is still in the game. How could their Lovi-guns still work? I want to go home; I haven't been home in a long time. The weather is too strong. When the weather gets better, I—"

I think I'm babbling, but then again, I'm not sure I'm talking at all. The creature is humming or whistling or maybe a mixture of the two.

"Articles of the Council:

Year: 2772

Subject: Jana"

Jana felt heavy as she awoke from a light sleep. The snow had covered her in a soft layer of white just as if she were a branch or a shrub. She started in surprise, and the majority of the snow fell, making a thud as it hit the ground. Her ears flipped up instinctively to check if anyone had heard the noise, and another round of snow slid off the top of her head. Her muscles tightened, trying to make herself smaller, but she stopped short that instinct too because she was too sore for any type of straining.

She scanned the surrounding area. Not too far away, she could hear noise from the village. Nothing intelligible, but the sounds of movement and chatter were soothing. Eto and the others were either being very quiet, or they had set off much earlier, making it to the village long before Jana had woken.

Restless minutes passed in which she tried to get up the courage to leave the safety of the tree. If they were still there, they might shoot her just like they had Grel. She wasn't sure why but this thought instilled fear in her. Her friends were acting so strangely the night before that she still wasn't sure of what she saw. The sun rose up through the branches, and she waited until it reached her eye-level before climbing down.

She listened for wildlife to calm her nerves. A rustle, a

heartbeat, a ruffle of feathers, nothing. Could it be possible that they were reacting to the same sense of danger that she felt? Maybe they could sense her fear and they acted accordingly. After all, if the top predator is nervous, shouldn't they be? Whatever the case, they had likely moved beneath the ground where heartbeats couldn't be heard.

She moved into a light jog, testing her strength. The forest of Silatines created shadows across the snow, leaving areas of cool darkness to contrast painfully against the unbearably bright spots of sunlight reflecting off of the white snow. She moved slower, walking through the area that the others had disappeared in the night before. The evening wind hadn't yet begun to blow, and the footprints left by her friend's morning travels were still visible, but just barely. She felt silly as she looked further down the line of prints; she had wanted to avoid encountering them, but why? There had been nothing to fear; the others had simply gone home.

The first breeze of the evening wind caught her by surprise. It whistled softly and then died out. Then came the arrival of a second, longer gust of wind. It picked up for a moment to the point where it was almost a howl, and as she hunched up her shoulders, someone moved out in the white. A short yelp escaped her before she could stop it.

"Who's there?" she called.

She stepped nearer, and then, upon understanding, stopped.

The wind must have pushed it over. They must have known she'd find it. The cry she had foolishly let out vibrated off the great trunks and echoed long enough to make birds scatter from the treetops. The wind must have pushed the body over.

"Netto?" she asked, but she didn't know why.

He had once lain slumped up against the tree. The snow

from the night before had blasted against the trees from the North, and when the wind had changed and blown him over, the outline of his body was still on the trunk. The body had slumped over into the snow; the ice in his fur was unshaken. His eyes were frosted over so that they blended in with the outer-covering of snow wrapped around him. And the snow was caked violet-red around his temple; the blood was undeniable evidence that it was not the elements that killed him. And the armband glowed "0," the number just as bright as—

She looked away. There was nothing else to do. Did they do this? It didn't make any sense. This didn't feel real. She left herself for a while; great gasps filling up her lungs, her vision blurred. She caught herself before she fainted, focusing on one area of the woods until her vision cleared and her breathing slowed. Her eyes focused on a strange red color. On the side of a Silatine which had faced away from the wind and snow, the bare, thin wood showed, peeled and shredded. Someone had vandalized the side of it, the utensil used still laying like the murder weapon beside its victim. A gooey, red sap oozed through the cuts. She moved away from Netto, entranced by the word the murderers had carved up the tree. Her feet stumbled, but she didn't fall.

"Why?" she asked.

"Congratulations," the tree oozed.

"Why?" Hysteria crept in.

"Congratulations."

"Why? Why? Why!"

She picked up the murder weapon and slashed through the word. At first, the tree didn't ooze, and then it did. Her breath caught.

"Congratulations."

Jana wretched violently.

When she had finished, her feet started carrying her toward home without asking for permission from her brain. When she got back to the village, they would tell her that she had just been away from home for too long and that she had started to hallucinate. They would tell her that Eto, Gentha, and Lantha were waiting to play with her once she got done eating a fine meal. They would tell her that Netto had arrived a few hours earlier and forfeited the game.

She looked back over her shoulder and could see only a lump in the snow. That's all it was: a lump in the snow. Running downhill, the world spun by faster than normal. She could already see the fence; she had only needed a little more time, and she could have been home the night before. The weather had not allowed this to be so.

The fence was built up high over the village, made from the full trunks of the Silatines. It appeared like a fortress, but the walls were meant more to block out the wind than to block out intruders. The posts were driven many feet down into the thick ice; originally they had not been half so deep, but the world kept freezing over, burying and securing the posts more each year. Jana slowed before the gate. She looked up, squinting to see the top of the fence, but it was hidden in fog. Then, with her face still lifted up, she called out for them to open the doors.

She backed up for the gate to let her in, shifting awkwardly on her feet to keep out the cold. There was a heavy cranking, and the door opened just enough for her to squeeze through. She instantly sighed in relief. A couple of people wandered outside the openings to the underground dwellings, chatting aimlessly. Her eyes settled on a group that was laughing loudly. A few pointed at a large Gluotain bird that had been skinned and was hanging from the happy hunter's hand. It was normal activity.

Then the male Octornian dropped the bird carelessly to the ground. It flopped there and the others laughed. Something was wrong. She focused on what they were saying, but the words slipped off her mind without meaning. She didn't understand them. Jana backed toward the door; the crank had already pulled it shut. The people who were standing near the tunnel entrance had stopped their conversation. One gurgled strangely and pointed. The wind hadn't interfered with her hearing, not within the tall walls of the village. She didn't understand them.

Lantha emerged from the crowd. Jana wanted to feel relieved to see her friend but there was something wrong. She was smiling.

"Congratulations!"

There was something strangely and sickeningly sincere about her. Despite all of her protective fur, Jana's blood ran cold. Jana almost ran toward the gate crank but fell short when her eyes caught sight of the Lovi-gun in the gatekeeper's hand. She whimpered. She had known the gatekeeper all her life, but looking into those solid, cold eyes, she did not doubt that if she made a move to open the gate herself, he would shoot.

"Aren't you going to thank me?" Lantha came nearer to her.

A couple more of the Octornians had come up from the underground. Grel and Eto were among this group. They stared and allowed it all to continue. Lantha was walking closer; her uncharacteristic confidence was unnerving. Whoever this was, it wasn't Lantha.

"Aren't you going to thank me?" This time it was more of a demand than a question.

Her heart crashed in her chest; she knew she was trapped, but she couldn't find any feeling of resignation. She didn't want to die. She couldn't beg for her life either. Prey cornered never gives in to its predator; even as the jaws come down, it squeaks in protest. Jana stared shamelessly at the Lovi-gun that hung loosely from the girl's index finger as if it were only a toy. The girl stopped advancing and Jana had to try.

"Lantha?"

The girl's lip curled; it was neither a snarl nor a smile. Somehow the name seemed distasteful to her, and yet it was hers. The hunter who had thrown down the Gluotain bird snapped something in his gurgling language. Lantha bristled and gnashed her teeth; the hunter became silent. Jana hunkered within herself. Lantha was much smaller by comparison to Jana, but whatever terrible sickness had come over her had changed her completely. She used her body to its full extent for intimidation. The others around her created an overwhelming presence, mimicking her motions.

Jana's eyes again moved toward the gun. Somehow, it had caused this. What illness did it carry within its rays? Lantha took another step forward, and Jana shirked away.

"What's wrong? You've never seen a Lovindian before?"

Jana didn't understand. Lantha lifted the gun and pointed. Jana checked the door again; it was still very shut. Her fur began to bristle as she realized she was being backed into a wall. A hiss of breath escaped between her teeth.

"This is the last Octornian standing!"

The others laughed their deep throaty laughs. Jana felt silly and vulnerable in front of the indifferent crowd with all of her anger and hate. She held a defensive posture, but there was nothing that she could do to defend against what was coming; she couldn't even defend against Lantha's mocking.

"This is the last Octornian standing!" she repeated. "Congratulations, you've won the game!"

She fired.

Jana dodged.

The beam blasted into her left foot, and the air pulse sent her sprawling into the snow. She desperately searched for some sign of pain, some confusion, as a man sustaining fatal injuries will search for his wound in the final moments of life. Jana pulled her knee to her chest and rubbed down the sides of her leg—no pain. Her hands found their way to her foot and she stroked it gingerly. If she had an ax, she could remove it and maybe—the armband blinked once, and the zero changed to a one.

Then Lantha grabbed Jana by her arm and helped her to her feet. Jana didn't resist her; she stood and stretched, yawning widely. Lantha laughed, enjoying the company of her friend.

16

Chapter 16

My vision goes in and out of focus. Finally, I make out the shape of a cup. Nyauta. I tilt my chin slightly downward to stare into the swirling liquid in the cup. I know the feeling of eyes on me well enough to know that the Lovindian is studying me carefully, without having to look up.

"You should drink that."

His advice seems far off; it's just a distant suggestion. My thirst wells up and decides for me. I reach out with both hands, uncoordinated like a child, and tip the drink into my mouth. The creature sighs.

"You scared me for a minute there. I thought—" he trails off. I know what he thought.

I clutch the cup at my chest. The nyauta in the bottom of the cup ripples. My teeth chatter. My body shivers. The creases in the creature's face are more pronounced than normal. Worry? He's almost as hard to read as a Gromptu.

"She didn't even feel it coming," I whisper.

"No," he rumbles. "Fortunately they don't feel it."

I shudder and the remainder of the cup's liquid swings up

to the rim. He would know. He was one of them.

"Do you hate me?" he asks.

"Hadn't thought about it," I cough in surprise.

I have always hated and feared Lovindians. It is difficult for me to look at the creature in front of me and know that he's a Lovindian. What other Lovindian would ask me if I hated it? I raise my head to meet it. It's not easy to tell, but I have the feeling that this creature is filled with immeasurable grief behind his stony eyes. There's a part of me that feels repulsed when he nears, but in the face of the enemy, I can't hate him. It has to be because he was banished from the rest of them. This one has to be different.

"She was just gone. I felt it—I felt it there and not her," I murmur.

The Lovindian leans forward, and its toughened skin almost touches mine. He's swaying back and forth—or maybe I'm swaying.

"I think you should go home and rest."

I laugh and it's hiccupy and painful. A Lovindian worried about the condition of a human. I hiccup and it almost sounds like a sob. My head spins. I sway.

I wake to the sound of someone humming. I feel the thick texture of the cot beneath my fingers. My neck is sore as I lift my head to see who is clanging and humming in the washbasin. He hears the cot creak and turns. A wet cloth hangs from one hand. He throws it into my lap, and the thing, drenching wet, soaks through my blankets immediately.

"Samuel!" I protest.

"Don't 'Samuel' me! You went and got yourself hurt again, and I want to know why. I know the explanation given to the Gromptu isn't true, so tell me the truth."

"Explanation?" I mumble. I finger a lump at the back of my head. I must have fainted and hit my head on the floor. How did the Lovindian get me home? I remove the towel from my lap and squirm out of the cold, wet sheets. The cold feels good on the lump. "What explanation?" I ask.

"I was waiting for you to return, and you never came. I didn't have anything better to do, so I came back the next morning and waited again. Then, suddenly you come in, or your ship does anyway, and the Gromptu started running about because your warning lights are on. Your transporter ship is flying all crazy because the atmosphere was having some wild winds and the autopilot wasn't compensating. They sent out another transporter ship to help guide your craft back in. They were furious, or I think they were; it's hard to tell."

"Samuel! What explanation?"

"Hold on!" he is obviously enjoying his job as an informant. He grins fleetingly, which is a nice relief from his more common nagging. "Then, when they get the ship inside the landing bay, you don't open the door. They finally have to force the door up, and they find you lying unconscious on the controls. I ask if you're alright and see them leaning over the flight entries—the compartment had been left open. Then they look at me with those big eyes of theirs and just leave you there. I guess they expected I'd either help you to your apartment, or you'd wake up eventually. I find you with dried blood all over your head, and I panic thinking maybe—well, you know! So I go over, and check on you—you're alright; then I look at the flight entries. It says something about you getting in a fight over a girl on Yahbi. I know that you can't get a girl, so what happened?"

"What happened after that?" I say, ignoring his jibe about

me being unable to get a girl.

"I dragged you back here. The damn Lovindians wouldn't help me, and I couldn't just leave you there bleeding."

"But did the Gromptu seem suspicious? Did they accept that explanation?"

"How should I know! I can't tell when they're happy or angry, let alone suspicious!"

I try to let this sink in. The Lovindian must have manufactured the story and typed it into the logbook under the guise of a Yahbiin official. It is a conceivable story except for the fact that there aren't any women on Yahbi that a human would risk a fight over. It is unlikely, though, that the Gromptu are wiser to this fact than the Lovindian. The lie isn't going to work on Samuel, though. I sigh and fall back into the cot.

"Jacob, I'm not going to keep bandaging you up. Next time, I might not be waiting for your craft in the shuttle bay," he says seriously.

His warning benefits me. I don't want him to wait for me in the shuttle bay. It's dangerous for him. I can feel his eyes on me, but nothing comes out of my mouth. I have to give him some kind of truth.

"I fainted and hit my head." I touch my forehead.

"Why did you faint?" he asks intensely.

I can't tell him everything. If I do, he'll only worry more, and he might become an even bigger target. The Gromptu have already seen him dragging me to safety and healing me numerous times. Samuel is like a brother to me, and I can't put him in any more danger. Which also means I have to be more careful. I can't keep getting hurt because it's making him more visibly connected to me.

"I found a—library that has recordings of history. I'm using it to learn the story of how the Lovindians rose into power."

He stares at me. I can tell he believes me, but maybe he hadn't expected me to be honest in the first place.

"H-how can something like that even exist?"

"Well, it's a secret place. The Talkers found it but never got to use it."

"That doesn't explain why you fainted."

He's right. I wince.

"I was weak with exhaustion and kept studying."

"Mmm, so who sent you home?"

"What?"

"Who made the log because it wasn't you. You said you were unconscious."

"The l-librarian."

Samuel looks at me quizzically but seems to accept it.

"A library that tells the stories of history, huh?" he says thoughtfully. "Does this library have—ah, never mind." A blush comes into his cheeks.

"Does it have what?" I frown.

"Well, does it have images of Earth?" He shrugs.

"Earth?" I hadn't even thought about it. I had been so focused on the Lovindians that I hadn't even thought about humanity's history. Could the Lovindian let me see humanity's planet?

"It would be amazing to see if the legend was really true. The idea of humans ruling their own planet is—" He trails off, unable to find a word.

"Incredible," I finish.

He nods. I'm stunned that I haven't thought of it before. I haven't even asked the Lovindian if Earth is real. My heart sinks. If Earth is real, is it still out there, stripped dry like

Yalk? Some people say Earth was covered in water and humans ruled the land, some say Earth wasn't ruled by humans at all, and others say that Earth is just a fiction created by fanciful Yalkians. Some people even believe that Yalk *is* Earth, or the only planet that humans had ever lived on.

"I have to go back," I say to myself.

Who knows how much time I've lost to being unconscious? I am still on borrowed time. I make my way toward the door.

"You can't!" Samuel catches my sleeve.

"Why not? I have to get back to the library."

"The Gromptu have canceled all interplanetary travel."

"For how long?" I exclaim and shake my head in frustration. "Since when?"

"They put signs out the morning after you returned. The signs say that the shuttle bay has been closed until further notice. Who knows how long that will take."

Through the door, I can see two Gromptu stationed in front of the door to the landing bay. Two signs are posted on either side of the exit. They must be the ones that Samuel is referring to. A few walkers have already begun to stir between the buildings. I glance nervously at Samuel.

"You better get home."

He shuffles awkwardly, and a bright blush fills his cheeks. I follow his gaze. For the first time, I notice the additional cot in the apartment. He must have moved in to take care of me while I was unconscious. There is no way now that he'd make it back to his home with his cot before the lights dim all the way down. I can't let him get caught bumbling around in the dark.

"Oh!" I say awkwardly. "You can stay here for the night."

"Thank you so much!" Gratitude replaces his embarrass-

145

ment.

I should be the one thanking him. I slide the pull-out door shut to block out the view of the corridor. There is no need for the door to stay open; no one is going out there tonight. The room darkens; the lights are automatically set to lower when the room is closed off. Closed apartments are only for sleep and the privacy of couples, neither of which require light. I find my cot in the dark, and I can hear Samuel doing the same.

I haven't roomed with someone since I was a child. I should say something to end the awkward silence. The noise level outside starts to rise. Samuel is the first to break the quiet.

"Do you think you could play?"

I'm a child again—before I walked the hallways. I would lie in my cot, breathing the tense air into tightened lungs. Sleep would not come behind my closed eyes. I was restless like the people outside the door, but I didn't dare move. It's only when restlessness overcomes the fear of being trampled that children know that they're ready to join their parents in walking. As I lay uncomfortably rubbing my sweaty palms together, a sweet voice would break the dark.

"Do you think you could play for me?" Keren would ask.

My shaking hands would reach into my pocket as they do now and pull out the fragile fennele. How long had Keren saved up her credits so she could buy this from an elderly lady down the hall? The metal is decorated with an intricate depiction of two armies surrounding a small boy and a giant. It's strange seeing art featuring humans. From the moment I laid eyes on it, I loved it.

Despite being so ornate, the instrument is played very simply. Only three strings are strung on the neck of the fennele, each of which is made of varying widths of wire. The instrument makes a high twinkling, like little bells, when it is played.

I pluck each string to make sure that it is in tune. In the dark, I can still see Samuel's smile. Hard calluses are built-up on the tips of my fingers from playing the fennele. When I was first learning to play, the thin strings would cut the ends of my fingers, but now my fingers are hardened. I don't need to see the strings to play.

"Will you sing?" he asks excitedly.

I want to tell him no because I'm tired, but it is the least I owe him for saving me once again. There aren't many musicians on Yalk. To get an instrument, you have to spend your precious baunti allowance on something you can't eat. Also, you have to teach yourself to play because who on Yalk could teach you? I know very few songs; only ones that I have caught mothers singing to children, and I'm never sure if I have all of the lyrics right. I start, letting my fingers do the work, and the sweet, bird-like song of the fennele fills the apartment:

"Don't go near the light.
The Maker's mark is cold.
Don't go near the light.
These aren't the days of old.
Child, roam your field.
The Maker's mark is cold.
Child, roam your field.
These aren't the days of old.
And the dirt is red,
but we don't tell.
And the dirt is red,
but we will never tell.
Child, come back home.

The Maker's mark is cold.
Child, come back home.
These aren't the days of old.
No need for a grave.
The Maker's mark is cold.
No need for a grave.
These aren't the days of old.
And the dirt is red,
but we don't tell.
And the dirt is red,
but we will never tell."

The last twinge of the fennele rings through the air. The song feels so light and whimsical that the lyrics feel more like an inevitability than a mourn. I lay down, not knowing what to say. I listen for the long breaths that signal sleep but hear none. I wonder if he's lying awake, frustrated in his cot, wishing for sleep. I try to think of something to say to comfort him, to acknowledge his fear of what is outside, but I don't know any words. No one ever had any for me.

17

Chapter 17

I carefully push open the sliding door just enough to squeeze my body through. A ray of light falls across the room from the hallway, and Samuel stirs in his sleep. I shut the door behind me. The lights are still dim. I can't help but think of the morning that I followed Saul's father down the corridors. Things would have been very different if I hadn't ended up in that tent that night.

I walk past the landing bay doors, but the Gromptu still stand guard. My shoulders tighten. I can't return to the red planet. What are the Gromptu up to? I can't remember them ever closing off space travel before. A seed of dread buries itself in my gut. It probably has nothing to do with me. If they knew about my exploits, I would just be dead; they wouldn't cancel space travel. The Lovindian told me himself that the Lovindians don't care about people going to the red planet—but I've been more than once.

The eyes follow me as I walk away. Cold sweat beads on my forehead. I'd label it as paranoia if I were more naive. I weave down an alley to make the eyes disappear, but the sweat doesn't stop. I rub the back of my hand. They'll come for me. I know it. No one will even notice. I hope Samuel forgets me; maybe he will live longer.

A Gromptu stands at the end of the row beneath a vent that funnels our precious air through Unit B. A couple of its loose, downy feathers shake under the breeze. It isn't facing me. The hairs on my arms stand on end. I didn't know it was possible to see one of them before they see you. I take advantage of the opportunity and stare openly. Its skin trembles from the cold air, but it doesn't move aside where the vent isn't as direct. Is it dutiful to that spot for a reason, or does it not even register that it is cold? The creature tilts one of its tubular ears. Has it heard me? No. I hear what the Gromptu was quicker to spot.

"Please, you have to tell me if you've seen her."

It's a frantic whisper. The woman is obviously trying to be quiet for the sake of the rest of the sleeping humans, but desperation causes her voice to rise as I step nearer. The Gromptu I was watching shifts back and forth on its feet several times before slipping away. I follow it.

"She's been missing for too long now. I know she's a grown woman, but I couldn't imagine her changing unit buildings without telling me."

I recognize the voice before I see her. She's plump, with glowing skin and straight, soft black hair. In her grief, Samuel's mother has forgotten the appropriate distance for a Gromptu and a human to keep. She moves forward with outstretched arms. My heart squeezes painfully. The two Gromptu stare at her with those eyes. They chatter back and forth, and I can't tell what they are thinking about the situation.

"Please, you have to understand me!" Tears run down her

face.

"Mary, what's wrong?" I interfere, stepping as close as I dare to separate her from the Gromptu.

"Oh, Jacob! You must know where she is!"

Her eyes widen when she sees me. She brushes the dark hair away from her face; she looks sticky and red, like a child worn out from wailing.

"Who? Know where who is?" I grab her shoulders.

Her lips scrunch, but hope still lights her eyes. She looks up through thick, black lashes. Surely she was very beautiful in her younger days. What has this world done to her?

"Why, my daughter, of course!"

"Mary, I don't know where your daughter is, but I can help you look for her," I say trying to get her to come away from the guards. I'm lying to her. I can't help her, but I have to get her away from them. She can't make a scene like this. She has to pretend to not notice like the rest of them. She has to pretend like—pretend like... I lower my head.

"I thought you would know," she says softly.

"Why would I know?" I say confusedly.

Her lips form an "O" and a blush rises into the tops of her cheeks. I shake my head realizing what she might have suspected. There aren't many things for young people to do to amuse themselves. It wasn't uncommon for a young pair to spend multiple days together. I blush in response. I've never even seen her daughter before.

"I'm sorry; I don't know where she is." My stomach tightens.

She lowers her face, looking down at her feet, which are wrapped in the same beige cloth as my own. I look away, feeling an awkward silence. She slaps my arm suddenly and a

151

broad smile spreads across her face.

"Oh, you kids! Just make sure that next time before you go running off with my daughter you tell old Mary first, okay?" I'm stunned by the sudden switch.

"Mary, I don't know where your daughter is."

For a second, she stops, her mouth becoming a thin line, but then the Yalkian magic happens. Her eyes narrow a little as if she's deciding whether or not I'm lying.

"Just tell me next time. Okay?" she says seriously.

She is ignoring me. My shoulders feel heavy. She trots away happily. Unable to find an explanation for her daughter's disappearance that would fit her reality, she manufactured one. Now she can rest as easy as anyone else in Unit B. I watch her return to her apartment. She stops to wink at me and grins. I don't smile back. The door closes behind her, but I can't tear my eyes away. It's better that she believes this way. It's better that she doesn't suffer as my mother did. It's a shame my mother was less imaginative.

The Gromptu are long gone. They left as soon as I had calmed the bizarrely acting woman. They were probably relieved when I showed up to divert her attention. I shudder to think of what might have happened had I not shown up, but more so, I shudder to know the truth. I'm sure that Mary's daughter did nothing to earn her disappearance. So why? My stomach feels sick. I wonder if she was beautiful—perhaps a real prize for a Lovindian. I wish I could lie to myself like Mary and believe that she had run away with a young man.

I unfold the fennele from my pocket and play thoughtlessly. The notes trill sadly underneath the sound of the raging wind outside the dome:

Child, come back home.

The Maker's mark is cold.

Child, come back home.

These aren't the days of old.

The melancholy that comes with Unit B feels sweltering today. I tuck the instrument away. As I walk home, I note that the Gromptu had returned to its position under the vent, just as if it had never left. I cringe and look away.

When I open my apartment door, I find Samuel pacing. He's rarely talked about his sister before. I wonder if they were close—I wonder if he'll realize what happened, or if he will believe his mother's fantasy. What about Emmanuel?

"Thank you!" he exclaims.

"Is something wrong?"

"I thought you'd taken off without telling me! I knew you wouldn't do that again!"

"How could I have left with the Lovindians blocking the door?"

"You didn't see?" His face falls.

My heart leaps. I peek out the doorway and see that the sign has disappeared. I can return to the red planet. I need to put some space between me and this planet. I start in the direction of the landing bay.

"Hey, stop!" I stop. "Take me with you!" My head starts shaking before I even get the words out. I lead him back to the apartment by his arm. "Jacob! I want to see it too! I want to know everything about the past," he protests against me.

"I'm sorry, Samuel; that's out of the question."

"I could go in with you! I could help look for the Lovindian secrets!"

"Shhh!" My eyes dart wildly, but for once, there are no Gromptu to hear him. "Samuel this isn't a game! You can't

153

talk about this! You shouldn't even be thinking about it!" I usher him back into my apartment and attempt to close the door with him on the other side.

"Wait, wait, Jacob, don't go! How am I supposed to sit around waiting while you go to study? There's nothing to do here!"

"Go look for your sister; she's missing." It comes out colder than I want it to, and Samuel looks as if I've slapped him.

"Sister?" he whispers.

"Yes. You should be with your mother." I'm more tender this time.

"Which sister?" I hear him mumble, but I'm already running away.

I can't risk him coming after me. The more distant he is from this, the better. It was never even a question of him going. It's not his burden to bear.

18

Chapter 18

The planet is dark as I step through the massive door. The ground outside still resonates heat from the sun. I wonder if the shifts from night to day are abrupt on the red planet. The Lovindian's sudden appearance startles me as usual.

"So you survived!"

"Yes, you had a part in that." I scratch the back of my head.

"You're welcome. I think this time we should go a little easier on you."

I rub the back of my hand thinking about what I want to ask. Samuel's questions about Earth have me itching. I don't know how exactly my relationship with the Lovindian works. He has helped me by changing the flight logs and getting me home, but how far does his charity go? My cloth-covered feet are stained red when I look down at them. I've been taking an extra pair of clothes and sending my red clothes out the waste disposal on the way home.

"Are you sure you're recovered?" the Lovindian asks.

I can't tell if his stone-grey eyes are showing actual concern or not. My life rests in the kindness of a Lovindian. I guess that's not really any different than usual.

"I'm fine. I—er, I just had a question is all."

He sits down, crossing his legs and gestures for me to join him. I accept his cordiality and smile awkwardly.

"Your question?" he asks.

"Oh! I was just wondering if—" My face burns. It's just a question. Why do I feel so embarrassed? I can't know the answer without asking. I mumble, "I was just wondering if Earth was really real."

"Yes." He nods slowly.

Yes?

"Earth was real?" A smile breaks onto my face before I can hold it back.

"It was real. I didn't think humans would still know what Earth was."

"Well, I don't know that much about it," I say honestly.

"It's nice to hear, though. Most of them don't remember their home planets after they're relocated." The Lovindian sighs.

My chest fills with an unfounded pride. Somewhere deep inside, I feel that I have another home somewhere in the world, but also—I feel cold.

"I am sorry for what happened," the Lovindian rumbles.

"It's gone, right? It was stripped just like this one."

I try to feel the loss, but I never really had Earth, so the only emotions that I can conjure up are envy of the past humans and anger at the people who ruined it.

"I can show you," the creature offers, "but it might hurt."

"Hurt? Physically?"

"No, not physically. There are a lot of worse pains than that."

156

He's warning me that watching Earth be destroyed will be painful, but it can't be any worse than what I've already seen. My heart hardens, and the pit in the bottom of my stomach sinks deeper.

"Show me."

I can find good things and tell Samuel. There had to have been some good things. There had to be. I hold out my scarred hand. The flesh is still sore from the last time.

"Just open your mind. You'll feel it start."

And I do.

"From the articles of the Council:

Year: 2213

Subject: Susanna Webber"

"Scanthirin Sickness (pronounced: Scan-theer-in): an infectious disease introduced to Earth in the second-to-last Earth century of humanity's Earth dwelling. Earth Year: 2203. Named after patient Maxwell Scant, first-ever documented case of Scanthirin Sickness.

"The disease spread wildly, affecting a wide range of humans all over the planet. The initial effects of the disease were innocuous, a low-grade fever, aches, nausea, but there were more detrimental things happening beneath. The infection created intense swelling around the brainstem, and without a cure, the disease inevitably left its victims in a coma-like state. A human scientist by the name of Edgar Battinson developed a vaccine after only one of Earth's orbits around its sun. The vaccine proved itself to be effective in preventing more people from contracting the disease and, for a while, seemed to give significant improvement to people who had quickly reached the coma state. It was only after the swelling had decreased around the humans' brainstems that it was

157

discovered there was little to no mental capability left in the afflicted. These people came to be referred to as 'Shells'. This surprised Battinson, whose patients showed signs of cognitive function while in the coma-like state, and he was led to believe that when the swelling decreased with the vaccine, it damaged the brainstem. He believed something could still be done for those who remained in the coma-like state and who were cursed with the nickname 'Scans'. This belief launched him into years of remarkable research."

The distinguishable lines between the two places meld. New colors are mixed with new sounds, and I try to close my eyes and cover my ears, but there's no effect. I try to focus on just a single sound and a single sight, but they are fleeting, a slam, flash, crunch, all gone. There's a constant. I'm moving—walking, and a rumbling—talking. The constant is the hard, even stamping of my feet. No, it's her feet. I let the story take me.

Susanna Webber's shadow marched just ahead of her. Her mind's empty thoughts had led her down one of the random sidewalk paths that threaded the hospital grounds. The building had been a university before it had been a hospital, and the sidewalks were a convenient source of stress relief for the staff, patients, and visitors. The university had been converted to a hospital when the majority of its students had become Scans.

It wasn't right for her to walk so quickly while in uniform, it might scare the visitors or put the other nurses on edge, but Susanna was very determined to have time to eat her lunch in quiet solitude. The oldest oak trees were in this part of the ex-campus. A squirrel chattered at her for allowing her white-shoed feet to make so much noise, and she appeased it by slowing down to sit on her favorite bench. Her quiet corner of the grounds wasn't, however, only to be shared with the squirrel; another nurse, Adrienne, walked a Shell beneath the shadows. Susanna grumbled at the inconvenience and immediately felt guilty as she watched her coworker struggle to make the person walk beside her.

She had no desire to watch; Susanna focused on the bench instead. A spider practiced web making on the armrest, and she inched away from it. The plaque fitted to the bench, which her exhaustion ordinarily did not permit her to notice, prodded her uncomfortably between her shoulder blades. She let out an excessively loud sigh, immensely irritated with her inability to relax in her usually comforting place. All the benches had a plaque, and they all said the same thing: "Thank you, Dr. Battinson." The plaques had been fitted when the state had given the hospital to Battinson in exchange for his "dedication to humanity" and, of course, the continuation of his research.

She twisted in her spot, beginning to feel hot, and thrust her hand into her lunch bag. She didn't bother to note which gas station sandwich she had brought from the multitudes in her refrigerator before stuffing it into her mouth. They didn't taste much different after a while anyway.

There was an area of the path where the ground stepped up just a bit and which the Shells always stumbled upon. Adrienne's Shell was no different. He stumbled, fell flat, not even trying to catch himself. There was a time when Adrienne or Susanna might have fondled over the Shell, feeling horribly guilty in their negligence. There was a time when they had done everything they could to smooth out the path by adding more dirt or breaking up the vicious tree roots with a trowel.

Adrienne passed by the Shell, attending to him only by lifting him to his feet by his underarm.

Susanna wondered when the nurses' compassion had turned over to exhaustion, and when that exhaustion had turned over to dislike, then hate, then indifference. At some point, she had to admit that she had taken delight in watching them fall over in the dirt, occasionally breaking their noses or biting into their tongues. Then, when had this become bothersome, and when did she begin to avoid that particular section in the walk? More importantly, however, when did she stop making decisions at all but just walked around, narrating her life from above? When did her body take over and just react instinctively to the routine that it found itself accustomed to? When did her body become so self-sufficient that it no longer needed her mind?

Then she looked up incredulously at Adrienne and her patient and was shocked at what she saw. She tried to shake the image out of her head. The image that they were not Adrienne and her patient but just two Shells walking side-by-side. Susanna jumped up from the bench, stuffing the last overly large mouthful of what was now, clearly, a ham, Swiss cheese, lettuce, and tomato sandwich, and rushed back toward the hospital.

The hospital was too clean and fresh. It acted as a false pretense of hope for visitors. Susanna could see the small signs of dying passion for a cause that was becoming tragic history for those outside of the hospital. Acceptance is the enemy of conviction. Slowly but surely, the rest of the world was accepting what had happened... and moving on.

The flowers, on each perfectly dusted bedside, were realistic, but they weren't real. At some point in time, a nurse had become sick of buying new flowers to replace the dying ones, when the patients' families had started to visit less and less, and the flowers slowly stopped coming with their absence. The fabric flowers proved a long-lasting, pleasant, easy alternative. The person who had made this decision had likely done it for convenience. It was only the medical staff after all who had to watch them slowly die over-and-over. It wasn't like the patients could enjoy them. The new flowers were unchanging and permanent, not unlike their patients.

"Hi, Susanna, how was lunch?"

"It was good, thank you."

The friendly exchange between her and the receptionist was comforting to the listeners, even though neither was actually as cheery as they sounded. A couple of visiting family members smiled at them. So thankful. So thankful that they could consider their former loved ones cared for. It wasn't their responsibility to pretend joy. They could just look in, see their loved ones well cared for, and they could leave with the responsibility of them off their backs. She was so jealous; she hated those thankful smiles. Hated, hated them.

Room C29. The beds had little, golden plaques on the footboards, not unlike the plaques on the park benches thanking the good doctor. "Madison Bale, Wei Wen, Evan Wall, Derrick Webber," she stopped at the last name.

A piece of lint had landed on his forehead; she brushed it away with a gentle hand.

"You're a little early."

None of the nurses in the room had approached her; in fact, they had departed discreetly according to routine. The man who joined her now was also part of her routine, she realized.

"Doctor, you don't need to check up on him."

"It's really no extra effort; it gives me time to get away from it all."

Susanna smiled, a little genuinely. She couldn't help but feel that the doctor was, in all actuality, checking up on her.

"Why are you laughing at me?"

"I didn't laugh," she mumbled, still smiling.

"A smile for you is a laugh for the average person."

She openly grinned at this, realizing that his jest was probably true.

"But seriously, Susanna, why did you smile?"

"Because when you take a break, you come to the place that I have to take breaks from." She was still smiling, but it was a sadder, more distant, smile. "It just puts things in perspective."

Then she turned away from Mr. Webber and looked up at the doctor. The doctor could not have been past his thirties, but the last eleven years, three months, and forty-seven days seemed to have aged him much more than that. His blonde hair contained white streaks crawling up the sides of his head, and she estimated within the next few years it would reach the top. His face was clean-shaven, but it had an appearance like it didn't want to be. It was worn despite its kind demeanor.

She hoped that he didn't think it was weird of her to comment on his work. The silence between them, however, seemed to be only awkward on her side. He chuckled darkly and seemed to be putting together an appropriate response.

"Your job is no easier than mine. It may seem like the world rests on my shoulders, but in all honesty, it rests on yours."

"But that's not true. When anyone thinks of their loved ones, they are consoled by the continuation of your work. There are tens of millions of people counting on your cure, and that isn't even including the family members."

He wasn't smiling anymore, not even bitterly. Why had she said that? Why in front of this bed, of all places? It looked like she was scolding him. Of course, he already knew the terrible weight of his responsibility! She tried to save herself, fast.

"I'm so sorry. I didn't mean to say—I mean, of course, you knew the importance of your work."

"Nurse Webber," he looked so serious now, "the reason I say 'the weight of the world rests on your shoulders' is because the work you do every day is far more important than the work I do; the rest of the world just doesn't know it. My work is just hopeful thinking, something that the people can ease their minds on, but you are the person working every day to keep the people's loved ones alive."

"A soldier is nothing without their general."

"A general is nothing without his soldiers."

She stared at him incredulously for a second and was about to retort something that was hopefully clever when he stopped her.

"Let's cease this praise fest, can we? We are both wonderfully important to the cause, and we are both wonderfully tired."

"At least the latter thing I can agree with," but she sighed in relief that the debate was over.

"You're impossible to please, Nurse Webber."

She laughed, and then remembered where she was. They both did. Their whole conversation seemed silly—vain. Derrick drooled a little out of the side of his mouth; she closed her eyes painfully.

"Susanna?" Even though they were what could be considered friends, he rarely ever called her by her first name.

"Susanna, I have an idea, but I need your advice."

"An idea?" she looked up inquisitively.

He gave her a knowing look, and she understood. Her mouth opened just a bit, and her eyebrows escalated as she prepared to talk.

"You mean for *it*?"

"Yes, for a cure."

"That's fantastic!" Her whole face brightened, and when she spoke, she let out a huge breath that she hadn't knowingly inhaled.

He grabbed her for a second, and it was only then that she realized she had been collapsing. She looked up to him with wonder that changed over to bafflement after analyzing his features.

"Why aren't you happy?"

"I told you, Susanna. I need your advice."

Again with the first name.

"My advice? How on Earth could my advice possibly help?" She shook her head laughing. "What could I possibly advise you on?"

"Please. Could you just stay after tonight and come to my office? I know I don't have to tell you this, but please don't tell anybody about this. I don't want to raise any false hope."

"Oh," she said quietly, "okay."

"Thank you."

He still had a careful hold on her, and he only let go of her arms when it was certain that she was on her feet. She bewilderedly looked back to her husband, wiping the bit of drool from his face. Drooling, and mind distant from their bodies, the Scans always looked so dumb. So irritatingly, helplessly dumb. She smeared tears away from her face; she always hated herself for feeling this way. Suddenly feeling self-conscious, she glanced around her, but Dr. Battinson had already left.

Her eyes then dared to move down the row. Two beds over, a vase of flowers had been left on the bed stand. Not the fake fabric ones but beautifully untainted daisies. Ana Battinson. She looked back at her husband's permanent flowers and felt a little shame. Could she really get him back?

"Jacob, we're going to have to speed forward a bit, or you'll be exhausted." Says the Lovindian from far away.

"Edgar?"

She only ever called him that after hours.

"Nurse Webber! Thank you so much!"

He seemed genuinely happy to see her.

"Again, I don't know what I can help you with—"

"Come in, please!"

She was standing in the doorway but came into his office nervously. She had never been into his office before; it was usually only a privilege shared with leading neuroscientists and other prestigious colleagues. The good doctor sat her down quickly in one of the chairs that these various colleagues had often debated with him from. He, on the other hand, took a seat on the edge of his desk. They stared at each other for a moment until he finally smiled giddily, and she returned it, happy the silence was broken.

"I have a way to wake up all of the people originally infected with Scanthirin, without the effects of the vaccine."

Her hands, which had been folded, dropped to her knees in surprise. She stood up, amazed.

"You've done it then? Derrick, Ana, they're all coming back! It's a dream! This is a dream! I've had dreams like this!"

"I wish it were like one of those dreams," he whispered.

"But why isn't it?" She leaped toward him. "Why is it that you have only told me? Oh my goodness. The world has to know!"

At this, Dr. Battinson finally came toward her, removing himself from the desk. He gently moved her from the door and guided her back to the chair.

"But—but what are you doing?"

"Don't you understand, Susanna?"

She did not understand.

"This is the reaction I want to get! This is the reaction I deserve to get! The one I've worked so hard for, but I'm not going to get it; I'm not."

After this sudden exultation, he leaned against the wall. He slammed his fist and his framed doctorate shook on the nail. Susanna was moved by both worry and confusion. For a moment, she drew back into the chair; maybe he hadn't found a cure at all but instead was going mad. Perhaps he led her here to hear the excitement he would never get, but no, he didn't look insane. Upset, but not insane.

"Well, of course, you will get that reaction! You are about to save millions of lives." He started shaking his head. "I don't understand, Edgar; is someone taking credit for your work?"

"Credit," he laughed grimly, "who would want to take credit for what I have done?"

Perhaps he had gone mad after all. Again, this fear was assuaged when he looked up at her from across the room.

"Something is wrong with the cure," she finally decided.

"There is no cure," he whispered.

"But you said—!"

"It wasn't exactly true." He rubbed his forehead with both

hands—hard.

"How much of it wasn't true?" She struggled to follow his conflicting narrative.

"I can wake up your husband and," he paused painfully, "and Ana."

"But that's a cure!" She was becoming extremely annoyed with all of his torturous turns, and her exasperation showed through her voice.

"I assure you, nurse, it is not a cure."

He walked quickly from the room, and at first, she was too astounded to follow. After enough seconds had passed, he returned to the door, rolled his eyes irritatedly, and gestured for her to follow. It was only a few doors down that he stopped and ushered her inside. F32—the lab.

"Come, come! I need to show you what the great Doctor Battinson has done!"

Susanna wasn't very good with technology, and so upon seeing the thing in the center of the room, the only thing she could say confidently was that it was a machine. Doctor Battinson had cleared all of his other equipment to the sides of the room except for an assortment of tools spread out on top of his moving cart. The machine was made up of a base and an upper portion which seemed to be able to move up and down if needed. A couple of buttons dimly glowed, but otherwise, the object made no sound nor projected any light.

"What does it do?"

"It captures life in its purest form."

Susanna's brows cinched together, at first in confusion, but quickly in anger. "What on Earth do you mean? Doctor, please be frank with me! If you are going to tell me about this, then please do, or else I would like to go home!"

"I have difficulty understanding this myself! Please—give me a moment!"

She gave him a moment. It was a long moment as he rubbed his hands across his forehead and through his thinning hair. He finally settled on biting the side of his index finger for concentration before he gave up thinking and tried to explain again.

"Every living organism has life."

"Obviously!" She laughed at him in annoyance. She trusted that he had a point.

"No one knows how life and its consciousness are made." He was being patient, but he was clearly frustrated as well.

"God makes life," Susanna confirmed.

"I'm not here for a philosophical debate, Susanna. How life is made is not really the important detail here anyways. The important detail is how we can access the energy that is life."

"Are we talking about souls?" Susanna tried very hard to follow.

"Yes, in a sense; if that's what you wish to call it."

"We are talking about accessing people's souls?"

"Calling it a 'soul' makes it sound absolutely ridiculous!"

"Well, make it not sound ridiculous! I am confused and tired."

"Susanna," he stopped and there were a few short breaths of silence for the two to collect themselves, "the Shells don't have working brains anymore; there is no way to restore them. They are as bad as people spending forty years on life support in a coma. Do you agree?"

"Yes."

"But unlike coma patients, the Shells have limited cognitive function, enough even, to be awake and move around."

"Yes."

"The Scans, however, show cognitive function on a higher level, indicating that they are thinking, or at least, dreaming. That is what we have concluded from the brain scans, correct?"

"Yes."

"Unfortunately, the vaccine makes it impossible for us to reduce the swelling and wake the patients up without causing brain damage, turning them into Shells."

"Yes! Yes! I have cared for them for seven long years; I understand the dilemmas! I have read every single damned one of your papers!" She lost her temper.

"Then don't you see? I found a way to access their souls and get them out of their no longer functioning bodies! Instead of finding a cure, which is impossible, I bypassed the whole situation altogether and have come up with a horrific, atrocious solution!"

A lock of curly, dirty-blonde hair had fallen into Susanna's eyes when she had gotten agitated in her last remark, she now removed it gently from her face and placed it amongst the many others. There was some dark part of her that understood what he was suggesting, but she pushed it away. It was not even a possibility.

"Yes, Susanna, it is that bad. I saw it in your face for a moment there, but you didn't let yourself believe it."

"No, I think you misinterpreted my expressions."

"I asked myself the question over and over: 'If I can remove the soul of a Scan from its useless body, where would I put it?'"

"Couldn't you remove it, and then vaccinate the body? The body would be healed, and then you could return the soul."

169

"Think, Susanna! The body would be dead without the soul! You can't just vaccinate a dead body. The souls need a mindless, living vessel to go into, and we have plenty of them lying around."

"No." She felt sick.

"If we put the souls of the Scans into the Shells, millions of people will have their family members back."

She gasped. "And millions will have to see some other person living within their loved ones!"

"I don't know what else to do! You want to see Derrick, don't you? You want your husband back, don't you?"

"How dare you?" She was infuriated. "Of course I want him back, but not at the expense of another! It won't be him anyway; it will be the face of someone else, and how could I be with some other woman's husband, some child's father, some man's brother? How could you take some other person's daughter and make it your Ana?"

"It might look like their loved ones, but it won't be! Their loved ones have been dead for years! Ever since I came out with that goddamned vaccine! They could be paid, compensated!"

"It's not the same!" She was sobbing horribly, wiping her face on her hands, hot and sticky like a child. She was crying now like she had done when the epidemic was brand new, before she had felt herself go cold. She was choking on the liquid in her throat when she said, "And you know it."

Dr. Battinson guided her to a chair, and she accepted his help gratefully. She was repulsed by what he had told her, but in her emotional state, she did not mind being near him. Like a child who had just been punished, coming back to hug the parent who had just beaten her, she held his hand for comfort.

"We can't do this!" she whispered.

By being his confidant, she found herself feeling like a collaborator in the effort. Edgar watched her tiredly. When she looked up, wiping the little bit of running mascara to the corners of her eyes, Dr. Battinson finally conceded.

"No, we can't. I just can't help but think that it's worth it to try to save half instead of letting them all go to rot."

Susanna flinched at the last word. Her Derrick. For the first time in a long time, she remembered him as he was. She remembered him driving her in his black Hyundai Tiburon around twists and turns in the Blue Ridge Mountains. She saw him making pancakes in his underwear while watching hockey. She remembered when they were first dating and he agreed to go roller skating even though he didn't know how. He rolled his ankle in the first fifteen minutes.

"They're right there and we can't have them," Battinson whispered.

She pictured herself constantly cleaning, turning, moving those motionless bodies so that the various infections didn't get to their sedentary shells. She felt sick, but then it was probably from the crying. Strong emotions always affected her stomach.

"Go home, Susanna; I shouldn't have burdened anyone with this, but I had to confirm what I already felt."

He helped her to her feet and escorted her to the door of the building. It was only after she had said, "Thank you, I think I will be alright on my own from here," and had gotten to her car that she questioned whether the entire encounter had even happened. She was just too tired to know for certain.

19

Chapter 19

Susanna carefully folded the bed linens. It was well after visiting hours, and she was taking advantage of this time to change the sheets on the patients' beds. They were rarely ever soiled in any way, but nevertheless, they were swapped out every evening. She folded the last fitted sheet and stacked it on top of her pile. It was a shame that she would have to unfold it momentarily. She had chosen to do the "C" hall tonight, as always. C29 was the fourth room on the hall, but she always started with it first. To "get it out of the way," she told herself.

Caught up in her thoughts as she was, she did not, at first, notice anything different about the room. She set down the sheets on a stand located around the inside corner of the door and chose the one from the top. She turned, stopped. The sheet which she had opened fell to her feet, and she stumbled back against the wall. She stared long and hard; she could hear the air conditioning buzzing and a deep, warm hum of various machines. Her nose burned like she wanted to cry, but nothing came.

Suddenly, she felt as if her hair tie was pulling too tightly.

She pulled down her hair, and her thick curls came loose. She bent over at the waist. Her chest burned, and she felt herself dry-heaving for a couple of miserable moments. Susanna wrapped her arms tightly around her body, feeling herself slowly slipping down the wall to the floor. She closed her eyes and let out a sound that could only be equivocated to the sound of something breaking. When a tree limb breaks, it creaks, and then snaps. When a board breaks, it pops. When a person breaks... well, there is no other sound like it. When the sound was gone, she opened her eyes. Her eyes were wet at the corners, but her cheeks were dry. Nothing happened. Nothing changed. Nothing happened at all.

Somehow, she found the courage to stand up again. Still holding herself, she started to look around. Someone had already changed the sheets. Of course they had. Why had no one notified her? Had no one found the courage? She counted the empty beds; the plaques were still there. Six, six out of eighteen were gone. Her bed was empty, but then again, it had been empty for a long time. Her hand trailed along the tops of the plaques which still had their names, although the patients no longer laid there. She passed by "Evan Wall," "Derrick Webber." "Wei Wen." and finally paused at the end of the row.

"Ana Battinson." Someone had tried to scrape that plaque off. There were deep scratches on the footboard, but it had stayed.

"Oh, Edgar," she whispered.

She was racing down the hallway. People stepped back in surprise.

"Edgar!"

The surrounding staff turned and stared, so did Edgar.

173

Susanna had been out to lunch twice with the doctor since the strange evening that they had shared; both times she had intended to question him about it but decided to let the conversation rest. In the time that they had spent ignoring the subject, he had somehow grown more ragged. His hair was longer, and he had started slicking it back with gel so that it didn't matter whether or not he had time to wash it. The bristles that always seemed to want to come through on his face now often made an unwelcome appearance. She hugged him quickly but tightly.

"I'm so sorry, Edgar. I am."

"Thank you, Nurse Webber."

She stood apart from him, instantly embarrassed. She looked around, but things like inappropriate work behavior could pass in a place where nobody cared much about anything. They stepped, awkwardly nonetheless, into his office.

"I'm the one that should be sorry." He sighed thickly. "I was trying to catch you at the door before you saw for yourself. I thought it would have been best to come from me."

"No, no, I understand. It was better the way that I—" She thought to herself that she preferred that no one saw her reaction. She preferred to experience her loss on her own.

Without being asked, she had fallen into the same chair that she had sat in before. He dropped the box of tissues from his desk into her lap, and she blew, at first embarrassedly, and then snottily, into one. She wiped her face with a clean tissue, gathering herself enough to ask the question, "Was it the same illness that's been taking them for a while now?"

"Yes," he whispered.

"And we still have no idea what it is?"

He shook his head, "A fever of some sort."

174

She met his gaze and recognized that he was watching her closely. She now, in turn, did the same. Dr. Battinson seemed tired—no, exhausted, but what more?

"Edgar, are you okay?"

She knew he wasn't okay. He must have known for a while now that they may get the fever. He had had time to sit and process and dwell on the inevitable before it came. It explained his recent appearance, and it explained how distant he was now.

"I need to get back to work."

There wasn't any more actual conversation between them, but Susanna nodded understandingly as if allowing him to go. She told herself that everyone grieves differently, but somehow, she had imagined him as the type to be completely distraught. He seemed so cold, so horribly indifferent, and something else—ashamed. She looked sadly after him as he left; of course, he was blaming himself.

"Susanna?"

She looked up; a young technician had entered the room. Her eyes were dark, and dark circles followed underneath. Her white scrubs contrasted to make her seem hollower and paler. The bright, sterile light didn't seem to reach her darkened eyes.

"Yes?" Vacantly.

"Doctor Battinson told me to tell you that you can go home."

"I'm sorry?"

"Doctor Battinson says you can go home."

"Ah, okay."

The technician gave her a sad, concerned smile and parted from the door. Susanna passed through that door and moved down a hallway and another door and another hallway and a really long hallway and finally a really wide door. With no intention of ever passing through the other side again.

She hoped that Derrick could forgive her. She hoped that he could forgive her for the sick feeling of relief she had as she left for the last time. Hopefully, he would look down on her from a better place and know that she had tried to fulfill her duty to him. She had tried to love him until the end, and she hoped she had. She hoped that she had loved him.

20

Chapter 20

The room restores itself in fractured, little pieces. I hear someone sobbing, but I don't know who.

"Hey, hey, calm yourself."

The Nyauta sits welcomingly in front of me. I realize with embarrassment that I'm the one who is crying. I lift up my hands to see that they're shaking.

"Did Doctor Battinson do it?" My voice sounds distant.

"Next time." The Lovindian gestures toward the cup.

"But if he did do it, if humans created the ability to—"

"Don't get ahead of yourself; you're becoming fanciful, and it isn't helping you get any closer to the truth. Drink the Nyauta."

Nyauta. I think quietly about the shape of the word and drink. Flashes of Earth bounce around in my head. I see the hospital and all of its busy energy. Separating my emotions toward the planet, from Susanna's deep sadness, proves very difficult. It's almost as if her memories became my own.

It's as if I've always known Earth and as if I don't know it at all. It's as if I've known love and never known it. I can feel her heartbreak as thoroughly as I felt Jana's demise. In the end, I just feel heavy.

"How are you feeling?" the Lovindian asks.

"Overwhelmed," I say honestly.

"I can imagine." His eyes glint like he's telling a joke.

"So humans really did rule a planet?" I laugh tiredly.

"As much as someone can rule anything."

"Wow."

"The Nyauta will work faster if you focus on what is around you instead of trying to remember the experience."

To appease him, I tilt the cup back and chug the rest quickly. I immediately regret my decision. My throat and eyes burn, and I cough in surprise. The Lovindian rumble laughs.

"Sip the Nyauta slowly, and it's flavorless; chug it, and well..."

I'm too busy coughing to complain about not being prior warned.

"You'd better head out soon, Jacob. You need your rest."

I notice that the Lovindian looks physically drained. It's something about how his fur trails behind him as he walks across the floor. I never thought about how the process might affect the Lovindian. Is he risking his health to help me?

"I don't know what your reasons are for showing me what you have, but—thank you," I say earnestly.

The Lovindian doesn't respond. I watch as he hobbles away; the cape of fur snakes behind him as he walks.

When I land on Yalk, Samuel is waiting as always. I pause guiltily, remembering how I last left him. Is he still angry? Samuel jogs toward me with a bright, all-forgiving smile.

"It's such a relief that you're back!"

My stomach clenches. I can't explain it, but for some reason, it would be easier to face his anger rather than his blind forgiveness. The Gromptu chirrup and shift on their feet; their massive eyes seem to trail us. I glance and they stare heavily back. A cold sweat comes over me. I've never seen so many before. I start to rub the back of my hand, but I stop when I feel the coat of grime. All of a sudden, I notice the intense hunger that must have been staved off before by the Nyauta and the adrenaline.

"How long have I been gone?"

"You don't know?"

I speculate briefly. "A day?" I guess.

"Try three."

"Huh." It didn't feel like that long. No wonder I feel so exhausted.

We are silent as the Gromptu open the door. The alarms blare, and as they dull, the wind outside sounds almost silent in comparison. A woman walks quickly around one of the apartments and darts back into the maze.

"Martha never came home."

"Huh?"

"My sister, she never came home."

"Oh." I hadn't even known her name.

"Yeah, Maan isn't even worried about her. She has some notion that she's with you. I told her that was ridiculous, but she wouldn't listen."

"I'm sorry, Samuel," I whisper.

He turns away and wipes his arm against his face. I want to reach out and comfort him, but for some reason, I just stand watching him dumbly. We reach the apartment solemnly. His cot is still standing against the back wall of the apartment. It seems that I have a permanent roommate. I close the door behind us, and Samuel's head snaps up. He runs quickly to reopen it.

"The Gromptu just open them again if we shut them," he explains.

"Why?"

"I don't know. They usually don't mind if we shut them during the dark hours, though."

I don't know why this bothers me, but it does—deeply. Maybe it is to maintain better air circulation, but I doubt it. All I know is that, somehow, the open door seems terribly offensive. I stand and close it again. Samuel looks at me strangely but leaves it be. In the cool darkness of the room, I lie down on my cot, and Samuel sits on his own.

"What's going on here? I've never seen so many Gromptu posted on watch before. Why are there so many inside the housing unit?"

"Why do the Gromptu do anything?" He shrugs with a sniffle. Isn't that the truth? "So tell me what you learned." I'm happy for the change of subject.

"I saw Earth." I encourage him.

"It was real!" Samuel breathes, turning his face up to smile goofily at the ceiling. I can still see where his eyes are wet.

"Well of course it was real!" I chide him. "Did you think humans always lived on Yalk?"

"It feels that way sometimes," he says quietly.

I search my feelings, wondering if I have ever felt that way before. I'm relieved to find that I haven't. I have always believed that there had to be something before this existence.

"Is it like they said?" Samuel asks.

"Huh?" I'm caught off guard.

"Earth," he repeats, "is it like they said?"

"It is like nothing that could be said."

"What does it look like?" He asks enthusiastically

"It was so green! The sky was so blue. There were humans everywhere and other animals too. I saw a squirrel."

"What's a squirrel?"

"It's about this big— and there's a tail that's puffy." I gesture lamely with my hands as I try to explain.

"That's amazing!" Samuel exclaims.

"Humans really had their own planet." I trail off in remembrance.

"And you think that it's all gone?" His eyes are wide.

Susanna's memories are still fresh in my mind. It's so real. Susanna had lived her entire life on the planet, and I can't fight the feeling that Earth is something that has always been and always will be. I work hard at taking Susanna's biases out of my thoughts. Recognizing which memories are hers help me push them back. It feels a little bit like I'm waking up from a dream.

"Yeah. It's gone," I say with a clear head.

"But why? You didn't see it happen, did you? Oh, don't tell me you saw it all destroyed!"

"No."

"Then how do you know that it's gone?"

"Because if it still existed, not a creature in the universe would want to live anywhere else."

"It sounds like it would be crowded." He raises an eyebrow but seems to like the picture I'm painting. It feels good to help him take his mind off of his sister.

"No, there would be room on Earth for everyone," I say, knowing that I'm just making things up.

"I don't think that would work, Jacob."

"Of course it would!" I already have the vision in my head.

"But not everyone in the universe could possibly live and get along on just one planet!"

"Maybe not, but everyone would still be there, because even with the sorrow that the planet could endure, the passion, the beauty, the, the—um, the, oh, you know!" Samuel shakes his head. Of course he doesn't know. "Well, it would all make it worthwhile!" I finish lamely.

Samuel stares at me—mystified. I blush, smiling shamefully. Samuel copies my reaction. We sound like children. Samuel starts to laugh. More blood rise to my face. A warmness floods my chest, and I surprise myself by laughing too. Have I ever laughed this much before?

The door slams open.

The Gromptu stares in; his large, white eyes absorb the entire room. I suddenly know fear. The white light! He's going to use the white light! It gives a long, slow blink. The warmth I felt before is replaced by a chilling cold. I'm frozen. The Gromptu turns and shuffles away. Light pours in as the Gromptu leaves, but it's not the white light, just the artificial light from the hallway. The brightness forces me to shut my eyes.

Samuel sits stunned. I shouldn't have shut the door. This is why Samuel was so quick to open it again. This time, I'm able to reach out to him and put my hand on his back. He doesn't move. For a moment, he had been able to forget where we were. He had been able to forget his life and have a window into a world we can only dream about. With the door open, that kind of imagination is impossible.

"It's gone now, Sam." I awkwardly try to soothe him.

"They're never gone," he whispers.

"What do you mean?"

He just shakes his head at me as if I'm not capable of understanding. His hands tremble. I was an idiot for thinking he might not understand what happened to his sister. He's not like his mother—he can't pretend it never happened. He must think about how the last thing she saw was those white eyes. He's right. They're never gone.

21

Chapter 21

When she comes to me, her gold eyes are full of tears.

"Why are you crying?" I ask her.

She just shakes her head at me.

"Keren..." I reach for her, and my fingers almost touch her shoulder. I'm closer than I've ever been before.

"You're going to get yourself killed."

"No, I'm not. I'm going to save you."

"Save who? You can't even save yourself!"

"I'm going to win, Keren. I'm going to save you!"

"You left me! I grew up on my own! With no big brother to protect me! You were the last hope I had!"

The darkness is filled with round, white lights. The eyes! They're surrounding me, but as soon as I look at them directly, they disappear. My heart pounds relentlessly.

"You left me! You're a coward! You won't save anyone! It should have been you! He was the better brother!" she accuses me.

They're closing in. I look down to see that I'm standing on a box. They're coming to get me. They know. They're always watching. They know what I've done. They know and they're all coming. I scream and scream and scream.

"Jacob!" Hands are on me. I thrash violently. Stay away from me!

"Hey, hey, calm down," a voice whispers harshly.

"They killed him. They're coming for me. They know. They'll get her too!" I'm gushing words, and I can't stop myself.

"Hey, Scrab, come back for a second." A rough hand touches my forehead.

My eyes finally find his face.

"Emmanuel? What are you doing here?"

"Waking you up, apparently. You scared the scat out of Samuel screaming like a madman. What on Yalk did you eat to give you that kind of nightscare?"

"Where's Sam?" I ask scanning the room. The room is strangely empty. His cot is gone.

"He ran to get me when you wouldn't wake up. I told him it would be best if he moved back home. Don't you agree?" His eyes weigh on me in a way that tells me to accept his judgment.

I nod; my shoulders fall. The further they all get from me, the better. I'm not ready to protect anyone right now. I'm just a danger.

"Let's go for a walk." He stands in the door, smiling pityingly.

I get up and follow him. I doubt that I'll be able to return to sleep after that anyways. The walkers are long put to bed. I wonder if it is very early morning or very late evening. It occurs to me that I've never wandered Yalk at this time before. It's so dark. With no artificial light, it is pitch black.

I can only just see Emmanuel's outline. Emmanuel seems to

confidently know where he's going despite our limited vision. Does he go out at this time frequently? I realize that it's been a very long time since I last saw him. I haven't seen him since before my first visit to the red planet. There is a strange air around him that is different from before. He has always been more serious than his elder brother, but this is different.

"Where are we going?" I croak sleepily.

"You're not the only one working on things."

"What do you mean?" I ask apprehensively.

Emmanuel just laughs me off. I wonder what Samuel has told him. He breaks into a jog, and it's exactly what I need. It feels good to have air flowing in my lungs.

"Do you see that?" He points upward.

At first, all I see is the laundry lines hanging out the windows, then I see a flash of red. A little red triangle hangs from one of the laundry lines among all the beige cloth.

"What's the flag for?" I ask.

"You'll see."

We wind around corners. I keep my eyes up toward the clotheslines. Every once in a while, there's another flash of red. He comes to a stop suddenly. I give him a curious look, but he only smirks and points up.

"After you." He gestures at the fire escape ladder.

As we climb, I understand why we're not just going up the steps. The walkway for the top apartment either collapsed at some point or was taken down because the top apartment is only accessible by the fire escape. Emmanuel slips through the window with ease, and I follow after him. The room is packed to the brim with boxes.

"Um... Emmanuel, what is all of this junk?"

"Can it for a second," he says, shuffling around in the dark.

I hear a snap, and suddenly there's a flame. A candle! They're banned on Yalk! My eyes adjust to the new light, and I can see just how full the room is with boxes. They touch the ceiling.

"Where did you get that? Alternative light sources are banned!" I say in hushed tones.

"And altering flight logs is *totally* allowed."

I startle. "How do you know about that?"

He shrugs nonchalantly in response. It almost feels like I'm talking to a Yahbiin. I get the urge to put baunti between us to see if he will tell me more. He's brought me here for a reason, though. I highly doubt that it was to show me candles.

"What is all of this?"

"You're looking at Yalk's very own black market." Emmanuel gestures around the room with a smug look.

"Are you saying that everything in here is illegal?" I can't hide my shock.

"Yup." He grins and corrects himself. "Well, mostly. Some of it is just unobtainable."

Unobtainable. Then how does he have it? How did he manage to put all of this stuff in a room without getting the attention of the Gromptu? My head spins.

"Where are you getting this from?"

Emmanuel runs a hand through his black hair. "Yahbi, the other units, people harboring things in their drawers."

This is insane. If the Gromptu knew about this, he would disappear in an instant. Even if Emmanuel is careful, which there is no way that he can be, then the other members of Yalk won't be. If he's giving these to Yalkian people, they will undoubtedly reveal themselves. A Gromptu would notice if unavailable items suddenly start popping up all over Yalk, it wouldn't take any time to trace it back to Emmanuel.

"Why? What's the purpose?" I ask.

"Well, at first it was just because I wanted to cause trouble, but then it started to become a real operation. People began to request food items that they couldn't get on their panels, fabrics that weren't beige, and other basic things. I started by getting those on Yahbi."

"You fly?" I say with surprise.

"No—Cruiser flies. I communicate the messages through the com-panel."

"Who's Cruiser?"

"Don't worry about it." He waves me away. "Anyways, I can't leave Yalk because Samuel keeps too close of a watch on the landing bay. I manage it all from here. I meet the clients through the com-panel, and they communicate their needs and their valuables. I have Cruiser and Luwelt send it under the disguise of another product."

I decide not to ask about this "Luwelt" person. He'll only blow me off again if he thinks the question is unimportant.

"Since when do com-panels connect unit buildings and let you talk to Yahbiin merchants?"

"My com-panel is a little special. It's manmade. The Talkers picked a few of them apart and made their own modified version." He picks up an odd-looking piece of technology and shakes it at me. "It was Saul's Dad's. Saul gave it to me before he—"

Emmanuel's face flushes. I turn away to give him privacy. I can't believe he's been doing all of this under the noses of the Gromptu from a Talker's com-panel. Dangerous isn't a strong enough word. It's suicidal. Somehow, he's found a way to do something more reckless than I am. Samuel had warned me that Emmanuel and I had similar feelings. Why hadn't I gone to check on him? I could have dissuaded him from this madness.

"So what are the red flags for?" I say to change the subject.

"They're interested buyers."

"What's the point of all of this, Emmanuel? Besides being the youngest owner of an illegal empire, what are you getting out of this?"

"Power. Power like the Talkers didn't have. I have an endless list of contacts linking all of the Units on Yalk. You wouldn't believe what's going on. The Gromptu are ruthless bastards."

"How is Unit C?" My stomach flops.

"Fine," he shakes his hand at me, "but would you believe that they let them have fresh fruit over there? Unit A has been having all the trouble. Plague after plague with them. I can't send medicine fast enough. I've already exhausted all the families in Units B and C who would donate to the cause."

Emmanuel has been saving human lives while I've been running off chasing after stories of the past. He's been taking so many risks to do something so important.

"I could have been helping." My chest burns.

"I have a feeling that you're already on the tail of something."

"How do you know that?" This is the second time he's hinted that he knows what I've been doing. How could he possibly know?

"The Gromptu have eyes. I have ears."

"I think you might be the worse of the two."

"Scat off," he grumbles, but I can tell he's actually complimented.

Talking about the Gromptu reminds me of the one that opened our door. All of these extra measures, the weird way they were acting in the landing bay, Emmanuel's not the only one changing.

"What are the Gromptu up to?" I ask.

He turns his face so I can't see it. So he does know what's going on. I'm not sure who has been busier out of the two of us. One thing is for sure, I don't see any sign of the lazy kid who used to follow Saul around like his shadow. I wonder if Saul had seen this in him all along.

"All I know is that there have been shipments coming into Yalk that aren't from Yahbi."

"From where then?" I ask.

"There are rumors it's from higher gen authority."

"Firsts?" I ask.

"Firsts or Second nobility," he answers.

"Second nobility?"

"Yeah, the ones nearly as old and as prestigious as the Firsts and their children." He says it as if this is common knowledge, but it definitely isn't.

"That doesn't necessarily mean anything, does it?" I say hopefully. Just because shipments are coming in from higher gens doesn't mean that it's something bad.

"I don't know," he says honestly. He changes the subject. "Did you hear about Martha?"

I'm surprised that he's brought her up, but I guess he talks about Saul more easily than both Samuel and me.

"Yeah, I'm sorry." I look at the floor.

"A week ago, I found a notice on my door. I balled it up and threw it away. If Maan wants to believe she's run off with you and if Samuel wants to believe she moved to a different unit—more power to them." He blows the candle out roughly, and I'm amazed again by how dark Yalk is at this hour.

He found a note. That means she really was taken. He might be right about his mother, but he's not right about Samuel.

"Sam knows the truth," I say softly.

He tenses noticeably. For all of his harsh words, maybe he was taking comfort in believing that his family was innocent of the truth. He must have felt like he was protecting them by bearing the truth all on his own. Maybe Saul should have entrusted his dream to Emmanuel instead. He hasn't just accepted what happened to Saul. He took his motivation and formed a criminal empire. He's saving humans even in different units and bringing the joy of luxuries that the Lovindians prohibit, even at the cost of his life.

"They wouldn't have hung them before Saul died," he says unexpectedly.

"What do you mean?"

"The flags. They wouldn't have hung them before. Yalkians are changing."

I get the feeling that he thinks this is because of Saul, but I know that it's not. No one listened to Saul when he talked, and I saw for myself that no one cared when he died. This is Emmanuel's doing.

"I wanted you to see this, Jacob. I just wanted you to know that they don't see everything. I told you this started out as just a way to cause trouble, but it's turned into something bigger than me. The red flags are bringing people hope. They're learning that the Gromptu aren't gods."

"Just be careful, Emmanuel. Don't underestimate them. I've seen things..." I can't help but see flashes of white. I wince instinctively.

"Don't become a Samuel on me," Emmanuel chides.

I laugh, but I'm worried. His lackadaisical attitude could get him killed. I wonder if this is how Samuel feels about my escapades. At least Emmanuel isn't coming back bruised and beaten all of the time.

"So what is it you need?"

"I'm sorry?" I ask.

"To complete your mission. What can I get you?"

I think long and hard. Emmanuel searches my face.

"Just keep Samuel safe. Keep him out of this."

"Didn't need to tell me," he growls as if I've offended him. "There's nothing else?" he demands impatiently.

"What do you mean?" I ask.

"There's no one you might want to talk to?" He squints.

I start to sweat. I see her blaming me. Blaming me for leaving her.

"I don't have anyone," I say coldly.

"Crying her name into your pillow is the better way to go, huh?" he says with a smirk.

I swing at him before I even know what I'm doing. He dodges easily. I'm sure that even if I hit him, he would have been almost unharmed. His eyebrows are raised in amusement. I see a little bit of Saul's twisted humor there. I'm embarrassed that I tried to hit him but more embarrassed that I missed.

"She's none of your business," I huff. The admiration I felt for him before has disappeared.

"Just trying to help," he says with raised arms.

"Just watch Samuel," I order him, making my way for the window. "Don't get him caught up in this scat."

Emmanuel had said that he wanted to find another way to unite Yalk, and he had done it. Some part of me can't help but be envious of his progress. What have I learned so far? Nothing that gives me an advantage over the Lovindians. It's starting to feel like the Lovindian is just telling me the story to prove how invincible the Lovindians really are.

I turn back just as I throw my leg over the window. I can only just see him. Despite the fact I've just tried to hit him and I've threatened him, he grins at me with warm eyes.

"You be safe too," I add before hopping down to the fire escape.

22

Chapter 22

I don't return to sleep after my walk with Emmanuel. I try, but it just doesn't come to me. I'm nervous to go to the landing bay with the Gromptu so on edge, but I'm afraid that if I don't go soon, I won't get the chance. My chances to visit the red planet feel like they're slipping away.

The Gromptu standing guard at the bay doors shuffles from foot to foot when it sees me as if it's unsure what to do about me. After twitching its head from side to side, it decides that I must be acceptable because it opens the doors. As I pass through the landing bay, I don't make any eye contact with the Gromptu inside. I don't want to draw any extra attention to myself. I might be pushing my luck with this trip. I had only just decided to be more cautious.

When I exit my craft, I break into a run. A billowing cloud of red dust spins behind my feet. I run fast enough that my hair pulls back from my face, breaking the midday heat. I stop at the entry of the Council Building to watch the red particles slowly sink back down.

"I used to run around the whole planet when I first got here," the Lovindian rumbles.

I can't imagine this creature running. It must sound like the whole planet is shaking. If I kicked up that much dust, I can't imagine what it would look like if the Lovindian ran.

"What possessed you to do that?" I ask.

"When I first got here, I didn't know how to access the memory stream, and as you can see, there isn't a surplus of things to do on Roja."

"Roja? Is that the name of this planet?" I never even thought to ask.

"Roja is what the Lovindians named it. The original name wasn't as easy for the Lovindians to pronounce."

"I see."

The screen of red dust has lowered to about two feet off the ground. It continues to sink under the scorching Rojan sun.

"Did you come for a story today?" the Lovindian prods me.

"Yes," I answer. "What will I see?"

"The aftermath of some big decisions."

I swallow hard to abate my nerves as I follow him inside.

"From the articles of the Council:

Year: 2383

Subject: Derrick Webber"

"Earth, like many other planets with only one intelligent species, was divided by the humans who lived there into different sectors. In the Earth year 2214, it was announced by the titled 'President' of the sector known as the 'United States of America' that 'the Scanthirin sickness had been conquered with great sacrifice of human life.' This 'great sacrifice' was labeled 'the Battinson Decision.'

"In the third Earth year after Dr. Edgar Battinson completed the final phase of the rehabilitation project for Scanthirin

195

victims, the repercussions of the Battinson Decision became apparent. The victims at first appeared to be operating as normal within their new vessels, but later, studies by leading psychologists started to describe them as 'detached,' 'crazed,' or even 'psychotic.' Their outbursts were characterized by the three stages of Transfer Sickness.

"Stage one: subjects are disoriented in their bodies and feel apart from themselves. Stage two: subjects claim that they are beginning to forget themselves and develop severe depression. Stage three: if for any reason, natural causes or otherwise, a subject feels that their being is threatened, they become irrationally violent. This violence becomes more prevalent with age, and they begin to voice anger over the idea of their lives coming to an end.

"In the Earth year 2251, a new movement was formed by people who faced the consequences of the Battinson Decision. This movement called themselves 'Eterns,' derived from the English Earth word 'Eternal.' In 2252, the Eterns launched an attack on The Battinson Memorial Hospital. This attack resulted in the theft of large quantities of scientific research and technology. Additionally, bodies of many unfortunate Scanthirin victims, whose families had opted to wait for the possibility of a true cure, were also taken. These bodies were reportedly used by the Eterns to discover how to transfer their consciousness into new bodies. It is estimated that around 2255, the Eterns were successfully transferring themselves into new bodies. The entire planet panicked.

"The Edgar Battinson Law was passed shortly after, stating: 'Any subject of the Battinson Decision found to be living after the year 2340 would be considered 'non-human,' and therefore arrested on the spot.' This law worked to accomplish that no human could take another's body to achieve immortality. However, proving that someone was an Etern, a non-human, was not without its difficulties."

Derrick Webber sighed deeply. She was late—again. He would have to leave in the next nineteen minutes, whether she came or not. Professor Wall raised an eyebrow at him but only shrugged. Derrick couldn't help but be irritated by his lackadaisical attitude.

The professor had recently taken the form of a young man. He was tall and lean but was used to being short and stumpy. He now sat with his back against the concrete block wall.

"Professor Wall, why do you insist on sitting on this filthy concrete?"

"Don't walls always sit on floors?" The professor's laugh seemed too old to come from a twenty-or-so person.

Derrick grimaced. "Very clever."

Professor Wall laughed again.

The space they currently were forced to share had at some point been the parking garage area beneath an apartment complex, but it was now condemned. It now functioned as one of the twelve various locations that they could expect solitude. This didn't mean that Derrick could relax. It was still possible that a drug addict might scurry through, or a nosy police officer might peek around looking for drug addicts. Derrick didn't like having to meet the others. It left breadcrumbs, and he didn't need to be trailed.

"Stop pacing so much, Derrick, or we aren't going to hear her when she comes."

Derrick stopped; the professor was right but he wasn't going to admit it to his smug face. Wall was rewarded anyway because they could suddenly hear the sound of footsteps on the concrete. She walked down the ramp, blinking wildly as her eyes adjusted from the intense light of the midafternoon to the dark of the garage. Upon recognizing Derrick, she smiled widely and strode toward him.

"Isn't she wonderful, Dare?" She spun around for emphasis.

The woman before him was around eighteen years of age. She was athletic and thin. Her eyes were a warm caramel color that matched her mid-brown hair, which was cut sharply over her eyebrow, and the remainder fanned out over her shoulders. He brushed the bangs from her forehead, but they fell instantly back into place.

"Yes, those are annoying, but they'll grow out." She was obviously irritated that he hadn't complimented her yet.

"I kind of like them," he mumbled.

She smiled. Nice teeth. She had picked a good one.

"Oh, Professor Wall! I haven't seen you in forever! You're looking well!"

"Thank you, Ana! You are as fine as ever," Wall, too, was obsessed with appearances, "but I believe Mr. Webber has something he wishes to inform us of."

"Unfortunately, I do."

They fell silent.

"There have been rumors that the police are being equipped with weapons that can identify Eterns." He said solemnly.

"You mean without any type of testing?" The woman's eyes grew wide.

"Without any testing. The worst part is that no one actually knows how it is identifying them. An Etern last week was supposedly identified while taking the same daily walk his vessel had taken to work for the last fifteen years."

"I heard something like that from Wei; I guess it must be

true then." The Professor stroked a chin where there had previously been a beard.

"I came up with a design for an emergency evacuation vehicle, but I want your opinion."

"You mean you want my resources to help you build it," the Professor grumbled.

Derrick ignored Wall's comment and started to page through a notebook that he had stashed away inside an inner jacket pocket. He passed it to Wall, who begrudgingly began to look it over.

"Some kind of vehicle!" Wall gave a single sharp, barking laugh.

Ana visibly cringed at the sound, vigilantly looking around her as if someone might have heard it in the dark quiet. Derrick couldn't help but feel a little relaxed by her reaction; at least she had the intelligence to feel a little bit paranoid. She caught him looking at her, and she smiled. Wall shoved the book into Derrick's chest.

"Derrick, this is too much! The Eterns are getting out of hand as it is!"

"It's only for us! The Eterns will never have it! We just need some way to defend ourselves if one of these crazy cops happens to identify us!"

"It's not defending ourselves, Derrick; it's flat out murder and theft."

"What is?" Ana tried to grab at the book and was lightly pushed away by the professor.

"If any of us were to be caught on the street, you wouldn't feel that way!" Derrick snatched the notebook from his hands.

"Derrick, we are criminals."

"It isn't our fault!" Derrick yelled back.

"Not with this again." Wall threw up his hands in frustration. "It is most definitely our fault, and you know damned well that it is! You act like we don't have a choice whether or not we trick someone into getting hooked up to our little machines and steal their bodies."

"Professor," she dragged his title out like a whining child, "what is this 'emergency evacuation vehicle' that Derrick's talking about?"

"It's not any kind of evacuation vehicle at all, my love," he said through his teeth, his eyes not leaving Derrick. "It's a gun."

The professor snapped his coat around himself and shoved Derrick with his shoulder as he marched toward the exit. He always did have a flair for the dramatics. Derrick decided that he would have to play on this weakness if he was going to win.

"I know you've never actually taken the life of a sane man, professor."

The professor stopped and turned as he expected.

"That's true; all of my bodies have been victims of mental illness before I came to them. I have given their families hope in returning their loved ones to them, and I will not be a part of your murderous schemes!"

He always made himself sound like the hero, but somewhere deep down, Wall had to know that he was only returning the shell to those families; the person they had loved was gone. Even still, not one had ever suspected that their loved one was no longer there. Any difference in their family member would be associated with the recovery from the addiction or depression or whatever else plagued them. All Wall had to do was work as a family psychiatrist and tell them that the disguised Battinson device was a therapeutic device. Was mental illness a justification for murder? Derrick didn't think so, but he wasn't one to talk.

"Why are you condemning your dearest friends to death? Something even you can't bear to face? If you let us die when you could help us, then that's murder in itself."

"I'm not making you a gun even if it means the extinction of us all. Your gun would mean shooting innocent people who are trying to protect themselves from us. I'm not taking the body of any able man, even if he chooses to shoot me and you."

Derrick's ploy hadn't worked; Wall too firmly saw himself as a justified hero. He noticed Ana tapping after Wall; Derrick's notebook was in her hand. Somehow, the devil had managed to take it while they argued. She had seen his design. The professor was five feet or so away from leaving before she caught him.

"Professor, I do think you should reconsider."

He stopped for her. She wasn't playing her normal flirtatious game. There was something a bit sinister about the way she leaned slightly into him. She welcomed, and yet, also threatened. She couldn't overpower him now, he was stronger but she was ruthless when she wanted to be.

"Imagine if, just one day, I was walking the same walk I have been walking for fifteen years, and I was caught and executed. What would you do knowing that there would never be any interesting possibilities for us?"

"I don't have time for this."

The professor attempted to get away, but she had placed the toes of her high heels on the ends of his shoes. She leaned in toward him, and Derrick looked away. His fists clenched and his stomach burned. He didn't like to see her doing things like this but it was necessary. At first, Derrick could hear Wall protesting, but his protests became less and less.

A few moments of awkward silence passed for Derrick. She was whispering something to the professor. From his peripheral vision, he saw her hand disappear, and then she rocked back on her thin-heeled shoes and released him. The professor glanced at Derrick warily.

"Did she order it?" He asked.

The *she* he refers to isn't Ana. It's someone much more terrifying.

"She did." Derrick nods.

The professor sighs and shakes his head before taking his leave.

"You should have started with that. There's nothing else to be done then." He remarks softly.

Ana turned toward Derrick, her red lips pulled into a tight smirk.

"I'm guessing that your persuasions were successful." Derrick could hear the jealousy in his voice and frowned to think that she could too.

"Well, I think he agreed that giving you supplies for your 'emergency evacuation vehicle' would be in his best interest." She gave a wicked smile.

What did she have over on him? What did she say that she thought would persuade him? Tempting him with her figure wasn't going to be enough for Wall. She had said something to scare him, and Derrick didn't know what it could have been.

"I hope he got a good look at the layout because I need him to remember all of his materials."

"Don't worry," she laughed, "he got the layout."

"What do you mean?"

"I took it from your notebook and put it somewhere he

won't forget it." There was a suggestive smile after her statement, and he couldn't help but laugh a little back. She was encouraged by his laughter and continued. "If you need to make sure that I put it in a safe place, I can show you just where I put it."

He rolled his eyes as she waved his notebook at him.

"I have to get back to Candace." He knew the effect this would have on her.

She instantly drew away from him, and it was then that Derrick noted how close she had moved toward him during the conversation. She was glaring at him, and somehow, through all of her bodies, the glare didn't seem to change much. There was almost some of the original in that. She slapped the notebook into his hands.

"Candace won't last forever."

It was what she always said about them; it was the only thing equally cruel she could retort after he mentioned one of the women who came after her.

"Neither will Adam," he replied, referring to the name of the person whose life he had currently taken over.

"Adam isn't even alive now." She was really angry this time.

"Ana—" he started but didn't know where he was going with the sentence.

"Stop, Derrick; I already know." She marched to the exit and he didn't watch her go.

The rain was warm outside. The warm and muggy air seemed to stick thick to his skin. It wasn't a soaking rain but the type that almost felt like a heavy fog in disguise. He could hear the drizzling, but it was hard to see the falling drops of rain.

Ana wasn't visible; she had always had the ability to fade

into the background. Sometimes he wasn't sure that Ana actually existed, but then other times he wasn't sure that anything existed besides Ana. She was the one closest to him for many years.

After his first transfer, his life was a disaster. He woke to a nurse who he mistook for his wife, Susanna. It wasn't her. It was foolish for him to believe that it was her. All that time, he had still been able to feel her presence in the room as he wandered through the rooms of his mind, but suddenly she was gone. He was informed that after many years of waiting for him, she had just left one day and never returned. When he looked in the mirror, he was a man seven years younger than his original body. He lifted his arms, but they felt like prosthetics. Surely Susanna had stayed with him as long as she could and like this—how could he ask to burden her again? As for his remaining family? Many of them had died due to Scanthirin sickness, and others had changed so immeasurably in the years that he'd been bedridden that he didn't know them anymore.

Waves of depression encompassed his life. Nurses sped around him all hours of the day, and he was scheduled therapy appointments and analyzed by psychiatrists. They all wanted to ask him questions. Was he feeling the same emotional disconnect as the other patients? Was he feeling angry? Were there times he felt like he wasn't in control? At the time, they created the label "transfer sickness" to describe this phenomena, but that phrase would later encompass more dangerous symptoms.

It was on his fourth day back that he met that bastard, Battinson. He had been sitting in a waiting area, twiddling his thumbs while staring at the outdated carpet. Ana was screaming at Battinson, hitting him with two balled fists. He still remembered their conversation.

"They keep asking me if I'm angry! Do *you* think I'm angry? Does this look angry enough for you?"

"Ana, I understand that you're angry."

"You don't understand! I'm twenty years old inside my head stuck in the body of a nine-year-old girl that I don't know! I've woken up to a nightmare!"

"Listen," he brought his voice down to a whisper, but Derrick could still hear, "I didn't know that you were still so aware all that time. I thought that waking you up as the age you were when you left me—would give you back those years."

"Well I didn't leave, did I? I thought and felt for eleven years! You should have just let me die!" She stomped toward Derrick and grabbed his arm, pulling him from the chair with surprising strength.

"What are you doing?" Battinson yelled at her.

"I'm taking this person, and I'm leaving. I'm not coming back here again! Don't try to find me!" She pushed Derrick out the door as he tried to muster the emotion to protest.

"Tell me you know how to drive." She said to Derrick as they left.

Ana was true to her word. She didn't see her father again before he died. Derrick thought that it was a bad choice. He could say this now from personal experience. It had been nearly a hundred-and-thirty years since he'd chosen not to search for Susanna, and for half of those years, he'd regretted it. Now he couldn't even remember what she looked like. There was warmth surrounding her name in his mind but not much else.

Where Susanna had disappeared, Ana forced her way into filling the space. While she spent most of her time fuming, he spent his time grieving what he had lost. The disconnect created by the transfer gave him a constant hollowness and a feeling of being outside his body. Ana's emotions fluctuated violently as if the body's chemistry was desperately trying to fling her out. It was like she was a disease to her new vessel. Over time, Ana aged properly, and her anger turned to bitterness. Meanwhile, Derrick explored every spring of emotion that he could find.

For a while, they were very close. Ana helped to bring out the emotions in Derrick and he helped her to calm, but after some time, they both stagnated. They couldn't grow from one another anymore. About twenty years ago, they moved apart, and Ana became closer to Wei.

Ana, like the professor, and like Derrick, had her own serial killer way of choosing her victims. They were people that, in her own self-righteous way, she deemed unworthy of the roles they played in the world. Sometimes they were an abusive mother, sometimes a drug addict; somehow she found this theft more justifiable.

Adam's apartment was located on the border between the nicer and the rougher sides of town. His wife, Candace, was a secretary at a local tax firm, but she was still on maternity leave for Katie. Adam did something in industrial design, but Derrick hardly remembered what it was anymore. He had made a considerable fortune several lifetimes ago, and he mostly showed up at the job to sit at the desk and keep up appearances. Some day he would be fired, but it wouldn't be particularly surprising to anyone. The real Adam would have eventually been fired too.

Derrick could hear the crying before he even reached the second floor. He sighed. It was an unfortunate mistake on his part. He hadn't checked well enough into Adam's character. When he had learned that Adam Gavins had no children, he hadn't thought to consider the unborn.

"Oh, Adam, honey, thank God you're home! Katie has been crying all day, and she's running a low-grade fever."

"Did you call the doctor?" He grabbed a soda from the fridge and leaned on the door to look attentive. His wet coat dripped onto the tiles.

"Yes," she glared at the water on the floor, and he immediately went to the closet and removed his coat, "the doctor said if I can calm her down, it will probably go away, but I've tried everything and she just won't stop!"

It was obvious that Candace herself had been crying. Her eyes were as puffy and red as the child's. The child hadn't noticed him through her tightly squeezed eyes. She didn't appear to be shedding any actual tears, and he doubted that there had ever been much more than a watering to begin with.

Katie, at about nine months old, could be considered pretty for a baby, not that Derrick really thought of any baby as pretty, but in her current emotional state, she looked comparable to a red-faced gargoyle. Derrick took a swig of his drink and set it on the kitchen counter. He wiped the condensation from the can off of his hands and onto his pants. Then, tiredly, he reached out to take the child. He grimaced at the thing, hot and sticky from her own sweat. Candace had put mittens on her hands at some point because she had tried to take her anger out on her face.

"Katie," he called softly.

"Katie, Katie, Katie, look, Katie!" He wiggled his fingers

in front of her face, but she was twisting and kicking, trying not to look at them by turning her head. There was a sudden wash of heated frustration within him; her crying was so annoying. Holding her away from him with two hands, he gently dangled her from side-to-side; on a good day, this would have produced a giggle.

"Weeeee," he whispered, but the enthusiasm wasn't there, and Katie obviously found him unconvincing.

He sighed, bringing her to him again. Suddenly she stopped, opened her eyes as if surprised, and vomited down the front of her onesie. Candace, who had previously been leaning her elbows on the counter covering her face with her hands, looked up at the absence of wailing. Surveying the scene, she ran to get a towel to mop up her daughter's face and, afterward, the floor. She was smiling despite it. The child was silent with its tummy troubles put to rest. Quietly and efficiently, Candace changed her and laid her down in her crib. Derrick took another drink of his soda.

"I don't think I could have taken much more of that," she whispered to him. Evidently, the child had worn itself out because it was snoring breathy baby snores softly into its bed sheets.

Derrick smiled what he hoped looked sympathetically. She hugged him, and he set down his soda to return it. Contentedly she sighed into his chest and he looked down at the top of her head. Her hair was reddish-brown; he pressed his face into it, and she murmured something happily. She smelled like baby powder.

Candace was gentle, sweet, and good. He always wondered if somewhere deep down she knew that he wasn't Adam. If she did suspect anything, it was probably more subconscious than anything else because she never said anything about him coming home late and never tried to pry into what it was that he was doing. Maybe she was just so happy that he wasn't who he had been in the past that she didn't mind any of those things. She didn't mind when he couldn't recall old acquaintances or inside jokes. Somehow she even overlooked him forgetting vacations, birthdays, and her favorite activities.

She pulled away just enough to look up at him with her hazel eyes. There was that never-failing warmth that he was always surprised by just a little before putting on a synthetic expression.

"I am so happy you're home."

"You always say that." He chuckled.

"Well it's true!" She bounced childishly when she said it.

"I'll always come home," he whispered down to her.

Derrick didn't know why he had said that. These moments were the hardest about joining a family. He wished he were more like Ana, with her ability to avoid emotional entanglements, but Ana hadn't been married before. She had never loved anyone, except maybe her father, but she hardly remembered him. Derrick was not sure that whatever had been between the two of them was romantic love either.

He had let his thoughts drift too far, and Candace was staring up at him concernedly. He smiled to put away her fears, hugging her once more and lifting her a bit from the floor in doing so. She giggled, wrapping her arms around his neck, but as he set her back down, she was frowning.

"What's wrong?"

"Nothing—it's nothing."

"Candace, what's wrong?"

"It's silly." She brushed a piece of her wild hair back from her face.

He continued to look at her sternly, and she bit her lip, scrunching her forehead slightly. Derrick waited for her to find her words, brushing the wild hair, which had bounced into her face again, behind an ear.

"It's just—it's just that I thought. It's just that you've been so different lately."

"Different? How so?"

His gut tightened. A thudding started in his head. Maybe she had heard the public announcements, or maybe she had been watching the news. They had been blasting reports about finding Eterns for months now. What would he do if she had figured out the truth? Adam had not been a great husband, but she wasn't going to embrace him—a stranger that had been residing in her home, taking care of her child. He'd have to—Derrick shuddered. He tried to hide his apprehension as she opened her mouth to speak.

"I was just scared for a while, that you, well, that you wouldn't come home. You were just so depressed, and I felt like Katie and I were a burden."

He instantly relaxed, and in his relief, he even laughed a little. She didn't want Adam in the first place. Adam hadn't wanted her.

"I just needed time, hon. I was so stressed. You and Katie were never the burden; it was everything else."

"I know that now." She smiled, seemingly relieved to have said something. It must have been weighing on her for a long time.

"You're tired, Can, why don't you head off to bed? I'm going to finish my drink and maybe do a little paperwork."

"Okay," she kissed him lightly, "see you soon."

She undressed as she made her way to the room, leaving a trail of clothes. Derrick smiled and turned his attention to his soda. He didn't have any paperwork, but he pulled out the notebook from his pants pocket and set it on the counter. He turned over the front page to look at one of the sketches he had done for the design he had given to Wall.

Although he called it an evacuation vehicle, it wasn't like a vehicle that you could get into and drive, or fly, around in. The E.V. was a mobile version of what Battinson had created. He didn't understand how the science worked himself, but being an engineer, he could build working copies of the original by using the same materials and setup. It was Wei that actually understood it. She had attempted to explain it to him once. Wei described the brain as a computer, and taking over a new life was like overwriting the hard drive of another computer. She explained it like they were viruses that would wipe out the existing memory and replace it with their own data. In this small way, he understood.

The E.V. was mobile, but there were side effects of it being so small. For one, it couldn't keep your patterns for very long. Another risk of using it was that you had to target it yourself rather than using the targeting system of the original. This meant that if you missed, it was likely that you were zapping your existence out into nothingness. He honestly wasn't sure if he would even want to use it himself, but with the police getting the new scanners, he didn't know how much longer they would be able to hide.

He shut the notebook. He took it out too often. As much as he didn't want Wall to be right, it was a gun. The connotations of such a thing existing were unsettling. If Eterns, or even everyday humans, duplicated the designs, it could be catastrophic. He just wanted to keep himself and the others safe, not start a war between Eterns and humans. Derrick sighed deeply, suddenly wishing that the soda in his can was something a little stronger.

23

Chapter 23

"And local authorities are finally confirming that the Norfolk Police Department officially has the equipment to finalize the search for missing Eterns. If you have not yet submitted yourself to your doctor for your mandatory scans, please do so immediately. They are harmless, painless, and can be taken at any of the locations scrolling down your screen; for the official list, please visit our website at norfolknews.net. By not having these scans done, you are putting your friends and family at risk.

"Remember, if you suspect someone you know may have been invaded by an Etern, just tell your mobile device the Insta-Code: 413-911. Give the name of your family member or friend, and the Police Department will subtly test them with the new technology, sending an instant message to your device with the results. I had everyone in the studio tested. Right, Eddie?"

Eddie laughed with white teeth. His face is pulled back in an unnatural way, which could only be the effect of plastic surgery. "I wouldn't know, Kenna; you said they were discreet." They both laughed, and Derrick imagined that their chemistry was seen as charming, although he hated them both. Her perfectly brushed hair and pointed eyes staring at him through the computer panel that ran the length of the rail car stirred disgust in his stomach.

"Pretty scary shit, huh, man?"

Derrick removed his earbuds, digging around in his pockets for the little carrying case. He didn't know if they were more annoying with or without cords.

"I'm sorry?"

"I said it was pretty scary shit." The man leaned across him to point at the panel in front of Derrick that was still flashing the news broadcast throughout the rail car. Derrick forced himself not to recoil as the man brushed his arm against him. This was supposed to be a normal human interaction. In a rail car, where you sat shoulder to shoulder, it would be normal to converse a little. The man continued. "I saw it this morning as I was leaving for work. It's freaky even when it comes from a babe like Kenna Lloyd."

"Oh, yeah. Really makes you wonder about people." Derrick looked around at the other passengers with mock suspicion.

"Well, I think it'd be pretty obvious to tell. I can't imagine that people could just enter another person and completely convince everyone around them that they're the same."

"I don't know. I mean, the cops haven't caught them all yet; they are probably pretty good at impersonating normal people."

"Hah! Man, there ain't nothing normal about 'em. I could spot one."

"I sure hope I can!" Derrick smiled nervously while pretending to wipe sweat from his forehead.

The rail car came to a halt and the doors burst open, sending a tidal wave of people gathering their things and shuffling out the door. Derrick joined them, telling his companion courteously that it was his stop.

"Keep your head low, man! Don't let 'em get to ya!"

"Thanks, you too!"

The rail car drifted away, and he watched it go. He always smiled a little at the fact they still insisted on calling them rail cars, when really, they didn't have any rails at all. They used a system of positive and negative pulls from a series of magnets to glide upon. When the car was hidden by masses of people in the congested city center, he focused his attention on moving in the waves, through the shifts and shoves.

"Adam."

He turned to see no familiar face in the crowd. A hand suddenly entwined in his and he jumped. The hand held fast and began to pull him through the crowd. His head snapped in the direction of the hand, and attached to it, he found a blonde woman with rich coloring in her cheeks and lips. Her nose curved elegantly downward, and her eyes were sharp as they looked upward.

He recognized the face from the television. Wei was the leader of Grennel Technologies. Grennel Technologies was a research company that Wei had technically built more than a hundred years ago but continuously was bought out or handed down by successors. Wei took on the new bodies of the CEOs and continued to run her business. In every instance, she fabricated records that her old body had been sick. She raised her successor just to take their vessel.

"Wei?" Derrick mouthed.

Her eyes reacted with the angry twitch of her mouth. "Adam," she had called him Adam, which meant that he shouldn't have said her real name.

"Way, way too long since I last saw you, my darling," Derrick spewed theatrically, and she relaxed a little.

"Adam, you aren't looking well. You should see a doctor. I'd recommend you to mine, but he has made several mistakes in regards to my health and the health of people I know."

Not looking well? He looked the same as ever. No, what was she saying? Something about a doctor making mistakes. Wall. He had a doctorate in his first lifetime.

"Oh, how so? I hope your doctor made no severe mistakes." Her shoulders showed relief in his understanding.

"Well, he was looking at a friend of mine's files, and he sent them to another specialist. He allowed a clumsy nurse to handle them, and they were no longer sealed by the time they got to the other specialist. It would be bad if someone peeked inside my friend's files."

Derrick stopped walking, a rush of fear overwhelming him, but Wei continued to pull him along. Someone had seen his diagrams of the E.V. Did she know who? Which of their identities were compromised?

"Take off work today, darling. Don't worry about your wife. Let's go somewhere."

She was acknowledging that they needed to talk but somewhere more private. Casually, she lifted her hand to him, the one that was still holding his own. At first, he only kissed it, playing his part, but when Wei continued to hold up her hand, he inspected it more closely. The underneath of her index fingernail was glowing faintly blue. It was the result of a latex chip that reacted when it detected audio frequencies on specific channels. The latex was part of a new design that Grennel Technologies had dubbed "Lay-Tech." It combined the latest in microscopic wiring and latex design. Right now, by glowing blue, it was telling them that there was a bud nearby, likely airborne. Buds were small flying devices that had various purposes depending on their quality and programming. This was bad. Wei was already under suspicion if there was a bud on her, but by who?

"Where would you like to go?"

"Let's go for a drive," she stopped, and then added, "out of the city."

"Whatever you want. I could never deny you." She frowned slightly, showing her true feelings for a second, and then laughed raucously. She was telling him not to overplay his part.

She slowly pulled him to the left, their direction change interrupting crowd flow. He knocked into the back of a man, causing him to lose the contents of his briefcase. Derrick turned to apologize, but the person had instantly been swallowed by the masses.

Wei pulled hard on his arm, jerking him forward again to plow through arms and legs and shoulders. Then, unexpectedly, they were out of the mass and teetering on the curb. Her car was readily pulled up, and she quickly opened the door for him.

Wei was old-school. She was the eldest of them, already seventy-two when she was "eternalized" by Doctor Battinson. Only the truly rich used cars, and they were more of an attention-getter than anything else. The majority of people walked or used rails. As cities grew, there stopped being room and necessity for cars. All cars now were models of classics, which were built from kits. Wei was driving a 2270 hover model.

"You know it's based on the first car that was available to the general public that went from zero to sixty in under a second. I know they can go a lot faster now, but my great-grandfather had the original when it first came out."

Derrick knew that when she said "great-grandfather," she meant herself. She looked at him for approval, but he didn't respond. He didn't want to deal with the small talk, but her nail was still visibly glowing against the steering wheel.

"The styling is a bit different," she added, "but at least it has a steering wheel. The pad-operated ones just don't have the history. Not even to mention the ones they experimented with in the early two-hundreds, you know the ones that were so-called 'mind-operated.' Those things might have been mind-operated, but whoever's mind it was listening to, it sure wasn't the operator's. There were more accidents in those models than any before them." She looked at him in the rearview mirror and added, "Acted like it had a mind of its own."

Derrick nodded, half-listening, but mostly stared at her hand, waiting for the blue to fade. They were driving past what used to be a shipyard. Not long after the founding of the Mars Base, the shipyard was made into a historical site, and work no longer continued there. A new one had been built to replace it. Wei was taking him further out of the city, and into the broken outskirts. The outskirts of every city were surrounded by small mod homes provided by the government. The people who lived here had roofs over their heads, but not much else. These housings had become the slums, and if you were born in them, there wasn't ever much likelihood of leaving. Wei seemed to have a very clear idea of where she was going, and this assumption was confirmed when, very suddenly, the blue disappeared.

"Alright," he said, encouraging her to start.

"I'm sorry it had to be so complicated. I knew that the buds were following me, but they usually have a fairly short radius in which they can track. They work by downloading recorded images from camera feeds and sending the images or videos up to a satellite to pinpoint a location from our surroundings. We were around too many people, too much technology. Please turn off any type of recording device you have, we don't want the bud using it to track us." He didn't have any such device, and she continued. "It's not too difficult for it to find us out here, but it has lost us—at least for the moment. For this reason, I'm going to try to be quick."

"I'm listening."

"When I needed you to draw me up a containment unit for the Battinson Device, or the E.V., as you call it, I told you that I couldn't build it in Grennel Tech. I knew that you would have to go to Wall with your designs once you finished so that he could use his university's resources. Wall wasn't careful enough when he ordered the materials. Rather than slowly acquiring the materials, he convinced students to use them for their research projects. I don't know what the idiot was thinking. Several of the items on that list bought within the same state raise a terrorist alert regardless of the purchaser's information.

"Then the idiot did the unthinkable! He sent the final design plans directly to Grennel Tech. I don't know what he was thinking! I'm a molecular biologist and a neuroscientist! I raise enough attention as it is with my engineering department."

Derrick wondered what Ana had threatened Wall with. Whatever it was had made him lose his senses completely. Derrick's chest felt hot. Wall had panicked and exposed Wei, and Wei went to Derrick and exposed him. They were acting just how the government would like them to.

"If they are tracking you, Wei, they must know you are an Etern. Why on Earth did you come to me? Why would you expose me?"

"For several reasons, I found that 'exposing you,' as you say, was the only option I had."

"I can think of quite a few more!"

"Let me explain, Derrick; we can't have but about twenty minutes before that bud, or another one, catches up with us. There is a lot more going on right now than you know."

"Fine."

"I'm going to start by at least comforting you with the knowledge that you aren't yet exposed. They aren't yet capable of proving that I'm an Etern, let alone you."

"What about the police? What about their new technology?"

"Yes, yes, I know all about it. Trust me, I make it my business. Their scanners only work if they have the names and brain waves of the original humans. The E.B.L. Scanners work by constantly verifying that people's brainwaves haven't changed. Certain brainwaves can be found that are as distinct as blood or a fingerprint, and that's how they are finding Eterns."

"So if our bodies weren't scanned before we took them, then they can't match us."

"That's not exactly true. The E.B.L. Scanners can also match us to our brain scans."

"You mean—from when we were still Scans," Derrick shivered.

"Yes, but thankfully, Battinson kept our group off the record, so we are reported dead. God forbid the government learns he did human trials before getting any approval. I'm not sure if the government has put the brain waves of all the previous Scans in the system, or only the ones that Battinson admitted to transferring."

"So we may or may not be safe is what you're saying."

"I'm a celebrity. I'm sure I've been scanned a dozen times. At the moment, I think we're fine, but Ana..." Wei's voice trailed away.

Ana. He hadn't even thought of her. Ana was the most famous of any Etern. The daughter of Battinson—his motive for the legendary Battinson Decision. They would be searching for her foremost, above all others.

"You've made me a suspect, Wei."

"And I'm sorry about that, Derrick, but it doesn't matter anyway. I told you this is a lot bigger than just—" he interrupted her.

"And what about Ana? Ana isn't off the grid, Wei! She's practically the Holy Grail of Eterns! What are you doing to help her?"

"Well, Ana is one of the many problems we have. You, me, Wall, we are all going to be watched now because of our association. None of us can warn Ana in person without also bringing her under suspicion."

"But Wei, it's only a matter of time before she tries to contact us! What happens then?"

"I don't know, Derrick! This is part of why it was so important for me to talk to you! We have to be on guard every moment!"

"Wei, how do you even know that it's the police that

intercepted the plans? It could have been Eterns."

"I don't know! They were as capable of noticing the purchases as the government. Does it matter, though? I'm not even sure which of the two options would be worse for us."

"The police would be worse for us—Eterns worse for everyone else."

There was a momentary silence, and Derrick let it churn in his head. He thought of Ana. Not of the vivacious, manipulative, and vain woman, but the young, honest, and unfortunate girl who he had once known a long time ago. They had once had a connection, but they had squandered it with the degradation of their youth, and subsequently their virtue.

"My soul is old, Wei."

She laughed. "And mine older yet."

"No, your mind is older, but your soul doesn't seem to age as fast as mine."

She glanced over at him for a moment, concern wrinkling around her eyes. "That's something you'll have to consider. Perhaps you're too old for this. Perhaps we all are!"

"What do you mean?"

"Derrick, it's what I've been trying to tell you. It's why I risked meeting you! The Eterns are planning an attack, and today's civilization is going to come to an end. We have to go."

24

Chapter 24

Pain wreaks havoc on my body as I'm torn away from the memory. I collapse on the stone arm wrapped around me. Everything is heavy. Nyauta pours into my mouth, and I struggle to swallow; it runs down my neck.

"I'm sorry," the Lovindian murmurs. "I wanted you to see the whole thing, but I didn't know what kind of toll it was taking on you."

I cough. My lungs feel like they're breathing fire. My head swims. Where is Wei? What did she mean? I can't leave. My body is twitching, jerking, but I can't control it.

"Jacob! You have to stop thinking about the story! You're here! You're not on Earth! Jacob! Jacob!"

Jacob? The name feels familiar somehow. Am I on the floor? My vision goes in and out. I choose to focus on a single speck of red dust that sinks slowly to the tile.

"There, come back around for me. Relax for a while. You have to start taking longer breaks between the memories. I don't want to leave any lasting damage to your mind." His voice is distant, rumbling like rain on the outside of the dome.

It's dark when I wake. I sit up and brush the red dust from my face. I'm still in the Council Building. A sharp flash of white runs up the back of my head, and I see Katie's fat baby hands reaching up to me. A moan echoes through the columns. It comes again, and I realize that it is my own.

"You're awake." The Lovindian is suddenly beside me.

My stomach feels incredibly empty, but it's nothing compared to the aches in my sides and the heaviness of my shoulders. The Earth I saw this time didn't make any sense. It wasn't anything like the Earth I saw the first time, and then there were the Eterns. They were like Lovindians—but they were human.

"I don't understand," I croak hoarsely.

"I'm sure you have a lot of questions, but I think you need to eat something first."

I breathe in. The smell of a hot, cooked meal reaches me instantly. I grab my stomach instantly. A bowl of cream-colored mash is set in front of me. I don't recognize the flavor of what's inside, but I don't know whether this is because I've never had it before or because I'm inhaling it too quickly. I've only taken a few gulps, but the bowl is empty. I lick the bowl clean and wipe my mouth on my arms.

"The Eterns are like Lovindians. Are you trying to tell me that humans were like Lovindians?" I breathe.

The Lovindian's mouth turns downward.

"Humans are humans, and Eterns are Eterns. They became different species when they branched off in the Battinson Decision. The Eterns became parasitic, spectral organisms, while humans remained the same. The species split, but both survived. So you're right in one aspect; the Eterns were similar to Lovindians."

224

"'Were?' Are all of the Eterns gone now?" I ask.

"Yes. They were exterminated by the Lovindians."

I suddenly feel cold. If the Lovindians exterminated the Eterns, then did that mean...

"Did the Lovindians take the technology from the Eterns?" I ask.

The Lovindian pauses for a long moment. I follow his gaze, but all I see are columns. His shoulders hang down further than normal.

"Yes."

It isn't possible. It can't be. How can humanity be so closely tied with the Lovindians? Humanity was destroyed, and their creation was used to enslave countless galaxies, including their own. For the first time, I question whether I deserve to be free. If our legacy is that of a people who created the wretched power the Lovindians abused, do we really deserve freedom? Humans created an evil that destroyed billions of people—countless billions. Maybe on Yalk, humanity is atoning in their suffering.

"Jacob, those thoughts aren't going to get you anywhere." I blink in surprise. How had the Lovindian known what I was thinking? Did he read my mind? He continues thoughtfully. "The Battinson Device wasn't created to hurt people."

The effect of the Lovindian's words is instant. I remember the deep, empty feeling within Susanna Webber. I remember the dark circles beneath Dr. Battinson's eyes and the crazed frenzy in which he had discussed wild attempts to save his beloved daughter's life. He was just one sad, broken man who loved his child. Just one selfish man, who wanted to save thousands of lives, made a decision which ultimately killed hundreds of billions.

"It wasn't his fault," I whisper.

The Lovindian laughs. "Oh, no, it was his fault. That's what's wrong with humans and so many other species. They want someone to bear the blame, and it has to be someone completely evil. Completely cruel people don't exist as much as completely kind people don't exist. Battinson knew the evil he was making, but he used his own sense of self-made integrity to justify it. Susanna told him not to do it—she wouldn't do it for her husband. Everyone has their own brand of morality—what rules they will and won't break. You can't vilify or glorify anyone completely."

"If humans are capable of so much evil, then why should we have a place in the world?"

"Everything is capable of evil. A flower can choke away the life of a seedling just by blocking out the sun. Would you pull the fully grown plant from the ground? What you are suggesting is genocide. Don't just kill the one plant but all others like it. It's not like that, Jacob. Not to mention, what you're doing here, listening to the whole story, isn't just for humanity—it's for all the planets out there. In fact, because of what Battinson did, maybe that's why you need to be the one to hear the story. Maybe you need to earn redemption for a species that has now resigned itself to burying its head in the sand."

"Is it even possible for humanity to redeem itself for all that pain? I don't even know how many planets we're even talking about," I say dejectedly. "Do you really think you can show me something powerful enough to do that?"

"If I didn't think I could show you something that powerful, then I wouldn't have risked your life by asking you to return to Roja. As for your redemption—Jacob, your people can't be blamed for the faults of long-gone forefathers. You have to remember that humanity has been enslaved for over six hundred years. You have been receiving punishment for your forefathers since you were born. Remember their mistakes, and learn from them. You are only responsible for the people of now. How you help people now is the only way to define your character. If you do nothing, then you aren't helping anyone."

He's right. It's a heavy weight, but he's right. I need to find the Lovindians' weakness and set things right. I hadn't expected Earth to be so closely linked with Lovindian history, but in a way, it doesn't matter. Eterns don't exist anymore, and the current remnants of humanity are ignorant of the damage their species has caused. They're still innocent. They may need redemption, but they're still a species worth saving.

"How did the Lovindians defeat the Eterns?" I blurt out.

"Another time," the Lovindian grumble-laughs.

"No. There's no point in waiting. I'm recovered now."

"Jacob, don't you have a family?" The Lovindian's eyes narrow in a way I assume is confusion. "Won't they be worried about you?"

It's the most personal thing the Lovindian has ever asked. I'm immediately uncomfortable. He's still a Lovindian. The idea of him knowing anything about the people close to me is unnerving, even if he means well. On the other hand, he isn't wrong. I think of Samuel and Emmanuel. I don't know how long I've been gone, and my friends will undoubtedly be worried about me.

"I can't afford to go back yet. I need to know more pieces of the story," I beg half-heartedly.

"The next part is going to be stressful, Jacob; I think you

should get some rest. Your body is starting to react poorly to the story. The memories that the Historians kept in this part of the story are from more than one source, and they jump in time fairly frequently."

"I'm ready now."

"Look at your hand, boy." His voice raises.

The scar on my hand is hot and pink. I trail it with a finger; it's soft and painfully fleshy. I shake it away. So what?

"I'm ready," I say again.

"Well, I'm not. I'm going to rest. Go home, Jacob." He turns me down sharply.

The Lovindian stands and disappears into the pillars. I sigh. I guess he wins this time. I tear a piece of my shirt and wrap my hand tightly to numb the burn. I wonder if Samuel will notice this. I should keep it in my pants' pocket to avoid worrying him.

25

Chapter 25

I'm exhausted. The weariness hits me just as I see my apartment. I feel foolish for asking the Lovindian to show me another story. He knew I couldn't handle it. Samuel didn't meet me at the shuttle bay. I can't help but feel a little disappointed, even though I know that it's better if he doesn't.

"Oh perfect, you're back! Let's go!" A large hand wraps around my arm.

Emmanuel twists me around back the way I came. I pull my arm back, struggling to keep my balance. He pushes his hair out of his eyes and shifts the weight of two giant sacks on his shoulder. He sees me eyeing the sacks and smirks.

"Come on! I need your help."

"With what?" I yawn tiredly.

"Gotta get this to Yahbi."

"You want me to take you to Yahbi?" I say with surprise.

"Yep, gonna give that Yahbiin scum a piece of my mind. Thinks he can rip my clients off by refusing to deliver the salt to Unit C." He mutters a few choice words under his breath.

Salt? So that must be what's in the sacks.

"Why can't Unit C get their own salt?"

"Can't. It's not possible to buy through the com-panel in mass quantities."

"Why do they need mass quantities of salt?"

"They've been using it as a preservative during the meat shortages that come during the rainy season."

"We don't have meat shortages."

"Not in Unit B, but around Unit C, the electrical storms are a lot worse. It keeps the Yahbiin meat merchants from some of their shipments. The refrigeration units onboard make the ships a little on the bulky side, and it makes it difficult to navigate the storms properly."

"That's all and good, Emmanuel, but I'm tired. Only just got back. Your salt is going to have to wait."

"It's not about the salt!" Emmanuel growls, looking around us for Gromptu.

"Then what is it about?" I sigh. I'm regretting getting this far into the conversation.

"It's about the medicine needed in Unit A," he hisses.

"Medicine?" I vaguely remember him telling me about the plagues in Unit A.

"Yes, the medicine! Unit A is dealing with another variant of the wheeze, and I can't afford to sell it to them at a decent price without upselling the salt."

"Why don't the Lovindians get medicine for Unit A?" I ask.

Emmanuel chuckles, and I blink at him confusedly.

"You're serious!" he exclaims when he realizes I truly don't understand.

"Of course I'm serious!" I say irritably. I'm still feeling lightheaded even after the Nyauta.

"You're as naive as Samuel! I guess that's what happens

when you've never been through a wheeze before." He shifts the salt around again on his shoulders. "How do you think the wheeze gets introduced, Jacob?"

My stomach lurches. I remember the decontamination spray that is emitted after exiting the transporter craft. If it's not being introduced by Yahbiin merchants or transporter crafts, then how is the wheeze still popping up in Unit A? Before it was thought to be transported by unsafe Gromptu and merchant procedures but that shouldn't be a problem anymore. Unless— unless it was purposefully introduced.

"Why?" I ask, my voice trembles angrily. "Why do they do it?"

"To make sure that our bodies are inoculated? To be cruel? Who knows." He gives a half-frown.

"Why not a vaccine if it is inoculation?" I whisper. There has to be a deeper reason.

"Don't think there is one." Emmanuel shrugs. "So are you taking me, or not?"

There's no way I can say no. If I don't go, more people will die in Unit A. Emmanuel's giving me the chance to do something meaningful. Who knows if I'll even learn anything from the story the Historians left behind. Doing this will help me get closer to fulfilling my promise to Saul. I scratch the back of my hand. The pink scar burns on my palm.

"Alright, Emmanuel, let's get going before Samuel notices." I consent.

"Fantastic!" He gestures excitedly toward the landing bay, and I'm hit with another wave of exhaustion. Maybe I can sleep on the way to Yahbi.

The Gromptu watch us carefully as we pass through the gates. The salt we have isn't illegal, but it probably looks suspicious. Emmanuel has never even gotten on a transporter craft before. I shiver and rub my arms to make the feeling subside.

I hold up my wrist to tell my command key to open the hatch door. Emmanuel steps back awkwardly as it lowers. He runs a hand through his hair, staring at the boarding ramp nervously. He catches me watching him and grumbles irritably.

"Well, what are you waiting around for?"

He marches into the transporter craft, and I hear the salt hit the floor. I chuckle—he always has to be difficult. I follow him, closing the hatch door, and put Yahbi into the navi-system. Emmanuel gawks at a few of the controls but quickly becomes disinterested.

"Didn't you say you had someone flying for you?" I ask. It was Cruise or something like that.

Emmanuel finds a seat on the bench, blood rises into his cheeks at my question.

"Cruiser? Damned girls are so fickle."

"Cruiser is a woman?" I say with surprise.

"If you can call her that!" he snaps.

We're interrupted as the craft starts to leave the atmosphere. I flip the viewer screen so that we can watch Yalk disappear. Dust rushes over Unit B, hiding it almost completely. It might as well be a pebble rolling through the sand at this distance.

"Damn," Emmanuel whispers.

I flip the screen back toward Yahbi. His reaction makes my love of flying feel fresh again. I wonder if Keren has ever flown. She wasn't old enough to go on the trip into space yet when I left. She would have loved seeing the stars from space. My chest tightens. Maybe once the story is over, I'll have the courage to go back to Unit C and face her.

"Stay close to me," I mumble as Yahbi approaches on the viewer screen.

"Hey, Jacob?" The nervousness in his voice almost makes him sound his age.

"Yeah?"

"What's Yahbi like?"

"Crowded."

It's the best word I have to describe it. When we land, I can tell he sees exactly what I mean. The swarms of people make me feel even more tired. I try to rub the tightness out of one of my shoulders.

"Which market are we going to?" I ask above the roar.

"Market? I don't know what you mean; I just need to find that Luwelt bastard and get my merchandise to Unit A."

"Why didn't we just take it to Unit A?" I say confusedly.

"Are you a certified Lovindian Trader? If not, I'd rather not get my baunti fined for smuggling goods into Unit A. If Cruiser wasn't in such a piss-poor mood, I wouldn't have this trouble, but she's not going to deliver it, let alone make us any false certification papers for the salt. Of course, she was kind enough to make the false certification papers to get it cleared into Unit B."

"Why'd she do that?"

"To piss me off," he growls.

So that's what this is about. We're here to make sure that the salt has certification papers for trading. It doesn't matter if Emmanuel doesn't know where this Luwelt guy is in the market. It is annoying, however. He better pay me back the baunti because I'm sure getting this information is going to cost me.

"Human being!"

The Yahbiin grins his orange smile. His eyes only flicker toward Emmanuel. He's more interested in my hand going into my pocket. I pull out the coin and set it down on the table like always. He glances at the bandages on my hand but doesn't say anything about them.

"Sabo, we're looking for a specific Yahbiin trader."

"I'm hurt! If you have any deals to make, I could always be of service." He smiles slyly.

"We're looking for Luwelt," Emmanuel interrupts.

Sabo hisses, slipping a glare in Emmanuel's direction. I've never seen a Yahbiin hostile to any possible business propositions before. I don't have the energy to wonder why he doesn't like Emmanuel. I tap the number on the coin up, and I see Sabo's eyes dart downward.

"Why does that creature want to see Luwelt? He is a most devious trader."

I'm even more surprised by his behavior. That creature?

"More devious than a normal Yahbiin?" I say laughingly.

Sabo's eyebrows rise. He crosses his arms antagonistically.

"And you are being more small-minded than the normal Human!"

I scowl, but I see his point. I hadn't really thought of Yahbiins as having distinct personalities—just different levels of greed. I'm reminded of when Sabo had warned me not to go to the Talkers tent, and I feel a little embarrassed. Maybe I have made more of a friend of the money-grabbing little bugger than I knew.

"I'm sorry, Sabo; I didn't mean it that way." It feels weird to apologize to the indignant little creature.

"Are you trying to encourage that human to continue with his trading? Yahbiins do not like humans taking their place.

It is our pride to be a mercantilist society."

It's just like Sabo to already know exactly what Emmanuel has been doing. Apparently, Emmanuel isn't as slick as he thinks he is.

"He's just trying to do service to the units. I thought Yahbiins would like the additional commerce."

"You don't understand much." Sabo watches me narrowly.

"What do you mean?" I ask.

Sabo looks down at the coin, and I sigh but tap the number up considerably.

"I mean," Sabo continues, "that Yahbi is under Lovindian sovereignty. We are allowed to trade because it benefits the Lovindians. If we stop benefiting the Lovindians, then I wake up with a Second Gen in my head instead of me! It doesn't help when we have rogue Second Gens like Luwelt stirring up trouble and stealing proper business."

My stomach flips. Rogue Second Gen? I flash a glance quickly at Emmanuel. His eyes are wide. So he didn't know either.

"Will you give me the coordinates to his booth in my command key?"

Sabo scowls at me. I wonder if I've pushed our relationship as far as it will go. After a long-drawn pause, he holds out a stubby-fingered hand. I drop the coin into it reluctantly. He taps it repeatedly, and I don't stop him. I don't look at the number; Emmanuel will have to pay me back for this anyway. Finally, Sabo sighs, gives me an irritable side-glance, and taps it one last time before dissolving it into his com-panel.

This time he holds out his other hand, taking my wrist, and presses his com-panel against the command key to sync the coordinates. The blue arrow starts to glow. I'm reminded of the last time the blue arrow appeared above my wrist. Of course, it points to the southwest market—that place is full of trouble.

"Thanks," I say.

"Don't mention it," he growls.

Emmanuel keeps close to my side as I start to slip into the crowd. I'm already sweating. My head aches from lack of sleep.

"Didn't think this place would be so damn crowded," Emmanuel mutters.

"Be careful who you elbow. You'll end up dead," I say as he shoves through the crowd with his salt sacks using an annoying lack of awareness.

"Jacob? About what he said back there—about Luwelt; I didn't know."

"I should have. It makes sense that a privateer would be the one doing the smuggling." I interrupt his half-apology.

"Cruiser didn't tell me."

"Seems like you rely pretty heavily on this Cruiser person to go pissing her off," I say as the arrow flickers a little more west.

"You'll never hear me say it," he says with a half-smile.

I roll my eyes. Whoever Cruiser is, I'm taking her side. No details required.

"What kind of relationship do you have with this privateer, Emmanuel? I'm not about to get myself killed over some salt, am I?"

"It's not about the salt." His eyes narrow at me, but he answers seriously anyways. "You can trust Luwelt. His biggest fault is that he's odd."

It doesn't surprise me that I'm not more relaxed after

hearing his answer. Trusting people isn't my strong suit, and I feel like I'm already trusting enough Lovindians for a lifetime.

26

Chapter 26

The arrow bounces up and down above the command key. The tent in front of us is undeniably the one we are looking for. My feet hurt. I think a sand scretter made its way into my clothed feet and bit the bottom of my foot. I scratch at it; my patience for Emmanuel's antics is waning quickly. We enter through the sheer, purple curtain.

"No! No! Not there! Do you want them to get out of the crate? Because if they smell the sand, they'll burrow right through those wood boards to get down." An older Yahbiin man, with light purple skin and white hair, scurries about inside the tent.

"Where then?" a woman snaps.

"High! Up high!" he grates her.

"Put it up there yourself," she says, putting the crate on the table beside her.

The woman is of a species I'm not familiar with. Her skin is a bright red, dotted from the top of her mostly bald head with black, scale-like protrusions. A long, black braid that starts at the top center of her head hangs down her back. Her arms are crossed across the front of her, and she refuses to look at the Yahbiin man, who, although tall for his species, is much too short to put the crate anywhere high.

"Fickle as always, Cruiser." Emmanuel steps forward, throwing the salt sacks to the floor with a groan. He rolls his shoulder dramatically.

Cruiser turns her head quickly at the sound of Emmanuel's voice. Her skin flushes an even darker shade of red than its natural color. After she recovers, she shoots back angrily.

"What are you doing here, numskull?"

"Wouldn't you like to know?" he says with a grin.

"Who's this?" She gestures at me with a thumb.

"He's my captain," Emmanuel says to me with a wink.

"A human flying a craft? Makes me sick." She glares at me.

The Yahbiin man stares at me through a pair of glasses. Adjusting them higher on his nose, he approaches me.

"Resemblance is uncanny. Redling," he mumbles.

"I'm sorry?" I step back.

"Nothing," he waves me off, "don't worry about it. I haven't seen you in a while on Yahbi. I'd be interested to know what you've been up to."

"I don't know you," I say suspiciously.

"No, but it's my job to know you! You're an oddity. Watching a little human pup grow up wandering around Yahbi has been very interesting."

"Didn't know that a Second Gen was watching me so closely." I'm uneasy.

"That's how you know I'm a good one!" the Yahbiin says with a laugh that, although friendly, makes me uneasy.

Emmanuel finishes bickering with Cruiser and approaches the Yahbiin Second Gen.

239

"Luwelt, why wasn't my salt transported to Unit C? It doesn't do any good for me to have it dropped off at my door."

"I don't know what you want me to do, Emmanuel. My Lovindian contacts don't have any interest in certifying the salt the legal way. It doesn't benefit them."

"People are dying on Yalk." Anger rises into his tone. I notice just how large of a man Emmanuel has become as he stands beside the Yahbiin. He's still shorter than me, but I suspect it won't last long, and he's much stronger. I wonder if it's from lifting merchandise.

Luwelt waves him away. "People are dying everywhere, my friend! I'm a privateer. My interest in the common good can only extend so far."

"Then how can I get the salt to Unit C?"

"Well if you hadn't slighted a certain damsel, you wouldn't be having this problem to begin with." Luwelt's eyes land on Cruiser, who huffs loudly at them. "Anyways, Jacob, can you help me with this crate?"

He points to a shelf near the top of the tent, and I obligingly place it there. I don't ask how he already knows my name. I half-watch as Emmanuel steams toward the woman. I'm not sure what to make of the privateer and the smuggler, but if they were going to turn Emmanuel in, they would have done it by now.

"I've never talked to a Second Gen before," I say conversationally to Luwelt. It's not exactly true. I suppose I don't know what generation of Lovindian the Historian is.

"Don't use me as a reference point," he says with a laugh. "I'm not real well-embraced by my kind. The bastard of two Second Gen Yahbiin supervisors isn't seen as particularly delightful. Not many Lovindians like Yahbiins to begin with, let alone want to imagine their kind mating as one. It's... unseemly."

"So you've never transferred?" I ask.

Luwelt raises his thick eyebrows, and I realize the mistake I've made. I shouldn't know the name of that process without having spoken to a Lovindian before. He skims over my mistake.

"No, I haven't. Do you think I would have picked a Yahbiin body? I chose a different sort of path. Didn't go to Lovindian schools. I guess the Yahbiin is stronger in me than the Lovindian. Biology over the soul, you know?"

I nod and realize again that he was testing me. I shouldn't know how transferring works. I shouldn't know how the consciousness transfers. I feel my skin prickle. He looks at me with pointed eyes.

"You really are an oddity, human."

He gives a barking laugh, and I feel myself strangely relax. I decide a change of subject would make this more tolerable.

"What did Emmanuel do to upset the girl?" I ask.

"Who knows with them? All I know is that for the first time since the orphan brat came crawling in here, I've caught her smiling to herself." He gives an orange, toothy grin.

I roll my eyes. "So will he be able to get her to do the papers?"

"Not for cheap, if I've taught her anything." He gives another barking laugh.

I risk another glance over at Emmanuel and the young woman. The black scales on her arms flare a little in irritation when Emmanuel speaks to her. I've seen a lot of interesting beings on Yahbi, but I feel like I would have remembered seeing someone like her before. She shakes her head at him, and her thick braid swings around her waist.

"What species is she?" I ask him, lowering my voice.

"Couldn't tell you. She doesn't know either. The girl is an orphan. When I met her, she was only as tall as I am." He laughs fondly. "She had the same temperament even then. At the time, she was an expert pick-pocket and a professional vandal."

"A vandal?"

He chuckles. "Yahbiin merchants were paying her to er—paint images on the curtains of their competitors. I knew it was only a matter of time before they hit me. Being what I am makes me an easy target." He shrugs it off casually. "I waited for the vandal to come, but when I found this little girl, I just laughed. She was pretty cute back then." He smiles like a proud parent.

"You took her in?" I ask.

"Not at first. That stray wasn't very trusting."

"How'd you earn her trust?" It's odd to hear of a Lovindian having a relationship with a non-Lovindian.

"I kept feeding her. Isn't that how you tame anything?" he says with a surprisingly serious expression. I don't know how to respond to him.

Emmanuel bulls his way between us.

"Let's go, Jacob."

"So you got her to make the papers?"

"Yes, I've got them, now let's go." He turns to Luwelt. "Send them off this time!"

Luwelt tilts his head in a comical bow, a smirk plastered across his face. I glance back at Cruiser. She is pressing her fingers against a piece of paper. The black scales on her head and arms slowly flap up and down, and a black, ink-like substance pours from her fingertips onto the page. The ink forms the perfect "LT" logo of Lovindian trade. Emmanuel grabs my arm, ignoring my surprise and confusion. Luwelt said she was "painting" the tents when he met her. I suddenly understand what he meant.

"Let's get out of here before she changes her mind," he whispers, pulling me from the purple tent and immediately forgetting the traffic outside. He curses as he's almost swept away.

"How'd you get her to do it?" I yell above the crowd after we've found a crowd current.

"For the sake of my dignity, don't ask."

27

Chapter 27

First comes a thick, white spray of sanitization foam. I close my eyes just before It lands on the top of my hair. The foam burns the skin it touches, leaving pink patches. I stand bare, tender, and uncomfortable. Spurts of air come through the pipes before letting out a sporadic spray of water. This is my chance to scrub as fast as I can to get the sanitizer foam off before the water stops.

I gasp as the foam comes in contact with the soft pink scar on my hand. I clench it tightly. I have to bear through the pain and get the foam off fast. It will be worse if I let some of the foam stay on me to give me a chemical burn rash. I only have so many bathing times for the week, and the bathhouse is always full.

For the last few days, I've been letting myself recuperate. As much as I don't like to admit it, the Lovindian was right. I was neglecting my rest. It's odd that I still haven't seen Samuel since being back, but I'm happy that he wasn't at the transporter bay waiting for Emmanuel and me. The two of us are involved in too much. He doesn't need to be seen with us after a trip like that.

The water cuts off. I can still hear foam bubbles popping in my hair. I'll have to try to get the rest out in the sink. At least I haven't used up my apartment water rations. A wave of heat comes next to dry me. I clench my teeth. Why's it always so damned hot? Dry at last, I wrap the shirt around me. Purple bruises run width-ways across my ribs as a constant reminder of what happened to Saul. I try not to look as I tie the shirt in a knot.

My feet, which were missed by the dryer, feel wet and uncomfortable in the cloth wrap. I pad awkwardly through the walkways. A flash of red catches my eye, and I look up to see a small, triangular flag fluttering on a clothesline. I look on and see another and another. It's surprising to see the people of Yalk doing something so bold. Why had they opposed the Talkers so vigorously but are now willing to fly Emmanuel's mark of rebellion? If the Gromptu catch on, everyone flying a red flag is risking their lives, as well as their family's.

The sound of a bugger hitting a swatter catches my attention. It's shortly followed by raucous laughter. I hadn't even realized I was walking toward the court. I just wanted to move around some to dry my legs.

"You're letting the scrabs win, dammit!"

"Emmanuel! You're freaking them out! They're never going to learn that way."

"Scrap 'em then. Damned if I care whether they learn to play."

I use the laundry hanging from the lowest clothesline for cover to eavesdrop. A group of small children struggles to balance buggers on their swatters. Samuel rotates through the group like a worried mother, straightening their balance where he can and fixing their hold on their swatters. Emmanuel rests comfortably and unhelpfully against the wall. The children vary in height and age, but they are all similar in appearance. In Unit B, it's very common for the people to have dark hair and copper skin. All of them are lean and boney. The mash packets have the nutrients that we need, but they don't make it easy to gain weight. There are still people like Saul who naturally carry weight better, but the majority of young Yalkians are scrawny from activity.

The smallest of the four children has a particularly strangely shaped bread roll. He wobbles from foot to foot to keep it from falling, much to Emmanuel's amusement.

"The boy looks like he's got sand scretters in his pants!" Emmanuel hoots.

The boy turns red, and the bugger goes flying to the ground. Emmanuel points and laughs wildly.

"Scat off, Emmanuel!" A bread roll breaks over his head, and he laughs, rubbing his head.

"Mag!" Samuel yells.

"You scat off too! You're worse than mother! Let's start a game!" the little voice hollers.

"Maggie, we aren't ready for a game yet!" one of the little boys complains.

"That's fine! He can play with me."

"Who?" Samuel asks.

"The Scrab behind the sheet. He's hiding like a creep anyway; he might as well lose to me."

I flush red, coming out embarrassedly. Samuel's eyes widen, and Emmanuel matches the frown of the little girl. Side-by-side, the girl is a clone of Emmanuel. I cringe. The last thing the world needed was two of them. I look again. The girl is younger and petite, but that face...

"Jacob! Where have you been? I haven't seen you in forever!" Samuel runs toward me.

Emmanuel shoots me a quick glance. Of course, I'm not going to tell him about that!

"I've been busy," I say half-heartedly.

Now all three of them have matching frowns. I would have done better to keep hiding behind the cot sheet.

"Alright, I'm ready to play," she says, directing the statement to me.

Maggie grabs a bugger from the struggling boy beside her. The boy opens his mouth to say something but shuts it quickly. Even if they all look similar, the three siblings are nothing alike. This girl is a terror! For some reason, I want to play her. I smile at her narrowed eyes. She's so serious.

"Mag, Jacob doesn't have to play with you," Samuel says cautiously.

"Scat that, he was the one snooping on us anyways!" Her dark brows meet above her eyes.

"It's alright, Sam; I'll play." I gesture for his swatter.

Samuel's eyes widen in surprise, "You can't even play the game with two players!" Samuel sighs but reluctantly hands it over.

Maggie's grin almost makes me regret the decision. I bend into a wide crouch, and she pops the bugger up into the air. Out of the corner of my eye, I see Emmanuel smirk, and I start to feel a little uneasy. Samuel herds the other children back to watch. I easily tap it above her head. She rolls her dark brown eyes that match her siblings' as if I've done something childish and unimpressive. I chuckle teasingly.

As long as I bounce it above her head, there's nothing she

can do. I ease toward the goal, and I hear the others break into laughter. The laughter suddenly stops. I'm sent reeling forward as the wind is knocked out of me from behind. The girl is latched on to my back. She uses her unclothed toes to climb up my back, and I stagger to my knees. The bugger pops up above us and she propels herself up by jumping off my shoulders. I scramble up from my knees, laughing wildly.

Maggie sticks out her tongue, tapping the bugger up and down without looking. I dive toward it to snatch it back. She's faster. Maggie shoots the bugger up. I realize what she's doing, and I can definitely stop her, but something stops me. She jumps, and her thick, black hair swishes so that I almost don't see when she spikes the bugger.

It just misses the bottom rim of the circle. My heart drops. I wish she had hit it right in the middle of that open eye. Maggie huffs, turning to face the other kids.

"Who has another bugger?" she demands, unfazed.

Maggie's bugger is reduced to bread crumbs beneath the goal. The boys, who have probably gone through a lot of trouble to steal their rolls, hide them quickly behind their backs. Maggie huffs again and stomps back in the direction of their apartment.

"Later, creep!"

I guess that's me. I smile. There was a moment there that I felt like a kid again.

"Quite the lady Maan's raised," Emmanuel mumbles, picking dirt from between his big toes and rolling it between his finger and his thumb. Samuel takes a deep breath, closing his eyes for a minute. I wonder if their Maan gave up after Samuel. Maybe Emmanuel behaved so poorly that she stopped trying to raise them properly.

"Sam, what are you doing teaching these kids Scrab's Ball?" I ask.

The boys slowly wander off now that Maggie's gone, and Samuel stands with his head in a hand.

"They asked me to!" he states with a bit of pride shining through.

"That's not true," Emmanuel says, hooking his pinky toe to clean it properly. "They asked me, but I said no."

"Then they asked me." Samuel turns red.

"No, then you offered to teach them."

"Is that how it went?" Samuel shakes his head laughing.

"You're a real sucker for Maggie, ya know? She's not sweet." He flicks toe-dirt toward him.

"She has her strengths," Samuel says embarrassedly.

"Like me?" Emmanuel smirks devilishly. I roll my eyes.

"You have—" Samuel starts, but Emmanuel interrupts.

"Don't, you'll make me blush." He holds up a hand sarcastically and hops up from the ground on both feet at once. "Sam, you should probably return those spatulas." Emmanuel points at the spatulas that the kids left on the ground.

"Great, their maans will know exactly what we've been doing," Samuel groans.

"Yes, you're all such rebels," Emmanuel says, rolling his eyes. Samuel takes him seriously and blushes, rushing to pick up each one.

"We can help you return them." I laugh.

Emmanuel shoots me a glare for offering up his help. I grin at him.

"Are you sure?" Samuel asks.

"We're sure." I smile.

Emmanuel grumbles something under his breath.

"Helping you is worth about two sacks of rice; don't you think, Samuel?" I say innocently.

"Huh?" Samuel looks at me like I've gone crazy.

Emmanuel goes red, and I put my arm around him. He scowls at me but doesn't resist. It's about time this Scrab helps Samuel with something. Samuel stops before an apartment building.

"It's the third floor, door five."

"Emmanuel's got the first one," I smirk. He shoots me a deadly glare that says if I keep this up, I won't just have the Gromptu to worry about.

"Oh, okay." Samuel looks at us a little confusedly and hands Emmanuel the bouquet of spatulas. "I'm not sure which one is Aaron's, so just show her the bunch of them."

Emmanuel stomps loudly up the metal stairs without holding onto the railing and pounds on the apartment door. The door slides open with a smack, and a large woman fills the space. I see Emmanuel take a step back. I can't hear what is said, but Emmanuel leans back against the railing as if falling over is preferable to a confrontation with the person in the doorway.

Smack!

There's a loud clambering as Emmanuel rushes down the metal steps. The stairway creaks and sways as he rushes down. I explode into laughter. A red shape blossoms on his cheek that unmistakably resembles a spatula.

"Emmanuel? What did she say? Is she mad?" Samuel worries.

"What did she say? Who gives a damn what she said! She clobbered me with that swatter over a damned bread roll! That beast is half Rodavian at least!" he rages.

"Oh, I hope we didn't get Aaron in trouble; maybe I should just get Maggie to return them to the boys," Samuel says disappointedly.

"Scrap them all!" Emmanuel storms away.

I wipe the tears from my eyes. My stomach hurts from laughter. Samuel watches me curiously.

"You know, Jacob, you seem kind of different." His eyebrows bunch together.

"Yeah?" I've finally recovered.

"Yeah. It's like you're happier, or something." Somehow he looks worried even when saying something like that.

Am I happier? I do feel like I've been laughing more, but I'm not sure that it's that. I'm still angry about Saul, and I still dream about Keren. Maybe Samuel's just imagining it. A little, red triangle hangs on the clothesline above us. I stare at it.

No—he's right. There is something different. I have been achieving things lately. Emmanuel has been achieving things. I've been feeling a change in the air on Yalk. The feeling of burning activity.

"I just like keeping busy," I say.

"Yeah." His smile falters. "Just make sure you come and say 'hello' once in a while. It's been a while since I've seen you, friend."

Friends. I've only ever had siblings. I vaguely remember Saul calling me over for the first time to play Scrab's Eye Ball. At the time, I thought of myself as just the extra player they needed, but I guess I haven't been just an extra player for a while now.

"Were we all friends?" I ask.

"Huh?"

"Us, Emmanuel, and Saul?"

"Of course!" Samuel laughs uncomfortably, "What else would we be?"

My chest swells. I wonder if Saul felt the same way. I guess I'll never know.

"Thanks, Samuel. I promise that from now on I'll make time to see you," I say it and I mean it.

"Are you headed off again soon?" he asks.

"Tomorrow morning," I say honestly.

Samuel smiles. "I'll see you when you get back."

I nod at him. "I'll see you soon."

28

Chapter 28

"From the articles of the Council:

Year: 2383

Subject: Ana Battinson"

"Fifty-three Eterns were identified yesterday in New Texas. The arrests were made this morning by the Mars Base Authorities, but the suspects were not held for long. Authorities were forced to release forty-nine of the suspects due to the lack of an official holding facility and insufficient proof. What on Earth is happening on Mars?"

Kenna Lloyd smiled at Eddie Baxter as a way of handing off the story. Eddie continued in her place, "You can't help but wonder, Kenna, if the civil rights activists might have had a little pull in this decision. As many of you know, the civil rights group calling themselves 'Progress for Privacy' argues that the new police scanning systems, meant to keep the citizens safe, are an invasion of privacy! Another of their arguments made against the scan is that it cannot be relied on alone as proof of a person's humanity. If we choose to accept their view, then the scanners are insufficient alone to make arrests. They support these accusations with experiments done by Grennel Technology, which shows that the scans are only 91 percent accurate in identifying Eterns."

Kenna cut in. "My goodness, just imagine! You could be a law-abiding citizen and get arrested just because your biology is too similar to that of a known criminal! Arrested for unlucky biology; just imagine!"

Ana stepped out of the door. She had unlucky biology once. Three out of five people contracted Scanthirin Sickness. Seventy or so years after Ana was made into an Etern, they found a real cure, but by then, it was just done for the hell of it. How they praised them, though, the best and brightest minds of Battinson University. Why did it matter? Children were vaccinated with her father's vaccine at birth, and there hadn't been an outbreak of Scanthirin since. Every Scan which hadn't been transferred by Battinson or by crazed Eterns invading hospitals, had already died out by then.

Memories of her first life were the most disintegrated for Ana. It was the life that gave her existence, her most significant life, and yet it was so distant. The brain was not meant to store so many lifetimes, and she felt that with every switch, she lost a little more of her beginning. The times before Scanthirin flaked away, and the times shortly after were mostly gone with it. Derrick remembered it more, but he was either losing it too or didn't want to talk about it anymore. Once he had sat with her and talked about it with vibrant passion. He had focused his enthusiasm for life on her rather than focusing on the absence of people in his past lives. They had used each other as constants in a constantly changing world, but over time they, too, had changed too much to recognize.

The fog was so dense that the door to her apartment was gone after she had walked down just seven stairs. She sat down, watching headlights come and go in the street below. The headlights barely seeped through the fog, reminding her of butter soaking faintly through the other side of a piece of toast. She remembered the last real conversation they had had before she finally accepted that he had grown tired—tired of her and life.

"Which lifetime did you become such a cynic?"

She was frustrated when she had said it, and he had slowly grown to be cruel. His response affected her so deeply that she had continued to ask herself it for eighty or so more years.

"In which lifetime did you?"

Had she become a cynic? Which lifetime did she suppose she had? She didn't know, but she had stopped wondering why it was that Derrick married so often in his lifetimes. He had frequently made her a sort of adulteress to these other women. He never lived with her, though he easily could. No, he purposefully chose men who were already married or engaged and called it necessity that he chose them and necessity that he stay with the women to play his part. His excuse that it was necessity suddenly stopped being real to her. The truth was that he had grown to resent her because he resented himself, and after living so many years, they had become too much the same.

If he wouldn't be with her, then why didn't he just grow old with one of them? The fact that she knew the answer didn't make it any easier. The truth was that after living or existing for so long, it was hard to imagine yourself just fizzling out like a human. How could an end like theirs be satisfactory when you had been immortal? The transfer sickness would eventually take hold before they could become suicidal. They were trapped in the cycle of life like a phoenix bursting into flames, never to feel the cool flow of death seeping in to erase its pain.

Ana had missed her window for finding someone to grow old with while she had been holding out for Derrick to commit to her. It wouldn't be long now until someone discovered her. Whether it was the Eterns wanting to make her a member for her father's work or the police department wanting to get her into custody, it hardly mattered. She smiled, and tears wet her lashes; if that thought alone didn't prove her a cynic, it at least proved her a pessimist.

At some point, she had scrunched her legs up to her body and aches had formed in her lower back and between her shoulder blades. Unfurling herself, she laid back uncomfortably, counting the number of steps that her body took up—six, six steps. They were damp from the morning mist and her hair clung to them, adding to her general discomfort rather than easing it. She peeled her head up and propped herself onto her elbows, forcing herself, once again, to stare out into the fog.

It was still as thick and smeary as before, seconds had not changed its form, but this time, something was moving through it. The bud was smaller than usual, and it made her unsure, at first, that it was even a bud. It was spinning through the air much like a bullet would in slow motion. This motion allowed the bud to be smaller because a single sensor, rather than a dozen, could sweep the area. Ana reached out to it, and after confirming her identity, the bud glided out to land on her index finger.

The device delivered messages one-way. Wei said it was because adding a mic would make the bud larger and more noticeable. In private, Derrick admitted to her that Wei didn't trust her to talk only in secure areas; Wei was probably right. Ana placed the bud in her ear and tapped it four times.

"Stay indoors today."

She waited for more, but it had started to beep. She removed the device from her ear and placed it on the step. That was it. Wei had sent her one of her stealthiest buds, through the fog, just to tell her to stay inside. The bud suddenly condensed and became a fleck of useless metal. She stood up, noting the large wet spots on the back of her pants from where she had been sitting. The material stuck to her ridiculously, and she let out an aggravated sigh, "'Stay inside!' she says. No problem!"

Chapter 29

"From the Articles of the Council:

Year: 2383

Subject: Derrick Webber"

Her long skirt swished around her ankles, barely kissing the tops of her bare feet. He imagined that, someday, Katie would pad around her, hindering the way she glided through the small kitchen. Her twirling was a little messy as she occasionally misplaced a foot, but it was charming still. There was music, but it wasn't like the old music. The singer never strained with emotion, never cried out for relief, or rejoiced with revelation. The singer was nameless because it was actually a combination of vocals from many artists. Computer programs combined vocals to make sure that every tone was perfect. The voice had the delicacy of a coffee house singer and the strength of a powerhouse vocalist. There was no note, high or low, that the voice struggled to attain, and by using slight inflections, the voice could be any genre.

They made it into a philosophy. When they had killed the artist, they had killed the soul of music in Derrick's opinion.

Music wasn't meant to be perfect—it was just an expression of an individual's passion. The young had never known true music, and even the old humans were young by his standards. His life was so long, and often so dull. When he listened to music, he wanted to feel the passions of others, especially in the times which he felt passionless. Hearing the struggle of others made Derrick more comfortable with his own.

"Let's go out for the day, Adam."

He raised his gaze from the bottom of her skirt to meet her eyes. She was so vibrant that for a moment he allowed himself to get caught up in it.

"Where to?"

"I don't know," she laughed, twirling in the light that came in from the window above the sink. "Let's just go."

She came and sat beside him, taking his hand as she did. She smiled contentedly, pressing her lips against the back of his hand and then resting her chin on the top of his knuckles.

"Please," she mouthed.

Wei had told him that he would have to decide within a week. That was four days ago now. She was waiting for an answer, and every moment she had to wait was another moment she couldn't finalize the plans. The Eterns were posed to attack Mars Base. When they attacked, no alarms would be sounded. By Wei's calculations, enough hidden Eterns were posted on Mars Base in positions of power that the battle would be over before it even started. There was a meeting in an hour, and if he didn't show, Wei would know that he wasn't going with them.

He should tell Candace that he had been called into work. He should go now; it was better than naively waiting for the police to kick in the door days after the others had reached safety.

What would that do to Candace, seeing him towed away by the police? Derrick had never been caught betraying someone before. Could he stand to look in her eyes and admit to the murder he had committed?

"I don't know, Can," he whispered.

Her eyebrows pushed together, her mouth crinkling at the corners. She pulled away a little but kept hold of his hand. "What are you thinking?" She was timid—frightened.

"I have a hard decision to make."

"Tell me."

"I can't. It's too hard of a thing."

"I'll make it easier." She leaned over, being all gentleness with the kiss she placed.

His head was muddled, and some part of him enjoyed the lack of clarity. He was always so clear; he had to be. Ever since Wei had told him about the attack, he had felt helpless. It was the same feeling he had felt after waking up the first time. His limbs were phantom, his body phantom, and his mind floating through a ghost. They called it Transfer Sickness. It affected each Etern a little differently, but every Etern undoubtedly had it.

Candace was waiting for him. Her eyes were watching him with extraordinary intensity. There were not too many people who had ever looked at him with such concern. He was sure Ana had, but not for a very long time. He had a crazy yearning just to tell her all of it. She deserved to know. Of all the humans he had encountered, she was deserving of the truth, but how could he justify giving her the burden?

After all these years, he had thought he'd known himself! He had never been discovered because he was never foolish enough to confide his identity to anyone. Yet, here he was, on the verge of a huge mistake, and hardly able to keep himself from divulging it all to this very young woman. No, he couldn't; it was as dangerous as it was selfish.

"I have to go to work," he finally said. The decision was out there, and he stood up to finalize it.

"No." She shook her head firmly.

"What? Candace, don't be childish; I have to go to work."

"No," she was calm, "I'm not being childish. For some reason, I feel like if I let you go out that door, you won't be coming back. You've been so distant for the last couple of days. Tell me I'm wrong." Her hands were on her hips and her lips drew into a tight line. "I know it. I know you."

Derrick didn't say anything. She was strongly intuitive.

Her forehead scrunched. "Tell me I'm wrong," she whispered painfully.

"You don't know me." He didn't know why he said it, but its effect was immediate.

"Let me." Her hands held his face. "Let me."

Tumultuous conflict. Her eyes were brown, so deeply brown.

"I don't care what it is, Adam. If it means you stay, I don't care."

For the first time in a long time, his heart began to race. His mouth was open, words ready to spill out and destroy them both. Could he stand to look into her face and admit his murderous nature? He had a perfect view to see her disgust, then hate, then, then what else? He couldn't imagine what else. She would pull quickly away from him and hate him. He had, after all, killed her Adam and taken his place.

Should he let her decide for him? Would she tell him to leave or call the Norfolk Police Department? If she did, he hoped he wouldn't stop her. If she tried to make a call, would his transfer sickness kick in and the mania cause him to hurt her? He started to sweat.

She leaned her mouth up to his, and he accepted it. Her breath was soft, and she was soft too. It always surprised him how soft a kiss could be. He wasn't sure that he loved her but having a real human next to him helped to make him feel some of his lost humanity. Derrick had tried countless times to end his life, but the psychotic pressure of transfer sickness prevented him. He waited for an unpredictable accident to happen but his existence persisted. He wished to ask this human, this little moral compass, for her opinion on whether he should continue.

"Please, Adam, please tell me what's wrong. She begged."

"Last summer, things were very difficult for us," he started.

She nodded encouragingly.

"Last summer, July 26, 2842, Adam Gavins committed suicide."

Her eyebrows lifted. "Metaphorically?"

He shook his head. "No Candace, not metaphorically."

"I—I don't understand; you aren't making any sense."

"I know, I know I don't! You're so good, Candace!"

He grabbed her face with his hands. Why was he like this? He had cut and run enough times before. She didn't matter in the end. He could leave on his own will now, or he could grow old, and just as he came close to peace, the transfer sickness would grab him up. He'd leave her either way. They couldn't die together. It wasn't a possibility.

"Stop, Adam, you're upsetting me! Just explain it to me. Explain it to me; I love you." Her voice was quiet like she was talking Katie down from one of her fits.

"Candace—Adam is dead." He was shocked by his own

words.

He ran his hands up and down her arms, pulling her slightly. He had to tell her now, if ever. He had said so much already, and she was hanging to him, confused, scared. She was searching his face, not understanding. Her lips twitched downwards, and he wondered if for a flicker of a second she saw the truth.

"I'm sorry." He shook his head, backing away. "I'm sorry, this isn't right. I'm not acting right. I have to go now."

"No, no," she was backing up, "no, no, you can't do this I thought we were better! Are you leaving?"

"I have to," he said firmly.

Her eyes had become very wide, filling with tears; she shook her head and they spilled loose. He had betrayed her. Derrick had betrayed her, and she knew it. She didn't know how severely he had done it, but she knew he had done it nonetheless. Adam had betrayed her as soon as he started popping prescription pain pills. Derrick had seen the signs in him and stalked him. On a particularly bad day, he had switched the pain pills to sugar pills. Adam had betrayed her when he decided to take all of those sugar pills at once. Derrick had watched him lie back in his car and wait for death to take him, and it did, but just not in the way Adam had expected. It was Adam who decided to give up life and to give up Candace, but it had been Derrick who had promised to never leave her.

"You lied," she choked.

Hurt mixed with anger in her troubled brown eyes. Her face contorted and grew red; she covered a sob with her palm. She gasped, and that single sharp inhale of air seemed to poison her. She convulsed and collapsed onto the side of the couch. "You lied," she repeated. "You said you would stay. You lied."

263

The words came through coughs of pain; she clutched her throat and chest as if she could soothe the pain by holding where it hurt. Katie woke up from her nap and started to scream.

"I lied," he whispered, but she heard.

It was transitioning from late spring to early summer. There was a thick fog outside, moist and unsettling. Perhaps if it had been crisp and blue, he would have been able to breathe in the air confident of his decision, but instead, it was brooding and heavy. Even the weather hated him.

30

Chapter 30

"Jacob! There's still more to see. Why are you coming back so soon?"

With eyes closed, all I see is the same melting sensation that I saw the first time I tried to listen to Jana's memories. I'm not back in the room with the Lovindian, and I'm not in anyone's memories. My body shakes with sobs. I feel like a child again. I remember when I was just beginning to toddle; my mother would come running to me when I'd fall. To calm me down, she'd mix sweetened mash and thick cream in a bowl and give me big spoonfuls that we couldn't afford.

That was before she cracked. That was before she stopped holding out her arms when her children tried to walk. That was when she could still choose to comfort a crying infant instead of walking the corridors. That was before my elder brother, Isaac, disappeared and my father left her for a younger woman. The memories I've tried so hard to repress come flooding painfully back. I choke on my own tears. I see a young man whose face is so much like my own. I don't want to remember him— don't want to remember what happened.

That night, the light grew dim in the halls of Unit C, and she set down the crying infant Keren carelessly on a too-high cot.

"Mom?" I called.

But all I saw was her dark-red hair disappearing through the door. She didn't even close it to shield us from what lay beyond. Only a handful of years older than my sister, I rushed to her aid. Her little, pale hands reached up to me, her face growing red with anger. I kissed her little face, again and again, rocking her from side-to-side. It was uncomfortable for the both of us at first but we had no choice. She wanted her mother or the perfect older brother that was stripped away from us but she was left with me instead. We belonged to one another.

It was my job to protect her. To keep her happy always. I'm her big brother.

"I left her. I left her," I moan.

"Candace lived a long time ago. She's been gone for a very long time, Jacob. You didn't leave her. It's just the memories confusing your mind."

The Lovindian doesn't understand. It doesn't matter that I didn't leave Candace; I'm guilty of the crime just the same. My mother played her role until they took my brother away. After that, when the lights went out, she'd disappear unfeelingly into the dark. That's how I knew—that's how I knew she wasn't really there anymore.

I told myself that I would never fall to the pull of the walkers. I would never be like them, but I've walked just the same. I can't even resent them. I can't feel anything toward them—just Keren. Keren, who never knew a mother who didn't walk. Keren, who was dropped on the nearest cot, like a doll baby, when the lights went dark. Keren, who secretly stashed extra baunti when she submitted food orders so I could have a pretty, silver instrument to play to her when she was scared.

"Play for me," she'd say bravely, even as she shook with fear. Even as the stampede slammed their bodies up against the apartment walls on the bottom floor where we lived.

"I left her," I groan pitifully.

"Please focus, Jacob! You're being sucked into your own memories."

Hot tears burn my cheeks. My consciousness grows too weak to hold myself in this world. I start to feel the pull of the next memory. My mind feels as if it's slowly sucked into a tube and regurgitated out the other end.

31

Chapter 31

"From the Articles of the Council:

Year: 2383

Subject: Derrick Webber"

The air was warm and thick as it always seemed to be between tall buildings in the city. Wei had heard word from the Eterns that the coup on Mars Base had happened three days ago, and as she predicted, the humans didn't seem to know that it had happened. Derrick looked into the sky and wondered just how many Ex-Mars Base Authority war class ships were hovering just outside the atmosphere. It didn't have to be many, since most of the Earth's ships were currently out where they should be, in space, and not near home to protect against attackers. Mars Base made up the majority of Earth's ships, except for private-owned crafts. If the Martian Eterns had managed to get just three warships off of Mars, then they would probably have enough firepower to make any other Earth craft in space surrender to them.

Wei had admitted to Derrick that the Eterns had contacted her more than twenty years ago, boldly claiming that they knew her true identity. Wei continued as head of Grennel Technologies by passing down her company to a partner and then feigning sickness and transferring bodies while the partner visited her on her "death bed." To outsiders, the way the previous owners of her company died just after passing it down to their inheritor wasn't suspicious, but the Eterns were more adept at finding the trends of their kind than humans were.

It was only a matter of time before the Eterns contacted her—power was strongly attractive for them, and Wei had a surplus. When the Eterns had unearthed that Laura Grennel, and Grennel Technologies, had been taken over by one of their own kind, they had automatically reached out to her for help. From there, Laura Grennel, or Wei, had developed a tenuous relationship with the Eterns.

One thing was for sure, ever since learning about the Eternian invasion, Derrick couldn't stop staring at the clouds. Every once in a while, he would see a shadow cast along the sidewalk and look up expecting to see a United States Government war class ship. He usually ended up waving awkwardly to the driver of a P.F.V., Private Flying Vehicle.

Derrick wavered at the street corner, wondering if he should cross to the other side of the road, or stay on the path he was going. He decided to cross the street and then cut over about three blocks down to get back to his hotel room. He did mindless things. He did mindless things and could not keep from looking at the sky.

It wasn't fear that he experienced but inevitability. Somehow, this was worse. In considering the sky, he was considering whether he was ready or not for his long existence on Earth to come to an end. For a moment, he felt the fragility

269

of life such as he had not felt since his first life. Even for him, there was an inevitable end. Wei had said there didn't have to be; he could have a new beginning.

His backpack bounced a little as he walked, and the contents pressed uncomfortably into his lower back. He stared up at the sky. A cloud filled with an intense gray as a massive ship glided above it. The darkness passed, and the cloud appeared as white once more. Derrick shivered. He waited for sirens to blare off in the street and the panic to begin. The ship went unnoticed. It could have been a trade ship or a government ship; it really didn't matter. It was either under Eternian control at this point or soon to be.

A woman prodded at her child with a shopping bag. She didn't actually say anything to the boy because she was using a Murmur. The device came in various colors but was a form of latex technology, or Lay-Tech, which fit over the corner of someone's mouth. Fashionable people had fun matching them with the color of their hair or their outfits. The Murmur allowed people to merely mouth what they wanted to say when taking calls. It was considered polite to talk to people in this manner.

The woman nudged the kid forward too hard with her shopping bag, and he fell forward onto the sidewalk. She showed some kind of a maternal instinct by turning off the Murmur long enough to try to bend over in her long, spandex dress to fish around for her child. Every time she managed to grab his arm, her bags would swing around and hit him on the head and throw him into the sidewalk once more. Derrick's eyes met the boy's just before he was thrown into the sidewalk again.

He looked away as he passed. They weren't all like that—humans today. Derrick was reminded of Candace cooing softly over Katie as she rocked her to sleep. There was still the good and the bad as there had always been. He knew which category he belonged to and didn't pretend to be pretentious. He was the worst of all.

Derrick felt the flecks of metal leftover in his pocket from the buds Wei had sent to him throughout the day. Each one had an address, which he had listened to and then removed the bud from his ear before it condensed. Finally, he had gone to the last address, and all that was left was to return to his room.

The room he had chosen was in a bed and breakfast in the historic part of the city. There were only three rooms, and the woman who owned it hardly ever made an appearance. No one greeted him as he walked in; there was no suspicious manager glaring at him from behind a check-in counter. Derrick walked upstairs to his room and shut the door.

He unzipped the backpack and spilled the contents roughly across the short coffee table, knocking over a thin-necked flower vase. He had spent most of the afternoon walking into different areas of the city to get the random objects scattered around the table. Wei couldn't risk having someone guessing what the pieces were for, so she had each piece of the assembly made at different facilities. She wasn't careless like Wall, whose parts they desperately tried to distance themselves from.

He pulled out the notebook from his hidden jacket pocket and used a part of the weapon to hold the page open. It didn't look much like his drawing. For starters, it was much smaller. The end was a thin, cylindrical barrel that fit inside what would generically be called a chamber. Also in his inner jacket pocket, he retrieved a package that was somehow naturally keeping itself very cold. He was told not to handle it without protective gloves, which he hurriedly put on. The holding chamber was shaped rather awkwardly like a small grenade. It popped in easily between the handgrip and the barrel.

He loosely held it in his hands. Wall was right; Derrick could choose to call it by whatever name he wanted, but it didn't change the fact that it was a gun. There would be consequences to this. He sighed deeply and tucked it back into his pocket with the notebook.

With the deed finished and the gun put away, he allowed himself to relax a little. He recited the address that Wei's last bud had supplied him with: "157 New Standing Road." Good, he had remembered; he relaxed a little more. His eyes started to droop, and the floral comforter seemed to bait him. Maybe a quick nap.

"Time?" he asked the Automated.

There was no answer. The bed and breakfast clearly couldn't afford a very sensitive Automated, or maybe—. He scanned the room and found an early "push to ask" Automated remote on the nightstand. It had been a very long time since he had seen a remote like it. "You've gotten cushy, old man," he chastised himself. Derrick pressed down the button and repeated loudly, "Time?"

"Four forty-seven."

No time for a nap.

157 New Standing Road. He still remembered.

It was in the newer, renovated end of Norfolk City. He was going to have to take a rail car. The rail car system in Norfolk was called "The Tide." Sometimes as he stood waiting for his car, he imagined that he was just going to jump in and let it carry him wherever it liked, like a giant wave. He supposed that was the thought behind the name.

157 New Standing Road was, to say the least, not what he had expected. The building took up a little less than half of the entire block it was situated on. He couldn't see the top, and it was for good reason. 157 New Standing Road was the location of "The Luxury of Nature Day Spa." The outside of the building was a fresh seafoam-green color, and through the massive glass windows, you could see the outline of an enormous pine tree. Derrick sighed; this was a stupid idea.

The doors slid open, and he was overwhelmed by the instant heat of the corridor. A light misting of artificial rain sprayed him as he walked through an assortment of plants. The second set of glass doors opened, and the temperature was more bearable. After taking a deep breath, he then immediately sneezed.

"Oh, sir, I'm sorry about that!" A tissue was handed to him. "Do you have any pollen allergies that you are aware of?"

Derrick indignantly blew his nose into the tissue and looked at the woman who had given it to him. Her hair was peach-colored and she wore only a thin, coral, sheer-like material, which was wrapped around her in ways he couldn't comprehend.

"Of course I have pollen allergies, almost every human does," he growled at the pixie.

The woman, without asking permission, wiped a pale, yellowish substance across the bridge of his nose. Derrick, startled as he was, swatted her away quickly and tried to rub the stuff off of his face.

"Now, sir! Don't do that, or you'll be disturbing yourself and the others for the duration of your stay with unpleasant sneezing!"

He stopped and apologized as the woman collected her composure. She stroked her hair, and a remarkable piece of latex technology on the palm of her hand pulled the hair follicles back into place as she petted. It occurred to him that that level of Lay-Tech would only be available to one of Wei's employees. She had to own the building. All the technology he saw before him was thanks to her inventive team and wealth. The spa was a great way to intrigue rich customers with the new and mind-boggling products, such as the hair tamer that he had just witnessed.

"Please give me your name, sir, so I can get you to your appointment."

"Adam, Adam Gavins."

The woman tapped the matching coral Murmur on her ear and mouthed his name into it. She nodded once and then turned to him, smiling very broadly. His previous insult to her was instantly forgotten.

"Come right this way now; Mrs. Grennel will see you immediately."

Derrick followed the woman, or rather, followed the material of her dress that rippled and hung behind her on the floor as she walked. They turned a corner, and he instantly felt a sense of immense space. Immediately he knew why the building was so tall. A massive tree, the incredible centerpiece of the room, stretched up and beyond where he could see. He noted that it was not a pine, like he had initially thought it was from outside the building, but instead some type of mixed-breed which was likely created to fill the room. The tree was as tall as a California Redwood and the branches were as wistful as a Japanese maple's. Thick wisteria vines hung down from every open space.

Derrick stopped and inhaled deeply; he wondered if they enhanced the scent of the room artificially or if the plants actually emitted such an incredible smell. The room itself was giant. Derrick couldn't see any sign of rooms or doors, but instead every wall was covered with panels which created the illusion of infinite space. He looked for a flaw in the creation, but the artistry appeared to be seamless.

"If only such a place actually existed," he breathed. "This planet might be worth staying on."

"But it does exist, Derrick!"

Wei came up from behind him and wrapped an arm around his shoulders. She was wearing a similar garment to the woman who had led Derrick into the room. He shrank away from her embrace to turn and face her.

"So we must not have long."

"What do you mean?" she pouted.

"You used my name."

"Ah, well, no, we don't have much time at all. I figured this was as good of a place as any to appreciate our final days here."

He could think of so many better places that he had experienced in his days on Earth, which he would like to see again. It was just like Wei to want to spend her final days in a place she had created. Nothing on Earth was ever good enough for her as it was.

"Also," Wei continued, "this place has the advantage of being mine. We can speak moderately freely here. Every person employed in this building is one of us."

Derrick looked back toward where the other woman had disappeared. That made sense; many Eterns had a habit of picking particularly beautiful people as their subjects.

"Where are Wall and Ana?" he asked.

"Shhh!" Wei's eyes flashed angrily. "Never use her name! Especially not now! Eterns or humans, she will always be an outcast because of her father."

"How so?" He asked.

"Whether they want to burn her at the stake or put her on a pedestal, neither are something she, or we, desire. We are forever a neutral party and not part of the coup."

"I'll remember that, but where are they?"

"Wall is gathering a few trusted friends, and she is over there enjoying a remarkable view of the lake."

Derrick rolled his eyes at this. They didn't have any trusted friends, and the lake was an illusion. When did they start to live in such a fantasy? Rather, when had they started to embrace rather than reject it? A hundred years ago? Is that when it had become necessary, or was it just when society started to see reality as primitive and undesirable? Wei would say that this was reality because she had made it so. Was that how it worked? He didn't feel it was.

"You are here, Derrick; you've chosen to be here."

"You don't need to tell me," he growled.

He waved her away and moved in the direction she indicated Ana would be, but Wei irritatingly caught him first by the wrist.

"I think I do," she hissed.

A heat welled up within him, and the headache which he had been experiencing since he had woken up in the morning suddenly throbbed sharply. He pulled his wrist from her, but she knew he would and released her hold just as he pulled. Wei always won.

Ana rested her back against one of the trees, which had to have been strategically placed by the lake for this purpose.

There was something in the way that she swished her long, thin legs through the water that made something in his chest stir. Even with her so characteristically cold and authoritative exterior, Derrick was never able to identify Wei immediately when she got a new face. Ana was different. She was, and had always been. She carried herself in a light and youthful way, especially when she thought no one was watching. He would always know her, no matter what form she took.

He must have made a sound, or maybe she had simply sensed his nearness to her, because she turned and smiled. Lifting one hand off the ground, she beckoned him to come closer. His anger at Wei faded as he walked to stand beside her. Ana had folded up her skirt in her lap so it didn't touch the water's edge, and he fondly noted the neat way in which she had done it.

"Don't admire my legs." She grinned in an old-friend sort of way.

Derrick rolled his eyes and sat beside her, taking care to not return his eyes to her legs. She would only tease him again if he looked, and it wasn't worth watching her ever-escalating ego rise up a little more. He looked out instead at the surface of the "lake" and watched an occasional dragonfly skim down across the surface. Ana watched him smilingly but then changed into an insincere pout.

"No, no, I change my mind." She faked.

"What's that?" He laughed.

"I think you should definitely admire my legs. They are very fine, after all."

She lifted a leg out of the lake so that water slid off the top and poured down. Her skirt rose slightly as she surely had known it would, and once her leg was left only dripping, she lowered it back under the surface. It was only then that he realized the attention that he had paid this little action. She had undoubtedly absorbed even his slightest expression.

"See, Dare, that was much more fun." Her pleasure was obvious.

He grunted in response, triggering a slight chuckle from her. Instead of messing with him further, she picked up a stone off the ground and rolled it around in her palm.

"You wanna hear something funny?"

"Sure," he mumbled.

"The lake only extends out about fifteen feet in that direction." She pointed. "I was trying to skip stones and I found a flaw in Wei's program."

Ana picked up a small stone and sent it whirling across the top of the water. It only skipped once before there was a sudden burst of light, and the illusion of a lake was distorted briefly before it recovered. Derrick laughed and picked up a stone, managing to skip it twice before it hit the wall which wasn't supposed to exist.

"I guess that explains the 'No Swimming' sign," he said with a chuckle.

"It is the only place in the entire building in which you can touch the wall. Everywhere else, it is blocked by trees or vines. I was so proud to have found it." She bragged.

For a while they maliciously threw rocks across the water, competing to see who could skip it the most before it hit the wall. Ana reeled back to throw another, but her stone did not stop at the wall. Instead, it continued across the water into what was slowly turning into a sunset. Her little mouth formed an "O" of confusion before pulling into a tight, angry line of understanding. The computer had generated an image which made it appear as if the rock had continued on.

"It adapted! Damn it! Why does everything have to adapt?"

Derrick frowned. Ana clenched her fists tightly, staring out at where the rock had disappeared. Derrick followed her gaze with darkening eyes. He was angry, but he didn't reflect too hard on the reason why. He didn't need to analyze himself; Wei psychoanalyzed him enough as it was. It had been a long time since he had known himself properly. He excused this by telling himself that it was hard to remember who you were when you'd been so many people.

Ana finally unclenched her fists and two stones fell from her palms and into the edge of the water. She turned away from it and back to Derrick. Her bangs had grown longer and fell almost to her eyelashes. She brushed them away from her face angrily, and at the same time, brushed away the start of tears. Her face was red; she had re-clenched her hands.

"What are you doing, Derrick?"

"What do you mean?" he asked the question, but he knew what she meant.

"Why are you leaving with us?"

"What else would I do?"

"Don't play that." She rolled her eyes. "I know you care about Candace and the brat. You never got over Susanna, whether you'll admit it or not, but I think you've been better since you became Adam. You've been healing lately."

"What are you talking about? Ana, I don't even remember Susanna!"

"And maybe that's true, but you have always jumped right back into another marriage. You were a married man, Derrick. You were settled and happy! That's all you wanted to be! You should go back to Candace! You know I wouldn't say this if I didn't mean it."

"Anne, this is none of your business," he said sternly.

"I just want you to be happy."

"What do you know of happiness?" he snapped. "If I had wanted to settle down so badly, I would have just done it with one of the many relationships I've been in over the years."

"What do I know of happiness?" Her voice trailed away. "I don't know much about it, Derrick; you're right. Unfortunately, I do know a whole hell of a lot about sadness, and I know enough to know when people are unhappy. You, Derrick, are unhappy right now."

"Candace and Katie are better off without me. I'm neither a husband nor a father. My only true wife died when I got Scanthirin Sickness and she forced herself to be my caretaker for the duration of my near-coma. Dr. Battinson told me himself she wouldn't want to see me as I am now. Who would want someone like this?"

After that statement, Ana closed her eyes so that she didn't have to look at him. It took him a moment to realize what he had admitted. Ana was right; he had never gotten over Susanna. Maybe it wasn't her anymore that he wanted. However, the fact that he would never live a life in which was truly his, and would never return to the normality of his first life, was something that he battled with. He was non-human. There was something horribly saddening in knowing that you would never get to completely connect with a new person ever again. He could never really become open with another person, and maybe that was why, in the end, he always moved on.

He had tried so many times to be with Ana, partially because she loved him and partially because she was one of the only people that could still know him. Somewhere in the relationship, he had realized that Ana had just spent a little too much of her life asleep. She hadn't had her father for long after her awakening. Ana cut contact with her father and he passed away soon after. Dr. Battinson was assassinated not long after the Eterns had started their antics. It was a father who had done it—a man who had learned his daughter's body was walking around with another person at the controls. Derrick had always thought this somehow just.

There was something forever missing in Ana; after all, she had sacrificed her childhood to Scanthirin Sickness. Childhood gone, father gone, Ana turned to the nearest person available—Derrick. Over the years, she had learned so much from him and shared so many of his opinions that he no longer thought of her as an individual but as an extension of himself. Unfortunately, he hated himself, and over time, he grew to resent her.

However, time had once again passed. She had grown older, separate from him, and he started to feel that they had gone on different paths for long enough to make her different from him once again. For a brief moment, he almost voiced this to her, but bitterness took over first. He would never be able to let himself die; Transfer Sickness would rush adrenaline through his body until he was forced to change again. They would only go on and on until they hated each other once more.

Wei returned, making it so that conversation between Derrick and Ana was thankfully impossible. Wei had been joined by a man and a woman who were holding hands. The man was about forty and the woman was perhaps slightly younger. They seemed to be straining to make it obvious, with looks of affection toward each other, that they were a couple who were happily in love. He decided he didn't like them.

"Derrick, this is Mr. and Mrs. Gerald and Anita Cole. They are part of my engineering team and will be assisting me on my ships," she announced.

"Are we taking more than one ship?" Ana asked.

"Three of my ships will be launched tomorrow afternoon, carrying the people you see in this room, including yourselves. They're cruiser class ships, meant for relaxing and sport, not battle. They're very fast, but if we can't get past the Eternian fleet's weaponry, then we may never get to show how quick they are."

Derrick looked around him. He estimated there were only several hundred people in the room. Derrick couldn't help but feel how his fate and the fates of these other people were forcibly intertwined. Wei followed his gaze.

"These are only some of my contacts. There will be just over six hundred of us. It would be too dangerous to have everyone here," she informed him.

"I see," Derrick nodded. "Wei, how long are we going to be flying in these things?"

Wei gave the Coles a look that demanded instant privacy. Gerald gently escorted his wife away where they seemed to recognize another person who lounged by the base of the giant tree. Once it was just the three of them, Wei sighed and began her answer.

"I'm not going to lie to you two. This could very well be a suicide mission."

She paused to study their reactions, but they stayed expressionless, waiting for her to continue.

"There is enough fuel for us to last two years in space. If we get clear of the stolen Martian Base armada, we should be fine. My cruisers are the fastest known to man, and we will get out of range from their scanners fairly quickly."

"So where's the risk," Ana asked.

"I was getting to that," Wei snapped. "As it is now, we haven't located a place to land. There's nowhere that, with time, the massive space cruisers won't eventually find us. We have to settle somewhere that hasn't been charted. Which requires us traveling as far as the fuel will allow and finding resources in a relatively safe, unknown planet which can at least sort of support human life."

"What if we don't find anywhere that fits that description?" Derrick asked.

"Then we're in trouble."

32

Chapter 32

From the Articles of the Council:

Year: 2383

Subject: Derrick Webber"

"Things are so different than they were only just thirty-two hours ago. We are still in shock from the loss of life that occurred yesterday afternoon and the fighting undoubtedly continues right now. Among the men and women lost, we mourn fellow co-host Eddie Baxter who was on-scene during yesterday's attack. We encourage all humans to stay indoors. Evacuation from the city is impossible. All roads are blocked, and any private flying vehicles would risk being fired on if they attempted to flee.

"For viewers watching on a country-wide scale, it should be emphasized once more how detrimental this blow is to our military. Norfolk is a major naval base, as well as being a major airbase. We were told only three hours ago that the Eterns have assumed full control of the airbase. There are rumors that shots continue to fire at the naval base, but we cannot be sure. It is confirmed that all but one of the Mars Base war class ships have been compromised by the Eternian rebels. There is also confirmation on the loss of at least four trade ships, one of which we know is not from our planet.

"Please, I repeat, please do not go outside under any circumstances. Please sit tight and wait for the military reinforcements to arrive. I give my final message to you now, as I have been told that it is no longer safe, or possible, to keep streaming to you even from our secure location. Thank you for watching. This is Kenna Lloyd signing off and sending my heart with you on this dark day."

Derrick watched it all from his seat inside of one of Wei's reconnaissance crafts. Wei said that the vehicle they had strapped themselves into was nearly invisible to scanners. Derrick had to take her at her word for this because fifteen minutes had gone by, and he had still not felt any blast near the craft.

There was only a short silence after the video had ended. Wei gave control of the vehicle to the person beside her and stood up to lecture details of the plan a final time.

"Listen, all of you are going to have to execute your roles very quickly. When we get to the top of my building, there will be unfriendly Eterns guarding my ships. I have this remote control," she held up a small pad-like device, "which gives me the power to control the very ships that they believe to have stolen from me. They will recognize me upon arrival. We have to hope that the facade of friendship we have worked so hard to create over the last twenty years will give me enough time to distract the guards. We have less than a minute and a half for you to knock out all the communications and weapons control from this building and get to my ships positioned over the roof.

"You will have to activate the Lay-Tech on the bottom of your shoes to climb the air up to the cruisers. Step straight upward and don't look below you. I hope you had time to practice before today because your life is going to depend on it.

"Once you get on board your ships, it is imperative that one of you puts your bud into the ship's navigation systems. I have given you each a bud in case some of you are lost in the process of getting to the ships. Remember which ship you have been assigned; we can't afford to have fifteen engineers in one crew and only four in another. We will be arriving in about four minutes. Be ready."

Wei returned to her seat, and everyone remained silent. Derrick looked to Ana. She twiddled her thumbs nervously and he searched his mind for conversation.

"You never told me what you threatened Wall with to make him work on the evacuation vehicle."

Ana smiled at him.

"I threatened to tell Wei that he's the one who has been tracking her with particularly evasive buds for the past ten years."

"Why is he doing that? How did you find out?" Derrick lowered his voice.

"I didn't know until he confirmed it for me," she grinned. "It was an easy guess. He's one of the only people able to outsmart her in technology and he's the only person as obsessed with Wei as she is herself."

Derrick smirked at her answer but noticed that she had returned to fidgeting.

"Are you scared?" he asked.

"I'm mostly scared of air walking. I'm not a huge fan of

heights and I hate the feeling of falling. I don't get adrenaline junkies."

Derrick nodded understandingly. He was also nervous about the Lay-Tech stuck to his shoes.

The people involved in disabling the communications from Wei's building were already hard at work tapping away at random panels positioned throughout the craft. Ana was beside Derrick watching the rows of people hard at work. The craft itself was not large enough to be any sort of threat, but it was larger than any private flying vehicle. Derrick had never seen anything like it. Somehow, it seemed small from the outside, but the interior space was so well managed that it held well over four hundred people. This was amazing except for the fact they were all tightly bound side-by-side, elbow-to-elbow in long columns back-to-back.

Wei still had over two hundred allies working inside her building. They were to shut down the building's defense functions which could only be disabled from the interior. Their jobs were the most important and also the most dangerous. If outward communications weren't knocked out before Wei's people inside deactivated the defense perimeter and started to air climb off the roof, then the unfriendly Eterns inside would trigger the alarms and set every ship in their armada after them. They had only a very calculated minute and twenty-three seconds before they would be out of time.

Ana grabbed his arm as the craft descended onto the rooftop. Quickly, Wei hopped out of the cabin and shut the door behind her so that prying eyes would be kept away from the people inside. A microphone bud placed on Wei played her conversation with the man who ran to meet her. Meanwhile, the technicians in front of Derrick speedily tapped at their screens, feeding code to fight the defense system.

"Hi, I'm Wei Wen, the Etern who took over Laura Grennel's enterprises."

"Ma'am, we are very thankful for your cooperation, but until the fighting dies down, you cannot expect to hear from the general. Also, ma'am, you cannot land here, this area has been confiscated by the New Eternian Alliance."

"Oh, I'm so sorry! I was just hoping to get some questions answered that I have about the temporary confiscation of my property and laboratories."

"I'm sorry, Ms. Wen; we can't give you any information of that sort at this time. If you contact the general, I'm sure he will try to respond to your request as soon as possible."

"But you see, my scientists were working on this project to create a new sort of umbrella, which is actually just a hat that creates a broad energy field above your head to deflect the rain, and it would be profitable for me to access our research."

"Again, I'm sorry, but I'm going to have to request that you leave. This area is not safe for civilians, and you are such an important Eternian figure."

Wei had done a very good job of securing their affections, or rather, their toleration. Derrick wondered when the man would run out of polite denials and inevitably call security. Anita Cole, who was sitting in front of Derrick, suddenly stopped rapidly pounding her fingers against her screen.

"I got it! Weapons control available." She gasped in relief.

"Just give me one more second, Anita; I'll have the alarms off," replied a boy beside her.

"You've got twenty-three seconds," Anita said and then added, "but please don't use them all."

The young man beside her started to sweat, and the momentary relief in her face turned into fear. Her eyes burned into her neighbor's screen. The time was ticking.

"Give me the problem on my screen," she demanded, taking over.

He swiped his finger and it took her only a second's hesitation before she tapped at it with precise mechanical motions. Her head spun to her husband, Gerald, who sat diagonally from her, and they locked eyes before she turned to Derrick.

"We aren't going to get it in time. We need to go now if we're going to have any chance."

Neither she nor her husband waited for a response. They both unbuckled the straps holding them into their seats and leaped for the hatch door. The door rose. There was a gut-wrenching silence as the people in the craft realized what had happened. They would have to run. Derrick struggled with his straps, his hands shaking. A flash of dark-brown hair whipped past his face and Derrick looked down to see his straps already undone for him. Ana. She was already out the door. No one was as desperate of a survivor as Ana, but she had still taken a second to unlatch him from his seat. It was happening fast. Adrenaline made the blood pulse loudly in his ears.

He wasn't as quick as Ana. People were already flooding into the sunlight. He heard the "pop, pop" of compressed air rifles. Get in the middle. He needed to get in the center of it. Herd immunity. Derrick was pushing hard against the person in front of him, and he couldn't make himself stop. He had to get out. He had to get out. Mass panic. His blood pounded. Live. Live. Live!

Then in one lunge, he felt the person in front of him go down. He struggled to step over them. A hand clawed at his ankle. How many people were down there beneath his feet? It didn't matter. He shoved through and into the overcast gray sky. On top of the building, the wind whipped. "Pop! Pop-pop!" An air rifle cut three clean holes through the man in front of him, but the man continued running as if he didn't feel it. An antsy, uncomfortable feeling itched at the back of Derrick's brain, and he tried to hold it back.

Derrick knew their sick, demented actions were just symptoms of the Transfer Sickness, but it didn't matter. They couldn't stop themselves, no matter how they tried. There was no way to think clearly when their lives were on the line. He clicked his heels together and heard the sound of the Lay-Tech activating. He needed to get on the lowest one. How many others would go on the first one just because it was the closest? Derrick remembered Wei's warning that they needed to get on the right cruiser.

He stepped upward as Wei had instructed. It felt no different than climbing stairs. It was difficult to measure how far his strides should be. He kept his focus on the bottom of his assigned cruiser even when the whishing sound of air rifles flew by him. A surreal feeling prickled at his neck as he watched people climbing the air like stairs being plucked from the sky.

He couldn't see Wei. She had likely entered one of the ships as soon as she realized the direction the situation was going. Wei was too smart to have fallen to an air rifle.

The hatch to Derrick's cruiser had already been lowered. He floated into the room and landed heavily on the floor as the Lay-Tech on his shoes deactivated. No sooner than he entered did he realize the chaos continued inside. Two men stood arguing over the top of the navigation board.

"Wait until everyone gets inside!"

"There's no time for that! Every Eternian vessel in Earth's airspace has alarms going off because of us!"

The man, who wouldn't wait longer, was tall and broad-shouldered. He towered over the hero who wanted to wait for the others. Derrick winced as the man of the people was shoved across the cabin and into a display panel. The tall man placed his navigation bud into the navi-controls, and there was a whooshing sound as the door sealed itself air-tight.

Just as they began to move, the entire ship was suddenly rocked, and everyone who was not strapped in was slammed into the nearest wall. Derrick found himself reeling in pain. A fellow crew member was screaming to his left, but he couldn't see them. Some kind of alarm was going off, but whether it was inside his head or outside, he couldn't tell.

Derrick looked through blurred painful eyes to see Ana strapped to her seat and desperately trying to reach him.

"Recovery procedure in action. Apologies for evasive maneuvers. Ship damage being assessed," the ship's Automated alerted them.

"Who was it?" He heard screaming somewhere.

"Which ship was it?"

"Wei? Come in, Wei!"

33

Chapter 33

Nyauta circles in my mouth. I cough and spit it up, but it's poured in again. This time I swallow, and the sharp pains in my head slowly ease. Am I back again? Sirens continue to blare in my head. I concentrate on drinking more nyauta so that they fade. If I think about anything else, my mind might try to travel back.

A damp cloth is laid over my eyes. I want to thank him, but instead I grunt. I rest in the cool for a while.

"What happened to the humans?" I whisper.

A wave of dust sweeps up against my face as the Lovindian sits down beside me.

"The Eterns maintained control of Earth until its demise six hundred years later," the Lovindian says tiredly.

I cough. "That didn't really answer my question."

He lets out a long sigh. "The Eterns colonized Mars Base and ruled above from star cruisers. The humans were watched every second of every day, and the Eterns made themselves like gods, plucking humans when they needed bodies and using them for their resources."

"That sounds familiar." I laugh bitterly.

"It only lasted until the Lovindians arrived," he adds.

"How ironic."

"Life often is."

The cloth is dry; I peel it from my face to stare up at the vaulted ceiling. So Earth is gone then. Humans hadn't ruled it to the end... Humans were weak even then.

"Why did the Lovindians bother to take humans from Earth? There have to be better, stronger forms that they could take." Something is still not adding up.

"You're right. There are many better forms they could take. Physically, humans are especially good at tasks that require dexterity, and that is part of the reason they are still considered valuable."

"And the other part?"

"Humans... are not too different from Lovindians. Their kind evolved to Eterns, which as you already said, bare similarities to Lovindians. They are an ideal life form for transferring into because of a similar evolutionary history. Also, humans are one of the Lovindians' more favored trophies. The battle against the Eterns was not an easy one. Additionally, planet Earth was overflowing with resources and technology."

"Ah," I mumble. So the Lovindians considered them prized livestock.

"Jacob, I think it's time for you to go home now. I'm not sure how much time has passed, but I'm sure the Gromptu are concerned about their missing transporter craft."

He's right. I'm too tired to go back into the memory stream. It's time for me to go. This time I will go home with a story. I knew that humanity would lose everything, but this wasn't how I wanted it to happen. Maybe I'm still a child, but in my mind, I had pictured Earth's strongest men fighting to the very last against the invading Lovindian army. I had thought that by seeing the past, I would find the same fury that I have in me, inside of them—the same desires. The humans were defeated long before the Lovindians even showed up. It was a disappointment.

It's time to go home.

As I speed back toward Yalk, regret wells in my stomach. How long have I been gone? What is Samuel thinking? He's probably sick with worry. Yalk grows larger on the viewing screen. I enter the atmosphere, and the three Unit Buildings look like massive blemishes on Yalk's already dull surface.

I start to feel uneasy as the craft approaches the shuttle bay doors. Something doesn't feel right. Aren't the shuttle bay doors usually lifting by now? I grip the controls. Am I going to have to veer away at the last moment? I drift toward the door. Is it going to open? What am I going to do if it doesn't? My stomach turns. Yalk is a prison, but what would I do if I couldn't go back? It's still my home.

I tense, ready to pull up the controls. The door lurches suddenly. They're opening, but are they going to open in time? I grit my teeth. The ship slips through. The landing gear catches hard because I come in too low to the ground. I jolt forward in the seat. I'm stunned at my own actions. Why hadn't I just pulled up and gone around for a second run?

The hatch door falls, but I haven't told it to lower. I stand up quickly.

"*Ach- tch- gracht.*"

My reckless entrance hasn't gone unnoticed. The *krik-krik* of its talons against the hatch door makes my skin crawl. Its feathered head is turned down, a three-fingered hand reaches

294

for the flight logs. I cringe, even knowing that they are already doctored to say that I was on Yahbi. It stares for a moment and then turns its gaze. I sweat. It feels the same as it had in the Talkers tent all that time ago. The white eyes penetrate me, and there is no way to tell what the Gromptu is discerning. Carefully, it turns and leaves just as it had come.

I breathe out; I had held my breath the entire time. I wipe the sweat from my forehead. Do I have a death wish? I wander out of the craft, but the Gromptu has already blended in with the others, and they are ignoring me fully. That would have been normal except for there is something about the way they are chattering to each other. What were they so preoccupied with that they don't care about my dangerous entrance?

They're crowding something. I stare openly because, for once, I'm not being looked at. The oily, gray skin between their molting feathers twitches when they move. Are they agitated about something? A head swivels around abruptly. The round eyes stare menacingly. I freeze for a moment, and the Gromptu shifts back and forth on its feet. I startle at my own stupidity and look down, but not before I catch a glimpse of their object of interest. They are looking into a crate but I cannot see the contents. I'm not supposed to look at them; it's a rule that doesn't need to be communicated verbally.

What is in the crate? I don't dare venture another glance. I blink heavily as I approach the Gromptu controlling the gate. It's been too long since I've slept. The housing doors open to let me in. The air is still in the compound. It is quiet—quiet even for Yalk. How long have I been gone?

The housing door siren peals. My head screams. I see Derrick's ship again. Had Wei's ship been destroyed? I hear the passengers screaming as Derrick slips into unconsciousness.

295

I bend over in pain.

"Jacob!" The voice calls me back.

"Samuel?" I groan through the noise. The hand drags me by my arm, and my vision is split between showing me images of inside the cruiser and inside of Unit B.

"Come on, Jacob, you need to get inside. It's not safe for us to be in the corridors. The Gromptu have been—things have been changing."

34

Chapter 34

I'm dropped onto my bed. I moan painfully. The alarm continues to screech in my head. I'm on Yalk. On Yalk. I'm Jacob. I groan and grab my head tightly around my temples. The pressure helps to hide the pain.

"Jacob! What on Yalk happened?" Samuel yells.

I try to focus on his voice—anything to make the noise stop.

"What the scat are you doing? Where have you been racking up for the past four weeks?"

It doesn't sound like Samuel. I open my eyes. Immediately, I realize my mistake.

I cough weakly. "Emmanuel?"

"Yes! Where on Yalk have you been?"

"How long have I been gone?" I ignore his question.

"Weeks! The Units are in havoc! I've lost contact with Unit A completely. I can only fear the worst of my contact."

"Where's Samuel?"

Emmanuel goes pale. He drops to a squatting position.

"Emmanuel?"

He looks down. I watch as he presses his hands together one

fingertip at a time.

"We were hoping... he was with you."

"With me?" I stand up too fast and my head spins. I ignore it. "What do you mean you thought he was with me?"

"I just—I just hoped." His voice breaks. "I wanted to hope."

My pulse starts to beat between my ears. A sinking feeling flows from the top, dropping down into my feet. This isn't real. It's not real.

"You don't—you can't, it's not—" I stumble through words.

"He disappeared shortly after you left." Emmanuel's face falls into his hands.

Disappeared. I shake the word away.

"That doesn't make sense, Emmanuel. You would have gotten a letter. If I've been gone for weeks, then there should be a letter." The thought snags hope in my chest. "There was no letter. You didn't say there was a letter." I fight desperately.

"No." He won't look at me. "No letter."

My heart beats heavily. I'm shaking. No letter. No letter. Emmanuel won't look at me. He looks at his hands. Tears drip down onto his thumb. He doesn't blink. They fall uncontrolled. His expression doesn't change.

"There wasn't a letter, Emmanuel." I search him.

"No," he whispers. His bottom lip trembles.

"Emmanuel—," I cough but he just shakes in response.

His chewed fingers reveal the sickening truth.

I can't feel anything. Nothing but the rage.

I can't hear anything. Nothing but the thundering in my ears.

"Things have been changing," Emmanuel mumbles. His eyes are empty.

My heart falls. I ball my cold, damp hands into fists.

"Ah."

I don't feel anything but the burn. Lack of sleep and anger mix together to blur my vision. I don't feel anything as I walk toward the closet and pull out the long, metal rod meant to hold my clothes. My throat tightens, and it feels like a sharp blade is being pressed into my neck.

"What are you doing?" Emmanuel's voice is far away.

"Stay here." My voice is distant.

I step into the corridor. The air coming in my nose is fire. I grip the metal rod so tightly that my fingernails cut into my palm. A Gromptu guards the end of the hall. It stands still and vigil. The feathers on its shoulder lift a little from the breeze beneath the vent. The wind wails outside the dome of Unit B.

I let the end of the rod fall and clang loudly. The Gromptu ruffles its new-grown feathers and turns its giant orb eyes to meet mine. That's it. Watch me. I want you to see. I meet its bottomless, uncommunicative gaze. The Gromptu doesn't seem all that large to me; it's not like that Gromptu that had joined me on my first voyage into space all those years ago. It didn't kill the Talkers in the tent.

I make my approach. It eyes me more carefully, but it's too late in establishing the dowel rod as a weapon. I rush forward, feet slamming into the ground, propelling me forward. It opens its little mouth just as the metal falls across the side of its head. Only a small gurgle comes out. It collapses.

I roar. The inhuman sound echoes again and again down the corridors.

The silence is broken.

My fury lights the air. Down and down the metal rod goes, crunching on what is beneath those white eyes. I see it now. I see what the Gromptu is feeling. It is strange that I never noticed their emotions before.

Another Gromptu blinks dumbly at the assault. It lets out a short, surprised barking sound and shuffles closer. I look up, still hunched over my kill. Why is it hesitating? Then I understand. I finally understand. It's scared. This Gromptu is scared—of me. I grin.

I charge. The creature heightens itself as if it's about to run, but it's too slow. I swing up with the weapon, and the Gromptu screeches in pain as the rod falls across its head and its bones snap. He drops instantly and lies in a motionless heap. It was so easy. I could have done it a million times. I took two of them just like they take us. Just like they took—

"YOU KILLED HIM!" I scream.

I slam the weapon again over its lifeless body. Blood splatters, staining my beige clothes. They bleed red too. I pound again and again until I can't see its eyes anymore. I can feel the creature's innards under my wrapped feet. It's disgusting. I'm no better than them. No better than them, but they will feel my pain.

I feel eyes burning into my back. I turn quickly, raising the rod. I will show them what a human can do.

"JACOB, STOP!"

I stop just short of his nose. Emmanuel. Tears pour from Emmanuel's eyes, and I touch my own cheek suddenly, realizing that I'm crying too. He is spurred back into life.

"What have you done? Damnit I had a plan!" he yells at me. "Damnit, I understand. I understand." He wipes tears from his eyes with the heel of his hand, but they keep coming.

"You don't want to be a part of this, Emmanuel. Go back home."

"You're damned right I don't!" he hollers.

"Go home." I rest my bloody hand on his shoulder to comfort him.

"Shut up," he snaps.

"I don't have a plan." My heart thunders with adrenaline.

"No, scat."

He fiddles with something on his wrist. A blue glow encompasses his fist. I gape. It looks just like something Wei would have made.

"Where did you get that?"

"I'm the sole leader of the Yalkian black market," he snaps.

Humans have slowly crowded around us. They look down at the bodies in silence; they are almost unrecognizable. Just a pile of feathers and blood. A child kicks it with his foot. The arm flops uselessly.

"Are you the Wind Wraith?" A woman steps toward me. Her eyes are locked on mine. "Have you come to save us? Have you come to get revenge?"

Save her? She wants me to save them? Her hand reaches for my pant leg, and I step back. She flinches, turning her face away. Does she think that I would—? I look down at the blood on my hands. My chest burns.

"We've got to get off this planet," Emmanuel says, pulling me away.

"There's no way we are going to get to the transporter craft," I mumble.

"If we don't get to the transporter craft, we are dead," he states plainly.

He starts running, and I'm forced to follow. The dowel rod swings at my side. My hand still vibrates from the metal connecting with bone.

Grah-aht! Grah-aht-ach!

The Gromptu are in motion. Their odd chirruping mixes in with my panted breaths. For a second I think I see one, but when I turn to look, it's gone. They're trying to beat us to the door.

My lungs swell. I don't feel my feet touch the ground. Faster, faster—keep looking forward. I definitely see one now. It darts between apartment buildings. I catch glimpses of them in the alleys. I follow Emmanuel blindly. If there is anyone who knows the fastest ways around Yalk, it's him.

They flank us. Their bodies lift to reveal thin, stick-like legs. I never expected them to be so fast. They reach the door first. My stomach turns. The Gromptu chatter at each other as they creep closer. They weave from side-to-side so that it is impossible to keep your eyes on just one.

"They're going to jump us!" Emmanuel yells.

"It's about time to show me what that blue thing does," I say nervously.

"I hope it's what I paid for. Here we go." He adjusts it with his other hand.

Blue explodes from his fist. The thing sprays blue, crystal-like light. Three of the Gromptu collapse in a spastic fit.

"Yes! That was great! Do that again!" I holler.

The Gromptu ignore their fallen. They continue to weave in their menacing pattern. I keep my eyes on the Gromptu in front of me. I keep eye contact to follow its movements.

"Emmanuel?!" I yell nervously.

"I don't know! I've never used this thing before! It's not working!" He smacks at his wrist.

The Gromptu in front of me tenses suddenly. Downy feathers fly up into the air, and I swing. The other Gromptu screech and leap back in unison. As they weave back and forth, my mind starts to turn. I remember the night in the tent. I know the Gromptus' weakness.

In one quick motion, I jump forward and wrap my arm around Emmanuel's neck. I hoist the iron rod over his head.

"I'll do it!" I scream at them.

Emmanuel squirms, but he is still smaller than I am. "What on Yalk are you doing?"

I ignore him. I'm getting off this planet. The Gromptu I struck takes in heavy squalling breaths as it lies helplessly bleeding out. One of the Gromptu wobbles toward it. The others hardly reacted to the other injured Gromptu. I wonder if these two have some connection to each other.

"You!" I point at it. "Open the doors!"

The Gromptu stare. They are trying to decide what to do. It all depends on this. One of them lets out a sharp chirp, and they move toward us. They've decided to call my bluff.

I let loose a scream of rage and throw Emmanuel to the floor. I lift the iron rod and swing up.

"Jacob, stop! Jacob, please! I don't understand!" He holds his hands defensively above himself.

I must look more serious this time. They inch away slowly. I breathe in, and then I let it out.

"Open the doors!"

35

Chapter 35

No need for a grave.

   The Maker's mark is cold.

   No need for a grave.

   These aren't the days of old.

   And the dirt is red,

   but we don't tell.

   And the dirt is red,

   but we will never tell.

Emmanuel sits on the far end of the bench not facing me. He fiddles with the thing on his wrist. The broad-shouldered, loud-mouthed, black market leader looks very small. For a moment I see his older brother. My heart squeezes in my chest.

I feel heavy. I didn't even—see it. There wasn't even a reason. One moment there, next moment, gone. It doesn't feel like it happened, and it makes me all the angrier. I can't understand that he's gone, let alone know what I'm feeling. I'm just heavy.

"I'll see you soon."

That was the last thing I said to him. How many lies have I told? I'm numb, but I hurt at the same time. Emmanuel sniffs.

"Emmanuel, I'm sorry."

He flinches.

"Emmanuel, I—"

"I heard you the first time," he hisses.

Of course, he's pissed about how I used him. One more tic to my guilty conscience. Emmanuel launches at me, shaking my shoulders. His red eyes are the only sign that he's been crying.

"I had a plan, dammit," he hurls at me. "I had the start of something."

"A plan?" That's what he's mad about? "Emmanuel, there's no plan in the face of the Lovindians. They would have killed us all before we got anywhere. You can't win. There was never any winning."

"Oh, no." Emmanuel tsks, getting up off the bench. "Oh, no you don't! If you say that stupid scat, then you're making it all scrapping worthless!"

"What scheme could you conjure up that would save Yalk? Were you going to do it single-handedly with some illegal rice sacks?" I don't know why, but I can't control the anger. The sleep deprivation is having a hand in my emotional outbursts.

"That's right! Lash out, Jacob! That's what you're good at! Go ahead! Why don't you try to single-handedly club the whole Lovindian army to death? That's so much better than contracting defense weapons to liberate Yalk and Yahbi and using Yahbiin privateers to build an armada!"

I gape at him. Here I thought he was just shuffling food and medicine around, but he was actually building a cash supply for a rebellion.

"Emmanuel, that's a fantasy! You don't know the Lovindians. They would bring their warships and destroy Yahbi in
seconds. They don't care about us! What makes you think the
Yahbiin people would even put themselves at risk? They make
all their profits off the Lovindians! Who would they trade with
if they allied with us—if they became independent?"

"At least I am doing something! What are you doing?
Escaping all the time on some kind of sacred mission! Acting
superior all of the time! I've been doing the best that I can
with what I have! Do you even know how many humans have
disappeared in the weeks since you were last on Yalk? Fifty-
seven between the units! They're doing something! They're
counting down on us, and I don't have many moves to make."

He's right. He is doing the best that he can, but it's not going
to be enough to take down the Lovindians. We need something
else, something better. I need to hear the end of the story. If
we could find a Lovindian weakness, then Emmanuel's plan
might actually have some merit. We have to be able to hold
something over them, or else—or else we'll never have any
measure of success.

The inside of the transporter craft is quiet as we hurtle
toward the red planet. We won't have long before they have us.
It's only a matter of time. It has always been only a matter of
time for me, though. Ever since I decided to punch the Talker's
coordinates into my navigational system, it was only a matter
of time.

If people really are disappearing at the rate Emmanuel said,
then all of Yalk is in danger. Emmanuel was working hard,
creating a united system in the units, and here I have gone
and ruined it for him.

"Why did they let us go?" Anger is still in his voice.

I sigh. "They let us go because they didn't know what to do with us."

"I don't get it." He grunts.

"Gromptu are incapable of improvising. All of their orders come from the higher ranking Lovindians, and without their instructions, they are immobilized." It was just like in the tent.

"So why did they open the doors when you—" His voice falls short and I cringe, hating myself for how I had used him.

"Lovindians consider humans to be prized livestock. The Gromptu couldn't determine what was more valuable, stopping us from leaving or losing a human. When they couldn't make the decision, they stopped fighting us because it's a lot easier to track us down in space when we run out of fuel than it is to explain why a perfectly good body was lost."

"Oh," Emmanuel whispers.

In the silence, all of my emotions rush over me. I think about how the rod came down against the Gromptus' flesh. The acts of violence repeat again and again in my head. I feel my anger go into each blow once more. I could have kept myself together, if only they hadn't just kept taking from me. They. Just. Keep. Taking. Emmanuel sighs loudly.

"Hey," he puts a hand on my shoulder, and I feel its comfort, "keep it together. We can't think about it yet. We have to survive first." He's mending our argument for now.

I know that by *it* he means Samuel. I can't take his advice because I know what they've done to him. To that kid with the sweet, round cheeks and ever-smiling face. The first person I called a friend. He's still out there. Just like Jana and the Historian. Wandering around with one of those things inside his head. Just a shell. How long will Samuel walk around

307

mindlessly, soullessly, until they consider his body too old and trade it in?

"I have a story to tell you," I say softly.

"Finally going to tell me what you've been up to?" Emmanuel turns on the bench to face me fully. I notice that he's shaking even though he's trying to sound strong. My own hands are shaking too.

"Yeah. You should know what the Talkers died for, what Saul died for without knowing, and what has happened to Samuel."

I explain it to him. His eyes light up at the young Octornians, at Earth, and at the sweet innocence of Katie. Dread replaces the light at the death of Jana, at the terrors of Scanthirin Sickness, and at the rise of the Eterns. I just wish that I had a better story to tell.

36

Chapter 36

The shuttle comes into orbit around the tiny planet. I feel the craft slow.

"So the library is here?" Emmanuel asks. That must have been what Samuel had told him.

"It's not exactly a library so much as a person," I say as the craft lands.

"A person?"

"Yeah, and there's one more thing." The craft door opens.

"What's that?"

"He's a Lovindian."

"A Lovindian!"

Emmanuel chokes on the heavy, red dust that spills in. He stands coughing and spluttering. I had my shirt over my face first but hadn't thought to tell him.

"Jacob!" The deep rumble seems to shake the planet. "I've seen the reports on my com-panel! Jacob, what have you done?"

I am stunned momentarily to see the Lovindian walking outside of the council building. He looks as if a creature emerged from the rocky bowels of the planet itself.

"I've sped things up a little." I walk quickly.

"You murdered two Gromptu!"

"It's hardly murder when you're killing murderers!" I call.

"Jacob, that's not the point. The Lovindians won't see it that way. You've just put a massive target on your back!"

"Then we are going to have to work fast. I need the rest of the story."

"I won't have time, Jacob! They'll be here in a maximum of three days. You're just lucky they don't have any First Gen Lovindians in this part of the galaxy."

"I need as much as you can give me of the story."

"And then what?"

"Then I will die with the knowledge that those bastards can be beaten."

"That's no plan, Jacob! There's no future in doing something like that!" His deep voice rumbles through me in anger.

"I never thought there was a future for me. There was only the story." I laugh.

"That's not why I started telling it to you!"

"Well, I am sorry that I didn't live up to your purpose." I never did get to learn what that purpose was. "Nevertheless, will you grant a dying man his last wish?"

The Lovindian roars in frustration. I pretend like the sound doesn't make my skin tremble.

"Damn you!" he relents. The Lovindian lets out a big sigh. Then his eyes squint. I see him looking past me. His eyes widen. "Who is this?"

I turn to see Emmanuel, whose eyes are fixed to the Lovindian.

"He's a friend," I say.

"You shouldn't have brought him here, Jacob. He would have lasted longer on Yalk." He isn't angry this time; he just sounds tired.

"Does it matter?" I shrug.

"Were you the one to decide? He might have lived happily there."

"They've killed too many of our loved ones for that."

The Lovindian looks at me with surprise. I realize that this is the first time I've told him anything about myself.

"They're taking people from us left and right. Will they clear the whole planet?" My voice sounds cold, almost as if it had come from Derrick's mouth.

"I don't know exactly." His voice trails away.

I have the feeling that he does know exactly. The Lovindian gestures for us to follow him inside, and we do. Emmanuel stays behind me. I turn to him.

"This is the storyteller, Emmanuel. He is the last Historian."

"But," he whispers, "how can you trust him?"

"I don't." I giving a barking laugh, and the Lovindian responds in his own chortling laughter despite his anger.

The Lovindian explains the process to Emmanuel so as not to startle him. I notice that Emmanuel doesn't stand too close to the creature or meet his eyes. I don't blame him. The creature is monstrous in size and would be unsettling to be near even if he wasn't a Lovindian.

"I am sorry to meet your acquaintance." The Lovindian holds out a hand.

"Gee, thanks." Emmanuel looks at the hand uneasily, not knowing what he's supposed to do with it.

"It's an ancient human custom. You shake it upon meeting."

Emmanuel takes his hand and wobbles it from side-to-side awkwardly. The Lovindian rumble-laughs and bobs their hands up and down. I wonder if it's because of the memory stream that I knew that it should look that way.

Emmanuel gapes at the great halls of the council building. I smile sadly, wondering if that's how I looked the first time.

"I'm not sure I understand what's going on, but I'll trust you, Jacob," he says nervously. "Before you do this, I want you to know that I'll have a plan by the time you're back. I heard you tell that guy that you plan to just let the Lovindians grab you, but that's not going to happen. I didn't risk my empire just so you can listen to some story and die. You owe me, so keep fighting."

"Okay," I say without much expectation.

Maybe humans didn't fight to the end for Earth, but I promise to fight to the end of my life. I sit down with the Lovindian for the last time. Emmanuel watches with fearful eyes. I smile at him. Even if it isn't going to be okay, I hope that my smile conveys it will be. I take the Lovindian's hand.

"From the Articles of the Council:

Year: 2386

Subject: Derrick Webber"

"During the three-year flight from Earth, Wei Wen's two remaining cruisers wandered through space. Near the end of their voyage, rations began to run low and tensions were often high. With very little privacy and no comfortable sleeping quarters, the Eterns under Wei's management grew irritable. The manufacturing of functional E.V.'s was one of the only things that focused the crew during this time.

"By the end of their flight, every Etern was equipped with

their very own E.V. The E.V. had three settings. The first setting was to kill. The second setting was used to paralyze and the third was for transfer. It was uncertain when they would get the opportunity to transfer again but preparation for the future and protecting themselves were the two thoughts that most occupied the minds of the Eterns."

Derrick awoke and immediately vomited all over himself. He vaguely remembered Ana strapping herself into the seat beside him. He turned his head and felt another wave of nausea. She wasn't there. A thin moan livened his senses. Derrick clumsily fumbled with the straps around his waist and shoulders.

For three years they had time to plan their landing, but something had gone wrong. Derrick wasn't a pilot, but he remembered hearing them bicker about electrical storms in the planet's atmosphere before it had all went black. Adrenaline pumped through him, and his hands found the way to release himself.

His knees dropped to the ground. His head was swimming; something had knocked him into unconsciousness, and it was hard to fight the throbbing pain in the back of his head. A loose wire, still alive with electricity, shot sparks across the metal floor, and they sizzled as they met his hand. Derrick flipped away from it so that his stomach was turned upward toward the ceiling. He raised the hand, which he had pulled from the sparks to his mouth. The back end of the ship had been crumpled. The lines of seats across the walls had been mashed together. If the ship had been crushed only two feet more... He tried to back away, but the ground was angled sharply upward.

The moan became a scream. It was coming from the copilot's chair. Four seats remained in the main cabin, including

Ana's. The two on the other side hadn't fared as well as him and Ana. A metal beam had shot out of the wall and decapitated the first; the second had either not yet awoken or had no intention of waking up again. There was another yell from the front of the ship. He recognized the shape of Ana at the foot of the copilot's chair.

"No, don't start that yelling now, Mr. Cotrelli, you're going to be okay. We have to keep quiet. Shhh, shhh, it's okay."

"Ana?" Derrick called out.

"Goddammit, Derrick, be quiet!" she whispered angrily, unfazed by the death around her.

"What's going on?" He lowered his voice.

"Shhh, Mr. Cotrelli, it's okay. I just need you to focus right now."

The man was sobbing violently. Derrick managed to get to his feet and lunge for the doorway to pull himself the rest of the way up. There was a loud cracking noise as he almost pulled a panel from the wall. Mr. Cotrelli yelped in surprise. Ana shot him a hateful glare, but he was too busy gathering himself to return one.

"No, no, don't worry about him, Mr. Cotrelli. No, he's just another passenger."

Derrick finally stumbled up to where he could see the scene playing out on the destroyed cruiser. Mr. Cotrelli, who appeared to be in the body of a young man of about twenty-two, was fish-gasping for breath. Derrick grimaced and shook his head. It wasn't good.

He noticed that an open medical kit had been set in front of the display panel so that it wouldn't slide down toward the main cabin.

"Did you run a mediscan?" he asked Ana.

"I did," she said.

"And?"

She didn't answer.

"Where's his puncture site?"

Mr. Cotrelli started his howling again.

"Shhh, Mr. Cotrelli, shhh. I need you to focus now. Tell me how to run a body signature and a topography scan."

Derrick took the mediscanner from the medical kit. The last evaluation was still on the screen. He held the mediscanner up to Cotrelli, and his internals lit up on the screen. There was no definite puncture site. There was an option prompting him to choose an area of Mr. Cotrelli's body for further evaluation, but he could see why Ana hadn't bothered. Mr. Cotrelli was bleeding internally in multiple locations. His ribs were puncturing his lungs; one had already collapsed. There was no hope. The pilot had broken his back upon landing.

"Mr. Cotrelli, please. Just focus on my voice. Tell me how to run a body signature scan."

Derrick held up the scanner to Mr. Cotrelli once more.

"Please, Mr. Cotrelli. What should I type in?"

Mr. Cotrelli stared with wide eyes.

"He's not going to be able to help you, Ana."

"He has to!" She snapped.

"Ana, his second lung is collapsing."

Mr. Cotrelli only gurgled.

"It can't!" She had broken her rule of not yelling.

In her insane desperation, she began shaking the man, but he was already gone.

"Ana." Derrick stared and didn't know what to feel.

She let go and flung Cotrelli back into his seat. Her arms wrapped instinctively around Derrick, who held himself up painfully with the control panel. Ana, who was clearly in shock, yelled unintelligible nonsense through her tears. Cotrelli's head had fallen to where his name was stitched into the fabric of his clothes. Derrick wondered if it was his real name or the name of the person he inhabited. Derrick could now make out Ana's words better. She was still talking about running a body signature scan. He sighed.

"Why is it so important that we get a body signature scan? I understand the topography scan. You want to figure out the safest way to exit the ship without making the whole thing roll down whatever is causing this incline, but why do we need the body signature scan?"

Ana wiped the tears from her face, and he noticed that at least one of her fingers had been broken.

"You noticed my fingers?" She sucked in air through her teeth. "I was stuck awake for two hours, unable to undo the straps hooking me to the wall. They've almost stopped now, but I still hear them quietly muttering."

"What? Ana?" Ana shook her head, avoiding his question. "Ana, what's muttering?"

"There's some type of creature out there. It understands our language, and it's mocking us."

Derrick listened. He hadn't heard the sound at first, likely because of the ringing in his ears, but now as he focused, he thought he heard a dull mumbling sound from outside the ship. Ana was right; it did sound as if there was a voice. Something outside was alive. That was why she wanted the body signature scan. He hadn't understood at first because the planet they had chosen showed up on their scans as void of intelligent life.

"They're mocking us," she whispered.

"What do you mean?" He stared at her strangely.

"They are quieter now, but those are the screams. Those are our screams. The voices are perfect matches."

"Are you telling me that whatever is out there is copying the screams of our fellow passengers?"

Derrick listened and was chilled for a moment as he thought he heard it. He got up the courage to yell out.

"Who's out there?"

"No!" Ana grabbed his arm, shaking.

"Shut up, Ana!" He shook her away.

There was a short pause, and then to his horror, he heard whatever it was shout back.

"Who's out there? Shut up, Ana! Who's out there? Who's out there? Shut up, Ana!"

The voice was definitely his own, but more troubling was that the sentences were overlapping. Whatever was out there was not alone. It was impossible to tell just how many creatures were outside of the cruiser.

"They're mocking us!" Ana cried, covering her ears with her twisted fingers. Derrick's stomach flipped at the sight of them.

"Ana, they're not mocking us. They're not from our planet; they can't even understand us! Whatever is out there cannot even be intelligent life. We saw no signs of civilization when we ran the scans before, not even primitive civilization. Whatever that is out there is mimicking us."

"Make it stop!"

Derrick rolled his eyes. "We need to reset your fingers, Ana; you're going to need them if we are going to survive here long enough to rejoin Wei."

The creatures outside had gotten quieter, but he could still hear them. It was unnerving at first to hear his own voice repeated over and over, but it quickly became just annoying.

"Ana, have you tried voice commands yet?"

"What?" she said dazedly.

"Have you tried to use voice commands? We can ask the computer to display a topography scan or give us the instructions for repair."

Ana opened her eyes and looked around her. She laughed a little. Derrick didn't understand initially, but it was probably due to the concussion he undoubtedly had and the nausea that accompanied it. Then, quietly, he looked around. The screens were destroyed. They showed some light on the panels, but they were unusable. The walls were crumpled like tin foil. The computer wasn't turning back on. He was thinking just about as clearly as she was.

Their best chance was to release the hatch door and face the consequences. That didn't come with out dangers. The ship could be perched on a ledge, ready to complete the crushing of its still-surviving passengers. Whatever was outside could be dealt with later; for now, they had to get out.

Derrick unsteadily made his way back to his seat; he tugged on the drawer beneath it to no avail. The ship was bent, and the drawer wasn't pulling out.

"Ana, I'm going to need you to find me something to pry open this drawer with."

"Why, what's in there?"

"Ana, please."

She dug around in the maintenance box with her good hand. The box was fully equipped with the latest technology. The devices were ideal to preserve space and keep the ship light but none of them in any way resembled a crowbar.

"Damn it," she muttered, "why couldn't we just stick to

hammers and screwdrivers?"

"Come on, Ana! Is there really nothing I can use?"

"No, no, wait—I have this thing!"

The device was a long, thin, metal prod, which was wrapped in rubber except for two inches below the top. It was meant for detecting electrical currents, and a small reader lit up on the handle. Derrick grabbed it quickly and pried open the compartment. From it, he retrieved his backpack and began hauling himself back up toward the door. There were two levers. One was meant in case the computer had an error and would cut the wiring to the door to release it automatically. The other turned the door into an escape hatch and would throw the door off its hinges with pressurized air as a last resort. He flipped up the plastic case and pulled the first of the two. The door started to lift but was prevented from going any further by the dent in the side of the ship.

"That's what I was worried about." Derrick sighed and ran a hand through his hair.

"What's wrong? We can pull the emergency hatch; it will come off fine."

"Yeah, but depending on what this ship's sitting on, the force of it flying off could have us falling off a cliff," Derrick huffed.

"Oh."

Derrick unzipped his backpack and threw the medical kit inside to fix Ana's fingers later. His hand grasped around the lever. Their eyes met; the air was heavy.

"Ready?" his gaze asked.

She gave him a small, confident nod, her uninjured hand wrapped around its damaged companion. He yanked hard, setting the world into motion. The ship lurched hard, but as soon as the door opened, Derrick jumped through the opening, pulling Ana with him.

They were instantly sliding—sliding down. Derrick thought he felt his ankle roll, but he couldn't be sure until he stopped moving. Dirt and rocks flew wild, and then he stopped. The dirt settled, and he wiped it from his eyes. The massive, dark shape of the ship's black hull loomed over them. The hillside was not as steep as it had felt from inside the ship. The cruiser had already slid down to the bottom of the hill.

Somewhere near, he could hear Ana sobbing. He slowly inched toward her in the dim light. She was on her knees, clutching her hand to her chest. She must have knocked it against something on the way down, erasing the initial shock and adrenaline which had prevented her from feeling the pain before.

"Ana, give me your hand," Derrick called.

"Ana, give me your hand. Give me your hand, Ana. Ana. Ana, give me your hand."

She turned to him, her eyes massive. Tears spilled un-endingly from her wide eyes. She opened her mouth to say something but then put her tightly bound hands over top of her lips. Derrick hurriedly fumbled in his bag for something to light the area. One of the voices was close.

"Ana, give me your hand."

Crouched as he was, he spun on the balls of his feet, feeling the pain in his ankle. From the bag, he pulled out a flashlight, which seemed to light up the whole world, and instantly revealed the culprit. Ana immediately started to laugh, and the creature laughed back. Derrick sighed angrily at himself and at it and at her. The furry, little mammal had a rounded, fuzzy face with massive, round, fleshy ears, that bounced as sound vibrated off of them.

"What is that thing?" She laughed through her tears.

With a jolt of pain, he suddenly thought of Katie. He remembered all the times he distracted her in her fussy states. Infants went so easily from tears to laughter.

"I don't know, some kind of wombat," he replied irritably, opening up the medical kit.

"What's the name of this planet again?"

Derrick looked around. They were in a very old forest full of what looked similar to Earth's prehistoric fern trees. He wondered how many of the grasses he rubbed against on the way down were poisonous. The planet had a thick layer of dust hanging around it just outside the atmosphere, which blocked out sunlight and gave the surface of the planet a foggy, golden hue. He ran hypotheses through the ship's computer weeks ago; it simulated different events that could have caused the dust to form around the planet. All he could tell was that it happened about the same time as the formation of the moon.

He pointed his flashlight down into the bag searching for something to numb Ana's pain before he tried to reset her fingers. Beads of sweat built upon her forehead, and he touched her gently with the back of his hand. She was on fire—feverish from the broken bones. He needed to run the mediscanner over her hand.

"Derrick?" Ana whispered as he neared her with the device.

"Huh?" She shook all over, but she was acting strong. It pained him a little to watch her carry on like this. He wondered if she was distracting herself from the pain by rambling on.

"I asked what the name of this planet is?"

"Yalk," he grunted.

Ana pointed with both of her hands at the funny looking

creature.

"That would make you a Yalkian Wombat." She giggled into the dark, and the dark seemed to giggle back.

37

Chapter 37

After three days on Yalk, Derrick had started to do a bit of a study on the Yalkian Wombat, as Ana had named it. It had wide, fleshy, satellite-looking protuberances on both sides of its head. He assumed that this was its way of bouncing voices. It wasn't even mimicking—it was more like echoing.

At first, he didn't understand what the purpose of such an adaptation would be, but that was before he met one of the predatory, bird-like creatures that stalked the planet. The bird-creatures hunted in flocks and seemed to communicate in a complex series of clicks, chirps, and hoots. When the wombats started their echoes, they effectively eliminated any clear communication between the predators. The birds were luckily too small to be a threat to him and Ana, standing at just beneath his knee and fleeing when he flashed a light at them.

The time that he hadn't spent thinking about their annoying pest problem he had spent combining efforts with Ana to construct a base and heal their wounds. Once they were feeling stronger, they wanted to return to the ship and search for food.

They were hoping to reach some of the food packets which were placed into each of the crew's backpacks like the one Derrick had salvaged. They had spent enough time healing; it was time to reap the rewards. Derrick went for the flashlight in his backpack.

"What are you doing?" Ana questioned him.

"What are you doing? What? What are you?"

"What do you mean, 'what am I doing?' We are out of food. I have to go in there to get supplies."

"But—the others..."

"Death shouldn't be anything new to you, Ana," he said coolly. "You've killed enough times."

"You've killed enough times, you've killed enough, times, you've killed."

Ana didn't say anything in return, and Derrick didn't wait for her to do so. The Yalkian wombats echoed on. The E.V. rocked as it hung from his belt.

The air on Yalk was always heavy with humidity. The heat trapped beneath the layer of dust in the atmosphere was palpable. It was impossible to wake up in the morning without a thin layer of moisture on everything. The dust prohibited the planet from being well-lit, and the tree canopy assisted in the effort. Derrick could smell the ship as he approached. He faced the open emergency hatch door and was hit with sweltering, damp heat. If he had eaten more than the rations found in his backpack, he would have wretched.

He remembered his own words, in part because they were still circulating through the air: "Death shouldn't be anything new to you." Still, it felt the same every time. The air inside was heavy with more than just the trapped humidity. He paused to focus on lowering his heart rate; he needed to minimize the amount of breathing he would be doing. The stench made his eyes water immediately. He gagged but fought hard to keep his mouth closed to avoid breathing in air that way.

He turned on the light, and a Yalkian wombat rushed into the darkness. Derrick grimaced; the damn things were apparently not limited to eating vegetation. He was thankful that Ana couldn't see this. He coughed into his fist and started to look around the cabin area. He couldn't see any backpacks. Extra provisions were in a foldout shelf in the wall, but beneath the shelf... Derrick didn't want to look, but it was impossible not to. He scooped the remaining packages into his bag.

There were still other places to search. The two unlucky passengers in front of him should have had backpacks as well. The compartment beneath their feet, like the one his backpack had been tucked away in, was bent in a way that meant it had to be forced open. He sighed, knowing he didn't have the strength to open it. He was still recovering from a concussion that caused constant sharp headaches. His ankle continued to throb. The mediscanner had proven to him that his ankle was not broken but sprained. However, the swelling had gotten severe from walking around on it over the past several days.

Derrick needed to quickly turn his attention elsewhere. Before anything else, he needed to find the Mineral Seeker. The Mineral Seeker was a two-part device. The first part was a bud, which soared up into the air and collected a satellite image of the ground below. It sent these images, along with a topography scan, to the handheld device, and then the device would be able to predict minerals beneath the surface. If they had any hope of contacting Wei or finding a stable fuel source, they would need some materials to work with.

He squeezed his eyes tight to shake off the wreaking air and focus through the stench. He'd find food later. He couldn't even think about food now. Derrick walked hazily back to the controls, where the pilot and copilot still hung from their chairs. Derrick smiled a little through his grimace. There was a bulge in the pocket behind the back of the pilot's chair. The Mineral Seeker was still exactly where it should have been. If only he had been thinking clearly when they left the ship the first time; he could have remembered it then.

When he stepped back into the daylight, he took in a gulp of fresh air, forgetting that the air was never fresh on Yalk. Steamy, swamp-scented air filled his mouth, and he spat angrily. If he ever left this planet, he was going to make sure it was utterly destroyed before any intelligent life had the misfortune of forming on it.

The bud flew from his hand and into the thick, foggy sky. "Transmitting. Warning: get to highest elevation possible." He looked up the hill that their ship had slid down from. If he could reach the top of that hill, he would have a much better chance of getting the handheld to receive the signal. His ankle started to burn at the thought of the climb, but his mind was set.

"Derrick, please tell me you won't climb with your ankle like that." Ana surprised him by appearing.

"I have to. You don't know how to use the mineral scanner and your injured hands won't make it any easier for you to make the climb than me."

"Be careful. I'll wait for you at the bottom," she relented.

His feet stumbled over one another. A rock that jutted from the ground skinned the side of his bad ankle. Derrick gritted his teeth and focused hard on the screen. A vine full of thorns caught at the side of his shoe, and he could feel it down through to his sock. Derrick pulled away angrily. Occasionally, he looked down to see Ana staring up with her hand above her eyes. The peak was almost in sight. He lifted his knees higher to avoid the front ends of his shoes catching on the rocky ground. Many rocks were covered in a coat of mossy slime that made them impossibly slick.

When he reached the top, he held out the device above his head and over the land. The screen lit up with watercolor-like patches blending into one another. He felt his jaw drop.

He was not this lucky. He was never this lucky.

"Yes! Yes! Ana, we have it!" He danced with the device above his head for her to see. She lifted her arms up excitedly, but he couldn't hear what she said. He hollered to the air above him, "Yes! I can't believe it! I can't believe it."

"I can't believe it. I can't believe it."

Derrick started. The creature had somehow gotten to be at his feet. He was so sick of those stupid little creatures. He kicked the thing as hard as he could and missed it. The rocky mud beneath him slid loose, and his ankle gave way. There was no saving his balance; he was tumbling down the hill. Derrick felt the ground connect with his side, his head, his arm, his leg. Something sharp lodged its way into his back, and he suddenly stopped.

The tree leaves above were either clear or muddled; he couldn't tell. His brain felt like a camera that could only sharpen its focus on one item at a time while the rest was completely fuzzy. Heat gathered at the spot where his back connected with rock, and the warmth in his hands and face was quickly fading.

'I'm dying,' he thought.

'Am I okay with this?' he asked himself. The pounding in his ears was muffled. The soft rhythm worked to ease him to sleep. His eyes began to shut.

'Yeah, I'm okay with this.'

He wasn't scared. The adrenaline pumping through his veins pumped blood into the mud and rocks beneath him. He wasn't dying fast enough. The dark warmth that he was fading into started to become uncomfortable. A whisper of sensibility told him that this was transfer sickness and he should ignore it. Fear crept in upon him.

"I can't believe it. I can't believe it. I can't believe it."

His own voice. He was dying to his own voice. From the corner of his blurred eyes, he could see the ugly thing. Ana was right. It was mocking him. A hot rage sent warmth back into his body.

"I can't believe it."

"Derrick! Derrick, where are you?"

He couldn't hear her, but the rodent could, and that was enough.

Derrick decided he didn't feel as dead as he did before. It couldn't be over for him already. His body twitched uncontrollably as his control over himself waned. Derrick slipped his hand through mud and rocks, not feeling the skin cutting against them. His fingertips brushed his belt where his E.V. was strapped, but the ends of his fingers felt as if they were made of mud too. He needed to focus.

He saw what he needed to do in his mind. The gun was slowly removed from its strap.

"Ana!" he screamed with all the force left in his body.

"Ana! Ana! Ana!"

His arm shot out, and he fired.

38

Chapter 38

"From the Articles of the Council:

Year: 2386

Subject: Ana Battinson"

"Ana! Ana! Ana!"

Ana crawled on all fours as she tried to get down the steep rocks faster. The thick heat invaded her head and made it difficult to think carefully. She had started down after him as soon as she had seen him fall. The world was lit up with his voice. He was screaming for her. He needed her. Her feet hit the ground.

Warm mud splattered her pant legs and sucked at her shoes, making it difficult to run. She wanted to call out his name, but then she might lose him in the many voices of the tangled, swampy woods.

"Ana! Ana! Ana!"

It was becoming louder as she neared the source. Jump a log, turn a tree, step over a rock. She slid suddenly to a stop. At first, her heart wouldn't let her believe that the decrepit form in the mud was his. Such a crooked, motionless, bleeding thing couldn't be her Derrick. He was just calling to her moments before.

"Derrick, no!" she whispered through her fingers.

"Ana! Ana! Ana!"

The thick, black mud around him streamed tiny veins of red. His pale, thin body was enveloped in mud and was posed at cragged angles as if it was growing from the ground. She didn't have to go to his side to know, but she went to him still. Her still-healing fingers intertwined with his.

"Ana! Ana! Ana!"

Ana blinked away a few tears, and they joined the mud and blood beneath her.

"Ana! Ana! Ana!"

His last tortured scream yelled out to her still.

"Stop it!"

She turned to the creature with vicious hate. It stared back at her with cold, unmoving, beady eyes. Her eyes widened. She was staring down the barrel of a gun.

"No," she whispered.

Her blood ran cold. She went hollow, more hollow than she had ever been, and then a deep sickness came up within her. It was like no other sickness. Not like the sickness that came from the smell of the other passengers rotting away. It was a different kind of rot. The Transfer Sickness reared its head. Her brain felt like it was boiling a thick, white froth over top of her thoughts.

The creature sat immovably upon the gun. It was so ridiculous, so hatefully ridiculous! She wouldn't end this way! He couldn't do this to her! Her knees and ankles had sunk deep into the mud as she crouched to be next to Derrick's empty body. There was no way she would escape in time.

"You couldn't!" she shouted at it.

"You couldn't! You couldn't! You couldn't!"

"No, don't do this!"

"Don't do this! Don't do this! Don't do this!"

"I love you!"

Blue light spiraled through the darkness, and there was no escaping the wide rays. Derrick stepped quietly around his body and picked up the mineral scanner from his limp hand. He kicked his old form away and watched his face sink into the ground. He had felt his mind fading away inside the head of the simple-minded creature that he had transferred himself into at the moment of his death. If she had just been a little slower—he wouldn't have been able to do it. If she could have just been a little slower...

"I love you! I love you! I love you!"

39

Chapter 39

"From the Articles of the Council:

   Year: 2386

   Subject: Wei Wen"

Wei Wen awoke to find herself hanging limply from the straps of her seat. Her first thought was that she needed to get her console working, her second was that she was thirsty. She brushed her arm across the screen on her side of the console, but the controls were set to the copilot's side. She must have fainted before Wall had. She looked to the professor now. He seemed to be unconscious.

"Wall?" She coughed.

He didn't respond, and she grumblingly unstrapped herself from her chair. Wei stood, stretched her back painfully, and then looked around the cabin. She noted that among the people moving was Anita. She was trying to care for her barely conscious husband. Wei sighed; Anita should be running a systems analysis.

"Anita, if you don't try to get systems back online, we aren't going to have anything to diagnose crew injuries with."

Wei knew it was the right thing to say to get her moving. Its effect was instant. The woman quickly scrambled to the back of the ship, abandoning her groaning husband. Wei hobbled to Wall's side of the console, noting that the ship was settled on uneven ground. When the third ship had been destroyed by the Eterns, Wei's ship had been clipped. The landing gear had been disabled along with a few minor systems, which was why they were forced into the crash landing. Normally, stabilizers would have been enacted after a landing to keep the ship steady, but these too had been destroyed with the landing gear.

She grabbed ahold of Wall's chair for support.

"Wall! Goddammit, Wall, get up!"

Wei Wen glared irritably down at him. His blonde hair was filled with dust from the metal panel above his head, which had been crumpled in the crash. Wall let out a small groan and flittered back into the world momentarily, only to fall back into sleep. She held a hand to her temple to ward off the growing headache. Why were they all so incompetent? Wei reached for her copilot's controls and slid them to her side of the control panel.

The fuel light blinked impudently at her. It had been alarming them of the decreasing fuel for ten days now. She huffed at it and deleted it from the screen. She would be happy if she never had to lay eyes on it again. She went through a few procedures to amplify the communication signal to Derrick's ship, but they failed. She hadn't thought they would work, but she had to go through the procedures dutifully so that she didn't overlook anything important.

Two days ago, they had been lucky enough to find two fairly uninhabited planets that could support human life. When

333

they had embarked on this crazed adventure, Wei had realized their first problem was going to be finding a fuel source. They couldn't stop in any local solar systems because the Eternian fleet would be looking for them. That meant they had to go into an unclaimed territory, where a natural fuel source would have to be found on the planet's surface.

They had spent a long time arguing about which planets would be most likely to have the needed minerals. Any planet with useful, untouched ore would have to be very far away. So far away that it would be inconvenient for any Earth-known higher intelligence to get to. That would mean the cruisers would have to almost completely run out of fuel to get there. Wei had split up the ships so that if one planet was a bust, the other team might manage to find success. She would be lying if she said she didn't choose the best planet for herself. The planet the other ship had landed on collected low levels of radiation from the sun. If they didn't preserve their medicines wisely, they would be dying of radiation sickness within an Earth month.

Wei knew they would have to get started immediately on her planet as well. Food and water would not be a problem for six hundred days—longer if a few of the crew had perished in the crash. They could find food on the planet they had landed on, but none of this mattered if they couldn't find a fuel source. If they were stranded on the planet, then they couldn't switch bodies, and they would slowly all submit to Transfer Sickness.

The ship shook a little and then sputtered to life. The lights flickered on. Anita had outdone herself! Wei clapped her hands, even allowing herself a smile.

"Anita!" she called, "run a shipwide mediscan on the whole crew, show injuries on the main console." She then directed herself to face the other wandering eyes. "Do we have any survivors with a history in the medical field?"

It didn't really matter because the mediscanners could automatically diagnose and direct treatment for any injury, but Wei knew that some hands and minds were more capable of such things than others.

"I was a dentist not that long ago."

The voice came from a kid around the age of nineteen. He was a scrawny, dorky-looking thing. This guy was doing it all wrong. Who the hell lives forever and chooses to be a dentist?

"Can you operate a medikit from a mediscanner?"

"Oh, yeah, definitely. We used them for all of the surgeries."

Why wasn't he already moving? He stared at her dumbly, and she flicked her hand at him to make him move.

"Oh, yeah, of course. Yes, ma'am."

Wei turned back to the main console, where Anita had put the display from the mediscanner. The mediscanner worked by detecting organic materials. After finding all the life in a room, it was automatically set to diagnose the health of all the organisms. The organisms, which were Wei's crew, showed up only at first as colored outlines of themselves. Alive was red, blue was dead, and anything in-between was in-between.

Wei looked at her own outline standing by the console. She was all red, except for a yellowness to her forearm. Wei lifted it up and was shocked to see that her arm was coated in blood. Calmly, she opened up the drawer under the pilot's chair for the second mediscanner. The cut wasn't diagnosed as immediate. The amount of blood was mostly due to the adrenaline of the crash pumping it more quickly.

Wei returned to her seat. It was time to start asking questions. She slid her hand across the console and the

335

automated option appeared.

"Automated."

"Wei Wen, what can I do for you today?"

"Access results of the shipwide mediscan."

"Accessed."

"How many humans are alive on board this ship?"

"Two hundred twenty-one."

That wasn't bad. They had only lost one.

"Automated, how many of these humans are in critical condition?"

"Two."

Wei turned away from the console. The dentist was babbling awkwardly to some man, clearly in shock, whose seatbelt had jammed. There had to be someone more competent for this job. This fool should have been on the ship blown up by the Eterns.

"Dentist!"

The boy jumped, and Wei rolled her eyes.

"Dentist, come here."

He listened, leaving the man who was kicking and grabbing at the straps of his chair. She lifted the mediscanner so that the dentist could see it.

"Do you see these two passengers? They come first. Get it done. If you find they're impossible to save, come to me immediately. No more of us can afford to die."

"What do you have in mind if there's no saving them?" His eyebrows came together.

"Dentist, people are dying. Follow your orders."

He scurried off, and Wei returned to the console. Unlike Derrick and Ana's planet, Wei's ship had detected some primitive kind of civilization on their planet. There had been large masses of heat signatures on the screen. They needed to figure out just how close they had landed near the natives.

"Automated, yesterday afternoon I was scanning some life forms on the planet's surface."

"Displaying all matching life forms on screen now."

"Put our location on the screen for reference."

"Complying."

That's what she had been afraid of. The screen was lit up with life signatures. When Wei had originally chosen this planet, she had been pretty surprised to find that only half the planet seemed to be alive. The computer hypothesized that the planet had been hit with an asteroid at some point in time, creating deep craters on half of the planet. The other half of the planet was ancient woodland. From space, the cruiser was able to pick out hot spots for life, which were the most likely points for civilization. Wei then had analysts look at the topography to pick out signs of development. The best they could predict about the intelligent life that lived there was that they lived in the trees, and they were fairly large in size. Neither of these things was particularly comforting to Wei.

There had been a lot of debate as to which side of the planet they should land on. They really couldn't afford a confrontation with the natives, but they needed to crash near a water source. Where they were forced to land was not ideal. What finally decided their unlucky location was the disabled landing gear. They couldn't safely hope to land in the woodlands without the landing gear. That meant they had to narrow their search for a runway down to clearings within walking distance to a water source. After several days of debating and losing fuel, they decided on this crash site that had a small clearing just around the lake. If they had been off by even a small margin, they might have ended up swimming for dear life.

They had successfully managed to land next to the lake and not in it, but that was only the first of many problems. The lake they had landed beside was surely a watering hole for many lifeforms on the planet. The life signatures of the lifeforms she was most concerned with were fast darting away from the location. They were fleeing from the commotion of their crash. She was lucky that they were able to be scared off so easily. For now, at least, they weren't in immediate danger. It wouldn't last for long, though, because they had been forced next to a hotbed of the natives.

"Ms. Grennel?"

Wei turned confusedly to see that the dentist had returned. All of them had been working for her before the Eternian revolution. Had she met him previously? She squinted at him, trying to place his face. Nope. Didn't know him.

"It's Wei," she corrected him.

"Ah, erm, yes. Sorry, Ms. Wei. Um, Ms. Wei?"

Damn. This pathetic creature didn't have a backbone. How could you live that long and still be such a failure?

"Please do spit it out, dentist."

"I managed to stabilize both of the passengers in critical condition, but one of them is being kept in an induced coma. He's battered up pretty bad. I don't think he's going to make it."

"How long do you think he has?" Her eyebrows rose.

"Er, well, I don't know."

"Then ask the computer," she snapped.

"Oh, yes." Momentarily he fiddled around with the mediscanner. "Best estimate is a couple of days, maybe a week at best."

"Fantastic."

Wei flew back to the main console irritated. The ship was showing that it was evening outside. She needed to get out, look around, and set up a perimeter. The forest-dwellers were nervous about the ship now, but maybe later that night they wouldn't be so cautious. They needed to set up some type of defense. Even if in the best circumstances the intelligent life permanently evacuated the area, there could still be other predatory life on the planet.

"Anita, how hard would it be to set up a safety perimeter around the ship?" she barked.

"It depends... we rerouted most of our electrical power to fuel the ship when we started running out of fuel. What we have left needs to be used to power the computers."

"Get creative. You have twenty minutes."

Anita scurried away, giving orders to those that were already up and moving. The dentist had returned to caring for the rest of the injured people and had employed some help. Wei gave a small, satisfied half-smile, which she made sure that nobody else saw. She loved progress. Her empire had been built on her progressive nature, and her new empire would be the same.

A funny thought crossed her mind.

"Automated, what's the name of this planet again?" she asked contemplatively.

"You are currently located on the planet Lovindo. Would you like to request further information on the planet?"

"No, that's fine."

What a stupid name for a planet.

40

Chapter 40

As night darkened the planet, there was a stillness that Wei didn't think she had ever felt before. The reflected stars seemed to glow from up under the lake instead of from above. There was a gentleness to it all. Untouched. For a moment, she almost liked it, or at least thought she might understand why other people liked it.

Wei turned away from the lake and followed the outlines of her people creeping around in the dark with little glowing, red lights. They were finishing setting up the perimeter. It would create a ten-foot-tall, magnetic field which did not wholly satisfy Wei. The computer had said that the natives lived in the trees. If they were descendants of a primate-like race, they would probably be okay, but what about something more... avian?

She would post sentries during the night. It was the only way they could guarantee that they wouldn't be attacked from above. Wei snapped her wrist, and her handheld screen unrolled like cloth and became solid. She was tracking heat signatures, specifically those of her intelligent neighbors, which had slowly inched closer to the lake throughout the day.

At the rate they were approaching, the computer predicted that they would be surrounded in less than a half-hour. The perimeter needed to be fully operational by then.

"Ms. Wei!"

It was the dentist again. Wei sighed and turned away from her handheld.

"Ms. Wei, Mr. Matthews is not doing well." He was referring to the patient in critical condition.

"I didn't expect he was."

"Oh," he said annoyingly.

"Are you going to tell me your evaluation?" Wei snapped.

"Oh, um, yes. Mr. Matthews is showing signs that he's slipping away from us." The induced coma they had forced him into was pushing him toward death more easily than if he'd been awake. Still, she couldn't afford to wake him up. She couldn't handle a crew member that had Transfer Sickness. It would only cause trouble for the crew and make them uneasy.

"How much longer does he have?" she asked

"I'm not sure we have much longer than afternoon tomorrow."

They were interrupted by a sudden, throaty howl. Wei shook a little. It was a sound somewhere between a wolf's howl and an owl's hoot. The first call had followers. The area was lit up with whoops and calls.

"Ms. Wei! What on Earth is that?"

"Not on Earth," she corrected him irritably.

"Huh? Oh, yes, ma'am, I guess not, but—"

Wei didn't have to look down at her handheld, but she did anyway. The outside edge of the tree line was filled with green blobs. Lifeforms. How had they arrived so fast? She had been projected a half an hour. Had her handheld malfunctioned?

"Ms. Wei, what is that?" He shuddered.

"That's a call for Mr. Matthews." Wei whispered darkly.

Wei turned away quickly, leaving the dentist staring dumbly into the dark. She looked at her weapon, turning the proper setting on. The last thing she needed was to accidentally shoot herself out of her body. The gun glowed white. White was lethal.

How had they advanced so suddenly? Maybe it was better to ask "why?"

"Anita!" Wei hollered, running back to the ship. The tall, gangly woman appeared in the doorway.

"Wei, it's not good news."

"The perimeter isn't up?"

"And it's not going to be for at least another hour. I had to reroute some of the circuits for the fence, and when I did, it shut down some of the ship's main functions including the ventilator, which we're using for Mr. Matthews. We almost lost him, but Kendrick revived him." She gestured at the dentist, who was following Wei like a lost puppy.

So that was the dentist's name. Wei looked down at her handheld and held it up to the tree line. She released a bud, and it zipped up and winked out in the dark.

"Display outer visual of lifeforms in real-time."

Blue lines shone out in front of them, showing the topography of the land around them. Shifting in the woods were hulking, red outlines. They were big. The computer was doing calculations to interpret their size and agility. Through the eyes of her technology, she was getting her first look at her adversaries. This would burn a lot of battery that she hadn't wanted to use.

The computer was creating a hologram of her foe from the bud's visual. It was about seven feet tall and two and a half feet wide from shoulder-to-shoulder. Avian ancestry for sure. The hologram etched feathers and then wings.

"Flight capabilities?"

"Unknown with current data."

Wei froze. The bud came face to face with their enemy, and a hideous mask was shaped.

"Connection lost." Her bud had been destroyed.

She stared blankly at the screen, the heat signatures of the birds were starting to jitter around in an aggravated manner. They were going to make their move shortly; it was only a matter of time. The horrific hologram that the bud had managed to create for her stared back at her—it was those eyes.

"Get the perimeter up now!" Wei ordered, marching into the ship.

"What about Matthews?" Kendrick asked.

"He won't make it if we don't make it first. Anita, you and your husband stay to maintain the perimeter." She pointed at the two of them. "Dentist, I need you to stay with Matthews; keep him alive for as long as possible without the ventilator. Get some people and make sure he's tied down before you turn off the ventilator. When I call, I need you to drop everything and get Matthews outside."

"Outside?" Gerald whispered.

"Yes? Can you do that?" Wei snapped.

"Yes, yes, we can," Anita asserted for her husband.

"Good. Everyone else, if you can walk, come outside with me. Turn your guns to level two at first; if they keep coming,

343

don't hesitate to turn it to level one." Level two was orange, paralysis. Level one was white, death.

There was a pause. These were men and women who were used to running, who were used to split-second decisions, but this was a whole new ballgame. The hooting had increased, and now there was even a smacking sound that confused her. What the hell could that be?

The handheld projected the outline of their heat signatures in the tree line so that everyone could see them. They seemed to fall back and forth in a way which at first seemed to be barely repressed aggression, but on second look, it was obvious that they were using some very complex, coordinated movements. Somehow, they were very slowly moving forward and shifting places without ever revealing an opening into their center. It was an angry, territorial dance that made the phalanx of ancient Sumer look like child's play.

They were clearly fast when they wanted to be. If they wanted to, they could advance quickly and overtake Wei's crew. She wracked her brain for ideas of how to combat the enemy. They had retreated deep into the woods when they crashed, so that meant that they were skittish. Maybe if they could frighten them again, they would back away. It wasn't just that they retreated either; they retreated for many hours after the crash, which meant they were cautious animals.

Wei thought of those massive eyes. The hologram almost made them seem like they glowed.

"Murmur, connect with Anita Cole."

Lay-Tech was the best thing she had ever come up with, or at least the most profitable.

"Wei, what do you need? I'm about to turn on the perimeter."

"I need you to find the brightest spotlight you can, and then shine it in the clearing between us and the woods."

"What for?"

"Just do it; you might be saving us all a confrontation." She added as an afterthought, "Where's Wall?"

"I don't know; he's been acting bizarre since the crash. He was just working on the perimeter."

"Get the light on and the perimeter up." She would worry about Wall later.

Wei turned off the murmur. The handheld showed that the natives were only about a half-mile away. That meant they were probably already out of the tree line. If it wasn't so dark, they would be able to see them. If Wei's suspicion was right, a spotlight might help them with more than just sight.

She could hear them closing in around them. The intensity of their shouts and whoops had increased. They were becoming more agitated as Wei and her people failed to remove themselves from their claimed land. She could hear bodies swishing around in the tall grass. Wei fought the urge to close herself off inside the ship. It wouldn't provide much protection, and she had to keep her eyes on the surroundings.

Her people were already walking around in the night, setting up the perimeter. She couldn't abandon them.

"Anita!" Wei shouted far above a murmur.

"Perimeter up... now!" She had never been so happy to hear Wall's voice.

There was a sudden crack of electricity going through the lines. A screech of pain blasted into the night as one of the natives had been caught in the perimeter. Squawks of rage soon followed. Her heart sunk. There were heat signatures inside of the perimeter. They had been too slow.

345

"We're not alone; be ready to fire at hostiles," she murmured into the device to her people walking around in the tall grass.

No sooner had she said it than a blast of orange light spilled through the night. She was startled by how near to her it had been. In those few precious seconds of light, she watched one of her men collapse under the weight of a massive, angry beast into the knee-high grass. Wei fired into the dark. The creature which had lifted itself up, undoubtedly to strike again on Wei's fallen man, collapsed under the orange light.

Then the dark was no more. Anita procured a makeshift spotlight, and it shined with brilliant intensity. Wei blinked, trying to clear her vision. She recovered quicker than their attackers. Wei felt her courage falter at the size of the monsters. The two remaining creatures, which had been backing down on an unlucky systems analyst, stopped suddenly, paralyzed by the light. Their massive eyes struggled to focus, as Wei had hoped; they were temporarily blinded. She shifted the setting on her gun. She fired twice and then twice again. It was a thick, white light that hardly registered under the spotlight. For a moment they stood and then collapsed on either side of the systems analyst who whimpered pathetically.

"Coles! I need Matthews outside immediately!"

The effect was instant. Anita had taken Matthews' legs and Gerald his arms. They were lucky that the man was still unconscious, because if he had been in a frenzy, it would have been hard for them to get him outside. She had to remember to add a stretcher to the medical kit. Wei ran to the place where she had shot the first of the creatures. She had shot it with the orange light setting, so if she was lucky and its physiology was not terribly different from theirs, it would only be temporarily

346

paralyzed. It still read a life signal on her handheld.

Kendrick and Wall had followed the Coles, carrying medis-canners and a medikit. As Matthews was set down into the tall grass, Anita's eyes froze on the spot where the native creature lay.

"Wei..." she started concernedly.

Wei held up a hand to her, staring back at her meaningfully.

Anita gasped. "No, you can't be serious!"

"I am very serious, Anita, but it's not my choice to make."

Kendrick stared confusedly, clearly not catching on to what was happening, but Professor Wall and Gerald Cole laid eyes on the monster on the ground.

Wall, used to speaking his mind, was quick to start. "What choice? You don't mean you expect him to transfer into that *thing*!"

"I do."

"Wei!" he protested.

"Listen," she snapped, "Matthews is going to die. It is inevitable. We are on a foreign planet, and I don't see any humans leaping around out here in the dark begging for us to use them as transfers. We will ask him what he wants, but I think we already know what his answer will be. Transfer Sickness will have a pretty thick hold on him by this time."

Anita shivered but didn't try to argue with Wei again. Truthfully, Wei herself was very disturbed by the task at hand. Quietly, however, she unstrapped her gun from its holster and put it on the blue setting for transfer. The handgrip grew blue as she laid it into Matthews' palm, and his veins started to glow brightly. If Matthews fired that gun, who knows if he would even be able to inhabit the creature. She gritted her teeth; he could be shooting his soul away into hell.

"Hold him down so that he can't fire at one of us, but allow him a shot at the native if he chooses to take it," Wei ordered.

She gestured for Wall and Gerald to hold down Matthews' forearms while still allowing for him to point the gun toward the native. She didn't need him getting any traitorous ideas. Friendly fire was not something she was prepared to deal with right now.

"Wake him up now," she said uncharacteristically softly.

Kendrick obliged her request. The man did not behave like a lunatic; he was too close to death's door. Instead, he weakly opened his eyes, staring up into the strange constellations. Kendrick had given the man until tomorrow afternoon, but she could tell now that he wouldn't make it to the morning this way.

"Matthews, you are in mortal danger. I'm sure you can feel the Transfer Sickness." When she spoke, it was soft, but her regular firmness was underlying.

Matthews blinked, and she assumed this meant he understood.

"We have temporarily paralyzed the body of an alien native on the planet Lovindo. It is of avian ancestry. We do not know if it will be suitable for transfer. You may quietly die looking up at those stars, or you can pull that trigger."

Matthews' eyes followed up his arm to the hand where the gun was held. He clearly had not been able to register it in his hand before. She saw the vicious thought of betrayal pass through his eyes, even in this depleted state. He was measuring his strength and deciding if he could shoot one of them instead. Wei lowered down to whisper into his ear.

"I'll kill you if you try it."

Wei opened her mouth to say more, but the man blinked

with furiously psychotic eyes; a tear budded at the corner of each eye. He understood. She didn't need to say anything else.

In the silence, blue light scorched the night air. Matthews' body lit up blue along every vein and then dimmed and went pale.

"Oh my God," Anita whispered, as all of their eyes followed to the native whose hulking, feathered body remained paralyzed but breathing in the tall grass.

"Is he—is he in there?" Kendrick cautiously approached the spot where it lay.

"How do we tell?" mumbled Gerald.

"I don't think we can know until the paralysis wears off," Wei replied flatly.

"It's horrible," Anita said, more to herself than the others.

"What is?" Wei snapped, feeling at first that her judgment on how she handled the situation was being questioned.

Anita startled a little at Wei's tone, but then replied faintly, "Transfer Sickness."

"Oh." Wei relaxed, but a little uneasiness broke through looking down at the frozen face of what used to be one of her men.

"He—he didn't hesitate," whispered Anita.

"No," Wei returned coldly.

"It's just that—would I?"

"Even the tamest animal will lash out when its back is against the wall. We are not tame animals, Anita. Who knows what a man will do when cornered, desperate, and scared?"

Anita stared down at the man in the grass. The insanity that had contorted his face before the transfer was still there, though it was not as powerful as it had been when life was still in him. She looked hard at this picture in the grass.

"We are not men."

41

Chapter 41

It had been just over two weeks since the crash when conflicts arose both within and without Wei's small encampment on the planet Lovindo. The natives still called from the tree lines at night, but it was comforting, at least, that they had stopped trying to ram into the perimeter after the second evening. Still, the looming threat was not forgotten. The effect it had on the crew was disheartening. The low, thrumming hoots at dusk and through the dark hours were a constant reminder of what was kept beneath the jagged shadows of distant treetops.

Wei watched her men work in silence. There had still been no success in contacting the second ship, but that had turned out to be the least of her worries. Despite her need to land on the side of the planet which contained much-needed water, it became apparent through many days of computer scanning that their best chance of finding minerals that could serve as a fuel source was near the crater site on the barren side of the planet. It was Gerald Cole's job to run manual scans on the planet. This took much longer than the computer's automatic scans, but he could get them far more detailed, especially when he enhanced the ship's range and sent out a bud to take topography scans.

Meanwhile, the native which Matthews had transferred into didn't have the vocal cords to speak any Earthly language. Although Anita had tried speech therapy with him for many hours, they were yet to have any successful communication with him. It was impossible to know how he was coping with the situation. It was also apparent that although none of the native's consciousness had remained, Matthews was picking up behaviors that were undoubtedly not human. For instance, he had taken on the unnerving habit of preening himself over and over again. His companions would watch uneasily as he combed tediously through each individual feather with his beak.

None of this, however, was what unsettled the crew about Matthews the most. It was the discovery that his taste buds were no longer the same. Cooked food no longer appealed to Matthews anymore, and since the ship's food stock failed to contain any raw meat, he was forced to live mostly on a diet of dried fruit. Wei had been sought out numerous times by crew members giving complaints about Matthews, who insisted that they were "very uncomfortable" working in his vicinity.

Wei, who spent as little time as possible worrying about their newly transferred crewmate and focused on searching for a fuel source, eventually went to Wall with the concerns.

"Wall," Wei snapped.

Wall was currently working on creating portable Geiger counters instead of using the one embedded in the mainframe. They would need them for the trip they were to inevitably make to the crater site. When Wei spoke, he lifted his head from his project and gave her a disinterested frown.

"Wall, it's been brought to my attention recently that Matthews has been making the crew nervous. Why is this a problem?"

Wall raised an eyebrow at first as if to question her seriousness and then chuckled at her.

"I don't need this, Evan," she said, beginning to walk away. "I will just ignore it until one of the crew members finally decides to tell me what it is about Matthews that is causing them to stop their work and interrupt mine."

"Wei! Wei, come back!" Wall said, still laughing, and Wei reluctantly returned. She hated humbling herself, but he was undeniably reliable with these sorts of problems.

"Well?" she shot at him.

"Well," he smiled, "apart from the obvious fact that Matthews is some type of alien bird monster and the fact that the other members of his species would love to get into our perimeter and tear us apart," he grinned wider, "he also seems not to be preferential to his current diet."

"What do you mean? I thought he's been eating."

"Lord, Wei! Do I have to spell it out for you? The damn monster puts those big, soulless eyes on you, and you can't help but wonder if it's looking a bit peckish! Ha! Peckish!" He snorted.

Wall continued to snicker at his play on words, and Wei's gaze shifted to Matthews. His head turned, and the white-colored eyes gazed back. For the first time, she started to feel what the others had been sensing for days. Matthews was hungry for meat, and he wanted it raw. She shuddered. Wall saw her recognition and added more seriously.

"You're a phenomenal entrepreneur and scientist, Wei, but we aren't back at Grennel Technologies. You've got people to

353

lead. They need someone to take charge and lead them in the right direction. Anita was right; we aren't men anymore."

Wall always had a way of being melodramatic, but what he was saying did strike a chord with her. It was obvious that the mental and emotional states of her workers were starting to interfere with their duties. Wei tried with some difficulty to put herself in their shoes. What would they want to hear? No. What did they *need* to hear?

Wei watched her men work in silence. They talked in low voices, passing glances occasionally to Matthews, who was sitting uselessly outside as Anita attempted to communicate with him. The best she could get out of him was some low, guttural noises which the crew desperately tried to ignore. They turned their heads and winced when they heard it. There was an undeniable heaviness in the atmosphere. There should have been a whirring mixture of activity from some of the greatest, oldest minds to ever grace the Earth.

When Wei discovered that they would have to make a trip to the crater site, the news had not been announced to the crew but had slowly and gloomily passed from crew member to crew member by word of mouth. Wei realized suddenly that this system was flawed. She was losing them. They were becoming disconnected; they weren't a unified, driving force like she needed them to be. Slowly but surely, the crew was weighed down with the events that had passed since they had left Earth, and not addressing them had left much uncertainty in the minds of her people.

She coughed loudly to grab the crew's attention, and each hand paused where it was, almost eager to stop. Seeing that she had something to say, they stood and walked forward obediently to listen. It was as if they had been waiting for her—she needed to get it right.

"Tell me. Why is it that you chose to come here?" She demanded of them.

There was a repeated silence, and Wei sighed.

"Men, listen to me, we are not men. Many of you are uncomfortable with Matthews' transfer. There are mutters of his inhumanity, and I can feel it beginning to weigh on our ship. This I want to make very clear to you: none of us are human. The humanity of Earth has named us "non-humans." The Eterns have made us their enemy. Today, my non-humans, my Non-Eterns, we are Lovindians.

"You are here because there is nowhere else. There is nobody else for us. We are all alone out here—even our sister ship is planets away. I understand how we all feel. We spent several lifetimes on Earth and found a home there; we were born there. It is fine for us to feel a little lost, to feel a little lonely, and tired. However, there has been some question as to how I have been leading this crew, and that's where I step in.

"What happens when you grow old? What happens?" Wei demanded of them, and when there was no response, she continued angrily. "Your Transfer Sickness will set in, your mind will become rabid, and just like Matthews, you will not have a human to transfer into. You are not men! Look at him. Look at Matthews!" She pointed harshly.

Resolutely, they all looked to the fidgeting creature, which stared back at them with hollow white eyes.

"This is what we are!" Wei exclaimed. "Look hard! This... is our evolution!"

The room settled, and Wei saw a mixture of emotions before her. Faces with fixed expressions of self-hate, faces of acceptance mingled with tears, and faces of non-accepting horror. She finally looked back at Wall, who gave her a grim sort of smile and returned to his work. Where was the hope, the purpose, in such a future as she had just foretold for them? With a certain sadness, she realized that she hadn't given them anything, so she continued, this time not sure of what she was going to say.

"Follow me." Their heads rose to look at her. "I do not know who we will become, but I promise that we will become the vastest empire in existence and take back the world that was taken from us so long ago."

"How?" The voice belonged to a man whom she could only identify as being one of her engineers. Wei addressed them all rather than just the one man.

"By fueling our ship with the minerals at the crater site."

Many heads bowed respectfully at this statement. She did not have to tell them her entire plan. She did not owe it to them, but she had given them a goal and a promise. She had given them what she owed.

"Ms. Wei! Ms. Wei!"

Gerald Cole stopped quickly in the doorway and looked around at all the new solemn but determined faces with mild confusion. His crazed eyes found Wei. She felt her pulse quicken forebodingly. Wei started to move forward so that she could speak to him in private, but Gerald burst forward with the news upon seeing her.

"There are others." Wei didn't understand him.

"Gerald..." Evan Wall had gotten up and was attempting to quiet him but to no effect.

"Not the natives. Not the bird creatures. These beings are living beneath the planet. Tunnels. Civilization. By the crater site." Gerald panted heavily, his sentences short and rapid.

Evan Wall stopped, stunned. All eyes turned to Wei. Her face darkened with anger. She was angry at the idiocy of Gerald Cole, angry at the new looks of fear spreading about her crew, angry at the audacity of another intelligent species living on her newly claimed planet. Wei answered challengingly.

"If this is true, if a civilization is here, then they have paved the way for our success."

42

Chapter 42

"Jacob! You have to get up, Jacob! They're almost here!"

The world blurs round and round. A worried face and a massively tall figure, walls, walls, walls, the faces again.

"Who's there?"

I'm shaking. Am I being shook? I'm not sure. The person comes close to me. I hear his voice, but it is a mangled, strange sound.

A cold rag is placed on my head. A hand covers my mouth, but it is gentle. I quiet. It's too difficult anyways. Something hot burns down my throat. Why didn't I know I was so cold before? Now I feel like I'm lit on fire. My brain tells me that I'm squirming, fighting, but my eyes aren't so sure. The world is still going round and round.

"What's happening? What's wrong? Is this normal?"

"No, no, it's not. No being is supposed to be in the memory stream that long, but he had to know. He didn't get a break from his last trip here. I knew that he didn't have much time. He's your last hope. You have to—"

The voices fade out. I start to feel myself falling backward, but I'm not falling at all. I'm still on the floor.

"Oh, no you don't, boy! You can't go passing out on us. They'll be entering the atmosphere soon."

More of the liquid is forced into my lips, but it is less hot this time. In fact, it is almost soothing to the pain in the back of my head. I cup it willingly with my hands, but they slip. Stronger hands hold the cup steady and pour.

"Ah, there we go," the voice says comfortingly.

Emmanuel stands over me looking worried. The shadow of his brother in his face haunts me. He looks down on me with grief and pain in his eyes.

"I'm so sorry, Emmanuel," I whisper. "So sorry."

It doesn't amount to much, but he grabs my hand and squeezes tight. My head is slamming. Part of me still sees the worried eyes of Wei's people staring up at her.

"Jacob, the Lovindians are coming. Wei is coming. I can't protect you from her. You have to understand," the Lovindian says forcefully.

"Wei? From the story?" My mind spins.

"Boy! Did you learn nothing? It was never just a story! How do you still not understand? You didn't get to see it all, but you had to have seen enough to know the truth!"

I've never seen the Lovindian so agitated before. I want to tell him that I learned everything I needed to from the story, but it's still so fractured in my mind. My head is too foggy to think straight. I struggle to please him.

"I'm sorry, I just don't understand! How is Wei here? How is she coming?"

A massive wave of air blows dust around the room, and a little, red dust tornado dances and dissipates beside my hand. Darkness falls over the Lovindian's face. He lifts my limp body with his stony hands and props me into a sitting position against the wall.

"I would hide you, but it doesn't matter anymore. You should have been gone by now. You spent too much time unconscious, and I hadn't expected them so soon. It's my fault too." He hangs his head low.

"How long have I been out?" My words come out crackling like leaves.

"In all? You were gone two days in the memory stream and unconscious for a whole day before we could even try to wake you. We would've given you more time, but we didn't have it. That dust that just rolled in was from their ship landing. We're simply out of time. I should have sent you off by now, but I just wanted you to see more." His voice is full of regret.

I look to Emmanuel and my guilt grows. If I hadn't killed the Gromptu, I would have had time to finish the story. I have failed everyone. I have to remember the story. I have to think back and connect the dots. I think aloud.

"Wei was a woman who was struck by Scanthirin Sickness. She was saved by the transfer and became a marked Etern. She refused to join the Eterns and defected from Earth and the Eternian movement. Her crew landed on Lovindo—and..."

That was right. Lovindians came from Earth. It was us all along. Why did the Lovindian try to hide it from me all this time? The Lovindians hadn't stolen the technology from Eterns because they were Eterns. How did this happen? How did we do this to ourselves? My chest burns painfully.

"Quick, Jacob, think back to Jana." The Lovindian straps something to Emmanuel's back, but I can't tell what.

"They discovered two intelligent species, but one was still tribal in nature, while the other had developed a modern civilization," I continue on.

"Think of Jana. What did they do, Jacob?" he urges again.

"They infiltrated the civilization of the intelligent species, they stole their resources, and they fixed their ship." That wasn't it, though; that wasn't the end of the story. "What happened to—?"

Emmanuel tugs at my arm. "Jacob, can you stand?"

"What happened to Derrick?" I ask, ignoring Emmanuel's question.

Sharp, trilling laughter stops him from answering. "Oh, indeed! What did happen to Derrick?"

The words sound playful, but the tone is so cold that I recognize it immediately. The tall, thin creature standing in the doorway of the council build is humanesque but clearly alien. Its height rivals the Lovindian, and its limbs are too long. Its structure is too thin, and its skin a little too shiny—a little too pink. It is her, though. She might as well have been the blonde woman I had seen in the memories.

"You didn't tell him yet? How rich!" she barked. I look to the Lovindian, but he reveals nothing. "You know, that face really suits you, old friend. In fact, I think maybe only you could pull it off. So... sociopathic." Wei smiles and shows a row of teeth that are just slightly over-curved at the tips.

Old friend? I don't understand. The back of my throat suddenly becomes sticky, and my heart tightens. Wei walks closer, a stream of almost blonde but too-white hair follows her, sliding around as if it is too slick to stay still over her sheer, blue jumpsuit. Whatever species she is, makes me feel very uneasy.

"Jacob." She's so close I could touch her. She turns her back to the Lovindian without apprehension. Her eyes narrow to small, yellow slits. "Let me tell you a story," she says through her teeth. "There once was a man who got sick and wanted to die but woke up bright and new. This man hated himself so much that he vowed to live in unhappiness because he could not force himself to die. Again and again he betrayed every gentle being he ever knew and cared for. His chest grew heartless, and before long, he was less human than you see me now. Then this wretched creature that roamed the Earth killed the most loyal lamb he had ever laid eyes on, only so that he could live on in the universe he hated so incredibly much.

"So he waited for his friends to return and save him, still posing as the poor, innocent creature he had murdered. I came for him, and with my new Lovindian eyes, I saw him for who he was just as clearly as you recognized me. What did I do? What did I do when I learned he murdered one of his own?" She pauses as if she's asking me, but I know that she's not. I don't have the energy to respond to her anyways. She gnashes her teeth at me. "I beat him again and again in his body, which was weak with age and radiation sickness that he feebly tried to prevent. He stayed imprisoned in his pathetic, old body and watched as our strength and numbers grew. Oh, how he groveled for a new lamb to be slaughtered in his favor! I let the Transfer Sickness sink in deep. I let him age and age because, like wine, pain is richer with age.

"Finally, though," she flips her hand, "amid his craze, I started to see a look of peace befall him, but that wouldn't do! I pictured poor Ana in my mind, and I knew it could not be enough! So I made a deal with him as he died. I would give him a new body, but he must work in it for me for many years with never a single day's rest. It would cause him terrible pain to use this form, but he could have it, and it was new. Even better! It could live for a very long time without losing any of its vigor! The murderer agreed, of course. I gave the cursed body to him, and I banished him to a small, little red planet to crack again and again in constant agony."

I turn to look at the Lovindian. His face is expressionless, but as Wei smiles at him, I see his eyes start to burn behind his stoic mask.

"It's quite a good face for him, really. He never had much emotion as he was before. Unfortunately, for you that is, that is not the end of the story. You see, Derrick worked for many long years doing what he was told with the realization that after several hundred years, the body would eventually become feeble. He would be at risk of death again, if not from age, then from learning how to access the memory stream and using his telepathy. Once again, he would need a new body. I did, after all, need a creature to survive on with the knowledge of the memory stream. What lies in it is very valuable to me. The universe's history is valuable.

"Once again, I was gracious to the murderer; I told him that he could have a new body as long as he transferred over the stories first. Again and again, he tried and failed; the bodies were too weak! We decided we would find specific children who had natural bred-in defiance, and we would lead them to the little red planet. Their willpower might give them the strength to travel through the memories. We whispered rumors about a place with a story that could defeat the Lovindians. We brought hope to dying races. Willingly, these noble, sacrificial lambs came to the little red planet from near and far, but none could take the story's power. But here you are, a victor, and a human, no less. Poetic, in the end."

"Are you finished?" Derrick growls.

"Do you deny any of it?" She smirks.

"Of course not," he sighs, "the transfer sickness will always get us in the end."

"So you think Ana would have done the same?" she snaps.

His face crumples "I don't know," he whispers.

He's betrayed me. Of course, he has! I have been an idiot. Samuel—Samuel—if I hadn't kept going to the planet, hadn't had faith in the Lovindian—Samuel wouldn't have—I could have been there to protect him.

I grit my teeth through the tears. My thoughts race, but I can't think of anything to say. I'm a stupid human after all. Not an exception. Why had I never been stopped from traveling to the Roja so many times? Why had the sensor disabler been sold so cheaply? Why had it all been so easy? How hadn't I seen it? How had I not seen Derrick staring me in the face when I saw Wei immediately? Except—I only saw through Derrick's eyes, and I never saw Derrick himself except after he was dead. I've been so blind. I made the mistake of putting trust in a Lovindian. My enemy.

I look to Emmanuel and see that he holds a pack over his shoulder. He inches toward me. I shake my head at him. He needs to stay far from Wei. I try to keep her attention.

"It doesn't matter—" I cough.

"Of course it matters. Everything you've done was only as we planned. You accomplished nothing, and no one will even notice you disappear."

I spit. It's mostly blood. I chuckle darkly. I'm going to die, and I can't even stand up. If I distract her, maybe Emmanuel can still escape. He said he would have a plan. Maybe he can still survive. I keep talking even though it's difficult.

"Maybe there won't be any Historians left to record my milliseconds in history, but losing to you is still worth knowing the truth. I can't stand up, but I'm not on my knees."

"I don't distinguish a difference," she snaps.

I know her better. I know she understands.

"You're going to die, Wei." I feel a warmth in my stomach.

"Not before you," she spits.

"Give me the gun, Wei. There's no need to gloat. Let me end him for you," the Lovindian says.

She turns away from me. She smiles at Derrick, but it's only filled with cold and analytical amusement. I frown. Wei unholsters her Lovi-gun and rolls it around in her hands.

"Unfortunately, Derrick, I don't listen to murderers." She waves him off. "You see, Jacob, the story I was telling you is finally at its close. Believe it or not, I don't believe that if I handed Derrick this gun he would shoot you. Oh, you look surprised, but you shouldn't be. See, I think that if I handed him this gun, he would instantly shoot me, and I'm not altogether certain what he would do with you and this... child." At this last bit, she gestures with a flick of her hand toward Emmanuel and her eyes glue him to the spot.

"Derrick, you're too trusting for a thief. I don't need you. You're expendable. You don't even realize that you've passed the memory stream on to him. Through the access point on his palm, I can retrace the science behind how the Historians went from telepaths to memepaths. All I have to do now is give him to a telepathic Lovindian, who can skillfully leech their way through the connection point. If only your weak body had allowed it years ago. Anyways, I will at least commend you for the job you did here. You have served your sentence well, and I will finally give you release."

Wei lifts her gun, and this time, it's not playfully as she had done before. It glows white at the end.

"You'll lose," I breathe, desperate for a distraction.

Wei laughs viciously. "How?"

"If I can find your weakness, then there will be others. Others who will come after I'm gone." I challenge her.

"Weakness!" Wei hisses. "I have no weakness!"

She puts her finger around the trigger, savoring what she's doing.

"Emmanuel," Derrick lays his eyes on him instead of me.

Derrick rushes forward, quicker than anyone could expect a boulder could move. A savage flash of white light bursts like a flame from the mouth of Wei's gun. Its power far outreaches the power it has in my memories. Derrick moves at an incredible speed, but the white light springs into his side and forces him to stumble sideways. My heart leaps for him. Wei was right; he hadn't betrayed us after all.

The gun doesn't stop him. Why? Is the effect not as strong on his species?

"Time to go!" Emmanuel hisses into my ear. He grabs my underarms and starts to pull me along the tile.

My muddled mind tries to make sense of it all. I process the world around me excruciatingly slow. I let out a whimper as I'm jerked roughly over the front steps and into the red dirt. The building shudders as the white light flashes against the inner walls. My heels drag limply across the red dust ground. I'm coated in red. The doorway flashes white again. Emmanuel is struggling. My underarms ache as he groans and yanks me forward. I have to get to my feet. I put my mind to making my legs move, but I'm too weak. All I manage is a kick.

A pinkish form emerges from the building. My skin prickles. I try to energize my body again but can only watch as I'm slowly led away. Too slowly.

"Boy! What is your plan? You cannot run!" Wei yells approaching at an even pace.

"You don't know what I can do!" Emmanuel retaliates boldly, but I hear the pain and the fear in his panting breaths.

"Emmanuel! Please go! Don't let me be the death of you like I was your brother! You can't save us both!"

"Shut up, Jacob! You didn't kill Samuel; they did. You drug me into this mess, and I'm dragging you out of it. Hang on, it's not much further!"

"You don't know her! You don't know Wei!" I plead with him.

"Without you, it doesn't matter if either of us makes it! You're the one they're scared of!"

He won't go. I panic. What plan could he have that he is relying on so strongly? What's the point of plans? I just want to save him. If I could just save one person!

Wei points her gun. The angle is too high to be aimed for me. She aims at Emmanuel. If I hadn't loved the transporter craft, if I hadn't wanted to know the story, if I hadn't gone to Yahbi and bought the device—could I have protected them? If only I had just stayed with my family in Unit C and been a responsible son.

Wei stops; her finger poises on the trigger. Here it comes. Suddenly, the ground rises up around her, and a wave of red dust falls across the ground. I hadn't seen him, camouflaged by the rock, but now two massive arms wrap around her pink, spindly body. Her back bends almost to the point of snapping before Derrick drops to the ground in exhaustion, holding her back with his remaining strength. Emmanuel lifts me into the transporter craft.

"Emmanuel, Emmanuel, stop! We have to take him with us! They'll kill him!" I yell fanatically.

Emmanuel doesn't hear or pretends not to. Derrick raises his massive head. Even through the dust, I see the trace of a smile. My heart wrenches in response. After all that happened, after all that he'd done, he was still one more person I couldn't protect. I'm fully inside the cabin now. Emmanuel rushes around behind me, hurriedly trying to get the craft started. Derrick won't be able to hold her back for much longer; I could see the exhaustion in his smile. I want him to know. I want him to die knowing. I reach toward the planet and scream with my remaining strength.

"I know their weakness! I know their weakness!"

My gargled words are swallowed up in the sound of the craft. The red dust glows white, and Wei's outline stands in the midst. I'm screaming. I'm screaming. I'm screaming. The last Historian falls backward. The hatch starts to close as we leave the ground. Wei has already disappeared. The autopilot glides over the scene below. The craft pulls the dust behind it, and a small opening in the dust appears. The last Historian is dead, fists clenched, eyes wide open. The manic fury of Transfer Sickness took hold of him in his last.

The small, silver craft hurtles out of the atmosphere and glides into space.

Made in the USA
Columbia, SC
20 September 2022